Guilty Pleasure

By Lora Leigh
and published by Pan Books

Dangerous
Forbidden
Wicked Pleasure
Only Pleasure
Guilty Pleasure

Guilty Pleasure

Lora Leigh

PAN BOOKS

First published 2009 by St Martin's Press, New York

This edition published 2014 by Pan Books
an imprint of Pan Macmillan, a division of Macmillan Publishers Limited
Pan Macmillan, 20 New Wharf Road, London N1 9RR
Basingstoke and Oxford
Associated companies throughout the world
www.panmacmillan.com

ISBN 978-1-4472-5798-1

Visit **www.panmacmillan.com** to read more about all our books
and to buy them. You will also find features, author interviews and
news of any author events, and you can sign up for e-newsletters
so that you're always first to hear about our new releases.

For Mom. For believing in me. For years of supplies and for understanding the imagination. For being proud of me and for being there for me. Now, if we could just work on that stubbornness issue you have . . . :)

I love you, Mom.

A big thank-you to Holly, for the hours of research and frequent phone calls to keep my life organized and running smoothly, so I could get the edits done.

Thank you to Bret, for jumping in when I need you to, and for the hugs and understanding. Don't worry, son, you'll get to drive alone one of these days.

A big thank-you to Donna Hershberger, who takes care of the little details. Nursemaid, armchair psychologist, and general sounding board.

And a big thank-you to Sharon. For driving, listening, and all the little things you do that make my life run easier.

prologue

"Traitorous fucking bastard!"

Marty Mathews stared at her boss, division chief Vince Deerfield, with a hidden sense of surprise as he threw the thick file on Khalid el Hamid-Mustafa across the desk.

The dull, yellow folder hit, slid, then fell from the desk to scatter loose sheets of information and pictures at her feet.

Khalid el Hamid-Mustafa. The bastard son of a Saudi sheikh suspected of terrorism. His father, Azir Mustafa, was a religious hardliner, a man who ruled one of the more barren sections of Saudi Arabia, on the Iraq border. He had tarred his sons with his own brush and in doing so had subjected Khalid to years of suspicion by the United States.

It was the reason Marty had been tailing Khalid for the past two years. As an FBI agent, one on the low end of the totem pole as far as her boss was concerned, Marty had been stuck playing babysitter and peeping Thomasina to one of the most sexually active men she had ever laid her eyes on.

A dark, brooding, dangerous man. There was no doubt in her mind that Khalid Mustafa would be a very dangerous man to cross.

If she had doubted it, then the information her godfather had given her over the past years would have confirmed it.

There was a reason why she had never reported any of the more suspicious activities Khalid had engaged in. Quite simply, it was because he engaged in them at the orders of her godfather, the director of the FBI.

"No comment?" Vince snarled, his heavy brows lowered, his hazel green eyes spitting fire and brimstone back at her.

"I'm the agent who's followed him for the past two years," she replied politely. "As my reports state, there's no evidence to support the suspicion that Mr. Mustafa has any ties to a terrorist community."

Vince threw himself back in his chair and glared at her now. That glare was nerve-racking. It boded ill to any agent on the receiving end of it. Unfortunately, she was the agent in question.

"Two years," he snapped. "I gave you two years, Agent Mathews, to find just a shred of evidence to support the suspicions we have against him. Two years. I could have convicted a five-year-old with that amount of time on my hands."

No doubt he could have but, on the other hand, he wouldn't have had a godfather who was director of the entire FBI going over his reports, editing them and deleting minor points that could have supported that suspicion because Khalid was currently his favorite mole.

"A five-year-old wouldn't have the decadent lifestyle Mustafa has." She rolled her eyes at the thought of it. "I rather doubt the man has the time to consort with terrorists. He's too busy playing with his little friends."

That was more truth than fiction, actually, no matter how much her godfather liked to smile and deny it.

Her boss stared back at her as though she were a slug under a rock that somehow had dared him to touch her. The very fact that he couldn't fire her without bringing down a heavy barrage of interest in his office was only the tip of the iceberg of reasons he hated her.

The man was slowly committing career suicide and didn't seem to have a clue. Her godfather was Zachary Jennings, the director of the

FBI and Deerfield's boss. She didn't run crying to Daddy Zach, but that didn't mean he wasn't well aware of the treatment she had been receiving in this office since being assigned to it.

"Well, you can stop protesting the assignment," he bit out, his tone malevolent. "You're off. The operation is dead in the damned water, thanks to your godfather and your incompetence. What did you do, go crying to him?"

Marty sat up straighter, a frown line forming between her brows at the accusation she had thought of only moments before. "I've never discussed this assignment with my godfather," she informed him, bristling at the insult, but thanking God that her godfather had taught her how to lie when she was young. "And I stopped crying to him when I was three."

"Then I don't have to worry about a protest on my desk when I tell you that you have to be one of the lousiest agents I've ever had in my division," he stated derisively.

"The only report you have to worry about is the one I may file, sir." She stared back at him, fighting to hide her anger. "Perhaps it wasn't my lack of skill so much as your lack of foresight and inability to accept the fact that Mustafa is guilty of nothing but his own sexual excesses."

She kept her tone respectful. She assured herself there was none of the animosity that brewed inside her leaking into it.

He sneered back at her, and it was all she could do to keep from telling him what a fruitcake he had become over the years.

His determination to find any shred of evidence that he could procure against Khalid had become a running joke within the office. He refused to listen to reason, refused to see that there was nothing to tie Khalid to any terrorist. Except those that her godfather had him secretly meeting with.

Now wasn't that fucked up?

"My lack of foresight has never been an issue." He rose to his feet and paced to the wide windows that gave views out over D.C. as he blew out a hard, disgusted breath. "Either way, the operation has been shut down. You're off the case, Mathews. You can finally begin the vacation you've been crying about for the past two years."

Crying about? She rather doubted it. She had submitted the request the month before she had been assigned to Khalid, and had merely resubmitted it every six months. She deserved her vacation. She hadn't had one in over three years.

"Thank you, sir." She just barely managed to keep the mockery out of her voice.

Not that Deerfield was fooled. He glared back at her as he clasped his hands behind his back and straightened his shoulders to stare down his hooked nose at her.

"You're excused." He grimaced, as though there was a smell that offended him. "I'll see you back here in one month. Hopefully by then I can find an assignment worthy of your mediocre skills."

Damn. She could wait longer than four weeks before returning to this office or Deerfield's questionable mercies. The man was a fiend. She would have nightmares while on vacation concerning her return.

"Thank you, sir." Rising to her feet, she gave him a short-lived, less than sincere smile. "I'll see you in a month."

Marty turned on her heel and walked quickly to the door, desperate to get away from the malevolence she could feel pouring from her boss.

Running to her godfather wasn't going to be a problem, though, because she had a feeling her time at the agency was history. At the moment, she was being courted by more than one private protection firm and she was seriously considering one very lucrative offer.

Closing the door behind her, Marty strode quickly from the bureau's unassuming offices and into the heated warmth of a D.C. summer day.

The first day of her vacation. A month free of strife and Deerfield's screaming rages because she hadn't managed to come up with so much as a shred of suspicion against Mustafa.

If the man only knew exactly who Khalid was to the bureau. His code name was Desert Lion and the missions he had successfully completed for the bureau had been imperative, both nationally and in the Middle East.

But why didn't Deerfield have the information that Khalid was one of her father's independent agents? Why had she been told but he hadn't been? That was information that Zachary Jennings still hadn't given her, but she had her own suspicions.

Deerfield was likely on his way out, if she knew her godfather. Otherwise Vince Deerfield would have been given the information that would have exonerated Khalid of the suspicions Deerfield had against him.

While she was striding along the sidewalk, a small smile tipped her lips. Two years investigating Khalid and she knew more about him than she may have known about herself. She knew the brooding, dangerous reflection of the man that hid behind calm, often amused black eyes. She knew him for the male sexual animal he was, and as the aloof "other" lover he played in his relationships.

And often she wondered what would happen if she wasn't an agent, if she wasn't shadowing him, if she wasn't the goddaughter of the director of the Federal Bureau of Investigation and a woman who he knew wasn't content to merely "play"?

Would he be in her bed or simply demand to be a third, should she choose a lover within the circle of his friends who shared their lovers?

It sounded depraved. Perverted. Marty knew the protective and loving lifestyle environment her parents had created for her instead. Her father, her mother, and her godfather.

Walking into the parking lot behind the FBI offices, she moved quickly to her car, engaged the auto lock, and pulled the door open before sliding inside.

Her hands gripped the steering wheel as she stared along the walkway in front of her, the profusion of flowers and shrubbery holding her gaze with their splashes of color. She had one month to attempt the seduction of a man who seemed determined to remain as aloof as possible.

She had four weeks to steal his heart. If he had one to steal.

THE CLUB, SINCLAIR ESTATE
VIRGINIA

Khalid watched as U.S. Senator Joe Mathews and the third he had chosen more than thirty years ago, FBI director Zachary Jennings, walked into the bar of the club, glancing around until they spotted Khalid.

Lifting his glass of whiskey, Khalid took a sip of the dark liquid as he tracked their progress through the room to the small seating area where he sat. If their expressions were anything to go by, then the news was good. Perhaps. The somber seriousness that had tightened their faces for the past two years had eased, and with it, hopefully, their tempers as well.

The two men were both trim, fit for their ages. The senator was nearing sixty, the director was only a few years behind, but both men appeared years younger. They swore it was due to a peaceful, stress-free home life.

There were days Khalid sincerely doubted that. He knew who they claimed as a daughter.

"Khalid." Zach sat down in the settee across from the leather recliner that Khalid was currently relaxing in. The senator took a seat in the chair beside the director, leaned back, and allowed a self-satisfied smile to tip his lips.

"Consider your problems over," Joe announced softly, his deep voice tinged with amusement as Khalid's brow lifted in curiosity.

"Really?" he drawled. "All of them?"

"The majority, perhaps," Zach chuckled. "The FBI has dropped their investigation of you. Deerfield was forced to pull the assignment this afternoon. Marty's on her way home for a vacation, and I'll be submitting my report on Deerfield next week. We should have his resignation within the next month."

"Before Marty returns to the office, I assume?" Khalid felt his fingers tingle with the need to curl into a fist at the thought of the hell Deerfield had been putting her through.

There were agents in the club, men who reported to Jennings, and who had revealed information concerning Marty to Khalid. Those men had kept them both apprised of the insults Deerfield had heaped upon her concerning her inability to find evidence against Khalid and his supposed terrorist activities.

"Before Marty returns to the office." Zach nodded, his expression tensing with anger. "The bastard has stepped over the line one time too many."

"And still your daughter refuses to file a report against him," Khalid murmured.

Zach nodded heavily. "Marty's not a snitch. I can get his resignation without her, but it would have helped."

"And have you asked her for her help?" Khalid sipped at the whiskey as he glanced at the two men.

Zach shook his head emphatically. "If she finds out we know about her problems with her boss, then she'll begin to question our sources. I don't want that. Keeping an eye on that girl isn't always easy. I don't want her to know just how well I keep tabs on her."

Khalid refrained from objecting. He wasn't a believer in hiding information in this situation. Marty was an intelligent woman who lived a potentially dangerous life, despite her godfather's attempts to ensure that she was protected. She would only be hurt and angry if it appeared that her father had no faith in her abilities.

"He still disapproves." Joe nodded in Khalid's direction.

"It is not my place to approve or to disapprove." He shrugged. At least, not yet it wasn't. The battle he was fighting to steer clear of her was becoming harder by the day, though. It was a battle he might yet lose.

"It could be." Joe's gaze was somber now. "If you were serious in your intentions."

Khalid had to chuckle at that. "Gentlemen, this is the twenty-first century, not the eighteenth," he informed them. "We're not Southern gentlemen seeking to protect the honor of our daughters. My intentions are as they have always been. I must plead guilty to seeking pleasure alone."

Joe grimaced as Zach shook his head at Khalid's answer.

"Marty isn't a toy," Zach stated, his voice firm, his tone warning. It was a familiar argument, though one Khalid rarely started or participated in.

"Tell me." Leaning forward, Khalid slid the recliner back into its folded position. "Is there any chance that Deerfield could learn what happened in Saudi before I left?"

What had happened ten years ago had nearly destroyed him. And there were still men who would love to see Khalid el Hamid-Mustafa broken, least of whom were his two half brothers.

"We're taking care of it," Zach promised him. "Deerfield's resignation will strip him of his clearance and ensure that he never learns your secrets."

His secrets. More like his nightmares. The bloody, shameful past that haunted his days like a dark specter. Khalid nodded as he rose to his feet. This conversation was at an end as far as he was concerned. If he stayed to socialize with the two men it inevitably would return to Marty. To the one woman he ached to possess with a hunger unlike any he had ever known before. She was the one woman he was forced to deny himself.

For too many years he had contented himself with being merely a third to other club members' lovers or wives. He had no desire to form a commitment to any woman, or to any relationship. He had no right to do so. He had lost that right long ago in a desert filled with blood and betrayal.

"That doesn't mean that the threats your half brothers represent is at an end." Zach sighed as Khalid fought to hold back the anger building inside him. "Have you taken care of hiding the girls yet?"

The girls. His daughters. Six young women whom his father had sent to him as little more than slaves when they had been no more than children, ten years ago. He had adopted them, raised them, and they were now beautiful young women making lives for themselves.

Khalid nodded. "They are with Mother and Pavlos."

Pavlos Galbraith, the Greek multibillionaire, had done every-thing required to ensure their safety, as well as that of his wife—Khalid's mother—and their daughter.

"Good." Zach nodded. "Until we know the repercussions of the operation that unearthed that cell in D.C. last month, it's best we stay on the safe side."

Which meant, it was best if he stayed away from Zach's daughter, Marty.

Which was no more than the truth. And still, it was a truth he hated facing.

"If you'll excuse me." He nodded to the two men as he moved away and headed for the bar's exit.

He had no desire to discuss Marty at this point, just as he had no desire to face another night filled with arousal and nightmares, and the memories of a past he could never change.

+·+·+·+

"What do you think?" Joe sighed, as he watched Khalid before turn-ing back to the man who had been his best friend most of his life.

"I think I'd prefer it if our daughter were interested in another man," Zach said, as he ran his hand over his jaw and tried to hold back the concern building inside him. "He's a hard man, Joe."

"He won't stay away from her." Joe shook his head at the thought.

"If he managed to, eventually, she would find him." This was a truth Zach was certain of. "She's as obsessed as he is."

"She's protective of him," Joe countered. "And she's curious."

Zach sat back in his chair and breathed out a heavy sigh. Marty was like the wind, soft and gentle one day and blowing fierce and hot, or icy cold, the next. But one thing remained constant, and that was her loyalty to those she cared about. For some reason she had focused on Khalid when she was no more than a girl, and that fasci-nation hadn't abated.

Joe knew Zach had lived in fear in the past years of that dark fascination that often filled their daughter's eyes whenever she saw Khalid. The man would break her heart, and Joe didn't know if he could ever forgive Khalid if he hurt her. But he knew Zach would see to it personally that Khalid regretted any tears Marty shed.

While rubbing his hand over his face, Joe gave Khalid's retreating back a final glance before lifting his drink and finishing it. Zach would take care of the problem of Vince Deerfield and get him off Khalid's and Marty's asses. Joe would help his daughter do what Zach had made him promise not to do. And that was to help her to attain what he felt would make her happy. But even more, he had a feeling it was what would make Khalid happy as well. Eventually. The boy needed something to fight for. Someone to fight for. He was growing lax in his own protection.

Sometimes a man could just sense when two people were meant to be together. Khalid and Marty matched in ways that defied description and, as a father, Joe wanted nothing more than her happiness and Khalid's peace.

Over the past two years he had watched the anger build inside Marty as Deerfield went after Khalid. Each order that had gone out to tap his phone, search his home, or follow him to whatever function or event he was attending had struck a sensitive nerve in the girl.

Each time she had been forced to remain on surveillance while he played his "games," as she had called them, she had changed a little more. As though the knowledge that he was sharing another woman's bed only angered her further.

Unfortunately for her godfather, keeping her away from Khalid would be impossible. Joe figured he might as well do as he always did and help if she asked. Then again, he knew his daughter well. She wouldn't need much assistance. He had a feeling she just might be the woman to tame the Desert Lion's heart and to heal the wounds in his soul.

Or she would end up sharing them.

"Stop worrying, Zach," Joe ordered firmly, as he picked up a paper on the table in front of him and sat back to read. "She's a grown woman. You have to let her live her own life at this point."

"So says the man who has standing orders out that she's to be covered by a protective detail at all times," Zach grunted. "Don't give me that crap."

Joe's lips quirked in an amused grin. "Where bullets are flying, I tend to remain cautious. Where Mustafa is concerned?" His grin widened. "He's a drowning man. Give her two weeks, he'll be like the rest of us. Putty in her hands."

"He doesn't have a heart, Joe," Zach said, causing Joe to lower his paper and frown back at him.

"What the hell do you mean by that?"

"His brothers destroyed any part of him that he could give to another woman in that damned desert," he said, thinking of what had been done to Khalid so many years before. "They ripped his heart out of his body. That's why he needs to stay the hell away from our daughter. He can't do anything but hurt her."

Joe prayed he was wrong, if for no other reason than his daughter's sake.

1

Heat surrounded Marty. A sizzling, sultry, humid heat that washed over her naked body, lapped at her sensitive nipples, and tingled at the juncture of her thighs. It glistened and shimmered over her oil-coated body and sank inside her flesh, almost reaching that spot inside her that always seemed empty, always dark.

Behind her closed eyelids soft color existed, compliments of the sun pouring down around her. There was just the summer surrounding her, heating her, causing her to tingle from the tips of her bare toes, over her waxed pussy and her pale breasts, to the top of her head.

She stretched beneath the heat, luxuriating in it as she hadn't been able to do for far too long.

She should have joined her mother and aunts in France, she thought. They were sunning themselves on the beach, drinking fruity little drinks with umbrellas in them, and relaxing. If she'd had any idea of the surprise her insane boss had intended for her yesterday, then she definitely would have made plans to join them.

She would have enjoyed the laughter that always resulted when her mother and aunts got together.

Instead, she was lying here, wondering what she was missing and why the hell she was here alone.

Just as she would have been doing if she were in France, she thought with amusement. She would have fussed internally every day she was there as she wondered what she was missing at home.

She would have wondered what Khalid was doing. Sexy, charming, brooding, secretive Khalid.

She blew out a heated breath as the image of him rose behind her closed lashes. So tall, broad-shouldered, lean-hipped. A fantasy come to life if all a woman was looking for was the pleasure to be had from sex alone.

There were times she wished she could settle for just the sex. The stolen moments in the darkness of night, a few hours of satisfaction before she went on her way. If she were more that type of a woman, she wouldn't be as tormented by one man as she was by Khalid.

Stroking her fingertips along the bare flesh of her abdomen left a sense of sensual weakness washing over her. There were days, nights, when she ached for his touch. When every nerve ending in her body, desperate for his caress, seemed to throb just under the skin. A touch she had never known.

She almost laughed at the thought. She was pathetic, and the older she got, the more the ache seemed to intensify. She couldn't get him out of her fantasies, or out of her mind. She wondered if she was obsessed.

Marty never obsessed over anything, and definitely never over a man. Khalid seemed to be the exception to her rule. Rolling over on the thick towel cushioning her from the cement surrounding the pool, Marty drew in a hard, deep breath and tried to force the ever-present erotic images of Khalid out of her mind.

She had decisions to make while she was on vacation, decisions that did not include Khalid's arrogance and sexuality. Decisions that could change her life as well as the direction she had once chosen for it.

The private security firm she had been approached by last month had made an offer she found hard to refuse. An offer she might yet accept.

Climbing the ladder in the bureau was beginning to look next to impossible. Her godfather's position as head of the federal offices held her back in ways she hadn't anticipated. She was protected and watched over, and then Deerfield had the nerve to accuse her of "crying" to Zach when things didn't go her way.

The wall to advancement that she was facing at times seemed insurmountable.

The private security firm, on the other hand, looked promising. She had no blood relation working there, no friends, and, even better, her father and godfather weren't involved in any way. She would have a sense of freedom, fewer rules and regulations, and more action and satisfaction. It seemed like a win/win situation so far.

So far.

She hadn't told her fathers about it yet, she hadn't discussed it with her mother, and every time she considered doing so, something stopped her. As though the thought of it were suddenly abhorrent. But she was an adult; she wasn't going to feel like she had to ask permission to play on the other side of the playground.

And while she was considering options, was she going to pull her towel over her naked body sometime before Khalid Mustafa stepped from the family room to the patio where she lay?

Peeking from beneath her lashes, she watched as his shadow lingered for long seconds at the French doors before he stepped into the brilliant rays of the sun.

Like a shadow come to life. Black eyes, black hair, deeply bronzed flesh. The man was like a living sex god. Hard muscle shifted beneath the white silk shirt he wore, just as lean, powerful legs flexed inside the form-fitting jeans that covered them.

"You're going to burn." His shadow eased over her, dulling the heat that had been sinking slowly into her back.

"I never burn." She fought to keep the arousal that whipped through her out of her voice as she lay beneath his gaze. "What are you doing here? Zach's at Dad's house. Next house down the street, if you're not sure where that's at."

"I know where it's located." Deep, dark, his voice washed over her senses with a velvety rasp that shouldn't have had the power to send her juices spilling from her vagina.

Why Khalid? she asked herself. What was it about him that made her so damned hot she rivaled the sun, when other men seemed to leave her cold? So cold that the thought of actually having sex with one of them was impossible to consider.

"Then why are you here?" She lifted herself up on her elbows and raised her head as he squatted in front of her, his dark head tilted, his thickly lashed eyes narrowing on her.

"You look like a virgin sacrifice. Laid out, naked, and tempting the sun to ravage as it chooses."

Wow. He sure as hell had a gift for words. She had known that about him; she just hadn't expected to have him use it to pay homage to her in quite that manner.

"It hasn't ravaged me yet." She looked up at him. "No matter how much I tempt it."

What was that flaring in his gaze? There was more than simple lust there, though the lust was there in spades. A hunger echoed through her body, tightened her nipples, and caused her abdomen to clench in anticipation of pleasure.

And how the hell was she supposed to know it would be pleasure? She had to be the only twenty-seven-year-old virgin left in the country. A woman who knew more about sex than the highest-paid call girl and yet had never known the touch of a lover, because she had to be the most stubborn woman in the world, too. She wanted Khalid. She had wanted him since she was fifteen, and no other man was going to do.

"Some would say you're tempting it as you speak," Khalid stated, his gaze flickering down to the rounded curves of her breasts.

Marty swore she could feel the swollen mounds hardening further, her nipples aching, throbbing with the need for his touch.

This was what he did to her. What he had always done to her.

"Tempting it as I speak?" She glanced up at the clear blue sky before turning her gaze back to him. "So far, it hasn't responded."

His lips lifted in a half-smile. "You might be surprised."

"I rather doubt it." Rolling over she sat up, drew the light robe from her side, and pulled it over her as she rose to her feet.

Turning to face him once again, she reminded herself that this man was way out of her league and a damned sight more male than she might be able to handle. That didn't keep her from wanting to try.

"So why are you here if you know Dad and Zach are at the other house?" she questioned, as she gathered up the towel and her gun and the tanning oil beside her towel. "Shouldn't you be there?"

His gaze flickered to the holstered gun before coming back to her.

"I didn't say I knew they were there. I said I knew where it was. Your father is scheduled to meet me here soon. He did not mention the meeting changing to his home."

"You'll have to wait, then." She shrugged.

"I can see this becoming a problem."

Response slammed through her. The rough edge of his voice was just enough to slice through any doubt she may have had that for the moment his attention was focused solely on her.

"It looks like you're stuck with me until he returns then." Her heart was racing, and excitement was building inside her until it felt almost impossible to contain.

"That it does," he agreed.

"No objections then?" Stepping through the French doors, she turned and headed to the kitchen. "That's quite an about-face. The last I noticed, you enjoyed making certain there was an absurd distance between us."

He rarely spoke to her, especially during the past two years while she had been following him on her rabid boss's orders.

"It could be well measured," he chided her, as she stepped to the fridge and pulled it open. "And perhaps that distance is best for both of us."

And he had stated that several times. As they danced at the parties they both attended. Or during her visits to Courtney Sinclair's home on the Sinclair estate that housed the men's club he was a member of. Each time they had come in close contact, he had warned her against it. Warned her until she did no more than roll her eyes at the warnings now.

"Fine. It's not wise. You can leave now." Pulling a pitcher of sweet iced tea from inside the refrigerator, she shot him a look that dared him to go.

Did she have the courage, she wondered, to be the woman she wanted to be? Seducing him was her dream, but did she have the courage to face possible rejection? More than once?

Pulling two glasses from the cupboard, she poured the tea before setting the pitcher on the counter and giving the glass to him.

"Thank you." His eyes locked on hers as he lifted the glass to his lips and sipped.

There was pure sexual hunger in his gaze. Lust filled it, shaped his sexy lips, and tightened the skin over his cheekbones. He watched her like a hawk watches its prey: narrow-eyed, intent, hungry.

"How much longer are you going to wait, Khalid?" She set the glass on the counter as she confronted him. "Forever?"

He stared back at her silently for a long moment.

"What do you want, Marty?" he finally asked, his tone darker now. "You can't know what you're getting into here. You can't know what you're actually reaching for."

"I want you."

Yes, she knew exactly what she wanted, who she wanted. Just as she knew he wanted her. He could deny it until hell froze over, but the truth was there in his eyes, in the hard contours of his face and the sensual fullness of his lips. He seemed to freeze. Like a predator suddenly catching scent of prey, his nostrils flared, his gaze narrowed as it flickered over her and seemed to reflect an intent, dangerous hunger.

He wasn't a man to play with; she had known that for years. There was something intrinsically predatory about him, a silent warning that nothing about him was as it seemed. Unfortunately, that something drew her in ways she couldn't fight.

"Stop tempting me, precious. You may not like what you find on the other side," he said harshly.

Marty inhaled slowly, allowing her tongue to run slowly along her lower lip, as though hesitant, as though considering his warning.

His gaze flared with hunger, with dark, gleaming lust.

Oh yes, he wanted her. Perhaps almost as badly as she wanted him.

She let a smile curve her lips before lifting the tea and sipping it slowly. She wasn't going to argue with him any longer. There was nothing to argue about. They both knew what lay between them like a fire threatening to blaze out of control.

"I understand." She finally nodded. "I'm not a woman who already has a lover. It's rather hard to remain unconnected from a woman when she's your lover rather than another man's."

He was known to share other men's lovers instead of having one of his own. He was the perfect third, from what she understood. Kind. Caring. Considerate. And having absolutely no desire to capture the heart or the loyalty of the woman he slept with.

"Perhaps," she continued, "I should simply find someone willing to consider my choice of a third. Would you be interested then, Khalid?"

She had to admit that the thought only infuriated her. It was Khalid she wanted, totally. His bed she wanted to share, his life she wanted to be a part of.

"I may become murderous," he murmured, before cursing himself for allowing the words to slip free.

Khalid watched Marty now in ways he hadn't allowed himself to before. The threat of another man coming into her life pricked at the darkness that brewed inside him. A sense of possessiveness, of dominance that he had sworn he would never feel again, roiled inside him like a beast struggling to break free.

He had fought too many years to stay the hell away from her. The fascination with her that had built inside him. It was a desire that ate at his soul.

He shouldn't allow himself to touch her. He should never tempt himself as he did now. To touch her would be to risk her, and he knew exactly the cost of that risk.

As he watched her, he realized not for the first time how incredibly fragile and delicate her small body was. It made him see how easily she could be taken, broken. And he had enemies who, though they had remained silent in the past ten years, would strike at her at the slightest opportunity. But even the knowledge of that couldn't still the hunger tearing through him or the desperation that thickened his cock and left his balls pounding with lust.

"I completely understand how such an offer could frighten you, Khalid." Her tone was as gentle as a Southern rainfall, and yet as cutting as ice. "After all, I do believe such things are against club rules, aren't they? The member himself chooses his third. Perhaps I should stick with a lover with a tad more possessiveness."

He almost laughed in surprise. The little wench had managed to turn this around on him and leave him scrambling to find his balance.

"Fear is not quite the emotion I would attribute to what I'm feeling at the moment." He let his gaze rake over her, remembering in exact detail how she had looked glistening beneath the sun, as she lay by the pool's edge.

He watched her flush and saw the innocence, despite the knowledge in her gray eyes. She was self-aware, independent, and, her father swore, willful. But she wasn't a woman who shared herself easily; he rather doubted she had shared herself at all. Yet here she stood, daring him to take her, challenging him with those quicksilver eyes of hers and that damned mocking smile.

They had been playing this game for ages, it seemed. The thrust and parry, the challenge and retreat had gone on so long that he had nearly given in more than once. Until he had learned that she was investigating him.

Did she know, he wondered, how he had missed the flirting, the teasing, the choice that had been taken from him when he'd learned he was a suspected enemy of his country?

There had been nights when he had thought of nothing more than touching her, than filling her eyes with knowledge rather than curiosity, with lust rather than innocence.

The nights he had nearly broken down, had prayed that his past was that, in the past, and that he could reach out for her.

It was that past that held him back. The knowledge of the horror and the blood that could so easily repeat itself. Yet still, he longed for her with a hunger that was nearly impossible to resist.

She had been built for touch, for pleasure. Her sweetly compact body, the full, high breasts, and the gentle curve of her hips were God's gift to any man who set eyes on her. She was beautiful in ways that other women could only hope to be.

From her button nose and pouty lips to her determined chin and stubborn expression, he could see the willful, independent little minx she was. But her eyes. Those eyes truly were the windows to her soul. If the look in them was any indication, then he knew she would burn him alive.

He let his gaze travel over the delicacy of her body once again. He wondered if her skin was as soft as it appeared, if her nipples tasted as sweet as they looked?

His entire body clenched at the thought, while his cock throbbed in heated anticipation. He could touch her, he thought. He could taste the sweetness of her and still pull back, he could still walk away.

He'd never intended to develop more with her than a very close friendship. A friendship that would allow him to share her with whichever lover she eventually chose. If she ever chose one. He'd be damned if he wasn't getting tired of waiting. Of wondering.

"Tell me, are you still a virgin?" He couldn't hold back the question, the need to know. Just as he couldn't hold back the desire that tormented him.

"Are you?" Anger shimmered in her tone, in her gaze. Better the anger than the invitation that glimmered in her eyes moments before.

"I? A virgin?" He grinned at that thought. "Sweetheart, I was born sexually aware. I don't believe I've ever been a virgin."

Of course, that wasn't exactly true, but he loved seeing her eyes narrow with interest and disdain. It made her all the more tempting, made anticipation burn through his loins as he considered all the ways he could touch her, challenge her, be challenged by her.

There was something about her that made him wary, made him fear the man he would be when he touched her. But on the flip side of that coin was the knowledge that inside this woman burned the soul of a sensualist—a lover who would meet him, match him. One who could burn down the night with him. For a while. If he could keep her safe long enough to learn all the intriguing secrets that shadowed her eyes.

"Yes, I also sincerely doubt you were ever a virgin." She gave a soft, ladylike snort at the very thought of it. "That doesn't mean it's any of your business if I'm one or not."

His brow arched at the challenge in her tone. Damn! She could make him harder faster than any woman he had ever known in his life.

"I don't know about that," he murmured, his gaze flicking over her. "When I push my fingers up your tight little pussy, I'd like to know if I should go hard and deep, or if I should merely tease and save such a delicacy for my cock to taste."

Before he finished, her face was flushing a brilliant hue, but her gray eyes were filling with arousal. He would bet his trust fund her pussy was silky wet now, slick and sweet, as her juices spilled from her.

The thought of it had his mouth watering for a taste of her before his common sense could reassert itself. He could easily go to his knees before her, spread her legs, and feast on the soft, silky flesh. She was naked beneath that robe. Her pussy was bare, waxed of the curls that would have shielded it. It would be sensitive to his touch, to his lips and tongue.

He could taste her, just for a moment. Just a moment wouldn't endanger her, surely.

"You're joking," she breathed out, her voice rough, her hands shaking as one lifted from the robe to swipe at the strands of dark blond hair that fell from the clip atop her head. She seriously believed he wasn't serious. He could see it in her eyes.

"Joking?" He tilted his head and watched her curiously. "Because I want to fuck you? Precious, there is no joke in the least in such a desire. The thought of touching you, of having your sweet flesh suck my cock inside you is enough to make me weak in the knees. I never said I didn't want you. I said it would not be wise to give in to such desires."

Her smile was scoffing. "It's not nice to tease like this, Khalid. What happened? Did you lose your little black book? Need a little entertainment to fill in the few minutes before my father's return?"

She watched the grin that tugged at his lips. She had never seen Khalid smile fully, she realized. A tug of amusement at the corner of his lips, a little quirk of a crooked smile, but never a true smile.

"As I'm certain you're aware, I'm never at a loss for playmates," he assured her, as amusement shone in his eyes.

Marty breathed in, slow and easy, fighting the dark fear that wanted to take hold of her as she saw the pure need that filled his eyes.

He hadn't touched her; he had only moved closer. She could feel the heat of his body but not the touch of his flesh. Still, it was enough to make her feel fevered, flushed. She couldn't seem to move away from him, to break the hold he had on her as his gaze stayed locked with hers.

"So I've heard," she mocked him lightly. "The 'playboy sheikh,' I believe is what they call you. Quite a reputation to have, Khalid." And one that bit at her every time she thought about it.

He reached out, his fingers feathering along the strands of hair that escaped her clip before brushing against her jaw. That smallest touch, that lightest stroke, had anticipation racing over her nerve endings.

"Oftentimes a reputation is no more than a shield to protect oneself," he said, his voice quiet, reflective. "To hold at bay the very things you know you cannot have."

Bullshit. This game was growing old, and it was one she was tired of playing.

"Stop messing with me." Stepping back from him, she fought to keep her breathing under control, to hold back the desire that assailed her.

The sexuality that was so much a part of Khalid was beginning to wrap around her, to work its way inside her. She could feel him holding back, feel him fighting himself. The thought that he felt he had to stay away from her confused her, left her wanting to push harder, to find out the limits of the control he was imposing on himself.

"You believe I'm playing?" He reached out to her, slowly. His fingertips touched her cheek and smoothed down her jaw, and she forgot to breathe until his thumb rubbed against her lips.

Swallowing tightly, Marty forced herself not to shake, not to whimper with the response that tore through her. God alone knew how desperately she needed that touch, and how unwilling she was to beg for it.

"Of course you're playing," she scoffed. "You've proven it over the years, Khalid. What's wrong, frightened of me?" She pursed her lips and blew him a mocking kiss.

"Fears are tricky things," he said softly, the flavor of his accent whispering across her senses as he ran the back of his fingers down her arm. "They lock themselves inside your mind and become rooted in your very soul. Fighting them is never easy, but once you learn how to control them . . ." He lifted his gaze to stare into her eyes, to mesmerize her, lock her to him. "Once you learn how to control them, precious, then you control yourself."

She wanted to roll her eyes at the teasing in his tone. She would have, except she heard the faintest thread of sincerity there.

"Then," he continued, "you learn that control can be your best friend. Your wisest counsel. When tempted by a woman who you seem to have no defenses against, it comes in rather handy." He whispered the last sentence softly against her ear. "Just as it comes in handy while showing a woman what should have always been hers."

"And that would be?" If he didn't kiss her, she was going to die. If he didn't touch her again, her flesh was going to burn to cinders from the need.

"A woman should always know pleasure."

She watched as his head began to lower, as he continued to whisper.

"A woman should revel in her sensuality, in that side of her nature that aches for touch, aches to be possessed." His voice lowered, rasped, throbbed with desire as his lips finally brushed against hers. "A woman, precious, should always be able to fulfill the desires that haunt that sensual core of her being. Tell me, Marty," he breathed roughly, "what desires haunt your woman's core?"

"Desires for you," she whispered back, and her breath nearly caught at the flare of response in his gaze.

He haunted her. She ached for his touch. She ached for his kiss. Her lips parted slowly as a near brutal need began to thunder through her body.

She had tracked him for two years. Followed him. She had seen the sexual excesses he immersed himself in, and she had seen the lonely nights where he stood in his window and stared down at her.

He had always seemed to know where she was, where she hid to watch him, how she ached. In his expression she had seen the brooding sensuality and a dark shadow of torment. A torment that sometimes reminded her of her own.

"I want to kiss you," he said. "Sweet candied lips. I look at them, and my body tightens with the need to possess you, Marty. To fuck you until you're screaming for more. Screaming for me. Common sense warns me to pull back. But the thought of those sweet lips keeps me coming back."

His voice hardened with a surge of lust as his eyes flashed with an inner fire a second before his fingers slid into her hair.

He didn't grab the strands. His large palm cupped the back of her head in a gentle if unbreakable grip as his head slanted and lowered.

Why she had expected a rough, bruising kiss, she wasn't certain. But what came was anything but ungentle. Firm lips touched her own, parted them as a cry left her mouth.

She was shaking in his grip, her hands lifting to hold his wrist as his other hand gripped her hip and held her to him. She could feel her nails digging into his flesh, feel a plethora of sensations rocking through her system as it seemed to overload on the most exquisite pleasure that she could have known.

Electricity filled his kiss. Sensations unlike anything she had ever known whipped through her, destroying her senses as his tongue licked at hers, touching it with slow, thorough pleasure and destructive heat.

When he drew back, Marty could only stare back at him in shock. It was her first kiss in years.

She fought to draw in oxygen. She fought to simply stand upright as his head tilted, his lips moving along her jawline to the shell of her ear.

"So sweet," he whispered, as her lashes drifted closed and she became immersed in the sensual, sexual world he was building around her. "I could take you just like this, Marty. So slow and easy, like a gentle summer rain."

His fingers were at her shoulders, touching the bare flesh beneath her robe, drawing the material over her shoulders as she felt her breasts throb with the need for touch now. His calloused fingertips sent a blaze of friction over her skin and had her suddenly pressing closer, needing more, needing his touch like the land needed the sun.

"I've dreamed of you," she said. "Of you taking me, Khalid. Fucking me slow and easy, fast and hard." Her breath caught as his body jerked, as though he had been struck, while lust became a brilliant flame in his eyes and urged her on. "I want to watch while you take me. See your cock press inside me while the pleasure burns me alive. I fantasize about it. I masturbate to it."

Her nails bit deeper into the flesh of his wrist as that image tore through her mind.

It was an image she gave him, an image she shared with him as his dark gaze locked with her own.

His hand slid to her breast as his breathing became harder, heavier. He cupped the rounded curve and dragged a shattered cry from her lips as sensation seemed to sear every nerve ending in her body. The stroke of his thumb over her nipple sent a near painful surge of bliss tearing to her womb, clenching it with a hard, tight spasm that stole her breath.

Jerking her head back, her gaze went to where his fingers cupped her flesh. A strong, dark hand, fingers outspread, her pale flesh cupped within it as he lifted the hardened tip of her nipple to his mouth.

"Oh God!" The sharp cry tore unbidden from her throat.

His lips wrapped around the pale pink areola, drew it inside his mouth, surrounded it with fire. His cheeks hollowed as he began to draw on her, his black eyes stared back at her, flickers of light trapped in a midnight sky, as Marty felt her pussy begin to burn, her clit to swell tight and hard, a near rapturous pleasure surging through her entire system. She felt the wet heat spill along the naked folds of flesh, surrounding her clit, sensitizing it further.

She couldn't breathe. She couldn't think. She could only watch as he destroyed her senses with his suckling mouth and wicked tongue.

When his head lifted, she flinched. The absence of sensation sent a violent, silent protest racing through her body, causing her to arch closer, to plead for more.

"So pretty." His fingertip touched her nipple before his gaze lifted back to her. "So innocent. Tell me, precious, would you flush with the same dazed pleasure if I sucked your clit instead?"

Her clit pulsed violently, the ache centered in the swollen nub, radiating through her body as it demanded more. She wanted to push him further, wanted to see him slip past the limit of his control but couldn't find the breath to speak, to tease.

"Should I suck that pretty clit now and find out?" The suggestion had her lips parting, the breath rushing from her lungs as another spasm of pure pleasure tightened her womb.

She wanted to scream yes. She wanted to beg for it. She wanted to watch his face as he touched her there, suckling her as he had her nipple, laving it with his tongue.

Her pussy convulsed, vibrating with a surge of such intense pleasure that she cried out from the sharp contractions.

Khalid blinked. Staring into her dazed expression he felt a punch of pure lust as the small orgasm rocketed through her from nothing more than his suggestion that he suck her clit.

Sweet heaven, what had he begun here? The innocence, the pure shocked delirium that filled her face at once humbled and terrified him.

He let his hand slide from her breast, down her stomach to the bare, wet mound of her pussy as she arched closer to him. He was a dead man if she was still innocent. He would expire there on the floor from both shock and regret.

She was twenty-seven years old. Surely to God she wasn't as innocent as she seemed. She couldn't be.

His fingers slid through slick feminine juices. The heat nearly scalded his fingers, the plump, tightly swollen nub of her clit drawing his attention as his fingertip glanced over it.

He needed to be inside her. His cock was pounding, demanding action. The need to fuck her was destroying him.

"Marty, we're home."

Khalid's gaze jerked from her face to the doorway as her father's voice sliced through the pleasure-dazed atmosphere of the room.

Hell, Mathews would fucking kill him. Jennings would drive a stake into his heart with a smile.

Before he could think, Marty jerked from him, her hands shaking. Her face flushed and filled with dazed confusion as she stared back at him and attempted to right the thin robe she wore.

"Marty?" Joe Mathews and Zach Jennings stepped into the room, and came to a hard, surprised stop.

There was no missing what they all knew had been going on. There was no mistaking the shock on Marty's face or the reddened rasp from the stubble of Khalid's beard against her neck.

Mathews took it all in, as did the other man. Eyes narrowed, they stared at Marty, then at Khalid.

"I'll just . . ." She swallowed tightly, panic filling her eyes now. "Shower." She nodded quickly. "I need to shower."

Like a teenager caught making out with her boyfriend, she turned and ran as Khalid watched her with amusement. The temptress, though still present in her gaze, fought to hide in the presence of her fathers.

While pushing his fingers through his hair, Khalid restrained the hard breath that would have escaped. He breathed in slowly, roughly, before crossing his arms over his chest and staring back at the two men with more arrogance than he felt at the moment.

That arrogance did little to affect the senator or the FBI director. Both men stared back at him in shock.

"I've lived the whole of her twenty-seven years and never had to catch her with a lover," Joe suddenly snarled, as he glared at Khalid. "I would appreciate never seeing it again, if you don't mind very much."

Khalid had to admit, he knew how she felt when she ran. He felt like a teenager caught with his hand in his girlfriend's pants, and damned if it wasn't awkward.

"I believe I could go the whole of the rest of my life and never have you walk in on such a thing again." Khalid cleared his throat uncomfortably.

Joe's outrage was a tangible thing as he stared at Khalid, but it was Zach's silence, the quiet, thoughtful look on his face that worried Khalid. Of the two, Zach was definitely the more dangerous.

Khalid refrained from giving in to the sense of discomfort that threatened to overcome him as Zach's look continued to pierce him with cool hazel eyes.

"Stay away from her unless you intend to do more than simply share her bed for a few nights," Zach finally stated, as he moved into the kitchen and over to the coffeepot. "She's not a toy to be played with, Khalid."

Khalid didn't miss the edge of steel in his voice.

"Of course she isn't. I realize that." He gave a sharp nod of his head.

He did understand. The world he was a part of existed on rules, rules that were not made to be broken, because of the very nature of the men involved.

Zach had given the ultimatum in front of a club witness. It didn't matter that the witness was also Marty's father or that he and Joe were both lovers with the same woman. Zach was Marty's godfather, equivalent to her father, and his wishes couldn't be discounted.

"Do you?" Zach turned back to him. "I've watched her obsession grow over the years where you're concerned, just as I've seen the way you watch her. But I also know you, son. You're not the forever kind. You're content to be no more than the other lover. That's not what she'll want from you. That's not what she needs."

"I understand, I need no lectures from you," Khalid bit out coolly, barely restraining his anger. "You may have caught us acting like teenagers, but that doesn't mean I'll be talked to as one."

"When you're caught acting that way in my house, with my daughter, then you can expect it," Zach informed him just as coolly. "Now stay the hell away from her unless you intend to force my hand in this. You don't want to do that."

Khalid stared back at the other man, assessed the degree of sincerity in his tone, and recognized the very serious warning he was being given.

And while he recognized the warning, he could have told the other man that it would be just as powerless against the hunger building between himself and Marty.

Instead, with a sharp nod, he strode from the room, then from the house. It was a warning he couldn't ignore, he told himself, as his driver, Abdul, opened the limo door and he slid inside. A warning he shouldn't discount. He wouldn't until he came against the fiery need in her gaze once again. And it was likely a decision he would pay for.

Zach wasn't just a member of the very exclusive club they both belonged to; he was also a part of the judicial committee that governed it and one of the most powerful members sitting on that panel.

The rules to their lives were simple, straightforward. They had to be for the club to have survived the past two centuries.

Until now, though, Khalid had never found them restrictive. Until now, he had never regretted them.

2

Marty escaped Zach's home, as well as her fathers' presence, without the lecture she had been expecting. Actually, she had managed to escape without so much as a fatherly talk. That one surprised her more than she wanted to admit.

Her fathers had never been shy when it came to discussing any aspect of life with her, claiming that they would prefer her to be prepared than to see her regret any actions she might take.

Khalid had already left. She had been disappointed that he wasn't there when she came back from her shower. Disappointed that the adventure in the kitchen had come to an end so soon.

Her lips quirked in a smile as she drove from Zach's home and headed to the heart of downtown Alexandria.

Kissing Khalid was more than an adventure, she thought. It had been a headlong flight into such the sensual core of pleasure that she would never have been able to pull herself free if he hadn't released her.

She licked her lips and remembered the feel of his. At first gentle, exploring and relishing, before becoming hungry, before consuming her with sensations she hadn't expected.

Damn. She wasn't going to survive the hunger raging through her. At this rate, she would burn to a crisp.

Making the turn into the downtown area, Marty directed the car to the restaurant and nightclub that she and several friends had agreed on for a nice little girls' night out.

Alyssa Stanhope had been a friend since childhood. She had always envied the other woman for her naturally streaked, blond hair, and soft, light blue eyes. For years, Marty had thought that Alyssa's life must be perfect, because of her tall, statuesque good looks. The truth was quite the opposite. Her father was a long-standing member of the U.S. Senate and an acquaintance of the Mathewses that they never socialized with because of Senator Stanhope's often cruel approach to his daughter.

Courtney Sinclair was Spanish, beautiful, and the wife of the owner of the exclusive, secretive establishment known merely as "the club." An establishment Marty had tried to investigate once. Her father had put a stop to that faster than she could blink.

She grinned at that thought. Her father and godfather, both of whom she had called Father, or Dad, on any given occasion, were members of that club. Men who shared their lovers or their wives. Men gathered together to protect themselves, their families, and their own reputations. It was an interesting concept, she had to admit. From what little she had learned over the years, the concept was one that had kept many high-standing social, as well as political, members out of the hot seat when it came to their personal and even their business lives.

Alyssa and Courtney had an odd relationship. They argued like enemies but seemed to stick together like sisters. As different as night from day, the two women had still managed to find common ground.

While making her way from the parking lot to the restaurant, Marty glimpsed Khalid's limo from the corner of her eye. His driver and bodyguard, Abdul, threw his hand up as he cast her a huge grin.

As she moved toward him, she smiled cheekily, knowing he would have something to say about the short skirt, snug top, and high heels she wore. Not to mention the makeup.

And she was right. He was now scowling as she walked toward him, his dark brown gaze filled with amusement and chastisement.

"So much beauty should never be displayed so indiscriminately," he sighed, as she approached him. "It should be saved for the husband who would better appreciate it."

"Give it a rest, Abbie." She laughed, as he flushed from the nickname. "How are you doing?"

She accepted a gentle kiss on her cheek before moving back.

"I am doing well, very well," he stated, with a sharp nod of his head. "The master, he is rather pissed with the world." He grinned back at her mockingly. "Have you been following him again?"

"Oh, so it's my fault he's in a bad mood?" She gave a light laugh. At least she wasn't the only one affected by the afternoon's adventure. "Trust me, Abdul, Khalid and a bad mood go hand in hand."

Abdul gave a heavy sigh, now staring at her with sad eyes, his weathered face creased into lines of concern. "I worry for him."

"Well, don't." She patted his shoulder as she moved by him. "Trust me, Khalid takes care of himself very well. We both know that one by now."

He took care of himself so well that he was one of her father's deepest undercover agents. Khalid managed to get information no one else could access, and infiltrated groups that no other agent could hope to slip into alive.

Striding along the cement walk to the entrance of the nightclub and restaurant, Marty threw an appreciative smile at the large doorman as he opened the door for her with a flourish.

Entering the building, she took the left hall and moved along the rounded wall quickly to the hostess's station and the smiling blonde standing in attendance.

"Ms. Mathews, it's so good to see you back." The hostess gave her a wide, toothy smile. "If you'll come with me, your party is waiting."

Her party wasn't waiting where they had promised they would be, in the restaurant itself. They were sitting instead inside a private balcony that looked out over the dance floor of the nightclub.

Courtney was staring over the balcony rail with a frown, her long brown hair cascading over her shoulder and the dark wood and brass rail, while Alyssa sat along the side of the wall, watching the other woman, also with a frown.

Alyssa tended to sit in corners, to hide, whenever she was in public. There were too many wagging tongues that were too eager to run to her father with the news of where she was and who she was with. And often, they were complete lies.

"Is she drunk yet?" Marty asked the other woman, as Courtney tried to find an angle that would allow her to see better. Though what she was trying to see, Marty couldn't decide.

"Not yet." Alyssa sighed, a small attempt at a smile tugging at her lips as she picked up her drink and took a long sip. "Give her time, though. She's pissed at Ian."

Courtney flipped around to glare at them. "I am not pissed at Ian. I am simply mildly displeased."

Marty glanced at Alyssa, then they both looked at the glass of wine as Courtney finished it.

"I give her an hour," Marty stated, taking her seat before turning and giving the hostess her drink preference.

"I give her less than that, actually," Alyssa said, as she shook her head, her blue eyes somber, her expression as carefully composed as always. It was rare for Alyssa to show emotion at all. She was the most carefully composed person Marty had ever met.

"I tell you both, tonight, I am not pissed at Ian." Courtney spun around, her regal stature spoiled by the frown on her face as she looked at Marty. "And you are late."

"So sorry." Marty almost rolled her eyes. "I was busy today."

Courtney narrowed her eyes at her. "I was by your parents' home today. I saw your car, and Khalid's, and I have been dying of curiosity. Ian has refused to tell me any gossip he may have heard." She pouted charmingly. "Tell me there is gossip, Marty."

It was all Marty could do to keep the flush from her face.

"Khalid was at the house to see Zach." She shrugged. "No gossip there, sorry, Court."

Lying to Courtney wasn't easy. Most people couldn't manage it. Marty had about a 50 percent success rate. Which wasn't that good, considering how many questions the woman could ask.

Courtney stared at her for a long moment before smiling beatifically. "You are such a liar, my dear. But I'll forgive you if you tell me the truth this moment. Otherwise, you will only force me to ask my good friend Khalid."

Marty arched a brow quizzically. "If you're such good friends, then he would have already told you any gossip there was to tell," she pointed out. "Now stop interrogating me. We're supposed to be having fun tonight."

Courtney sat back in her chair and crossed her arms over the brilliant scarlet top she wore as she glared, first at Marty, then at Alyssa. "Why do my good friends want to withhold the juicy details from me? It's not as though I ask for much."

"Is she becoming more spoiled or what?" Alyssa stared at Marty in mock surprise. "I think Ian's ruining her."

"I think she's the pot calling the kettle black." Marty turned back to Courtney with a sweet smile. "Tell me what you know and I'll tell you what I know."

And, of course, Courtney couldn't agree to that one. Marty watched as her friend glared at her once again, before huffing and picking up her drink.

"Are you still investigating Mustafa?" Alyssa asked Marty seriously. "You know Courtney won't give you any information on him."

"I want other information." Marty shrugged. "The investigation is over. It's personal now."

Courtney perked up. "Personal?" She propped her elbow on the table and cupped her chin in her hand. "How personal? Merely friends and concerned or 'wanting to jump that luscious body' personal?"

"She's always wanted to jump his body." Alyssa spoke low, in a too serious voice, as though afraid someone would hear her. "I believe we were fifteen at the time." A smile almost tipped her lips.

"Almost sixteen." Marty frowned back at her. "And that is really beside the point."

Courtney rubbed her hands together gracefully, her smile wrinkling her pert nose. "Ahh, the downfall of Khalid. I could get into this. I really could."

Marty simply stared back at her for long moments before leaning closer. "Who is his latest liaison?"

Courtney blinked back at her. "His latest lover? I don't believe I've heard."

"Who is he playing a third to?" Marty simplified the question.

Courtney narrowed her eyes, as though considering the question, before sighing heavily. "That information is not mine to give if you do not already have it. You know how this works, Marty. The rules are clear, and as a child of this world, I know you understand them well."

Marty hated the rules. There were times she hated the world she was born into. The club. That damned club that her fathers were part of, that Khalid was part of. They guarded their privacy like America guarded its gold.

No one admitted to being part of the club, no one ever confirmed anyone else's membership, and no one sure as hell revealed relationships. Especially Courtney, the wife of the too-arrogant, too-secretive owner of the club.

"Look, it's not as though he'll get involved with anyone else if he does start a relationship with you, Marty," Alyssa stated then. "Khalid is very well-known; his reputation as a man who keeps his word is beyond reproach. While you're with him, he wouldn't be involved with anyone else."

"That's not the point," Marty told them, as she leaned closer to the table. "To catch him, I first have to make certain I don't have someone else standing in my way. Why make a fool of myself otherwise?"

The idea of seduction was slowly taking hold in her mind. Could she do it? Khalid was more experienced than she was by far. Other than the lapses today, he had managed to keep a careful distance between them.

"Trust me, there is no relationship." Courtney waved the thought away. "The path is clear, my dear, and I'm certain we could help you if you were of a mind to truly capture our elusive Khalid. No other woman has managed to snag his heart before. You may be the first."

She would be the only. Marty was determined in that. If she managed it, her intent was to seduce more than his body. She wanted his heart. To reach the heart, she just might have to take other paths first, though.

"How do you capture a man determined to stay away from you?" She sighed. "More than ten years, Courtney, and I'm still trying."

"Men are stubborn." Courtney shook her head in confusion. "They know they want us, want to possess us. They want the heart and the soul of a woman. The more they want it, the harder they run from it. Trust me, if he hasn't taken you up on the invitations you have thrown at him, there could only be a few reasons why. One of which could be how much he does need you." She shrugged as though it were the only logical explanation.

Could it be that simple?

Marty concentrated on her drink, the idea rushing through her mind with the force of a tidal wave. She knew he wanted her. He wanted her badly enough that he had nearly taken her in Zach's kitchen. And his response hadn't been lukewarm. He had been burning for her.

"Has something happened?" Courtney leaned closer. "Tell me, Marty, has our beautiful Khalid made a move?"

Marty glanced up, smiling. "Maybe."

A soft, excited scream escaped her friend's lips as a wide smile finally crossed her lips. "Tell me about it," Courtney said. "What did he do?"

"Not much." Marty laughed as Courtney's expression fell from excited to disappointed.

She wasn't comfortable giving her friends details. Besides the fact that Marty was aware that Khalid had once played in Courtney's bed as the third in her relationship with Ian Sinclair before their marriage, there was also the fact that sharing such intimate details wasn't something Marty could ever do, at least not easily.

"I should interrogate Khalid instead," Courtney grumbled, her brown eyes filled with amusement. "Perhaps I could get the truth from him."

"I doubt that one," Marty retorted. "I don't think Khalid gives anyone the truth about anything at any time."

Courtney fell silent, her gaze thoughtful as she stared back at Marty for a long moment.

"Perhaps because no one has demanded the truth from him." It was Alyssa who broke the silence.

Though she was serene and composed, her regal features somehow were heartbreakingly set into lines of thoughtfulness.

"No one has ever gotten close enough to him to get the answers they demand," Courtney interjected. "Making him invest himself will be the hard part. That's not something Khalid does easily."

There had to be a reason for that, though. As the waiter appeared with menus the subject was dropped, but Marty had to admit the questions the conversation had raised intrigued her.

As Courtney said, Khalid didn't invest himself in his relationships. The women he slept with weren't his own; they were the wives or lovers of other men. He was the third in the relationships she had managed to uncover.

Not that it was ever easy to figure out who Khalid was involved with. But over the years she had developed an internal radar where he was concerned. She could sense whenever he was with a woman and if he was sleeping with her.

What would it take to get Khalid to invest himself in her? To steal his heart? God knew she had waited for him long enough, hungered for him with a power that kept other men at arm's length despite the loneliness that often plagued her.

She wasn't a one-night stand. And she couldn't force herself to begin a relationship with another man only to manipulate him into bringing Khalid in as a third. That would never be enough for her. It could never satisfy the need inside her.

"Speak of the devil." Courtney said, drawing Marty's attention as the waiter refreshed their ice water. "There is our elusive prey, my dear. Watch how he moves through the crowd, his gaze scanning, searching faces. Perhaps he's looking for you?"

Marty's gaze was drawn to the dance floor where, as Courtney pointed out, Khalid was moving through the throng of dancers, his gaze restless, his expression predatory.

Dressed in that white silk shirt and those blue jeans, he looked every inch the dangerous creature he truly was. Silk could never hide the strength in his body or the determination in his eyes.

Marty watched curiously as he paused at the edge of the dance floor, his gaze sweeping around once more before it lifted, and within seconds met hers.

A brutal punch of sensation slammed into her womb as his black eyes captured hers and held them. Heat flushed her body, bringing her nerve endings to life as they sizzled with anticipation and the memory of a touch so filled with pleasure that they ached for more.

Her breasts became swollen, her nipples hard. Her clit swelled instantly and throbbed as she felt her sex begin to heat, to dampen.

Her lips parted as she watched him, her breathing became harder, rougher. The memory of his touch swept through her, weakening her until she wondered whether her knees would hold her up if she actually stood to her feet.

For long, brutally intense seconds he held her gaze, stroking her with his eyes alone before his attention was pulled from her, leaving her shaking and fighting to hide the effect he had on her.

"My God," Courtney whispered at her side. "I don't think I've ever seen anything quite like that."

Swallowing tightly, Marty looked at her with an edge of desperation. "What are you talking about?"

"Dearest, he was eating you with his eyes." A satisfied smile curled Courtney's lips. "I don't believe I've ever seen Khalid stare at another woman quite like that."

"He hasn't," Alyssa stated. "Khalid is always cool and composed. It's his trademark."

"Tonight, he lost that trademark." Courtney fanned her face with her hand. "I'll definitely have to tell Ian about this."

"Why? According to you, he doesn't share information with you," Marty stated in irritation.

"Well, this is true." Courtney nodded. "But perhaps he just needs a bit of a nudge and a small incentive." Her gaze twinkled in knowing amusement. "Sometimes a woman simply must use the right bit of bait to lure in the information she needs."

"Or the man she needs," Alyssa murmured, her gaze catching Marty's. "Stop holding back, Marty. You keep waiting for him to come to you, and we all know Khalid has a will of steel. He can control himself with exemplary strength. But he can't control you. You're your own ace in the hole."

"Damn, she's good." Courtney sat back and looked at Alyssa in admiration. "Aly, I want to be you when I grow up."

"You'll never grow up," Alyssa shot back, her expression never shifting, as she flicked a look Courtney's way. "You're frickin' Peter Pan."

"Well, if I ever do." Courtney shrugged with a laugh. "But I do believe you've pinpointed Marty's problem."

"Of course I have," Alyssa responded archly, as she sat back and straightened her dress. "She's always watching and waiting. Khalid's always standing back and finding other things to distract him, simply because he's a man. If she wants him, then she's going to have to stop worrying about getting hurt and throw herself into the ring."

Marty turned and found Khalid in the crowd once again. He was at a table with two other men. She knew those men. Sebastian De-Lorents, a Spaniard and one of the newest members of the social set Marty had been raised in.

If she wasn't mistaken, he used to work for Interpol and was now the new manager of Ian Sinclair's club and had been a friend of Courtney's for years. However, it was the man sitting with them who had her gaze narrowing. Shayne Connor was an undercover CIA agent who worked out of the Middle East and often infiltrated terrorist cells known to be moving into the United States.

He was a deep-cover agent, and a very dangerous one. A man that even the FBI was often wary of when working with him. Her question was, what the hell was he doing in Alexandria with Khalid and Sebastian?

"Interesting," Alyssa murmured at her side. "Now what makes you think those three are *not* discussing the latest stock reports?"

Marty almost snorted at that one. Each man's expression was carefully composed as they spoke. They appeared relaxed; they even smiled; but there was something about their eyes, about the tense set of their bodies that told another story.

"Shayne Connor," Courtney stated, her voice low. "I haven't seen him in years."

"You know him?" Marty's gaze swung to her friend.

Courtney nodded. "He and Bastian partied extensively in Europe and especially in Spain for a while. Shayne's family disowned him, you know, though a sizable inheritance from his American grandfather allowed him to maintain the lifestyle he had been raised in."

"Disowned him?" Marty's brow arched. This was a story she hadn't yet heard on the ever elusive Shayne. "Why?"

Courtney turned back to her, a hint of worry in her gaze now, before she breathed out roughly. "For his suspected involvement in a bombing in Spain. Bastian never believed he was involved, but his parents are very rigid. They threw him out of their home and publicly disowned him. It destroyed him. Shayne spent several years trying to exonerate himself before he simply disappeared."

He hadn't disappeared; he had been recruited, instead. She'd known he was born of a Spanish father and an American mother, and that they were considered wealthy. She'd never heard he'd been disowned, however.

"He and Sebastian are friends, then?" Alyssa asked, her normally quiet gaze glinting with the barest hint of curiosity.

"They were very close as boys, I know." Courtney shrugged as she and Alyssa sat back, their attention shifting between the three men. "Even as young men they were more like brothers before Shayne was sent away by his parents. I saw him only a few times after that."

Marty kept the three men in her peripheral vision. Interesting. An undercover FBI asset, a CIA operative, and a former undercover Interpol agent. What did the three have in common besides friendship?

It could be a chance meeting, she thought. Sebastian was friends with Shayne, just as he was with Khalid. This was a very popular establishment. It wouldn't be a surprise that the three would come together. Unless you knew for a fact that two of them had ties to information and resources that placed them squarely in some very dangerous situations.

Finishing her drink, Marty wiped her lips with her napkin before collecting her purse from beside her plate and smiling at her friends.

"I'm heading home," she told them. "It's been a long day for me."

"Already?" Courtney pouted. "I was hoping we could have a few more drinks before we left."

"Not tonight." Marty shook her head. "I'm driving. But next time, I promise."

"She's being a spoilsport, Aly." Courtney turned to Alyssa. "Do something about her."

Alyssa shook her head as a smile tugged at the corner of her lips.

"She's not the only one who needs to make an early night of it," she said. "I need to head home as well. Perhaps next time."

"You're both going to give me a bad reputation if I begin arriving home before midnight," Courtney stated ruefully. "Ian may begin to believe I'm actually settling down."

"I'm sure you can convince him otherwise." Rising to her feet, Marty gave the other two women a little wave before moving from the balcony and heading along the wide hall to the stairs. As she left the restaurant she noticed that Khalid was no longer at his table.

She needed to get home to her computer, from which she could pull up the information she needed on the three men. There was a connection among them; there had to be. Despite appearances, those three should not be together, for the simple reason that they all had something to lose if the wrong people saw them together. Someone like Deerfield, or one of his agents.

Shayne Connor might be an agent, but only a few within the FBI knew that. The operation that had brought her in contact with him had necessitated her keeping his true purpose for being there a secret. He was a valuable contact to have, and one she didn't want to cross.

Making her way from the club Marty strode along the sidewalk to the parking lot, preferring to walk rather than use the valet.

Shadows stretched along the area despite the lights that surrounded it. Customers milled around as they chatted and moved to and from the restaurant. No one appeared interested in anything other than their own concerns. No one paid attention to the lone woman walking through the parking lot until she neared her car.

"You didn't mention you were going out this evening, love." Khalid spoke from the shadows of the trees, stepping just close enough to allow her to make out his dim outline as the darkness wrapped around him like a jealous lover.

Leaning against the BMW she crossed her arms beneath her breasts, refusing to tread into the darkness where he watched her like a dark, hungry predator.

"I didn't know that I should give you my itinerary," she drawled, watching as he moved closer, the hungry glint in his eyes fueling the adrenaline coursing through her.

"Perhaps you should," he stated, his voice low, deep, throbbing with a hidden power.

She swore she could feel him under her flesh, the heat of his body sinking inside her as he stopped just before her.

"Perhaps you're living in a dream world," she said, challenging him, challenging the command in his expression as he stared down at her, his gaze dark, seductive.

"And perhaps you are trying to involve yourself in matters that do not concern you."

He didn't touch her, but the need for it was a hunger she could feel wrapping around her.

"I'm always getting into things I shouldn't. That is my job description. Remember?" She straightened, bringing her body closer to his, the heat of him nearly flush against her.

"Stop." His fingers curled around her upper arm as his expression tightened, his gaze narrowing on her.

"Stop what?" Brow lifting, she stared back at him archly. "Remember, Khalid, you sought me out, it wasn't the other way around."

"I know you," his voice was a heavy growl. "You're about to make a mistake, Marty."

"A mistake?" Her hand lifted, pressing lightly against his chest. "I'm not the one that made this mistake. I believe that was you."

She could feel his heart beneath her hand, beating hard and heavy, racing with the same power that she felt in her own.

"Your father warned me to stay the hell away from you." His fingers tightened on her arm reflexively. "I believe he should have warned you instead."

A smile tipped her lips. "He knows better." She moved closer, watching his expression, feeling the power of her own inexperience and the desperate need tearing through her. Seducing him was her goal, but it was going to take more than standing in the dark with him.

"You should know better than this." Suddenly, as though the power of her own need transmitted to him, he pulled her against his body, one hand pressing tight and hard against her hips to hold her flush against the strength of his erection.

The heavy, erect width of his cock pressed against her lower stomach, the heat of it sinking past his slacks and the silk of her clothes as her breath caught in her throat.

God, she felt like one of those damned stupid fainting misses from the old romances her mother used to read. The ones who swooned seconds before the pirates had their way with them. Yeah, the ones she had laughed at for so many years.

"Why should I know better?" Her hands slid over his chest to his shoulders. "Because you're meeting with a deep-cover CIA agent known to share his women, just as you do? Or perhaps you and the CIA agent are meeting with a man known to have ties to both of you? Tell me, Khalid, does my godfather know you're up to fun and games with the CIA and Interpol?"

It had been no more than a suspicion at first. Sebastian De-Lorents was a hell of an actor, but seeing them together, hearing the history Bastian and Shayne had, it had finally clicked.

"You don't know what you're talking about." The slow tension in his body told her otherwise.

She almost laughed. The sound came out more as a suspicious little snort. "Really, Khalid, you are talking to the woman who knows all your little games and how you play them," she reminded him. "Tell me what games you're playing with our local spook and his Spanish cohort, and I might be nice and not tell Daddy on you." The facetious threat didn't go over well.

Or perhaps it went over too well.

A heartbeat later he lifted her, pulled her into the dark shelter of the surrounding trees. Before she could think to struggle he had her back against a tree, her body lifted to him, his lips covering hers.

And he wasn't stopping there.

Sensation raced across her flesh as pleasure began to stream through her nerve endings from her lips to her thighs. His hand pushed beneath her skirt, flattened against the upper roundness of her leg and lifted it until she was crooking her knee over his hip.

His cock wedged against the mound of her pussy then, throwing her senses into overload as his head jerked back, his lips tearing from hers.

Marty stared at him in ecstatic shock as his hips rolled subtly, the heavy erection beneath the material of his slacks pressing, stroking against the swollen bud of her clit.

"You will destroy me," he snarled, as one hand curved around the nape of her neck to hold her head in place as his head lowered again.

His lips nipped at hers, sipped at them for long moments before he drew back once again.

"How will I destroy you?" The question raged in her mind with each warning he gave her. "Tell me, Khalid, how am I such a threat to you?"

His fingers stroked her neck as the other arm curled around her hips, lifting her higher, holding her against him as her knees clasped his hips now.

The feel of his cock pressing between her thighs was exquisite. The slight movement of his hips against hers sent hard, racking shudders racing through her system as flames of pleasure raced over her flesh.

"Perhaps, love, it is I who am the danger to you."

There was no chance to argue, to retaliate, as her lips parted, his tongue stroking past them to hers, his lips sealing in the shocking, heated moan that would have torn from her lips.

She was drowning in the pleasure. Her knees gripped his hips tighter as her arms wrapped around his shoulders to bring him closer to her. His hands stroked her back, her hips, bunched the material of her dress between his fingers and dragged it over the curve of her ass before cupping the bare rounded rise of flesh.

He stroked, kneaded. His fingers clenched into the sensitive mounds and parted them, sending shooting arcs of sensation racing along the hidden entrance that the narrow cleft concealed.

She had touched herself there, just to see what it felt like. She had wondered what Khalid's touch there would do to her senses. Now she knew. His fingers slid deeper into the parted flesh, stroked, pressed.

There was too much pleasure. Sensation upon sensation began to attack her, building and flooding her senses with waves of nearing ecstasy as she fought to hold on to just enough control to memorize every touch, every arc of the hungry flames licking through her now.

"Damn you." He jerked back from her again, but he didn't let her go.

As she stared up at him, her body riding high on the pleasure racing through her, his fingers pressed beneath the silk of her panties and found the hot, slick juices.

"Stop pushing for this," he commanded, but still his fingers slid through the rich essence, gathered it and drew it back to the tight, shy entrance of her ass. "Before you destroy us both."

Her head fell back again as shock rounded her eyes and pleasure stole her breath. His finger pressed against the snug entrance, then entered just enough to send a pinch of pleasure pain tearing through her before halting.

"Khalid." His name tore from her lips.

"God help me." His eyes glittered in the darkness as his thumb pressed into the clenched opening of her pussy. "You're so fucking tight I ache to be inside you." His finger and thumb flexed, moved inside her, creating shards of sensation that threatened her sanity.

This wasn't the place for it, a part of her whispered. The other part, the woman dying for his possession, was screaming for it in silence.

Her knees tightened on his hips, her lashes fluttering at the exquisite sensations overtaking her.

"Then why fight it?" She was almost begging now. "You're teasing me, Khalid. Teasing us both."

"I'm drowning in you." His lips sipped at hers again. "And you're doing nothing to save either of us."

"But I don't want to be saved," she whispered against his lips as he rubbed his own against hers. "If I wanted to be saved, I wouldn't be here. I'd be in another man's bed instead of begging to be in yours."

And that was what she was doing. Begging. Pleading, in all but words.

"Damn you." He pulled back again.

His finger slid from the heated, too sensitive grip of her anus as his thumb slid free of her pussy. Feeling him release her nearly destroyed her. Her knees were weak as she took her own weight, her system overloaded with desperation and the ache for release.

"This has to end now," he ordered, his voice rough. "No more."

"Coward." Jerking back from him she nearly stumbled as she pushed away from him and the tree, glaring back at him as she fought to get her breathing, her emotions, under control.

"Be careful, Marty." His hand jerked out, his fingers curling around her wrist as she tried to turn and head back to her car. "I could take that as a very serious threat."

"So sue me," she snapped back, pulling her arm out of his grip and stumbling from the shadows. "Better yet, don't bother, you'd lose. The evidence is all on my side, sweet cheeks."

Jerking her key from the small hidden pocket of her dress, she grabbed her purse from the ground where it had fallen and stalked to the door of her car.

Releasing the auto lock she pulled open the door and stared back at him from the dubious shield between them.

"You could never understand," he said, his tone filled with dark bitterness.

"And you'll never have the guts to explain," she accused him. "But I'm at a point where I really don't give a damn. Seducing you is starting to bore me anyway. I think I'll go home and see if I can find out why the hell Connor is in my town and what the three of you are up to. I do believe I would find that vastly more entertaining."

He moved fast. Coming from the shelter of the trees he was nearly upon her before she slid into the car, slammed the door closed, and shoved the key into place.

She didn't look at him until she was backing out of the parking space, and what she saw then sent more than shock racing through her. There was a thrill of arousal, and a spark of knowledge.

Behind him, Shayne did nothing to hide the fact that he was there. In the second that she caught his expression she saw the hunger, and knew he had been there watching, listening.

It was no more than she had already suspected, but she hadn't anticipated her own response to it. If she had been wet before, then her panties were soaked now. If she had been aroused before, then lust was flooding her now.

All for nothing.

Reversing quickly she pressed her foot to the gas and shot from the parking lot. It was time she took off the gloves where Khalid was concerned and show him that she may want him until hell froze over, but he sure as hell wasn't the only damned man in the world.

And quite frankly, she was sick of waiting on a lover who did nothing but deny her. It was time to check out other possibilities. And perhaps to show him exactly what he was going to be missing.

3

A week later, Khalid stepped into the secured meeting room Sebastian had prepared and faced a part of his past that he had avoided at all costs.

Staring back at the man who could have been his twin brother, Khalid felt his chest tighten, felt the pent-up agony of guilt, and fought not to apologize once again for events he had been unable to control.

Abram cl Hamid-Mustafa rose slowly from the couch, his muscular frame standing tall and proud as fierce black eyes stared from a face that had turned to stone years before.

A short, neatly trimmed beard and mustache now covered his lower face. Thick, heavy black lashes would have given his black eyes a sensual, drowsy look had it not been for the pure ice that filled his gaze.

That ice melted as Khalid closed the door behind him and watched as Abram approached him. Behind the other man, Sebastian remained sitting, just as Shayne did.

They were the only ones to attend this meeting, the first in more than two years.

"Khalid, you are of course looking as decadent as ever." A glimmer of a smile warmed Abram's dark gaze as he took in the jeans, the untucked white shirt, and casual leather shoes that Khalid wore.

Khalid grunted at the description as he shot a disgruntled look at his brother's attire. "Slumming today?"

Abram wore a baseball cap, jeans, and a black T-shirt with the name of a popular hard rock band emblazoned on it.

"Ah, the things we must do to survive, eh?" Abram plucked at the front of his shirt before giving Khalid a brief, strong hug and murmuring quietly, "It is good to see you again, little brother."

"Five minutes doesn't make me your little brother," Khalid reminded him as they parted.

"Of course it does." It was their lifelong argument. "Just because you are the son of his prized, redheaded pigeon doesn't make you any less younger than I. It simply makes you luckier."

Khalid's mother, Marilyn Kobrin, a French college student who had been kidnapped while on vacation had had a brother, as well as a fiancé, who had been determined to find her. Marilyn hadn't been the type to sit around and wait on rescue, however.

No more than a few weeks after Khalid's birth, she had wrapped her child in a blanket, tied him to her back, and escaped the palace she had been locked inside, for the desert beyond.

She should have died. The desert was no place for a woman alone with a child to care for and very little water for her on her journey.

Fortunately, her brother and fiancé had managed to track her to Azir's lands and had been watching the palace as she scaled down the wall that had enclosed the gardens that the women were allowed to gather within.

Azir's "redheaded pigeon," as he had called her, had flown the cage and quickly escaped with the son Azir had claimed as his second heir. An heir he hadn't seen again for eighteen years.

"I'm not so certain about the 'lucky' part." Khalid shrugged. "It seems to me that neither us have much influence in the luck department."

"Luck is what you make of it." Abram sighed wearily as they both moved to the bar.

Sebastian and Shayne joined them, the two men remaining quiet as Khalid and Abram fought to find that comfort level they had once shared.

They had been nearly inseparable after Khalid had returned to the desert to meet, and to destroy, the man who claimed to be his father. Now, more than ten years later, Khalid wondered if he and Abram weren't the ones who would eventually be destroyed.

"So, I hear from Shayne that your woman has you running in circles." There was an edge of amusement to Abram's voice, as well as something else. Something darker, something edged with danger or warning.

"She's definitely making life interesting," Khalid agreed as Shayne poured their drinks and handed them across the bar.

"She's got him watching the shadows and pacing the rooms, Abram." Shayne grunted. "He doesn't know if he's coming or going."

Khalid's lips tightened as he turned away from the bar.

"There is no need for guilt, Khalid." Abram's quiet statement made him pause.

"Isn't there?" Khalid asked before shaking his head and continuing to the sitting area arranged in the middle of the room. "Why are you here, Abram?"

He couldn't imagine what would make his brother risk his life, as well as his place within Azir Mustafa's heirship, to visit his little brother.

"Actually, I managed to manipulate Azir into ordering the visit." Disgust filled Abram's tone as he spoke of their father. "He wishes the trip to remain a secret from Ayid and Aman. According to him, it would only upset them needlessly."

Rage ignited inside Khalid at the thought of Azir's loyalty to his two youngest sons. They were terrorists, men who sought to destroy everything the royal family, Azir's distant cousins, had ever fought to maintain.

Azir had protected them for far too many years. He had lied for them, defended them, stood in front of his king and swore that Khalid lied, and that, as an American citizen, Khalid had no loyalty to Saudi Arabia or to the ruling family. And therefore, there was no basis to believe his account of the death of Lessa Mustafa, Abram's young wife.

"And how did you manage such a manipulation?" Khalid sneered, thinking of Azir and his own manipulations where his two youngest sons were involved.

"There are rumors." Carrying his drink, Abram moved to the sofa across from Khalid and took his seat once again. "Azir has heard that you were involved in the capture of a small terrorist cell moving into D.C. several months ago. Two of the men were killed. Ayid and Aman were involved with this terrorist cell. Azir fears you're going to target this once again."

"So I have." Khalid sipped at his drink as he stared back at Abram, reading the hatred and icy rage in his brother's gaze.

It was a rage that filled Khalid as well. A rage born of blood and death, of deceit and hatred.

"Azir does to Ayid and Aman the same as he does to us." Abram grimaced in anger. "You know this well. He defends them, refuses to believe the truth. That we will destroy Ayid and Aman, no matter what it costs, and vice versa. The world he lives in is not one that reality touches."

"At least not in this matter," Khalid agreed. "Did the old bastard send you to beg me again not to kill them?"

Each time his brothers fucked up, Azir sent a plea to Khalid to stay his hand, to leave his brothers unharmed. Khalid ignored each plea, and with every bit of information and proof he could garner, he sought to take his brothers down.

"This is a fair description of the reason he sent me," Abram said, his tone rasping with fury and pain. "As though the past had never happened." Abram shook his head. "As though the blood of my wife does not stain their hands."

The blood of his wife, as well as the blood of Aman's and Ayid's own wives.

"They won't forget the vendetta they have against the two of you," Sebastian warned them as he and Shayne remained at the bar. "They're only growing in strength and numbers, Khalid. The men you helped capture in D.C. was only a small number of them."

Khalid was well aware of that.

"That mission you and Shayne cooperated with was one Ayid and Aman were counting on succeeding," Abram said as he leaned closer, his gaze becoming cold and hard once again. "It is only a matter of time, Khalid, before they learn for sure of our involvement. When they do, they will strike once again. I do not wish to see you lose what I lost so long ago. Your woman must remain safe."

"There's no way they can find out." Khalid shook his head. "I've learned how to cover my tracks, Abram."

That was something he and Abram both hadn't known how to do effectively during those years in Saudi. That inexperience had cost them Lessa's life, and nearly their own.

"Rumors are already surfacing," Abram argued. "Just as I know Shayne has warned you. One of the terrorists involved in the D.C. cell managed to escape back to Saudi. He carried the tale that he saw you when the agents swarmed into the safe house for the arrest. Were you there?"

"The chance that Ayid and Aman would be there was too great," Khalid said, his voice tight.

But they hadn't been there. They had returned to Saudi hours before the Homeland Security agents had overtaken the small cell.

It had been a far different scenario than the one of ten years before in Saudi, just outside Riyadh.

There had been no agents then, just a fighter jet and a bomb, and a small, mud hut beneath the blistering sun just outside the city. The eight-man terrorist cell had been gathered there, along with Ayid, Aman, and their wives. That time as well, his brothers' luck had ridden fast and hard upon their backs. Ayid and Aman had slipped from the hut to meet with a contact they had approached within the Saudi Royal Palace. A cook who had conspired with them to kill the king and his immediate family.

The Saudi Royal Air Force had struck before they returned to the hut, and the information that it was Khalid who had supplied their location to the Air Force had been on the cook's lips when he met with the brothers.

Ayid and Aman had known who to strike, just as they had known that Abram would have been involved in whatever Khalid was involved in. Abram and Khalid hadn't been at the palace when the brothers had returned, but Lessa had been. And because Abram had shared his wife's body with Khalid, Azir had stood back and allowed Ayid and Aman to brutalize her.

He had blamed Lessa for what he called Abram's and Khalid's "unnatural desires."

"Ayid and Aman weren't there, though," Abram informed him about the most recent mission. "Their suspicion that you and I were working together once again to provide the information of the movements of this cell have risen due to the information the terrorist carried back to Ayid and Aman's ears after the raid. He swore he saw you."

"And what does Azir think?" Khalid asked curiously.

"So far, he has Ayid and Aman on a tight leash," Abram sighed heavily. "It is a hold that may not last long. And it is one that Ayid, especially, will find a way to work around."

Ayid was older than Aman. He was the leader and the planner, while Aman was no more than the gopher, the pitiful sidekick who followed whichever direction Ayid took.

Khalid could feel rising inside him now the certainty that Ayid and Aman would strike against him.

And what better way to strike than to come after a woman Khalid claimed as his own?

Marty's timing was damned inconvenient, Khalid thought.

"Khalid, Zach has his men on this as well," Shayne said, his tone low as Khalid rose slowly from the couch to pace to the window that looked out over the gardens. "There's no way you can hide the fact that there's something between you and Marty. Not now."

Khalid wanted to shake his head. He wanted to deny that he had done anything, that he had ever placed her in danger. But there was no denying it. He had done just that. He had drawn her into the most dangerous game of his life, and he was damned if he knew how to pull back now.

"Ayid and Aman have sworn their vengeance against both of us," Abram reminded Khalid. "I cannot stay and help you protect her."

No, he couldn't stay. He would not be Khalid's third. Not that Khalid had planned to go that route. Abram had his responsibilities in Saudi, and Khalid had his here—despite the bond that had developed between them during the years Khalid had spent in Azir Mustafa's small region. The brothers, so close in looks and temperament, had found they had shared similar interests as well. Most especially that dark, driving hunger to share their lovers.

"When are you going back?" Abram never stayed long, never spent enough time away from Saudi to allow the brothers to suspect that he was doing more than attending business in Riyadh.

"In a few days," Abram answered as Khalid turned back to him. "I've brought with me the pictures and files I've put together over the months for Shayne and Zach Jennings. The training camp in the mountains, just over the border, has grown in recruits. I counted more than thirty men last week. Ayid and Aman were there, but, as always, their faces were covered. There's no way to prove it's them by pictures alone."

The brothers moved with a distinctive stride and their voices had a clearly recognizable pitch. There was no way to document it though without a recorder, and there was no way Abram could get close enough for that.

"Our main concern at this point is their next move," Shayne said. "As I told you when I arrived, Ayid and Aman are already accusing you and Abram of being part of the capture of the D.C. cell. That was too important to them, Khalid. They're going to come after you."

Of course they were. Sooner or later. They may even get lucky and manage to kill him this time.

Not that they hadn't tried hard before. Unfortunately, they were limited in the funds Azir allowed them, as well as in the freedom he gave them. And they would never be satisfied unless they could drive the stake into his heart themselves.

"I'll be prepared, then." He gave a short, brief nod to the three men watching him. "And I'll make sure Marty's protected."

"There is no more that I can do here, then." Abram removed the baseball cap to run the fingers of one hand through his hair before replacing the cap. He gazed back at Khalid regretfully. "I must go now."

Khalid moved to him, embraced him, and damned if he didn't also feel regret tearing through him. They had made a pact so many years ago, to always be a part of the other's lives. Now, not only distance separated them, but also the evil whose blood they shared.

"Kiss your lovely woman for me," Abram said softly as he drew back. "And watch your back, Khalid."

"Abram, I'll see you back to your hotel." Sebastian stepped from the small private bar, his black eyes in contrast to the dark blond hair that grew thick and long to the collar of his black shirt.

"Once again, I am in your debt, Sebastian." Abram nodded as Shayne also moved forward.

Extending his hand, Abram shook Shayne's firmly. "Watch out for my little brother." His lips quirked with amused fondness as he glanced back at Khalid. "See you soon."

Leaving the room, Abram didn't look back. He never did. Khalid saw his big bodyguard, Mohammed, step forward to lead Abram from the building. And then the door closed behind him and his brother was gone once again. Turning to Shayne, Khalid gave a weary sigh. "I must make a few calls. If you don't mind meeting me in the bar later?"

Shayne gave a quick nod and an amused grin as he strode to the door before turning back. "Tell Zach I said hi."

The panel closed softly behind him, leaving Khalid alone with nothing but his thoughts and his fears.

The fear that his past was rising against him now, and the fear that despite the battle he had waged against it, Marty would be smack in the middle of it this time.

Jerking the cell phone from the holster at his side he flipped it open and placed his call.

"Zach." The FBI director answered on the first ring.

"We have a problem."

4

A week. Khalid managed to stay away from the tempting little vixen one full week. He'd never realized how often he'd sought Marty out over the years.

When he had spoken on the phone with her godfather, a hunger—a need to bind her to him—rose inside him like a fever that couldn't be cooled. It had tightened his body and torn at his soul.

He felt like an addict needing a fix. In the past, just the sight of her had been enough, or perhaps a dance, a flirtatious remark, or a heated little exchange. But always there had been the knowledge in the back of his mind after those occurrences, that she was still his. That she still belonged to him.

Until the full seven days had passed with no sight of her and no small comments or tidbits of information from her normally too talkative father, Joe. And suddenly he needed all those things desperately.

Thankfully, Marty had shown no interest for any man other than him. So there had been no threat that she would be taken from him. But his past had always been the reason he couldn't reach out for her, either. Why he couldn't possess her.

As he stood, staring out the window of the room used to meet with his brother, Khalid watched as Shayne walked through the wide French doors leading from the bar to walk into the confines of the garden below.

His past was about to rise again with a vengeance. It was also the reason Shayne was in D.C. It was the reason Azir had sent Abram on his hasty trip from Saudi.

Azir was desperate to regain Khalid's favor. Favor he had never possessed, and never would. The man who had bought, raped, and tormented Khalid's mother was a monster to him. The only reason Khalid had agreed to go to Saudi just after he turned eighteen was to find a way to destroy Azir.

Azir hadn't been destroyed, though. Abram and Khalid had been the ones to suffer.

Staring out into the flowering gardens below, it wasn't the beauty of the perfect blooms he saw.

He saw his past.

He saw the blood.

Raking his fingers through his hair, he drew in a hard, frustrated breath before turning away and stalking back to the drink he had sat on the table next to the couch and tossed it back quickly. Grimacing at the burn as it traveled down his throat, Khalid wondered if he would ever erase the sins of the past from his soul.

His jaw clenched as memories and rage threatened to flood him. It had been ten years, and still he couldn't get the sight of it, the horror of it, out of his head.

He could still hear Abram's howls of rage as they echoed through their father's desert palace. He could see the woman he and Abram had pledged themselves to, spread out upon her marriage bed, naked, her gaze staring in blank horror at the ceiling above the bed, blood covering her body and the satin sheets, and pooling between her thighs.

And now, here he was, so many years later, tempting that horror to strike once again.

"The day will come, brothers," Ayid had warned them in a letter sent to both Khalid and Abram weeks later, *"when you will claim a woman that is yours rather than another's. The day will come when you will cling to one heart. And when it does, we will be there. We will strike. And you will know it was your actions that took the life of the one you love. Just as your actions took ours."*

Khalid knew he must be insane, because there wasn't a chance in hell that he could endure the pain Abram had endured when he lost Lessa. Should he lose Marty to the vindictive cruelties of his half brothers, he would go on a killing rampage unlike any Ayid and Aman could imagine.

Even knowing it was more than he could endure, he couldn't stay away from her. Not anymore. But more important, she had declared herself, and Marty wasn't backing down in spite of what she had said a week ago. He knew Marty too well. Even if Khalid didn't respond, his brothers would take notice of her eventually.

And with that knowledge came the realization that to have her, he would have to protect Marty as he had never been able to protect another. And there was one man, besides Abram, who he trusted to help him do that.

Moving from the meeting room, Khalid strode down the stairs to the main bar where he found Shayne sitting in solitude, as he normally did, a newspaper raised as he lounged comfortably in one of the recliners in the corner of the large room.

The CIA agent claimed, to the members who dared question his presence, that he was on vacation, though Khalid was well aware that the man had never had a vacation in his life. Not a true one. Shayne had been the first to warn Khalid of the rumblings heard in Saudi of the Mustafa's brothers' plans to strike against him and had helped set up today's meeting with Abram. He had come to warn him. But he would stay to protect the woman he had become fond of over the years.

"Shayne." Khalid took a seat on the sofa across from him.

The newspaper lowered slowly. The other man looked back at him, his expression curiously bland, though his light brown eyes danced with knowledge. "I will require a third." Khalid kept his voice low but his intentions clear.

Shayne folded the paper before laying it carefully on the low table between them.

"Do you think it's the best time for this?" Shayne tilted his head questioningly as his gaze darkened with a hint of disapproval.

"I believe it is." Khalid nodded. "Ayid and Aman are planning to strike, as we always knew they would. Marty is not going to back down, and resisting her isn't something I believe I can do for much longer."

Explaining himself wasn't something Khalid did well, but in this case, the explanation was required. How to protect her, how to shelter and keep her safe would have to be discussed, questioned, and planned in exacting detail. That would require more than just explanations, and he would have to face others besides Shayne. He would have to face her fathers.

Looking around the nearly deserted room, Shayne slid the recliner back into its upright position before leaning forward. "They don't know about her yet. There's a very good chance we can keep her out of this," he began.

Khalid waved that suggestion away. "There's no way to keep her out of it. She will draw their attention once they decide to make their move. The question remaining is how to protect her while we're resolving the situation."

Shayne nodded before his gaze narrowed and his expression became thoughtful, intent.

"We've always known this was a dangerous game we were playing where your half brothers are concerned. I had hoped we'd have the proof the Saudi government required by now."

Khalid sighed wearily. "They're smart. They wouldn't have survived so long otherwise."

"What about Abram?"

Khalid understood the question Shayne was asking, he merely preferred to ignore it.

"I do not require his permission," Khalid stated firmly.

"The two of you share a past in this," Shayne pointed out, his gaze narrowing at Khalid's deliberate attempt to avoid the subject. "I admit, I expected you'd make him the offer instead."

"Abram has other responsibilities, and what is in the past is long buried."

Shayne slowly nodded. "As long as that's where we stand. If you intend to introduce her to any other as a potential third, then I'll decline if it's all the same to you."

Khalid was more amused at the other man's attempts to control some part of this relationship with Marty than angry, though anger wasn't far behind. It was rather a good thing that he had developed the patience he had over the years.

"I understand." Khalid nodded soberly as he began to rise to his feet. "Forgive me for disturbing you."

Shayne glared back at him. "Sit back down you arrogant bastard," he snapped. "Hell, at least give me a chance at part of her heart."

"I will give you the chance to secure yourself as our third, nothing more." Khalid resumed his seat. "I have no desire to share more than I have stated. Her bed, as well as her safety."

Khalid found himself feeling rather possessive where Marty's emotions were concerned.

Shayne grimaced at the statement.

"Hell, I was hoping Marty would demand more along the lines of what her parents have."

"And you are prepared for such a commitment?" Khalid arched his brow in disbelief. He wasn't surprised by the rueful smile Shayne gave him in return.

"It would have been nice to play house for a while." Shayne finally shrugged. "She's a damned fine woman, and coming home to her wouldn't be a hardship."

The life Shayne lived was solitary one. He'd mentioned that to

Khalid and Sebastian several times. Evidently, he thought Marty could provide more than the sexual intensity a third was normally seeking.

"She's not a toy." Khalid found himself repeating her father's warning. "She's my woman, and she will be treated as such."

"And you'll need a third, one you can trust until the situation with your brothers is resolved." Shayne's expression turned serious now. "We're not going to have much time, Khalid. Ayid and Aman won't be held back by your father for long. Old man Mustafa may think he can control his sons and keep you from killing each other, but you know they'll make their move soon."

"Yes, I'm aware of this." He was, to the very darkest corners of his soul, aware of what he would have to do.

"You'll also have to come clean with Marty," Shayne told him. "You can't let this happen without warning her about what's coming. Her, as well as her fathers."

"You do not need to warn me about how I must handle this situation," Khalid said, his tone rough. "I am no imbecile, Shayne, nor am I uncaring enough to start something without first warning her of the consequences."

There was no way to hide his past from her any longer.

Damn, he couldn't get her out of his head, his heart, or his fears.

Shayne was watching him with that penetrating stare once again. "Marty and I are friends, Khalid," Shayne said, his voice serious. "I don't want to see her hurt. Are you certain you can't stay away from her?"

"Can you guarantee that once Ayid and Aman decide to strike that they won't also go after Marty simply because they suspect her interest is returned by me?"

Shayne's lips tightened. "I can't guarantee that."

"Once she learns why I have resisted her, she will run headlong into danger whether I allow it or not. Not informing her of the danger is just as dangerous. Tell me Shayne, what other choice is left?"

There was no other choice, and they both knew it.

"Then I have no other choice but to help you protect her." Shayne shook his head, his shaggy hair falling over his brow before he pushed it aside. "Damn. We should just kill those bastards and be done with it."

"If such a thing had been possible, then I would have done so already," Khalid informed him. "However, bring me a plan with a chance of success, and we'll talk."

Shayne ran his hand over his face in a gesture in frustration as he bared his teeth. "Sons of bitches," he finally snarled.

"No doubt," Khalid agreed. "It doesn't change the fact that we must protect Marty now."

"She'll shoot us if she finds out we're trying to protect her," Shayne told him.

Khalid shook his head slowly. "She will have enough of the truth to understand. And I will have the comfort of knowing that should anything happen to me, you will see to her safety."

Silence descended between them as Shayne continued to watch him carefully. Should his brothers succeed in killing him, then Khalid didn't want his woman left to suffer that alone. He wanted another to comfort her, to ease her grief.

"I'll do that," Shayne promised. "If needed. But let's see what we can do to keep you alive."

Shayne wondered if Khalid was aware of the demons that roiled in his eyes, the pain that gleamed within them.

He'd held out against Marty longer than any of the members of the Club had imagined he could. It had cost him, though. With the exception of Abram, Shayne knew more than anyone what it had cost him. He'd seen the darkness that filled Khalid. He'd seen the cost of the missions Khalid had completed as the Desert Lion in Saudi.

Khalid knew the region that Azir Mustafa controlled like the back of his hand. It wasn't unheard of for him to lead strike teams into the region to take down the terrorists moving across the border.

As the CIA agent assigned to the area, Shayne had worked with

Khalid as well as Abram, more than once. And in each man he'd seen the scars that the past had left. Scars that marred the soul rather than the body.

The Mustafa brothers, Ayid and Aman, were demons of the worse sort. Vicious, brutal, and filled with hatred.

Shayne had also seen how much it had hurt Khalid to turn away from the woman he ached for. There were times Shayne wondered if Khalid even knew that he was in love with Marty.

"When will you tell her?" Shayne finally asked.

Khalid sighed. "Tonight, perhaps."

How interesting. Shayne barely managed to restrain his smile.

"That might be hard to do."

Khalid's eyes narrowed on him, and Shayne found his suspicion almost amusing.

"You say this for what reason?" Khalid asked, his tone turning cold.

"She's attending a ball tonight with Senator Mathews." Shayne grinned. "I heard she actually approached another member of the club with an invitation, but it was very nicely refused."

Khalid's jaw tightened. Shayne had toyed with the idea of with-holding this information, certain it would push Khalid into claiming Marty, and had not been certain that it was a good idea. If Khalid had already made that choice though, then it wouldn't hurt to let him know that his woman was growing a bit sick of the game he was playing.

Khalid drew in a hard, deep breath, as though drawing patience into himself. It had always amazed Shayne how he did that, how he forced a certain control on his emotions when it came to Marty Mathews.

She was a weakness. And honestly it was something Shayne had thought Ayid and Aman would have already figured out by now.

"The Sinclair ball," Khalid finally stated emotionlessly. "She's attending it tonight?"

Shayne nodded. "It would seem so."

"Then I will speak to her tonight."

Shayne smiled. "I look forward to being a part of her pleasure, Khalid. Thank you for the offer."

A half smile tugged at Khalid's lips. "You merely want a chance to play house for a while, remember?" he reminded Shayne.

"Well, there is that," Shayne agreed. "There's also watching her tie you in ten different kinds of knots. That's will always be amusing."

"I'll remember that when you're tied up in those knots yourself, my friend," Khalid informed him with a knowing grin. "Trust me, your turn is coming."

Shayne inclined his head in acknowledgment, though Khalid doubted he believed him. Shayne called himself a lone wolf for a reason. He had learned years ago, just as Khalid had, the cost of love. And like Khalid, the day would come when he would fight for it again.

"I'll let you know then when you're needed," Khalid finally said as the other man picked up his paper again and shook it out, his light brown eyes still lit with amusement.

It was an amusement most single members had when they watched another fall into the silken arms of the only woman their hearts seemed to beat for.

◆─◆─◆

"Your father has called again," Abdul reported as he drove the limo along the curved driveway that led from the club.

Speak of the devil, Khalid sighed.

"What did the old bastard want this time?" A feeling of weariness descended over him like a heavy, wet blanket. Hell, there were times he wanted nothing more than to simply rest. To close his eyes without the worry of what tomorrow would bring.

"He wants to speak to you as always." Abdul's tone was without inflection.

The old bastard wanted to be certain Abram had come to D.C. as he'd asked him to.

"Did you tell him to go to hell?" Khalid asked with vicious politeness.

"I informed him once again that you have been quite busy." Abdul cleared his throat uncomfortably. "He seemed upset. More so than usual."

The son of a bitch called in a show of fatherly concern whenever Ayid and Aman were about to do something foul to him. If he needed confirmation that his brothers were ready to move, then this was it.

God, he wanted it over with. There were nights he actually managed to convince himself that he could fund the death of the old bastard and the sons that were no more than animals. And he would have, many times over, if his hand hadn't been stayed by the FBI.

"If he calls again, tell him I regretfully decline kinship with him and would prefer that he lay down and die painfully," he stated wearily. "In the meantime, please contact the estate and have my attire for the Sinclair ball laid out. It seems I'll be attending after all."

5

The Sinclair balls were impossible to ignore, especially for those who were a part of the Sinclair club, or who knew Courtney. Members of the club were given a personal invitation by Ian Sinclair, with several reminders not to forget his wife's ball. Those who didn't attend endured his glares for weeks.

Married or single, the members knew better than to miss one. If there was one weakness Ian had, it was his delicate little wife and anything her merciless heart desired.

The end-of-summer event was in full swing when Khalid arrived, alone.

He moved across the ballroom to the bar on the far side and ordered a drink stiff enough to burn through the hunger riding him as he searched for Marty and Shayne. Apparently they hadn't arrived yet.

"Khalid, thank you so much for being here."

Turning, he accepted the fierce hug from the petite sprite dressed in red. Courtney smiled up at him. Behind her stood her brooding husband, Ian. And Ian always brooded whenever his wife was surrounded by hungry males. At least, that was how he described them.

"I only obey the commands given," Khalid assured her, grinning, as she pouted back at him impudently, her chocolate-brown eyes gleaming with impish delight. "Though, I have to admit, your buffet is better than most."

"Ian, he's being mean to me," she complained, frowning back at her husband.

"Stop being mean to Courtney, Khalid," Ian ordered, with a mock glare that had his wife pressing her elbow sharply into his hard abs.

Khalid grinned at the move, though his gaze roved the ballroom, searching, as always, for that one delicate figure. If he hadn't needed to discuss the situation with Ian, then he would have never allowed Shayne to pick up Marty for the party tonight.

"I need to talk to you a moment, if you don't mind." Khalid stepped forward, his voice low as he drew Ian's attention.

"Of course. My study?" Ian nodded to the smaller doorway leading from the ballroom.

The newly constructed mansion boasted two stories and two wings. The shorter wing housed the ballroom and Ian's offices, while the main house occupied the larger wing.

Following Ian through a short hall, Khalid stepped into the study while he the other man watched him curiously.

"Courtney and her parties." Ian sighed as he strode to the small bar in the corner of the room and fixed two whiskeys. "I swear, you'd think they were world events the way she plots and plans around them."

"For Courtney, they usually are," Khalid drawled, accepting the drink.

"I believe Sebastian has been telling us all horror stories about the balls she and her mother used to throw."

Sebastian had known Courtney before her arrival in Virginia nearly two years earlier. Before she had made the decision to win the elusive Ian Sinclair's heart.

She had stolen Ian's heart, and the friendship of everyone else she had touched since then. That didn't mean they didn't live in fear of her disapproval. Or her anger. She had a temper that could make a grown man whimper in fear.

Ian tugged at the tight neck of his evening shirt and shook his head.

"You wanted to discuss Courtney's predilection to overdramatize her parties, or was there something more on your mind?" Ian asked as he walked to the desk and sat down, with a long, drawn-out sigh.

"Actually, there was more on my mind." Khalid shoved his hands in the pockets of his tuxedo pants before turning and pacing to the French doors that opened out into Courtney's personal gardens. "A situation has developed. I may need to make use of the club for a short time. And there could be some problems involved in it."

"What sort of problems?" Ian kicked his feet up on the corner of the desk as he leaned back in the chair, with the air of a man taking advantage of a small reprieve.

"I may need a place to run to." Khalid turned around, rubbing at his neck as he watched the other man carefully.

"Our doors are always open." Ian shrugged and he smothered a yawn.

"Marty might be with me."

He stopped mid-yawn. Ian stared back at Khalid as though he had lost his mind, before slowly lowering his feet to the floor and sitting to attention as his jaw snapped closed.

"You're joking." Ian's dark blue eyes narrowed on him in warning. "You know the rules, Khalid. They're not broken, for anyone."

"Even if it could mean her life?" Khalid asked. He regarded Ian as he held back his grin. "I believe, during the Civil War, a small hidden cellar was built to hide the wives of the club members. Two senators' wives and the wife and daughter of a general hid there for over week, while the club conducted regular business." Ian sat back in his chair, lifted his gaze to the ceiling then closed his eyes as though the search for answers had just become too exhausting.

"What the hell is going on, Khalid, that you may need to protect your woman here, in this club?" Ian finally growled as his eyes opened again. He looked at him in frustration.

"My past." Khalid sighed as he moved to the heavy leather chair on the other side of Ian's desk and sat down. "Or more to the point, my half brothers. They've learned of a problem I might have created for them. One that may have cost them a large amount of funds, as well as respect of their peers." Their terrorist friends. "They'll definitely come after me. When they do, that will place Marty in the line of fire."

Ian glared back at him. "You've been playing secret agent for Zach Jennings again, haven't you?" he snapped. "Son of a bitch, Khalid. Every member of this fucking club has managed to get his ass shanghaied by Jennings, and I'm getting sick of it. I thought you didn't enjoy following the crowd."

Khalid restrained his chuckle. "I was perhaps the first," he pointed out. "Needless to say, Jennings recruited me fresh out of high school, the year Azir Mustafa decided to assert his parental rights and tried to sue my mother for the years he had not been a part of my life." Anger still churned inside him at the thought of what Azir had tried to do to his mother all those years ago.

It hadn't been enough that he had bought her from her kidnappers, raped her, and locked her inside the walls of his palace, refusing to allow her to return home. But eighteen years later he had decided to torment her further by trying to sue her for the years she had kept Khalid hidden from him.

"Jennings can be a bastard." Ian rose to his feet, moved to the bar and poured two straight whiskies. Returning to the desk he handed a glass to Khalid before resuming his seat. "So Daddy Dearest is doing what then?" he asked.

"Perhaps it would be more accurate to say it's the evil half brothers who are now stepping in for him," Khalid explained. "As I said, I've cost them a fair amount financially as well as personally. It may become imperative that I find a safe place where Marty will be protected until the situation can be resolved."

"And you've discussed this with Marty?" Ian asked, still holding back his assent.

"I thought I should first make certain you had no problems with it," Khalid answered with mocking innocence.

"Don't fuck with me," Ian growled, his voice dark. "Does Marty know about the trouble that could be coming?"

"I'm certain I'll have to explain it," Khalid assured him, though it was something he wasn't looking forward to. Losing Lessa had been one of the dark points in his life, a failure he had never been able to forgive himself for.

"I'm fairly certain it'll be a requirement," Ian told him facetiously before a grimace tightened his face. "Hell, Khalid, you know I can't make this decision alone." He rubbed at the back of his neck in irritation before continuing. "But I don't see the request being rejected, considering she's the daughter of two of our more powerful members. But this is a hell of a position to put me in here. You know it's going to require notifying all six hundred members of the need to open a single room to female occupancy and listening to the bitching over it until the situation is resolved."

Ian had stated more than once that the majority of the club members were like ten-year-olds with nothing better to do than bitch and whine.

"I do understand the position this could place you in. Were it just myself, Ian, I wouldn't worry as much."

"Yeah, you proved how much you don't enjoy living the minute you let Jennings pull you into his little games," Ian said with a hint of mocking disgust. "I thought you knew better."

Khalid hid a smile. Ian and Zach Jennings rarely saw eye-to-eye over what Ian described as Zach's unconscionable use of knowledge and information that came through the club. More than once Ian had actually protested when the FBI director had managed to pull a club member into an operation. The reason Jennings got away with it was the fact that, so far, no one had been placed in any true danger.

"I appreciate it, Ian." Khalid rose from his seat as he finished his drink. "I better return to the party. Marty should be arriving soon."

"And Courtney will kick my ass if I hide in here all night." Blowing out a hard sigh Ian rose from his chair, a flash of irritation gleaming in his eyes.

"She'll kick both our asses," Khalid reminded him with a grin. "She's not the nice, tamable sort that used to be your norm, my friend."

"That she's definitely not." Laughter replaced the irritation as they left the study and headed for the ballroom. "And that is what makes life with Courtney so damned much fun."

The sprite made everyone around her laugh, Khalid thought as he re-entered the ballroom and spotted Marty on the other side of the room.

Sensation slammed into his gut, heated his insides and had his cock thickening immediately.

Damn her, she could do to him what no other woman could. Make him helpless against his desire for her.

"Mr. Mustafa, Mr. Sinclair sent you a drink." A waiter stepped in front of him, drink in hand.

Giving it to Khalid, the waiter moved away. Khalid lifted it to his lips, paused, and swore he would lose his breath as he watched Marty turn, caught her profile, and the smile that curled her lips as she and Shayne stood amid a crowd of her friends.

She was a beacon of light in the darkness, her dark blond hair pulled back from her face and glittering with sapphires. The short dress she wore was sapphire silk, riding high on her thighs and paired with heels matching in color that lifted her height enough to nearly match Shayne's.

Her sleek feminine curves were made even more sensual by the dress and heels. Her shoulders were all but bare, her breasts full and pressing temptingly against the material covering them.

Shayne stood at her side, his hand resting low on her back, his fingers splayed against her lower back with a hint of possessiveness.

Khalid hid his smile. Shayne *did* want to play house for a while, and in his estimation his relationship with Khalid and Marty would allow that.

Well, it was always best to let a man learn the hard way that such schemes weren't going to pan out. Marty's heart was his, Khalid knew, just as Shayne did. There was no jealousy required, but that didn't mean Khalid wouldn't silently put the other man in his place when needed.

⊹⊹⊹⊹⊹

"I can feel the dagger in my back," Shayne whispered in Marty's ear as she lifted the champagne glass to her lips while half-listening to a school friend recount her latest trip to the Bahamas.

Ignoring Shayne's laughing comment, she focused instead on a conversation she really didn't give a damn about, just to prove, incorrectly, that she really didn't give a damn. She wasn't in the least amused that Khalid had had Shayne pick her up for the ball rather than picking her up himself. When he had called and asked her to accompany him tonight, she had cautiously accepted, interested to see where he was going with this. He was up to something. She could feel it. And she wanted to know what the hell it was.

"Andrew's yacht is simply exquisite," Tanya was exclaiming, as Marty felt Shayne's hand press more firmly against her lower back in warning. "And Andrew does know how to throw a party. You should join us next month, Martha. It's so much fun."

She was going to gag. Martha. In all the years Marty had known Tanya, she had never had the good grace to use the nickname Marty's mother had declared Marty would be called by when she was a baby.

Martha was her grandmother's name. She'd been named Martha to fulfill her grandmother's dying wish, and Marty was proud to own it. But her name was Marty. She had been Marty all her life, and she didn't like Tanya's pompous little voice sneering out her given name instead.

"I'm sure it's just megawonderful, Tannie," Marty cooed back at her. "But I think I might have to work. You know how it is. Have to make the rent money."

Tanya's eyes widened, though she never for a second caught the small slur Marty had sent her way.

"Dear, I'm certain your trust fund could cover you," Tanya drawled with self-important sobriety. "After all, I do know your grandmother left you rather well off, even if your parents aren't inclined to do so."

Marty gritted her teeth. Her parents had taught her a strong work ethic—something that was uncommon among the glittering trust-fund babies and silver-spoon angels she had grown up with.

People like Tanya didn't realize the work that had gone into the fortunes they now lived off and rarely contributed to.

"And I still prefer to pay my own expenses." Marty's eyes rounded mockingly. "Go figure."

Tanya blinked back at her before turning to her husband, as though in confusion. The husband, an executive with Tanya's father's engineering firm, hid a smile.

"She's an aberration, sweetheart." Her husband, Mike Collie, sighed, as though he, too, was confused by Marty. "Remember how we used to pat her on the head when we were children and pray for her before sleeping?"

Tanya glanced back at her sympathetically.

"Yes, and now, Mike, I pray for you," Marty stated sweetly, as he chuckled back at her, clearly unoffended by her remark.

"And I appreciate each prayer, my dear." His blue eyes gleamed with amusement. He was one of the good ones. They were few and far between sometimes.

As pompous and arrogant as some of her childhood friends may be, most of them still had a sense of humor where it counted.

"Excuse me, I need to find my father for a moment," Marty said when she glanced to the side and saw that Khalid had managed to pry himself away from a small group of men who had delayed him and he was now trying to make his way across the room.

Perfect timing, she thought. No one made it through this crowd quickly, which gave her a few more moments before he got to her.

Keeping Khalid carefully in her peripheral vision as she hid her smirk at the frustration on his face, Marty and Shayne made their way to where Joe and Zach stood along with Ian Sinclair, and the owners of Delacourte-Conovers, a rising electronics development and manufacturing firm in the area. The Delacourtes and Conovers were heavy contributors to her father's political funds, as well as friends.

"Marty." Joe stood back, making room for her and Shayne as they entered the small group. "I see you finally made it." Turning to Shayne, he extended his hand. "It's good to see you again, Shayne."

"You couldn't at least consort within your own branch of law enforcement?" Zach muttered beside her, though she heard the amusement in his voice.

"I thought it best to have friends in all branches. Besides, it doesn't hurt to look outside the box," she replied, looking up at him with a smile.

"You can always look," Zach reminded her, his gaze moving over her head before coming back. "Doesn't mean you'll succeed."

She could feel Khalid now. As though his very aura had reached out, wrapped around her, and claimed her; she could feel him moving behind her.

"Shayne. Thank you for escorting my lovely date. I'll take her off your hands now." His voice was dark, brooding, sending a surge of sensation racing up her spine as she and Shayne turned to him.

"Evenin' Khalid. And I must say, it was my pleasure."

There were days when it sucked being at the mercy of what she liked to believe were no more than hormones. After all, how could you love a man who made you insane every time you saw him? It couldn't be love, therefore it had to be a biological/chemical/pheromonal reaction that bound her to him.

"Marty." Khalid turned to her then, and the force of those dark eyes staring into hers seemed to steal her breath and the last bit of common sense she might have possessed as his head lowered and his lips brushed hers.

"Khalid." She tried to pretend that her reaction to him didn't exist, but the brush of his lips against hers stole her breath and left her knees weakening in response.

"Dance with me." The tone of his voice as he gripped her hand and pulled her to him had Marty's heart racing as heat began to swirl through her body.

The dark edge of hunger in his tone was barely hidden, but it was his eyes, midnight velvet, so deep and filled with sensual promise that had her flesh sensitizing, her breasts swelling and her clit suddenly pulsing in reaction.

+ + + +

"I must admit Khalid, I didn't expect you to have your third pick me up tonight," she muttered as Khalid drew her against him and began moving her across the dance floor. "I was beginning to wonder if you had changed your mind concerning a relationship with me. Again." Innocence marked her face and belied the subtle mockery in her tone.

"I apologize again, love," he murmured, his thick lashes screening whatever emotion was in his eyes.

"Since he did pick me up tonight, that does rather make him my official date." Marty kept her voice calm, sweet. Innocent. "I believe, as such, he's entitled to certain privileges. Wouldn't you think?"

"I don't believe I would agree with that statement." He didn't beat around the bush. "Don't play games with me, Marty. We've gone too far for that."

"Really?" Arching her brows inquisitively she forced back the amusement she wanted to feel. She wanted what she was entitled to, all of him, or nothing. "So tell me then, Khalid, what game were you playing when you invited me to attend this ball with you, only to send Shayne to pick me up instead?"

"That is an explanation for another time," he answered, his tone brooding.

"Then perhaps this relationship that I've fought so hard for is meant for another time as well. I won't be pawned off like a reluctant responsibility. I'm certain there are other interested parties who would be more than happy to actually escort me themselves." Marty shrugged negligently, though she paid particular attention to the fact that Khalid was dancing them closer to the darkened hallway that led to the main house.

"You would only turn them down were they to extend such an invitation," he growled as he stared down at her, his expression darkening. "You rarely attend these balls with a date."

Which, unfortunately, was no more than the truth.

"I didn't always turn them down," she reminded him. "Just particular ones. There were several I accepted over the years."

"Men who had no chance of controlling you," he pointed out. "You dated men who had no chance in hell of naysaying you in any decision you should make."

The words had her lips parting in outrage as he stopped at the entrance to the hall before gripping her upper arm and drawing her into it.

"Couldn't handle me?" She glared up at him as he led her through an opened doorway into a small library before closing the door behind them. "Khalid, no man *handles* me."

Jerking her arm from his grip she rounded on him, every insult she could think of rising to her lips, ready to fall from her tongue.

"I do."

Demanding, arrogant, his voice lit a fuse to her temper that had her lips parting to inform him otherwise, quite vocally. Instead, she found herself in his arms, his lips on hers, his larger, broader body bent to her as the hunger and the need held barely in check at the best of times, flamed out of control.

This was where she needed to be. All arguments aside. All pride aside. God help her, but she needed to be in his arms.

Her fingers clenched at the fine silken material of his evening jacket as she felt his hands splay against her back, drawing her closer. Small, sharp kisses fueled an already growing demand for his touch as Marty fought to get closer, to crawl into the hard, heated body holding her tight to his chest, to his kiss.

She felt as though she were flying. The pleasure whipped through her body, slicing through any hesitancy, any shyness. This was Khalid. The man she had been much too aware of since she was too young to even understand what it meant.

She wasn't too young now. She was a woman, and though she may be technically innocent that didn't mean she didn't know what she wanted, what he would want, eventually.

"God, what you do to me." His lips moved from hers, traveling to her jaw, her neck. "You destroy me, Marty."

It was no less than he did to her.

His teeth raked against the sensitive flesh just under her jaw, causing rioting sensations to her nerve endings. Her nipples hardened beneath the material of her bodice; between her thighs, her clit throbbed, her juices spilling onto the silk of her panties.

Heat washed through her body, her thighs; her breasts tingled. His hands roved over her back, her shoulders, gripping the tab of the zipper at her back and slowly easing it down.

Weakness flooded her, a sensual, heated rush of pleasure rocking through her body and sending flares of sensation tearing into erogenous zones that she hadn't known she possessed.

The feel of the silk bodice slipping over her hardened nipples made pleasure steal her breath. They ached with the same white-hot need that possessed her clit, the core of her body.

She could feel the need tearing through her unlike anything she had felt before.

"You make me forget." The hard, hot growl followed by a sensual nip at her ear, as the cool air met the heated tips of her breasts, forced a strangled cry to escape her lips.

She wanted his lips all over her body. She wanted his hands lower, touching her, stroking her.

Sliding her fingers beneath the edges of his jacket, Marty sought to find a way to the warmth of his flesh beneath. She needed his touch. She needed to touch.

"Sweet. Sweet Marty."

His hands gripped her waist, lifted her until she felt the cool wood of a desk against her thighs, as her fingers tore at the buttons of his shirt to reveal the hard, muscular contours of his chest.

This was what she wanted. What she needed. Her fingers curled against the light covering of rough curls on his chest, her nails raking through them as she felt his hand sliding up her side to the curve of her breast.

"I need you," she whispered, as he pulled her closer, stepped between her thighs, and bent over her until Marty felt the desk meeting her back.

There was no time to think about where they were. They could be caught. Anyone could walk in on them.

Then his head was lowering.

Marty reached up, her fingers going to the leather tie that held back the long, coarse strands of black hair at his neck. When she loosened it, his hair fell around her fingers as his lips smoothed over the rise of her breast, his tongue licking, tasting her flesh, going ever closer to the aching peak of a breast.

Her fingers speared into his hair, her head tipped back farther, pleasure whirled through her system as her knees gripped his hips, her pussy cushioning the hard ridge of his cock beneath his slacks.

Shifting her hips beneath him, Marty felt the thick press of his erection as he thrust against her. His lips parted, his tongue licking over her nipple before drawing it into the heated dampness of his mouth.

The stroke of his tongue, the flex and suction of his mouth over the ultrasensitive tip, made her hands clench his hair tighter, holding him to her as she arched closer to the flick of his tongue over the heated tip.

The pleasure was torturous. She felt a searing sense of complete abandonment in his arms. Control had no meaning. Common sense had been lost long ago. There was just this, this man, this moment, this fantasy she had never been able to let go of.

"Do you know what you do to me?" The rough caress of his voice stole through her senses as her lashes lifted to stare into the black heat of his eyes.

"I know what you do to me." She fought to breathe through the pleasure, through the sensations tearing through her as he brushed his jaw over her nipple, the light stubble on his flesh abrading with sensual roughness.

Staring back at him, Marty fought to hold on to her senses as she felt his palm sliding along her leg to her thigh. The feel of his calloused fingertips was a sensual rasp of exquisite pleasure.

"Khalid," she panted his name, fought to still the trembling of her body as he leaned back enough to watch the progress of his fingers.

"Do you know how long I've wanted you?" His voice was dark, hungry. "Far longer than I should have, Marty. Far longer than I thought possible to want one woman."

Moistening her lips with her tongue, she drew in a hard, deep breath as those adventurous fingers moved along the elastic of the silk panties at her thigh.

"I should stop." The expression on his face, the dark hunger in his eyes weren't that of a man intent on stopping.

The fingers dipping beneath the elastic leg band of her panties definitely weren't those of a man intending to stop. Marty all but held her breath as those knowing, wicked fingers began to play seductively beneath the silk.

They parted the silken folds of flesh and his eyes locked with hers as she caught her breath at the feel of his fingers gliding through the satiny, slick dampness gathered there.

Lips parted, a cry trapped in her throat, Marty could do nothing but whimper as those diabolical fingers slid upward to circle the tender, straining nub of her clit and torture it further.

"All I can think about is fucking you." His voice was a harsh rasp of hunger that had her womb clenching in demand. "Day and night, for years, the hunger for it has tormented me."

She bit her lip, whimpering little moans leaving her throat as his head lowered, his lips finding a tender nipple and sucking it inside as his free hand began to push her dress higher up her thighs.

"Tasting you." He breathed against her breast as his head began to move lower down her body. "I need to taste you, Marty."

Marty stared unseeingly up at the ceiling as she felt her panties being pulled to the side, and a second later she felt the heated rasp of a hungry tongue as it licked up the slit of her pussy.

Pulses of brutal pleasure raced through her, flinching through her body as his tongue worked to her clit, circled it, and sipped at it before moving lower again.

She wanted to scream out at the sensations tearing through her. The desperate ache that resulted from each lick was torture. An agony of sensation washed through her body as his tongue flickered and licked, driving her crazy with the need for more.

Khalid ate the tender flesh like a connoisseur tasting nectar. A little groan vibrated against the tender bud, nearly sending her senses exploding in sensation before his lips moved again. His tongue licked lower, rimmed the clenched opening, then with a hot, wicked glide of his tongue, slid inside the clenched, ultrasensitive opening in a smooth, white-hot thrust.

Marty's feet pressed into the edge of the desk, her hips rising in a desperate jerk as her hands clenched in his hair to hold him to her.

She couldn't hold back the cry that tore from her throat, just as she couldn't stop the heated rush of her response from spilling to his tongue.

Knowing, hungry thrusts of his tongue had her reaching desperately for an orgasm he held just out of reach as his hands clenched her rear, lifting her closer to him.

Marty felt lost, suspended between pleasure and torture as sensation after sensation attacked her nerve endings. Heat blazed through her body, tore through her mind. The feel of his tongue fucking her drove her to a precipice she hadn't known existed as she fought to find release.

Male groans vibrated against her flesh as she arched, pressing closer, desperate mewls falling from her lips as she felt the blazing sensation building inside her body.

In that moment, the door opened and Shayne Connor stepped inside.

Embarrassment should have seared her. As he closed the door quickly, his hand clenched on the doorknob, his gaze turning from curious to a blaze of arousal, something ignited and flamed inside her as Shayne locked the door and swiftly moved closer.

Pleasure was agony. It was tearing through her body, burning her nerve endings as Shayne stopped at her side, his hands cupping her breasts, his fingers finding her nipples and tugging them deliciously as his lips moved to her neck.

Khalid chose that moment to slide a finger along the crevice below her pussy. Drawing her juices, stroking, massaging, the tip of his finger slipped inside the clenched opening of her anus as Shayne licked his lips in hunger.

Sensation detonated. Marty's lips opened for the scream that would have ricocheted from the room, but Shayne was there. His lips covered hers, his kiss stealing her cry as her fingers gripped his shoulders tight and she arched into the orgasm racing through her.

Her thighs clenched around Khalid's head. Her free hand clenched in his hair as she began to shake, to tremble. A surge of pure electric pleasure raced up her spine and radiated in static ecstasy that shook her entire body.

It was like flying, falling, burning, freezing. Nothing mattered, nothing existed but the pleasure and the pure heated release surging through her.

Nothing mattered but the men touching her and the knowledge of the hunger she knew she couldn't escape.

6

He was going to burn alive in the flames of need that had ignited inside his body as he felt Marty's release spill to his lips. The sweet, heated juices were like nectar, like the finest, silkiest syrup. He had felt the proof of her innocence, the virgin shield that no other had breached, just as he had felt, tasted, the heated honey of her response.

Staring up at her, he'd seen her desperate grip on Shayne's shoulder, the way her screams fed into the other man's kiss, and nearly experienced his own release with no more than the rasp of his clothing against his cock.

Her response destroyed him. Rather than embarrassment as Shayne touched her, she had instead exploded with a strength that still had him shaking nearly thirty minutes later, as he fought to move across the dance floor without stumbling over his own feet.

On her other side, Shayne seemed no steadier. He swore they both looked like drunks.

"We're leaving soon." He made the decision as he looked down at her now, still seeing her flushed features rather than her now composed expression. Her gaze was still drowsy, tiny wisps of hair lay on her forehead, still damp from the perspiration that had dotted her skin earlier.

He wanted her hot and damp, her body sheened from her juices and their combined perspiration. He wanted to hear her scream rather than feel her muffling her cries.

"It's about damned time," Shayne muttered.

"Why would we want to do that?" There was a hint of a smile on her face as she stared up at him. "I haven't even got to dance with my date yet." She cast an amused, teasing look toward Shayne before meeting Khalid's gaze once again.

"I'll get Abdul." Shayne's didn't bother to hide his grin as he moved away quickly and headed for the wide ballroom doors that had been thrown open earlier.

"And you won't be dancing with him, either," he growled. "At least not here."

A hint of a smile tugged at her lips as she stared back at him. There was no mistaking the clear, dark possessiveness in his tone.

That smile, so starkly feminine and filled with satisfaction had him reacting in a way he hadn't expected. He could feel the arousal tearing through him, building, burning hotter, brighter than ever before.

He swore his cock had never been so hard, his balls so tight. The blood throbbed through the thick, tight flesh, reminding him that she could make him hunger for her like he had never hungered for another woman.

"You're pushing." And it would take her places he was certain she didn't want to go.

Zach had assured him years ago that Marty wasn't the sharing kind. That when it came to a relationship, to the man she would eventually love, he had been warned not to attempt to draw her into the lifestyle that members of the club shared.

"How am I pushing, Khalid?" she whispered archly. "Wouldn't it be difficult to push much further than I've already pushed you over the years? Or further than you're trying to push me? Don't imagine for a moment that I'll tolerate any of it."

She was aroused. He could see the hunger in her eyes and in the soft smile on her lips.

She was more determined and certainly more stubborn than he had ever imagined.

As they passed through the open ballroom doors, Khalid felt the overwhelming need for her tearing at him again. His self-control was deteriorating by the moment. If he didn't have her soon, if he didn't mark her, claim her, then he was going to go insane.

He had to admit to a small bit of surprise when she followed him. They moved through the ballroom to the foyer, and without searching for Ian or Courtney, they left the party.

Shayne was waiting outside, leaning lazily against the tall column of the porch as he watched them curiously.

"Shayne will be coming with us," Khalid said, his body tightening to the point of breaking.

Marty nodded, breathless.

"Though when we get home, it will just be us," he said firmly.

Marty looked confused but said, "Ok."

Shayne gave him a quick nod to show he understood, though there was a question in his eyes.

Marty had saved herself for him and he would not share that gift even with the man he had chosen as a third. Still, he wanted her to continue to become accustomed to Shayne's touch and to the both of them giving her pleasure.

Marty wanted to close her eyes, to hold onto the fantasy, if that was what this was, and never let it go. She felt as though she should pinch herself, do something, anything, to prove it was real.

Her body was humming with sensation as the two men escorted her down the steps to the driveway where Abdul was pulling up in the limo. Khalid's hand rested low on her back, Shayne's arm brushed against her shoulder.

The heated sensations washing over her were sizzling. The clear intent in their gazes, in the careful positioning of their larger bodies against hers was unmistakable.

It was finally going to happen. So many years spent dreaming about it, fantasizing to it. And now that the moment was here, she was terrified she would awaken once again to find it was simply another dream.

"Courtney is going to skin you alive," she said, hearing the breathlessness of her voice, the nervousness as she slid into the back of the limo.

"Courtney will survive," Khalid informed her as Abdul closed the door behind them.

The dark interior surrounded them as Khalid pushed the button to raise the partition between them and Abdul.

Beside her, Shayne watched her silently, his expression tense, filled with lust. Only lust. There was no emotion aside from the affection of a friend, a lover. Khalid could read nothing in the other man that appeared to be a threat to his possession of Marty's heart.

Khalid's jaw clenched as Marty shifted, causing the bodice to tighten over her breasts. He wanted to lower the material, wanted to feel the firm weight of the swollen globes in his hands once again.

As he watched, her hand lifted, the painted tips of her fingers stroking over the upper curves of her breasts teasingly. Her fingers shook, but her expression, though filled with wariness, was also filled with curiosity.

Khalid watched her hand, as he knew Shayne was watching as well.

Khalid's eyes lifted to hers, his body clenching so tightly that he swore bones would break. He met the teasing glint in her eyes.

"I stayed away as long as possible," he said gently. "Remember that when you begin to learn things you don't like, little flower. I tried to protect you."

"You could explain." There was a somber edge of sadness in her voice.

Khalid glanced at Shayne and read the warning in his gaze. If he didn't tell her, if he didn't explain, he could lose her, and not just to the repercussions of his work with her godfather, or to his past. He could lose her by not warning her, by letting her face danger without being prepared.

Her head tilted to the side. "Did you grow horns and I'm somehow missing them, Khalid?" she asked. "Or perhaps you don't trust me with the truth."

"Perhaps the horns were there long before you were old enough to imagine what I would want from you. And I would trust you with my life."

There was blood in his past, the blood of an innocent, the blood of someone who had dared to trust him, dared to love him.

God knew that should he lose Marty in the manner that he had allowed himself to lose Lessa, he could never live with the guilt.

He was aware of Shayne watching, listening, waiting. He had no choice but to tell her the truth. The danger he would become to her from this one night onward would demand that she know the truth of his past, that she would see him for the man he was, rather than the man he wanted to be for her.

"I don't know, Khalid," she said quietly. "I rather doubt I'd find a monster. I'd probably simply find a man who found he couldn't control the world as he once thought he could."

Khalid sighed. "I haven't been as careful as I should have been in the work I've done for your godfather. My two younger half brothers have learned that I was part of a recent operation that has cost them financially, as well as personally. Because of that, I suspect they'll make a move soon to strike against me. I did not want you endangered, Marty. I wanted you safe, and that safety is no longer something I can guarantee."

Shayne watched as Khalid fought to reveal just the information Marty needed, and none of the painful truth of what had happened before he left Saudi Arabia ten years ago. He actually felt sorry for the poor bastard. As strong and as arrogant as Khalid could be, Marty could still bring him to his knees. And how she saw him was still something Khalid struggled with.

He wanted to be a white knight in her eyes, not the dark knight. And there were times he had never understood that it was the dark knight who actually ended up saving the day, the princess, and the world he believed in.

But what Shayne had known, and Khalid had yet to see, was the woman Marty truly was.

At Khalid's explanation her gaze sharpened, her eyes narrowed, and the agent she had become over the years slipped into the picture.

"What was the operation?"

Shayne had to hide his smile. She would be full of questions now, and hiding the rest of the truth from her would be harder by the day for Khalid. Just as it would be more difficult for these two people to continue denying the emotions they felt for each other. Others saw it. Shayne saw it in both of them. But neither Marty nor Khalid had yet to acknowledge it.

He also doubted that Khalid saw the depth of her love, but it was something Shayne saw, and almost envied. If he were ready to love, then he would definitely have to fight Khalid for this woman.

And Marty didn't recognize that emotion in herself because, Shayne knew, she had felt it for Khalid for so long, that it had simply become a part of her. It was now as natural as breathing.

"So you believe Ayid and Aman Mustafa are going to try to kill you because of the mission here in D.C.?"

Marty knew far more than she let on. She wasn't about to allow it to distract her now, though. As she spoke, she allowed her fingers to whisper over the rise of her breasts above the bodice of her dress. Back and forth, stroking, caressing her own flesh until even he could barely think for watching her.

"That is a reasonable explanation," Khalid murmured.

Shayne almost grinned at the sudden distracted tone in Khalid's voice. Not that he blamed the other man, watching Marty's fingertips caress the upper slopes of her breasts was making him insane as well.

"And this is why you've stayed away from me all these years?"

Ah, she had him there. Shayne would have glanced at Khalid for his reaction if he wasn't pretty certain Khalid's attention was still glued to those fingers as she caressed herself.

"Should we play this safe then?" she asked. "Should I choose another lover, Khalid, hope he's a member of your illustrious club, and then hope he chooses you as a third?" Her fingers played closer to the edge of the material that barely covered her nipples. "Then you wouldn't have to worry, would you?"

Shayne's mouth began to water even as he admired the very delicate, very subtle way she was learning exactly how to ensure that Khalid lost his heart to her. He wondered if she was aware he already had.

Damn, she was frightening. She should be an interrogator. Because she was going to wring every and any truth from Khalid's lips if he wasn't very careful.

"Would you enjoy watching me commit murder?" Khalid muttered, then nearly held his breath as she pressed her fingers beneath the bodice and slowly lowered it over the ripe, firm globes of her breasts.

Pale pink nipples, hard and flushed, met his avid gaze as he felt his mouth water for the taste of them.

A quick glance at Shayne showed that the other man was just as entranced. Just as eager and as hungry for a taste of her as Khalid now was.

"Would you commit murder for me?" Her inquiry was but a distant sound to his fogged brain.

"If another man tried to touch you without my direct approval, then yes, I believe I would," he stated, his attention never wavering as her fingers began to play over her distended nipples.

Damn, that was pretty. Watching her touch herself was almost as torturous as touching her himself. He knew the shape, the silky sweetness, the heat of the firmed flesh. He knew the taste of them, the feel of them against his tongue, and he ached for more.

The strain on his own control was telling. He wanted nothing more than to jerk her to him, pull her over his lap and release the aching length of his cock before pushing inside her.

Better yet, to have Shayne hold her, caress her, gently restrain her as Khalid parted her thighs and allowed the other man to watch his possession of her. To caress her, to push her pleasure higher than she could ever know with a single lover.

The fact that she was a virgin was all that stopped him. Though, leaning closer, his fingers going to her knee as her face began to flush with pleasure, he wasn't certain if either of them had the strength to pull back.

"You're beautiful," Khalid whispered as Shayne slowly moved to press her thighs apart and slide the short skirt of her dress nearly to her hips.

Sliding his fingers over the damp crotch of her panties, Khalid had to clench his teeth to hold back the need to fuck her immediately. How in hell was he going to manage to wait?

"Khalid." The breathiness in her voice stroked his senses as he pulled the silken material from the bare folds of her pussy and ran his fingers over the silken, slick flesh.

"Let us watch you play with those pretty nipples, sweet flower," he said as heat flooded his fingers. "I'll pet your soft little pussy for a minute. Just for a minute, Marty, then we'll be home."

Her head fell back against the seat as her fingers pinched at her nipples.

Moving closer, Khalid pressed one knee into the seat beside her as the fingers of one hand worked into the delicate clenched opening of her sex. His other hand tore at the restraints of his slacks, his eyes devouring the sight of her tweaking her nipples as Shayne began to touch her, to caress her thighs, to ease higher as Khalid slid his fingers free of her pussy to allow the other man to touch, to experience the softest flesh in the world.

Releasing the excruciating length of his cock, he had to bite back a groan. He needed her lips on him. He needed her taking him.

Shayne began to caress the delicate folds of her cunt. His control was shaky at best at the moment.

"Fuck!" As the thought of this passed through his head while his eyes had closed to hold back the demand, Marty had taken the initiative herself.

Staring down he saw her tongue rimming the swollen crest of his cock. Delicate pink and damp, it was like a stroke of fire as she licked him like a favorite treat.

He watched as Shayne pressed two fingers into the clenched tissue of her pussy in a shallow thrust, as Khalid fought for breath.

"We may not make it home before I fuck you." Khalid growled out the warning as her lips parted and her mouth began to consume him.

Wet heat. White hot flames. Her lips wrapped around the wide head of his dick and sent his senses drowning in pleasure as she began to suck him with delicate greed.

Nothing could have prepared Khalid for the sight of her taking him so intimately. Her face flushed with pleasure, with hungry demand, her eyes closed as the fingers of one hand attempted to wrap around the base of his cock.

Nothing could have prepared him for the pleasure. The erotic sensation of her lips, her tongue, moving over the swollen crest and sucking it deep inside the snug heat of her mouth sent bolts of electric pleasure racing through his balls, up his spine. His entire body felt surrounded by static sensation as it tingled over his flesh, stroking it with a phantom caress as her tongue whipped over his cockhead like wet fire.

He forgot about Shayne for the moment. He heard her moans, felt them on his cock as Shayne caressed her, touched her, and knew nothing but pure ecstasy.

"God, yes," he hissed out, fighting for control. "Sweet sweet Marty. Just like that."

He loved the way her cheeks hollowed, sucking at him hungrily, her tongue licking him greedily. No experience with any other woman had ever been as sensual as watching this woman taking him as though she were starving for the taste of him.

* ◆ ◆ ◆ *

Shayne's fingers stroked inside her pussy as she sucked Khalid's dick. He felt the generous flow of juices as she moaned around the flesh fucking her mouth. Pressing against the fragile barrier of her virginity Shayne drew back, ignoring the shifting of her hips, the slight arch of her body as she sought a deeper caress. Damn, she was sweet and hot, pure fire as he touched her while Khalid enjoyed the sweet heat of his mouth.

The gift of her virginity was Khalid's alone. It was a responsibility he didn't want, a commitment he had no intentions of sharing. Her innocence was the gift she had for the man she loved. He would enjoy only the pleasures she shared. And that was enough for him.

Stroking her, touching her. God, he ached to taste her.

Moving to the floor between her thighs he glanced up, met Khalid's gaze, and had to fight to hold back his groan as the other man gave a quick, hard nod in acceptance.

Hell yes, he would taste her. Fuck her sweet pussy with his tongue and fantasize about her lips wrapped around his own dick.

* ◆ ◆ ◆ *

Khalid felt his heart tightening, racing out of control as he stared down at Marty's flushed face, his senses exploding at the complete abandon in her expression as he took her mouth and watched as Shayne's head lowered to lick at the sweet delicacy of her pussy.

He could see her in his mind's eye, stretched out, at the mercy of their touch, steeped in pleasure so rich, so exquisite that she could do nothing but ride the waves of arousal as they washed over her.

Watching his cock press inside her mouth, feeling her cries vibrating around it. The darkness inside him became lost to the sweet pleasure that he knew he would find only with her now.

"Damn you." He cursed her as well as himself as her tongue rubbed erotically against the underside of his cock.

"I won't take you here. Not like this," he groaned, knowing he was so very close to doing just that. He was ready to fuck them both into oblivion here and now. If he did so, then Shayne would have her as well. The other man would press his way into the ultrasnug entrance of her ass and introduce her to a pleasure that she should only know later.

This first time. God help him, this first time had to be for her, for him. He couldn't bear the thought of another sharing it.

Her lashes lifted. Soft gray eyes had turned stormy, nearly black with the need filling her as he drew back. Watching as his cock pulled free, he wondered with agonized hunger how it would feel to fuck her pussy with the same soft, easy motions.

"You're killing me," he whispered as he gripped his cock in his fist and rubbed the head of it against her swollen, cherry red lips.

※ ※ ※

Shayne was in agony. Licking over the sweet, flushed curves of her pussy, the taste of her like nectar against his tongue, was nearly too much to bear.

She was so responsive, so sweet.

Glancing up he watched as Khalid rubbed the head of his cock over her lips and he couldn't resist. Cupping the cheeks of her ass in a firm grip he lifted her closer and thrust his tongue deep, hard, into the white-hot entrance of her pussy.

The taste of her exploded against his tongue. Silky, with the barest hint of sweetness and the delicate flavor of feminine heat. It combined to a subtle, addictive flavor that seeped into his senses and left him aching to fuck her as the muscles clenched around his tongue.

"Once I get you home I'm going to eat you with the same greedy hunger as Shayne is eating you now," Khalid groaned. "Is he fucking your pussy with his tongue, baby, like I did earlier? Is he making you crazy to feel my cock stretching you, taking you as no other man has dared?

She licked at the head of his cock as he held it back from her, crying out in need and in pleasure as she shuddered, her body rocking in Shayne's grip.

She was close. So close to release. A release he knew Shayne was holding back from her.

"Damn." Shayne's head lifted. "Fuck. She tastes like pure heat, Khalid. So fucking hot it burns."

Just then, the limo pulled into the driveway of the estate. Khalid pulled back from her as Shayne slowly released her then fought to get his cock back in his pants.

Marty looked erotically drugged as Shayne released her. She stared back at Khalid with the dazed, confused expression of a woman who didn't quite know how to handle the sensations racing through her. God knew, he understood exactly how she felt. Never had such pleasure racked his body.

"I need you." Her voice was thin and breathless as she tugged at the bodice of her dress to right it as the limo pulled into the driveway of the estate. "I might not survive how desperately I need you."

Helping her fit the material of her dress back in place over her breasts, Khalid stared back at her, rather humbled by the helplessness she saw on his face.

Independent, willful, his Marty wasn't a weak woman. Yet the pleasure they shared left her faltering, her hands shaking and her body trembling as Khalid eased her dress back over her thighs.

He leaned forward to touch her lips with his.

What he had meant to be a soft, gentle kiss turned into something more. Lips parted, his as well as hers, and seconds later their tongues were licking, stroking, lips melded together as if they were trying to consume each other.

Khalid drew back, knowing that they had to get out of this car right now. Abdul wasn't exactly an emergency. He stood patiently after opening the door, waiting on Khalid and Shayne to step from the vehicle before Khalid extended his hand to Marty and helped her from the car.

Sultry summer heat wrapped around Khalid as he helped Marty from the back, like the heat of her body, tinged with moisture, sinking into his flesh and warming the places inside him that had been cold until her touch.

"Abdul, you may retire for the night," Khalid informed him as he led Marty up the marble steps to the front door, Shayne moving ahead of them. "I'll see you in the morning."

A security guard opened the door from the inside, his impassive gaze flickering over them as Khalid escorted Marty inside.

Marty was silent as he led her into the house and up the curved staircase to his bedroom while Shayne headed to the opposite side of the house in silence. The fingers that he held in his hand still trembled, and her breathing, as well as his own, was still slightly labored.

His heart was racing in his chest. Like a youth, the sheer excitement of touching her, of knowing that soon she would belong to him, was nearly the last measure of pressure that his control could take.

"Would you like a drink?" he asked, as he pushed open the door to his suite and led her inside.

"No." Her voice was as unsteady as he knew his own would be if he didn't control it.

"Hungry?" He closed the door behind them before stepping closer to her and gripping her hips and pulling her to him.

Graceful hands landed against his chest, reminding him that his shirt was undone. Hell, he hadn't even thought to fix it before leaving the limo. At least his slacks were firmly zipped.

"I'm very hungry." The tone of her voice assured him that it wasn't food she wanted.

Her hands reached up, tugging at the edges of his jacket until he shrugged the material from his shoulders. His shirt followed, leaving him naked from the waist up as his fingers moved to the zipper at the back of her dress.

Undressing her took no time. The soft material slid from her body as his lips moved to hers once again, covering them, immersing his senses in the delicate heat and hunger of her arousal.

Marty had never known the desperation for another's touch that she felt for Khalid's now. Over the years she had ached for him, needed him, but never with such power that it made her body tremble and left her weak to his touch. So weak she had to fight to stand. To breathe. Her lungs labored as a fragile groan tore from her chest. Her hands gripped his shoulders, fighting to hold on to him as he lifted her against him, moving, gliding to the huge bed at the far end of the open suite.

He didn't pause as he laid her on the black coverlet. She heard his shoes thud against the soft carpeting, felt his hands tearing at his pants as his kisses grew more demanding and became edged with a sensual roughness that had her heart rate doubling.

Within seconds he was moving over her, hard, hot, naked. His knees parted her legs as his lips moved to her jaw, her neck. Hungry lips moved to her breasts, where he kissed with delicate greed before consuming the ultrasensitive point of her nipple with a hungry mouth.

Marty flinched at the surge of ecstatic pleasure that tore through her. Electric shards of sensation tore from her nipple to her womb; it clenched tight as her clit began to throb with excitement.

It was the most amazing feeling. As though the thinnest of nerve endings connected her nipples, her womb, and her clit. Each tug at the swollen tip caused a surge of heat to travel below, shaking her with the force of the pleasure tearing through her.

"You're destroying my control," he groaned, as her fingers curled around the thick erection between his thighs.

"Who needs control?" She could barely force the words past her lips as he moved to her other breast and drew that neglected nipple into his mouth.

Marty arched tightly, a cry tearing from her throat as the need became painful.

Parting her legs as she felt Khalid's hand stroking down her midriff, she prayed for his touch at the tormented flesh between her thighs. Her pussy throbbed in need, the ache centered deep in her belly and blooming with heat as his fingers slid into the narrow slit between the folds of flesh.

"Khalid!" She cried out his name as he circled her clit, never giving her the touch she needed as his lips began to move down her body.

"I'm going to eat you like candy, baby."

Sliding between her thighs, he pushed her legs wide, his hands pressing beneath her rear to cup it and lift her to him.

The first touch of his lips made her entire body tense, and a ragged moan echoed from her chest. They circled her clit, drew it inside, and then proceeded to drive her insane as he began to suckle at the little bud.

His tongue stroked over it, around it. Each touch was never firm enough, never fast enough to send her racing over the edge of release that she could feel just out of reach.

His fingers clenched her rear, parting the twin globes and dipping into the narrow crevice there. Drawing the juices that spilled from her pussy back to the snug opening, he began to massage it firmly.

There was too much pleasure. Too many sensations. Marty couldn't hold her careening senses in place as he stroked her in places where her own fingers had never ventured.

The tiny prick of pleasure pain at her ass had her pressing closer to the caress. The suction of his mouth at her clit destroyed her, the waves of pleasure tearing through her as she writhed beneath the destruction his mouth and tongue created.

Her senses were whirling with the extremeness of sensations. The feel of his calloused palms on the sensitive flesh of her rear had her twisting in his grip, the rasp of them stroking over nerve endings she hadn't known could be so sensitive.

It was his finger stroking, massaging, pressing against the tender opening of her rear as his lips and tongue sucked and licked at the too sensitive folds of her pussy that drove her to the edge of sanity.

She needed . . . she wasn't certain what she needed. She had never felt this. She had never known such pleasure. It built and built. It burned and ached.

"Khalid." She arched into his grip as his tongue circled her clit with rapid, heated strokes. It flickered over the swollen bud before he sucked it inside once again. At the same time, his finger slipped into the tight entrance of her rear. The alternating, blistering sensations were too much to process, too much to bear.

As his finger stretched her anally and his tongue stroked over her clit rapidly, something exploded, detonated. In a blaze of sensation, a white-hot heat she couldn't resist, pleasure ruptured inside her and sent her flying, as a strangled scream tore from her throat.

She was dying. She couldn't live through it. She couldn't survive it. Ecstasy was a brilliant conflagration whipping through her mind and body.

Marty fought to catch her breath, to still the rapid beating of her heart. Her body shook in the grip of a rapture she couldn't explain, and one she couldn't escape.

"Sweet baby." His voice stroked over her as his hands smoothed along her sides, his lips moving up her stomach to her breasts.

When they reached her lips, the need was burning inside her again.

Opening her eyes, Marty stared up at him, her breath catching at the extreme sensual hunger that tightened his face. That look was as arousing as any touch he had given her so far. The sheer desperate lust, the tightening of his features, the heaviness about his lips, the drowsiness in his eyes, the rivulet of sweat that eased along his dark face. The combination was like a hit of aphrodisiac that surged through her system.

"Khalid." She breathed his name as his thighs slid between hers, the wide crest of his erection pressing against her pussy.

"Damn. I've never done this before." His breath was heavy, rough, as she stared up at him in surprised amusement.

"You could have fooled me." She panted, her hands gripping his hard shoulders as he pressed closer, his hips shifting, his cock stretching the untried entrance of her sex.

He almost smiled. "I've never taken a virgin," he growled, as he gripped her hip and pressed closer.

Marty bit her lip as the blooming heat between her thighs sent pinpricks of pleasure pain racing through her nervous system.

"You still haven't," she pointed out, as she fought not to groan at the ecstasy building inside her again.

"So I haven't." His head lowered, his lips brushing against hers as he spoke. "Get ready, precious."

The moan she had tried to hold back slipped free as the head of his cock began to stretch delicate tissue, to stroke nerve endings never before touched.

Crowding sensations began to tear through her. The burning heat of the penetration, the shift and thrust of his cockhead inside her, never going far enough, never fully possessing her as the pleasure began to rise inside her once again.

Marty lost sense of what she knew was coming. She knew only what she wanted, what she needed. She needed him deep inside her. She needed the stroke and thrust of him against tender nerve endings suddenly blazing for touch.

Her hips arched, her legs wrapped around his hips as she writhed beneath him, reaching desperately for more.

"Easy," he groaned. "Slow and easy, Marty."

"No." Her head shook as she tightened around him, fighting to draw him deeper inside her. "Fuck me, Khalid. Now. Please God, now."

His hips jerked, burying his erection deeper inside her, the burn suddenly building, intensifying as he drew back once before surging forward with a hard, blinding thrust.

Pleasure and pain merged. Fiery heat and desperate hunger blended as Marty cried out his name, her arms tightening around his neck as he buried himself inside her to the hilt.

Excruciating pleasure. There was no other way to describe it, to sense it. A pleasure that bordered pain. A pain that bordered ecstasy.

"Fuck. You're burning me alive," he groaned against her lips as she felt his erection throbbing inside her.

"Now." She could feel the inferno beginning to blaze inside her, the building sensations, the desperation and need that he just move.

"Now." A gentle nip at her lips, and he was moving.

Marty stared up at him, watching the expression of building pleasure as it tightened his face, feeling the exquisite rapture racing inside her as he began to fuck her with deep, heavy strokes.

Pleasure began to escalate inside her, to whip across her nerve endings as her body began to demand more, her senses becoming lost in the hunger tearing through him.

Tightening her legs around his hips, tilting her hips to the stroke and drive of his, she let the building pleasure escalate. She didn't bother to fight it. She knew better than to try to control it. Ecstasy was just a heartbeat away, one last surrender to fulfillment.

She gave him that surrender. Her body tightened around him, the delicate muscles clenched and milked his cock as each thrust became harder, pushing inside her, stretching her, impaling her with heated hunger as the explosions began to detonate through her body.

The cry that echoed around her was her own. Her body tightened, arched, then began to tremble as white-hot impulses of sensation began to tear through it.

Raking her nails along his back, she cried out his name as she felt each thrust increase until a strangled groan tore from his throat. She felt the heated, furious blasts of his release inside her. The sensation triggered another fiery burst of pleasure through her body, another orgasm that drew her tight within his arms and forced a cry from her lips.

It was rapture. It was dying and being reborn. It was agony and ecstasy, and Marty knew in that moment that she had lost something in his arms that she may never be able to regain again.

She had, in all possibility, lost her heart.

Gently, Khalid cleaned Marty's exhausted body as she dozed. With a soft, warm cloth he wiped the perspiration from her face, her neck, and her breasts. From between her thighs he cleaned the sweet juices and the excess of their passion before toweling her dry and pulling the blankets gently over her body.

Donning comfortable cotton pants, he sat at the edge of the bed for long moments, trying to speak, trying to tell her the rest of the truth, the mistakes he had made. The reason why it was so important that he not lose her.

She was tired, he told himself. He could tell her when the sun rose, when he perhaps had more information on his brothers.

His contacts should know something by now, he assured himself. He would speak to them first, then he would speak to her.

Bending to her he kissed Marty's forehead gently then rose from the bed and quietly left the room to allow her to sleep.

He had to know where his half brothers were, what their plans were and if they had targeted Marty. And if they had, then he had a decision to make. Plans to put together. Killing in cold blood was far different than taking down a terrorist cell.

They would stop at nothing to kill Marty. And that was something he could never allow.

Now, he had to protect her, even if it meant becoming the cold-blooded killer his brothers accused him of being.

She wasn't going to survive the emotions tearing her apart. As Marty escaped the estate hours after Khalid had left the bed and disappeared into his study, she had to fight back her shame. It wasn't shame about what they had done. The pleasure had been so intense, so mind-blowing, that there wasn't a chance in hell that she could feel ashamed about it.

It came from the very fact that for some reason he hadn't been able to lie beside her, to sleep with her, once the sex act had been completed. The anger that had surged through her once she realized that he had no intention of returning to her had burned through her like wildfire and had sent pain into the very depths of her soul.

The next afternoon she still hadn't managed to get a handle on that pain and anger.

Khalid had called more than once that afternoon and the messages on her answering machine were becoming colder, and obviously angrier. And she was becoming more nervous. Khalid wasn't the type of man to whom a woman said no easily. If nothing else, bittersweet regret would linger in her memories for more years than it should.

And he wouldn't do it through physical intimidation. Oh hell no, Khalid would use his sexuality, his experience, and a woman's hunger to make damned sure she didn't escape him until he was ready to let her go. And that terrified her almost as much as the intensity of her emotions did. Her body was in conflict with her mind, and it was craving more of Khalid.

The phone rang again. Turning to stare at the offending instrument, Marty waited until the answering machine clicked on.

"Marty, it's Shayne." The amusement in his tone had her frowning. "It seems Khalid's upset with you, darling. Could you give him a call? I'm afraid he just might lose that legendary control of his soon if you don't."

Marty winced. Yes, Khalid's patience was considered legendary.

"Come on, sweetheart, don't make this harder on yourself than it has to be," he finished, just before the recorder clicked off.

Great. Now Shayne. She should have listened to her instincts where he was concerned. He was simply too damned dominating.

She bit at a fingernail as she paced the living room floor, struggling with what she wanted to do versus the anger and fear rising inside her. What the hell had he done to her the night before? Hell, it was just sex. Right? It wasn't as though he had grown two heads and tried to steal her soul. *Well, he hadn't grown two heads*, she thought, with a weary sigh. But the stealing her soul part . . . she wasn't too sure about that. Her entire body was too sensitive, as though being away from Khalid was putting her through some sort of withdrawal.

She wanted him again. Her pussy was wet, her breasts sensitive, her arms ached to hold him, her thighs tingled at the memory of the feel of him between them.

She almost scoffed at the idea of an addiction, but God, she just needed him. But she had needed him for years. The feelings raging through her were amplified from those that she had felt before he had taken her in that big bed of his. Before his release had spilled inside her. Before he had cleaned her with painstaking care afterward.

Why hadn't she believed the rumors that Khalid rarely slept with a lover? That in most cases the members of the club who more often played the role of a third did so because the responsibilities, such as sleeping with their lovers, were the very responsibilities they shunned in a relationship.

She had needed that sense of intimacy, though. She had ached for it with the same strength that she had ached for his touch, his possession. The lack of it now left her struggling with both anger and pride.

The problem was, she had no idea how to do anything about it. The most she had managed to do was perhaps piss him off because she had left before he was ready for her to leave.

And there was no doubt that he was angry. She had refused to answer the phone all morning, but he had still called. Several times. His voice becoming darker and more brooding each time. At least she had some satisfaction from that. Slight though it may be.

The phone rang once again.

"Have you ever been spanked?" Khalid's tone was dark, brooding. "Because I'm thinking that's just what you need, baby. Pick up this damned phone, Marty. Now." She stared at it as though it were a snake, coiled and hissing. The recorder clicked off as a surge of nervous energy began to race through her. If she stayed here, then there wasn't a doubt in her mind that Khalid would be there soon. She would have to face him eventually, but she had hoped to get a handle on whatever the hell it was she was feeling, and to get over her anger, before dealing with the situation.

If she only knew what to do now. How did you make a man provide the intimacy needed when he clearly seemed against it?

The other part of this intimacy problem was the half-truths he had given her the night before. He had given her just enough to warn her that danger could be coming soon, but not enough to provide a clear picture why.

That complete truth, the intimacy of sharing more with her than simply what he had to, was obviously something he couldn't give her.

She had chased after him since she was teenager. Now that she had made it into his bed she was learning that there was much more to seduction than she had ever imagined. She was going to have to figure out the rules before she went much further.

Unfortunately, she had the feeling her apartment wasn't the best place to do so. Khalid owned the damned building. Grabbing her purse and the overnight tote she kept packed, Marty rushed from her apartment to the parking garage.

Her mother was still gone, but her father was home. She wouldn't have to go into detail; she'd never had to when her emotions were like a cauldron ready to boil over. And when it came to Khalid, she imagined her father could be a font of information, if he wanted to be. Convincing him to give her just a few insights shouldn't be too hard.

Her father had always understood. He would understand now.

Sliding into her black BMW, Marty started the engine and put the car into drive. Driving through the exit of the garage, she threw a wave at the security guard on duty.

As she drove past she noticed his hand reaching for the phone and rolled her eyes. No doubt he was informing Khalid that she was leaving her apartment. She'd noticed that Khalid had a rather strong habit of keeping tabs on everyone in his life. Not that he had many friends, but those he did have also seemed to revolve in the same sphere of social, personal, and business alliances as he did, which made it easier for him to do so. She had now become someone he felt the need to watch over.

She hadn't needed a man's protection since she had left her parents' home. She didn't need Khalid's protection now. What she needed was far more important, something she was afraid she would never possess.

It was more than she had received last night, though. She just had to figure out how to get him to realize he wanted to give it to her. Then she had to figure out exactly how to handle it if he did.

The night before had been a revelation in many ways. From the second Shayne had walked into the Sinclairs' library, Marty had sensed that her life was changing.

Something she had only been curious about before had bloomed inside her. And in Khalid's eyes she had seen an affirmation that it was coming.

If she allowed this relationship to progress, then it would be far more than what they had shared the night before.

She felt a jolt of response at the thought of being the lover of two men. It had only been a distant curiosity for so many years, but the knowledge that it would happen if this continued suddenly had her wondering what it would mean to her own sexuality, and to the emotions she could feel torturing her now.

Over the years Marty had managed to get enough information to form a certain image of the club and the men she knew were a part of it.

Men who walked a certain dark edge, who found thrills in various forms of high-adrenaline lifestyles. Whether they were CEOs, leaders of countries, or agents of one of the world's alphabet agencies, they all shared a common tie: a darkness and a sense of danger that they carried like an invisible shield.

The ring of the cell phone on the seat beside her had her heart racing again. Picking it up, she glanced at the number, fortified her courage, and flipped the phone open to answer it. "Leave me alone for now," she ordered briskly, praying she sounded more determined than she truly was.

"You picked the perfect time to leave." Shayne's chuckle came through the line. "Khalid was on his way to your apartment as you pulled from the garage."

"That's what I pretty much figured," she informed him. "I need some time."

"You should have thought about that before you shared his bed last night." Shayne's tone became firmer. "What the hell is going on,

Marty? You're not some flighty kid. Why the hell are you running from him?"

Because she didn't know what to say, what to do. Because she wanted to dream of happily ever afters and she was terribly afraid those couldn't exist in Khalid's arms. He couldn't hold her after taking the innocence she had saved for him. He could only give her half truths. What made her think he would ever do more than fuck her?

She should have considered this; she should have thought of it. But she would have sworn he felt more for her than simple lust.

"I need to think," she finally breathed out roughly. "I'll call him later."

Shayne grunted at that. "Does Khalid seem like a man you can dangle on a string, sweetheart? I think you know better."

Yes, she knew better. And she had a feeling Khalid would reinforce that impression.

"I didn't ask for your opinion," she muttered.

"I volunteered it," he stated, his voice like dark silk. "If I were you, I'd return to the estate."

She laughed at the order. "Go to hell. Look, I'm certain you'll be talking to Khalid soon if you're not still at the estate. Tell him I'll call him later. I have some things I have to sort out, and I can't do that in his bed."

"You may not have a choice," he growled.

"Yeah. Right." She laughed into the line as she made her turn and took the road to her parents' home. "When I no longer have a choice is when you'll be burying me, Shayne. Now go away. I have things to do that don't include you."

"For the moment." Though low, his tone was intense, commanding.

"Good-bye, Shayne." Flipping the phone closed, she cut him off as effectively as possible and ignored its strident ring as it lay in the passenger seat.

No man ordered her around, and she was going to be damned if she was going to allow Shayne or Khalid to do so.

She could see this situation deteriorating rapidly, and she knew it was her own fault. She shouldn't have run. She should have faced this; she should have faced Khalid and demanded what she knew was her due as a lover. Spending the night in his study was not acceptable loverlike behavior as far as she was concerned.

But perhaps it wasn't just Khalid's fault. From the moment the intensity of her orgasm had begun to ease, Marty had known she had entered a realm of sensation and emotions that she wasn't prepared for.

She had been suddenly terrified of a broken heart. In the moments after that final orgasm she had sensed that she had already allowed herself to cross a line. She had invested much more of herself in a man than she had ever intended.

Pulling to a stop at the intersection, she waited for the car in the opposite lane to proceed first, her mind still racing to figure out how to handle her personal life.

She was distracted, and she knew better than to allow herself to do that. Khalid and Shayne had her off balance, but not so off balance that she didn't see the black car as it raced from its parked position farther up the street or the barrel of the rifle as it was shoved out the back window.

Bullets tore into the front of her vehicle as Marty jerked the wheel to the right, stomped the gas, and started praying as the window shattered. A scream tore from her lips as she ducked, and her foot hit the gas harder.

Another blast blew out the back window, and a second later she heard the scream of tires, horns blowing, and the sound of voices raised high in shock. The vehicle slammed to a hard, shocking stop, throwing her forward into the steering wheel. For a moment the world seemed to tilt on a crazy axis. She could hear sirens in the distance. Her cell phone was ringing again, that crazy "Who

Can It Be Now" ringtone echoing in her head as she fought to get her bearings.

She struggled to reach the phone on the passenger seat as she lay across the console, the world still tilting around her.

"Hello?" Her voice was scratchy, weak. It didn't sound like her, even to her own ears.

"Marty?" Shayne's voice was instantly concerned. "What's wrong?"

She tried to push herself upright. "I'll have to call you back. Someone just tried to blow my head off." She was going to throw up. "Bye, Shayne."

She could hear him screaming her name as she flipped the phone closed and took a hard, deep breath. Her stomach was roiling. A sense of vertigo plagued her, as she struggled to sit upright.

She hadn't hit her head. She hadn't been shot. The car had slammed into a tree, however.

"Lady, you okay?" a voice asked her from outside the broken window.

Marty forced her eyes open and focused on the officer.

"FBI." She forced the word past her lips as she tried to get her senses back into line. Pulling the small wallet from the inside of her jacket pocket, she flashed her identification at him and breathed in hard and deep once again.

Okay, she was going to get through this. She wasn't hurt, just a little shaken.

"Agent Mathews, an ambulance is on its way." The officer pulled the car door open and knelt beside her.

"Witnesses." She breathed through her nose to get past the rising nausea. "Plates on that car."

"My partner's getting statements on it," he assured her, rising and backing up as she started to pull herself out of the car. "You should stay put until the ambulance arrives, Agent Mathews," she was advised. "They're on their way."

"I'm fine." She waved his advice away but accepted his arm as he helped her step from the vehicle. "Did they get away?"

Of course they had gotten away. She couldn't have been lucky enough that they had actually stuck around to be arrested and interrogated. Hell no.

"Sorry, ma'am." The officer kept a firm hold on her as she swayed for a second. "You need to be checked out, ma'am." There was a concerned look on his face. "You're going to be bruised. Some of that glass got you."

She shook her head again. "Contact Director Zachary Jennings, FBI, immediately. He's my godfather."

The officer snapped into place as Marty gave him her godfather's name. Instant results produced instant action.

Within twenty minutes there were two detectives on the scene as well as a crime scene van and the personnel required to collect what little evidence could be gathered from the scene.

Pictures of the skid marks, witness statements, the bullets that had ripped into her leather seats.

It also didn't take long for her godfather to call her father. Within thirty minutes of the detectives' arrival Marty turned at the sound of screaming tires and watched her father's Porsche come to a shuddering stop.

Just what she needed, Senator Mathews going ballistic. His temper didn't explode often, but she had no doubt in her mind that it would be used today.

She wished she had allowed herself to pass out.

"Senator Mathews." The detectives were quick, she had to give them credit for that as they chose their unwilling spokesperson. "Your daughter's fine. She's refused an ambulance, but allowed EMTs to check her out."

"Get the hell out of my way." Her father pushed past the frazzled detective, and a second later she found herself enclosed in her father's embrace as he began trying to lead her back to the car.

That was her dad. He was already trying to rush her back into that parent/child world where he could coddle her and comfort himself.

"Whoa. Whoa." Pulling herself back wasn't easy. "Doesn't work this way."

He was icily furious. Marty pulled back enough to see the cold, precise rage burning in his gaze now. He had no idea what had happened and, for the moment, he didn't care. All he cared about was getting her somewhere safe.

"Don't tell me what works," her father growled. "I'm getting you the hell out of here," he told her. "Where's Khalid and Shayne? Damn those two to hell."

"Doesn't matter where they are," she told him firmly. She had to struggle to assert the independence he was suddenly trying to strip from her. What happened to her supportive father? "I have a job to do."

She hated it. It was breaking her heart not to stand there and comfort her father, to assure him that she was fine. To be a daughter. But to be a daughter right now would mean letting go of the independence she treasured. He was her father, and she understood his need to protect her. But right now, she didn't need his protection. She needed to do her job.

Her stride was hesitant, aching, as she moved away from him, only to come to a stop once again as she all but plowed into Khalid's chest.

She couldn't fight him. Staring into his intense black eyes, his savagely hewn features, she knew she couldn't fight him. She stared up at him instead, realizing he must have broken several speed limits to have gotten there so quickly.

As the warmth of him surrounded her, she suddenly had to do what she hadn't had to with her father. She had to force herself to be strong rather than leaning into his strength, and it was all she could do not to sink into his arms. He had a determination to protect her. Fighting against that would be much harder with Khalid for some reason.

Instead, she stood still as he pulled a handkerchief from inside his pocket and gently dabbed at the cuts on her face.

Staring into his eyes, she felt more connected to him now than she had in his bed last night when she had lost her virginity in his arms.

"You're bleeding, precious," he stated calmly, though his black eyes were filled with fury and concern. Concern for her.

"Not badly," she assured him.

He nodded before glancing at Shayne, who had just jumped from his car and was now headed toward them. "Do as you must. I'll distract your fathers and give you a chance to do your job. I'll have my personal physician ready when you're finished, and then we'll talk. Agreed?"

She swallowed. "Agreed."

She was caught. There was no getting out of it, and the sense of relief she felt was almost as frightening as the knowledge that she truly didn't want to run from him any longer.

"Talking won't be easy," she said softly.

"Most things that are worth fighting for are rarely easy, love," he told her, before pressing a gentle kiss to her lips. "But we'll muddle through, I'm certain."

The calm, easy demeanor was at direct odds with the flames of rage burning in his eyes.

"Go." He released her slowly. "Our time will come soon."

Hell. She was definitely in trouble now.

Letting her go was perhaps the hardest thing Khalid had ever done in his life. He pocketed the white silk handkerchief that was now stained with her blood and watched with hooded eyes as she and Shayne moved off.

"Bad idea," Joe snapped behind him. "She's hurt."

Khalid turned to him slowly.

"She would know if she was hurt badly," he told the other man, and prayed he was right. "She is on her feet and making logical decisions. As long as she is doing this, we have no right to interfere."

There was a long silence behind him then. He could feel the fury pouring off the other man as they watched Marty and Shayne move into the fray of witnesses and police officers that had gathered. Shayne was going to have a hell of a time dealing with Jennings once he arrived as well. Zach Jennings might make use of Shayne when he needed to, but on home turf, where his daughter was concerned, it would be a different story. The CIA wasn't exactly bosom buddies of Zach's. He was simply fonder of Shayne than he was of other agencies from that particular branch of covert operations.

"What the hell happened? I thought she left with you last night? Didn't you stay with her?"

The fury pounded at his back as Joe stepped closer. "I warned you she wasn't going to be as easy to control as you thought she was. That she would need more attention if you stepped into an affair with her."

There was nothing inattentive about what Khalid felt for Marty. But there was also fear. More fear than he had ever known in his life. Fear for her life, for her safety.

Still, Khalid nodded slowly. "So you did. It is a situation that will not be repeated. But in all fairness, Senator, I have never stated a desire to control her, nor do I feel the least bit careless toward her. My only desire was to ensure she was never harmed."

"If I find out your past is behind this attack on her, Khalid, then you won't enjoy dealing with me," Joe snarled, now at his side as he voiced Khalid's own fears.

Khalid turned to the senator, watching him coldly before turning his gaze back to the woman.

"If I learn this happened because of my past, then I will deal with it however I must," he said. "She's a woman. My woman. And I promise you, I will protect what is mine this time." He looked at Joe again. "No matter who she must be protected from."

He would protect her, whether from his past or from a father who wanted nothing more than to throw a sheltering blanket over her. Her fathers had tried. She had been placed within his sphere, and there danger always existed. Though he had not expected danger to come so soon.

Moving away from the senator, the concerned father who wanted nothing more than his daughter's protection, Khalid walked over to his sleek black Lexus.

Abdul was waiting, his craggy features creased into a frown as he watched Marty, his hand placed casually in the pocket of the jacket he wore—and on the he carried there.

"Contact Azir," he ordered. "See if you can find out if Ayid and Aman are involved in this. My contacts had no information this morning, nor do they know of my bastard half brothers' whereabouts."

Abdul shook his head. "This is not something he would discuss with me. Your brothers do not discuss their schemes with him. They work around him, below him, but never where he can stop their plans."

"Then contact the bastards," he snapped. "Tell them I will come after them, Abdul. I will hunt them, and they will die if she gets so much as another scratch."

Abdul stared back at him, his expression tormented and filled with fear. "This will only give them greater satisfaction and spur on their efforts," Abdul warned him. Go to them and you go in weakness. Stand silent and still, and you meet them in strength."

Khalid's lips tightened furiously. "I'd rather go hunting."

Abdul shook his head again before nodding toward Marty. "Seduce your woman. Love her. Use this time to tie her to you, so that once your deceptions are revealed she will not run from you. She is a delicate female, Khalid, and one deserving of your time and your care." There was a hint of censure in his voice then. "She is also strong. She is a woman of truth and honor, my friend. The day will come that this may be all that holds her to you. Then, when your brothers move, you will meet them in strength, not in weakness. This is my advice to you."

And it was advice he should heed. Khalid watched as Marty and

Shayne worked together. He acknowledged that the other agent was carefully covering her back, on guard, and watching everyone closely.

Shayne was a man of strength; Khalid had chosen him as his third for this reason. He would be there when Marty was in danger. And Khalid would be by her side as the man who held her heart.

Sharing her was something he couldn't pull back on. The danger that would always surround her would always weigh too heavily on his soul. Should she be harmed or, God forbid, should she be killed, then could he survive the loss?

He couldn't. He knew this. Sharing her life with another man, one he chose, one who he may not control but was in agreement with, was the only alternative. And thankfully it was an alternative he would be pleased to live with.

"Contact Abram," he told Abdul. "Let him know the situation as it stands. He should add to his own protection as well."

Abdul nodded. "They will attempt to destroy Abram, but only after they have destroyed you. Azir protects Abram for now, for Abram is the chosen heir."

That was what they suspected, it wasn't what they were certain of.

"Doesn't matter." Khalid shook his head. "They'll do what they can as opportunity presents itself. Abram needs to know what could be happening to protect himself against them. Make sure that he has the information he needs, and we'll work on our end to ensure our own protection."

Khalid wasn't a murderer. He had tried to distance himself from the politics and bloody infighting of his father's world for most of his life. Khalid had disowned the entire family after the horrors he witnessed ten years ago. And still, it wasn't enough for the half brothers determined to take over the minor throne their father held.

Watching Marty, he was reminded of that life of so long ago, and what he had lost there. He was reminded how easily someone could be taken from him and of the rage that could consume him. He wouldn't allow that again. He wouldn't allow the evil that infected his father's and his half brothers' lives to further disease his own.

It was a vow he had made to himself ten years ago, and it was a vow he wouldn't break now.

8

Something was changing inside her.

Marty sat on the side of her bed after a rigorous and grueling checkup by Khalid's doctor, as Khalid, Shayne, and her fathers waited just outside the room.

In Shayne's eyes she had seen not just his concern, but his affection. She didn't know what had happened, she had no idea why she had been targeted.

Now, if she just knew the rest of the story, the bits and pieces that both and Khalid and Shayne were hiding from her in regards to Khalid's past with his half brothers. Until she had those answers, she had other things to deal with. Not just her own protection, but also Khalid's. She needed to get with a few of her contacts and see what she could find out about Ayid and Aman Mustafa. She hadn't investigated them any further than what was in the file the bureau had given her. That had been a mistake on her part. Perhaps she would have known more about the vendetta they had against Khalid.

She kept her questions, as well as her suspicions, to herself as she assured her fathers that she was well. She listened to them rant and rave, then pretended a weariness she didn't truly feel to convince them to leave.

She loved them dearly, but their overprotective anger was about to smother her.

She had known for most of her life that where a relationship was concerned she would most likely end up involved as her mother was: with two men, rather than the socially acceptable one. Most of the men she knew were members of the club that her fathers were a part of. It was a legacy, a centuries-long tradition for the males of some families.

For Marty it helped knowing that her mother was one of the happiest women she had ever met in her life. Her fathers were just as satisfied and played roles in her and her mother's lives that had kept Marty as well as her mother secure and loved.

She had never considered who would play that role of a third in her relationship. She had certainly never expected it to be Shayne.

But she wanted them both. Admittedly, she wanted Khalid more; he was her center, the cause of a hunger she realized she wasn't going to escape. She had realized that the moment she knew Khalid had chosen Shayne as a third. And now, only hours after escaping death, she found herself needing it, aching for it.

She could have died. She could have lost so many precious moments in his arms.

As she rose to her feet she drew the pale gray silk of her robe tighter around her body and paced to the wide window that had been heavily shuttered. A dark privacy screen had been drawn over the window, blocking sight from the outside. It also blocked infrared and heat imaging. An amazing little invention created by one of the small companies that Khalid had acquired over the years.

The man didn't work a day in his life that she could see, but he had fingers in so many pies it was really amazing.

"You're restless."

His voice had her swinging around to the open doorway. She hadn't heard him open the door, hadn't heard him and Shayne enter, but there they were.

"Restless?" She almost snorted at the description. "That's an understatement."

Her gaze flickered between the two men and the hunger on their faces.

Khalid nodded gently, his expression, especially the dark depths of his eyes, filled also with sympathy and concern. But was there love? Was it even possible that they could fill with love?

She was focusing on that emotion when she had promised herself that she wouldn't take that path. She had promised herself that she wouldn't ask for anything more than to be his lover. If it was meant to be, then the love would come. If it wasn't, she would deal with that, too.

Her heart wasn't following that directive, though. It was aching, demanding that she do more, and, at this point, she had no idea what that more could be.

"Have you managed to find out why I was targeted?" She spoke to Shayne, knowing he would have been on the phone with his contacts by now.

"Nothing conclusive." He shook his head. "You know how it works, Marty. It takes more than a few hours."

"Knowing that doesn't help," she muttered irritably.

"I can understand your anger." Khalid moved closer, the sensuality, the sexuality that was so much a part of him seeming to surround her. "Though I feel I must point out, had you not run from me this morning, then this would not have happened, Marty. You would be in my bed now, filled with pleasure rather than facing the knowledge that you're in danger."

"Thank you for pointing that out to me," she said with false sweetness. "How ever have I made it through my life without you there to spread your little gems of wisdom?"

"Never fear, little flower. I'm here now." His smile was tight, his gaze narrowed on her. "I'll make certain you don't forget it."

Shayne's chuckle drew a glower from her. She didn't need his particular brand of amusement at the moment. Glaring back at Khalid, she wondered exactly what it would take to shake loose that smooth persona he insisted on wearing.

"The last I heard, you don't do straight relationships, Khalid," she stated. "How was I to know you prefer me to stay rather than sending me on my way, as you do your other women?"

Mockery filled his expression now. "I have never sent a lover on her way, precious, as I'm certain you know. As a third, I've usually been sent on my way."

"Poor guy, he's been so unloved." Shayne smirked as he leaned against the dresser and crossed his arms over his chest, watching them curiously.

He was definitely going to begin irritating her soon.

"That's your own fault," she informed Khalid as she ignored Shayne, her voice brittle now. "And rather beside the point."

Turning from him she pushed her fingers through her hair and fought to hold back the emotions trying to tear through her.

"I needed to think," she finally told him before turning back, his silent patience raking across her nerves. "And I need to work. I want to find out who the hell thought they could take shots at me and get the hell away with it."

"It's too late to regret your decision to come to my bed," he told her with a flash of dominance. "If this is part of why you need to think alone, then you can forget it."

Unfortunately that dominance did nothing to still the arousal burning inside her.

She arched a brow. "Did I say I regretted it? I believe I've made my position fairly clear, Khalid. It's been my intent for years to get into your bed. You're the one who was determined to keep me out of it."

"And now you will stay in my bed." The growl in his voice surprised her. "I'm no notch in a bedpost, love. You don't want to attempt to play such a game with me."

They had an audience, an amused one at that. Not that she was beginning to care. Shayne may as well learn the lesson Khalid was going to get into his thick skull sooner or later. No man dictated to her.

"Then perhaps you should put yourself out to stay in that bed as well," she snapped back. "I'm no notch, either, Khalid, and I won't be made to feel like one."

She felt too delicate, too female next to him. She didn't feel like a fully trained agent; she felt like a woman begging to be touched. A woman willing to give the man she desired everything he wanted, and she couldn't decide if she was pissed off or resigned to that.

"Be patient, Marty." Khalid shook his head at her accusation. "There is much I must deal with now that you're here. Things I must take care of soon. That will require many hours away from you. And perhaps from our bed."

"Patience isn't one of my virtues." She cast a glare at him before moving away, only to turn back to face him. "What's going on, Khalid? All the warnings, the dire predictions. I'm sick of waiting for the truth from you. What kind of trouble are you in?"

She was getting closer. The truth was there; at least at this point he was willing to admit that there was much more to what was going on here than whatever work he was doing for her father.

"A woman's patience is an inspiration, just as is her tenacity." A small smile tipped his lips as he watched the suspicion flicker in her eyes. He was evading her question, and they both knew it.

Glancing at Shayne, she saw his knowledge of it as well. What the hell was he keeping from her?

"Don't play word games with me, Khalid. You want too much from me to insult me in that manner."

She watched his eyes. They flickered with the truth of her statement as well as with an edge of regret.

"I would give my own life to save yours," he said, his voice harsh. "And soon, I will give you the answers you need. Until I can, I ask only that you stay here, within the house, and allow me to bring to you not just the answers, but also, hopefully, the knowledge of who targeted you and why."

She wanted to rage at him. The answers were there in his eyes and she knew it; he wasn't even trying to hide it.

"You can't trust me with your secrets, yet you can ask me to trust you with my body and my heart," she said, with an edge of anger. "Where's the fairness in that, Khalid?"

"I did not say there was fairness in it, Marty." Frustration was beginning to line his voice. "Very soon, the answers will be given to you. That I promise you."

"You can't give me those answers now, but you want my body now. You and Shayne. Together."

She glanced at Shayne, watched his gaze darken, the lust in his expression deepening.

Khalid's lips tightened. "No, it is not simply your body that I want, but if this is all I can have at this moment, then I'll gladly take what you will give."

This answer surprised her.

There was an edge of something in his voice that she couldn't pinpoint. A hunger, a need she didn't know how to interpret. Something deeper than she had expected from him.

"What if I just want you?" She pushed him. They both knew better, but the combination of arousal and anger had her pushing him, daring him.

He stared back at her for what seemed like long minutes.

"If I believed you wanted only me, then I would gladly take what you offered," he said finally. "But we both know that that is not true."

She couldn't evade him; she didn't even try. His arm curled around her waist, pulling her to him, his head lowering, his lips taking hers without hesitation.

The instant his lips touched hers, Marty felt herself melt, unable to fight the need or herself any further. She wanted this kiss; she wanted this man.

There was something about his touch that made her weak, that tore aside the shields she had built around herself for so long. She had made Khalid unattainable to herself, and in doing so had only driven the hunger for him higher.

She could sate herself with him. *It didn't have to be love*, she thought desperately, as his lips, his kiss, began to devour her. It didn't have to be a lifetime of strife or conflict. *It could be just this. Just what they wanted, what they both wanted.* And when it was done she could go on with her life.

She could do that.

Her arms encircled his neck, her lips parted farther, her tongue met his in a sensual, sensuous dance that became heated, desperate.

Thick black hair met her fingers and she entwined them in the silkiness in order to pull him closer. His hard, lean, muscled body sheltered hers, surrounded her as his arms held her close to his chest, his head bent to hers.

She felt sucked into another world. A world where nothing mattered, nothing existed but the hunger suddenly tearing through her.

Pleasure rushed through her system with each devouring kiss Khalid shared with her. It built, became hotter, each nerve ending in her body more sensitive as she felt his hands moving over her back, feeling the heat of his flesh through the thin material of her robe.

She wanted his hands on her naked body, touching her, skin to skin. She wanted his body covering her, his hands stroking her.

A hard breath caught in her throat as she felt his fingers move to the tie of her robe. Experienced fingers loosened it and drew the edges of the robe apart. His hands smoothed over her bare hips.

Shayne simply watched. This moment wasn't for him to share in, not yet. The emotions between Khalid and Marty were running too close to the surface. Too much desperation filled them, too many haunting secrets threatened to tear them apart. For now, he left them alone and merely watched as the hunger surrounding the two began to fill the room.

"You make a man desperate for you," Khalid groaned, his voice thick with hunger. "So desperate he would risk all that he is to have you."

Her lashes lifted, and her stomach clenched as she read the need to touch her, to have her, in his expression.

Had she ever been wanted with such ferocity by anyone?

"Marty, my sweet little flower." The sound of his voice, husky, deep, the words gentle, caused her heart to tighten as his hands lifted to push the robe from her shoulders.

Silk pooled at her feet and she watched his expression tighten, his black eyes blaze with lust.

Heat pooled between her thighs, preparing her further.

It had been too long since he had taken her, something whispered inside her mind. Too long since she had known his possession.

Her breath caught as his hands moved to her breasts, cupping them, his thumbs raking over her nipples, creating an exciting friction that sent flames racing across her nerve endings.

She felt on fire from the need rushing through her body.

Desperate fingers moved to the buttons of his shirt, only to grip the material instead and jerk it apart as his lips again lowered to hers.

As though that action had released a flood of lust inside Khalid, his kiss became rougher, more territorial. A wildfire of sensation rushed through her veins as she fought to hold on to just enough control.

But there was no holding on. Her hands gripped his shoulders, her tongue dueled with his, as they both fought for dominance of the kiss.

Khalid's clothes were disposed of quickly. His shirt was tossed to the floor, the rest landing wherever they dropped. Marty didn't know; she didn't care.

All that mattered was the feel of his body against hers—the light rasp of the hairs on his chest against her sensitized nipples, the feel of his lips on hers, his hands stroking over her body, cupping her breasts, plucking at her nipples.

The silken comforter of the bed met her back before she realized he'd moved her. It stroked against her flesh, another caress to burn through her senses as she fought to touch him.

His lips moved to her neck, nipping kisses drawing her muscles tight as her neck arched and whimpering moans left her lips.

Nothing mattered now but touch—sensual, seductive, heated. Taste. The taste of his flesh as she lifted her head, her lips moving to his shoulders, her tongue stroking, sampling the salty male taste of him.

There was more of him that she wanted to taste, more of him that she needed to taste.

His lips moved down her neck, over her shoulder, and to her breasts. His hands cupped the swollen mounds, his thumbs stroking over the nipples a second before his lips covered one tight peak.

Marty froze. The pleasure was a rush of adrenaline and weakening sensuality. It was a cacophony of such incredible sensations that she became lost in the waves of them.

His teeth raked against the tip; his tongue stroked it. His lips closed on the areola, sucking it with deep, measured pulls of his mouth.

"Khalid." She was surprised at the sound of her own voice. There was a plea in it, a desperation she couldn't hide.

Her pussy was on fire from the need. Her clit was so swollen, aching with such intensity, that she swore she could feel the swirl of air around it.

Anticipation tore through her. His hand stroked her, from her breast to her hip to her thigh. A whimpering moan left her lips at the building need for his touch where she had grown so wet.

His lips, teeth, and tongue worked at her breast as his fingers moved to her inner thigh. A cry tore from her lips, her eyes opening wide as she struggled to find a sense of balance in a world suddenly tilting on its axis.

He didn't tease. He parted the curl-shrouded folds of her pussy, and a second later two fingers began pressing inside her, stretching her, burning her.

"Khalid!" She cried his name as her hips arched, her thighs spreading farther apart as the initial penetration sent a shock through hidden nerve endings, exposing them, sensitizing them further.

Her hips writhed against the impalement. Thrusting, she fought for more, a deeper, harder caress that he gave instantly.

His fingers worked inside her, thrusting slow, then hard; easy, then fiercely. It was never the sensation she expected, never the caress she thought would come. His fingers scissored inside her, stretching her further as a ragged cry tore from her lips.

"God yes, Marty." His groan wrapped around her, the desperation in it tearing through her.

He wanted her. He was hungry for her. In her life she had never known such desire from a man until Khalid.

The knowledge of that hunger, the pleasure tearing through her, the feel of his sweat-dampened body, her own perspiration sliding between them, combined in such a powerful force that her orgasm tore through her without warning.

There was no initial tightening of her body. There was no rush of impending force. It was just there. A sudden, explosive wonder filled with light and sound as his fingers continued to work inside her, to stroke her higher, throwing her into a blazing conflagration that seemed never ending.

"Sweet Marty, burn for me." His voice was an echo of the pleasure in her head. A sensual, mental caress that sent aftershocks of release rippling through her.

In that moment, as the pleasure eased and another hunger built, a wisp of a thought, a desire shocked her senses. It could have been hotter. There was a component missing, something she knew she could have, something she was terrified to reach out for.

Fighting back that thought, she reached for the man destroying her senses and her sense of herself. As he rose to his knees in front of her, spreading her thighs farther, Marty sat up, one hand gripping his hip, the other curling around the thick, dark protrusion of his cock.

Khalid froze in front of her.

He had never known such pleasure. He had never known a woman who could give pleasure as she did with the simple act of coming around his fingers.

Now her slender, fragile fingers gripped his dick with silken strength.

"What now, precious?" He fought the urge to dominate now, to let loose the sexual animal that existed inside him.

It was hard, though, incredibly hard. Her hand stroked the length of his cock, her thumb whispering over the swollen crest to gather the droplet of precum that moistened it.

"You always manage to destroy my control."

He heard the emotion in her voice. That edge of fear there clenched his heart.

"What do you do to mine?" His fingers flexed with the need to dominate her now. "You do not know the edge you push me to, love."

Her tongue glanced over her lips, so close to the tip of his cock, his flesh so close to such extreme pleasure.

"What would you do if I asked you to lose that control?"

Khalid stilled at her question. There was something in her expression now, in the heat of her eyes that sent anticipation tightening his gut.

"Is that what you want, precious?" He touched her face, his fingertips relishing the feel of her satiny flesh. "No control? No limits?"

"What would you do?"

"I believe you know what I would do. I would give you pleasures that even your imagination could not perceive. I would ensure it."

He would give her not just himself, but Shayne as well. Whenever she wanted it, in ways she most likely couldn't imagine. Khalid knew, even if she didn't suspect, that his sexuality, his sensual hungers went far deeper than she had most likely considered, even knowing how sexual he could become.

"Right now," she whispered, that edge of anticipation and desperation still ever present in her voice. "Right now, Khalid, what would you do with no control?"

A part of him sensed what she wanted. She was a strong woman, a woman who had made her own rules long ago and had lived with them, no matter the cost to her heart. But now, in this one moment, only seconds after her release, she was wondering what that control had cost her.

It had cost her the knowledge of her own female strength, Khalid thought. His Marty had denied herself that adventurous, sensual core of femininity that lurked just beneath the surface of her control.

His hand slid into her hair.

"You want this?" he asked, hardening his voice, forcing himself to hold back. "All that I am at this moment, sweet flower? Is that what you want?"

She licked her lips again. He expected to see indecision in her eyes, a flash of regret or denial. Instead he saw an excitement, a flash of hunger and lust that he was certain she was unaware lurked inside her.

"Yes."

His fingers clenched in her hair, tightening, pulling at the strands with just enough force to send what he knew would be a rush of fiery pleasure pain through her already overloaded senses.

She moaned. Her lashes fluttered closed.

Gripping the base of his cock he pressed it to her parted lips.

"Suck my cock, precious. Slow and easy. I want to feel that sweet little tongue working over the head. It's my favorite fantasy. Your pretty lips wrapped around my dick."

His teeth snapped the last word off as she did just as he ordered. Her lips parted as she sucked him in, her tongue lashing over the sensitive crown as a low growl tore from his chest.

"Fuck yes." The words were torn from him.

Lightning flares of exquisite pleasure began to race through his body as he continued to flex his fingers in her hair, pulling delicately.

Her expression became a picture of perfect sensual pleasure. Her lashes drifted closed over her soft gray eyes, her face flushed, a delicate pink staining the creamy flesh.

Watching her, his body tight with the need for release and the demand to hold back, Khalid controlled her movements. One hand in her hair, the other wrapped around the base of his cock, he fucked her mouth with slow, easy strokes, letting the pleasure wash through his senses.

The deep, measured suckling of her mouth over the sensitized crest was nearly more than he could bear, though. In all his sexual years he had never known the pleasure that Marty managed to send rushing through his body. She was like a narcotic, instantly addictive, always desired.

Clenching his teeth, he fought the tightening of his balls as she sucked him deeper, her tongue stroking over his cock as he took her mouth with gentle greed.

Moving his hand from his cock he watched as she wrapped the fingers of both hands around the heavy flesh. He wanted to touch her, to follow the curve of her breast, to feel the hardness of her nipples.

Like responsive live pebbles, her nipples were tight and hard, silken and heated. At his first touch he felt the little moan from her throat vibrate against his dick and nearly lost his control then.

His hips jerked, his ability to pull back nearly disintegrating beneath the heated strokes of her tongue and the snug suckling of her mouth.

"Your sweet mouth is destroying me," he groaned, his hands tightening further in her hair. "Are you sure you want this?"

There was so much he wanted to do to her. So much he would do if she gave him the chance.

Her answer was a moan and the swirl of her tongue over his cock, and the leash snapped.

Marty didn't know what she expected, but when he pulled back, his expression, his eyes wild, she was certain it wasn't quite this, though "this" sent screaming waves of pleasure and anticipation tearing through her.

"Over." She sure wasn't expecting him to turn her, to push her upper body to the bed as he lifted her hips.

"Khalid."

"You asked for all of me." His voice sounded torn, dark and dangerous. "Give it to me now, because I need all of you."

She felt his cock tuck against the folds of her pussy, spreading her flesh as it began to push inside, opening her, searing nerve endings that seemed to have forgotten the last time he had taken her.

"Sweet. Fuck me, you're so tight and sweet." His voice was rougher, deeper, darker. "Fucking you is like drowning in pleasure."

He surged inside her. Half the length of his cock buried inside her in one firm thrust that had her fighting to lift her upper body from the bed in reaction.

A broad, calloused hand pressed her back down, held her there as he pulled back, then surged inside again. With each broad stroke his flesh buried deeper inside her, stretched her farther, and sent explosions of sensation erupting.

It was like being burned alive from the inside out with such incredible pleasure that there was no way to acclimate herself to it. She could only take it, love it, press back for more of it.

"Stay there." His hand lifted from her back. "Keep that pretty ass raised for me, sweet. Let me show you a mere shadow of the pleasure I can give you."

Marty's breath caught as his fingers moved along the crevice of her rear. Caressing, firm, demanding, his fingers stroked the juices of her pussy from the heavy layer coating his cock and the folds of her sex.

Slick, heated, his fingers always returned to her rear as she felt him like a thick, living wedge, buried inside her. The thunder of blood rushing through his cock pounded through her pussy as the heated rasp of his fingers began to press against the delicate opening of her anus.

She had never been touched there before Khalid.

Marty shuddered with the pleasure.

She had never been taken quite this way.

A desperate moan pushed past her lips.

His hips moved, his cock easing back as a single finger slipped just inside the sensitive opening of her ass.

"Khalid." She could only gasp his name.

He thrust inside her again as his finger eased back. Seconds later he pulled back once more, his finger slipped deeper into her rear, and Marty lost that last fragile thread of control.

"Damn you," she cried out, feeling her juices gush between them a second before his finger slipped free entirely to gather more. His finger slipped in, coated the opening, then slid back once more.

"Khalid." She was demanding. She needed it. She knew there was more than the gentle caresses he was giving her. She knew there was more he wanted to give her. Much more that she was willing to take.

"Then take it, sweet," he urged her, as he filled her pussy again, every thick, hard inch of his cock burying inside her. "Take what I have to give you."

He pulled back, and this time two fingers slipped into her rear and sent her senses reeling.

Pleasure pain. The most incredible burning, agonizing pleasure tore through her as his fingers slid inside her ass. Delicate, ultrasensitive tissue screamed out in ecstasy and in agony. Fiery pleasure enveloped her, brutal ecstasy threatened on the edges of her senses.

She couldn't help but clench on the invasions as she cried out at the sensations, the alternate strokes fucking inside her with wicked intensity, tearing away her control and her will to resist.

Pressing back, she took what he gave and demanded what he held back. Her nails clawed at the blankets as perspiration coated her flesh, and waves of lust and hunger surged through her with tidal waves of sensation.

"Harder." Her cry was a mix of desperate begging and demanding passion. "Oh God, Khalid. Fuck me harder. Harder."

She needed more. She needed to ride this incredible wave into the pure bliss she could sense just out of reach. The pinnacle of pleasure awaited her, and she wanted to fly into it.

Tiny shocks of sensation began to ignite inside her with every alternate thrust inside her pussy, her rear. She could feel the explosion coming, building. It was there. It was a golden ball of pure white-hot heat, and it sucked her in with such a burst of sensation that she feared she may not survive it.

Tension gripped her, tightened her. Her muscles gripped his cock, sucked at his fingers, and the white-hot conflagration of sensation building inside her erupted.

She felt Khalid, thrusting powerfully, his release powering inside her, heating her, filling her. His groan was a distant sound, his heavy body coming over her another pleasure mixing with the torrent of sensation already tearing her apart.

Was she screaming or just trying to scream?

She was shuddering beneath him, crying, locked inside the heavy pulses of agonizing sensation still tearing through her. She was his. In that moment, in that second, she sensed it like an animal senses its mate.

She belonged to him totally.

9

Khalid stared out the window of his library, three days later, a frown marring his brow. He watched the breeze drift through the trees surrounding the gardens. He looked tired, he thought, catching sight of his reflection in the window. Nothing like the charming seducer he was supposed to be. Or the carefree lover he tried to be with Marty. Though, he admitted, at the best of times, he was anything but carefree.

Working for Joseph Mathews and Zachary Jennings had done this to him, he thought, with a twinge of amusement. He thought perhaps he had earlier even glimpsed a gray hair or two in the thick black strands of his hair.

Of course, knowing his brothers would move against him didn't help things. A man could grow old before his time looking over his shoulder as often as Khalid was forced to. Not to mention the strain it had placed on him of all those years fighting his overwhelming desire for a woman who he knew would be placed in danger the moment she came to his bed.

Marty was in the thick of it now, and protecting her was his main priority. His brothers had sworn they would destroy any woman who held his heart, and he feared they were now making good on their promise.

Ayid and Aman should have been dead after the explosion that had been set off in the terrorist headquarters in Riyadh so many years ago, and the initial report had stated no survivors. Abram and Khalid had relaxed their guard for no more than hours. Just a few short hours, but long enough for Abram's father, Azir, to demand that Abram rush to Riyadh to find out what was going on. Just long enough for the brothers to contact their followers in the region and have Khalid kidnapped and held.

He rubbed his hand over his face and moved away from the window. Just a few hours. It had been enough to allow the brothers to make their way back to the palace and torture and kill the woman Khalid and Abram secretly had been sharing. The woman Abram had claimed as his own, the wife he had cherished.

Lessa had paid with an agonizing death for Khalid's part in the destruction of that terrorist cell. Simply because Ayid had somehow learned of the part Khalid had played in the attack against the terrorist cell's headquarters in Riyadh.

After Khalid had left Saudi Arabia, Abram had returned to being the son Azir had demanded. It was the only way to keep Khalid safe, he had claimed. Though Khalid knew Abram was simply biding his time, waiting until he could destroy his younger brothers without the threat of Khalid paying in some way for his crimes.

It hadn't worked, though. Khalid had never been safe, and now Marty was in danger as well.

She had worked her way into his desires, then into his heart. She was in danger because of him. He could feel it. The attempted drive-by shooting had been a clear message. Ayid and Aman were tired of waiting for their vengeance. For whatever reason, they were moving now.

And he couldn't still the fear that no matter her training and her abilities, he would still lose her.

His Marty was determined to always be the risk taker. At least, in some areas. Unfortunately, having her risk her life didn't sit well with his possessive male tendencies.

The sound of the door opening behind him caused him to stop his musings, and he turned from the window. He watched as Joe and Zach entered the room, glancing at him with concerned expressions.

"Khalid, you're looking tired." Joseph wasn't one to mince words when the situation warranted it.

"I have no idea what would cause such a thing," he answered, with subtle sarcasm. "Perhaps it's the late nights I'm keeping."

Nights spent trying to track the information that had come in that Ayid and Aman were tired of Khalid's interference in their terrorist activities over the years. That, added to the deaths of their wives, had exhausted their patience.

Zach moved to the bar and began pouring drinks. He hadn't spoken yet, but Khalid had a feeling that once he began, they would all need them.

"Have a seat." Joseph waved to the seating area in front of the cold fireplace.

"The news is this bad?" Khalid took a chair across from Joseph as Zach moved to him and handed him the straight whiskey that he had poured.

The situation must be grave indeed. The meeting the two men had asked for had surprised Khalid, especially when they requested that Marty not be made aware that they were arriving.

"The reports coming in are inconclusive so far," Joe stated. Zach took a seat on the short couch facing the fire. "Ayid and Aman crossed the border into Iraq last night. There are murmurs that they've sent someone to the area, but not against you. A single terrorist, rather than a cell sent to strike against a strategic target."

Khalid sipped the whiskey.

"Sheikh Azir Mustafa contacted the consulate when news of the attack on Marty was first reported and your name was mentioned as having arrived at the scene of the attack. He's demanding that they provide proof of your well-being."

Khalid snorted at such an idea. Trust the old bastard to use the attack to stage a display of fatherly affection that didn't exist. If the old man gave a damn about his eldest and youngest children, then the two sons who had struck against them would be dead now, not benefiting from their father's benevolence.

"Tell him to go fuck himself," he muttered, knowing his father had only demanded the proof because of his fears that Ayid and Aman was coming after Khalid. Should the Saudi king learn, for a fact, that Azir's sons were terrorists, then Mustafa would lose all hold they had on the region that they ruled.

"The ambassador thought perhaps a politely worded assurance of your health was more in order, all things considered at the moment," Zach retorted, his expression deadpan. "It seemed to require much less effort, and less bureaucratic red tape."

Khalid glared back at him.

"It's been years since there's been even a hint that they're still targeting you, Khalid," Zach pointed out. "Just because Shayne has heard rumors that they're prepared to move now, after the D.C. operation, doesn't mean you're more important to them than whatever strategic target they've chosen. We have time to figure this out."

"Think what you will. I know my half brothers. The attempt on Marty's life was ordered by them. I can feel it. Whoever your lone terrorist is, whatever his agenda—trust me, I'm high on his list of priorities, and Marty would be the perfect target to make me suffer before they came after me." Rising from his chair, Khalid moved to the bar to refresh his drink.

"If your suspicions are correct, had you stayed away from her as you were asked, then Marty wouldn't be involved in this." Zach's tone was hard and accusing.

Khalid stilled himself before lifting the decanter and refilling his glass. Forcing back the fury beating at him was nearly impossible. Zach was a shackle around his ankle at times where Marty was concerned. It was too bad that that shackle hadn't been enough to keep him from her.

"It's too late to fill the day with accusations." Khalid turned back to the two men. "I'll deal with my brothers as well as any other threat against Marty, in my own way."

Joe's brows lifted mockingly. "Really? And you've been waiting for what to take care of the situation with your brothers? Your funeral?"

Khalid leveled a dark, brooding look at the senator.

"I preferred to stop short of murder," he informed the other man. "I had hoped I could arrange their deaths through the operations we've fouled for them."

"Commendable," Zach drawled, with a hint of sarcasm. "But our attention is now split, which is something we can't afford at the moment. Shayne is attempting to locate the terrorist your brothers sent to Alexandria or D.C. Meanwhile, as I understand it, you've also chosen him as your third. Tell me, Khalid, how is he supposed to help protect her if he isn't here to do his job?"

Censure filled Zach's voice now, drawing a darker frown to Khalid's face.

"He will be here when he's needed," he assured the other man. "Should my suspicions prove correct, then Shayne will be available when he's needed. This is all that matters."

So far Khalid and Shayne together had managed to keep Marty distracted and off the subject of the truths Khalid knew he could not hold back from her for long. *That wouldn't last much longer,* Khalid guessed. He doubted it was working now. It wouldn't surprise him in the least to learn that Marty was merely biding her time with information she was learning on her own.

"You're going to fucking pull her in on this," Zach said furiously, as he sat forward in his chair to glare back at Khalid. "Aren't you? You've told her just enough of the truth to arouse her curiosity."

Khalid sipped his drink before answering.

"She will never thank any of us for attempting to protect her," he stated. "She has already been contacted by a private security firm. I know she's considering the move. Once she leaves your agency and joins that firm, she will no longer be under your control or your protection. Shayne is our only hope to ensure that she is always watched over as she fulfills the dreams *she* has. Not the ones *you* have."

Joe and Zach now stared back at him in shock.

"Shayne's CIA. He won't leave the agency." Zach shook his head doubtfully.

"Once my half brothers are dealt with, Shayne will be leaving the agency," Khalid informed them. "Should Marty decide to accept the position offered to her then he will be there as well."

"Son of a bitch." Zach came out of his chair furiously as he glared back at Joe. "You're in on this? We agreed that after she came back from her vacation to convince him to stay with the bureau. That was the plan."

Joe breathed out heavily as he stared back at Zach. "She's not going to stay, Zach."

Zach turned to his friend.

"Deerfield won't be there," Zach snapped, furiously. "I'm making sure of it."

Joe shook his head slowly. "She knows you're protecting her there. Holding her back. Marty knows she doesn't get the assignments she wants because you're pulling strings. Be thankful she's taking herself out of that equation rather than turning her back on us."

"She won't turn her back—"

"She will decide for herself what she wishes," Khalid broke in firmly. "She's an adult."

"And you're going to get her fucking killed," Zach yelled back at him. "Why the hell do you think I warned you away from her? I knew you'd do this. You and your damned determination that everyone has a fucking choice. That's bullshit, Khalid. Her choice will get her killed."

Khalid stared back at him, seeing a father's fear and rage, and he couldn't blame him for them. Marty was the child he had never had himself, for whatever reason. She was his daughter, and she would always be the little girl he had watched over.

It was hard for Zach to step back and risk his own soul, as he was being forced to do. Losing her could break him, no matter how it happened.

"Shayne will watch out for her while I cannot," Khalid stated. "This was the reason I chose him as a third."

"I can't believe you'd make this decision without consulting us." Zach stalked to the other side of the room, his arms crossing over his chest in a gesture of frustrated anger.

"Why would I consult you?" Khalid asked, his tone mocking. "You have warned me from her for years. Why would I think you would agree with any decision I made in regards to her?"

"Can you believe this bastard?" Zach turned to Joe in amazement. "He thinks he's God."

"Or the man she loves." Joe got to his feet as he glanced between Khalid and Zach. "I agree with him. Marty's going to take herself out of the bounds where we can protect her. In this way at least someone will be watching over her."

"Have you discussed this with Virginia?" Zach asked.

Joe's brow arched. "Did I discuss it with you? You and Virginia seem to forget that she's my daughter as well. And she's not stupid. She knows what's going on at the bureau; she knows why you allowed her to be stuck watching Khalid for the past two years. And, trust me, she already suspects that you warned Khalid away from her. She's not going to be happy with any of us if this continues, Zach, because she's growing damned tired of the fact that all you're concerned with is keeping her out of the line of fire."

"She'll be safe," Zach argued furiously. "There's no chance of her getting killed."

Joe laughed. "That's what we said about Virginia when we tried to maneuver her off a certain case during her first years as a prosecutor,"

Joe reminded him. "We nearly lost *her* then. I won't take that chance with my daughter."

Zach grimaced before casting Khalid a hard sneer. "I blame you for this."

Khalid shrugged. He really didn't care who Zach blamed as long as Marty didn't throw blame his way.

"This meeting is over, gentlemen," Khalid informed them. "Marty will be returning soon from her luncheon with her friends, and I'd prefer she not catch us in this little secret meeting. Her anger isn't something I wish to deal with at present."

The quirk of Zach's lips was filled with a faint satisfaction. A smile quickly hidden, one that filled Khalid with suspicion.

Manipulating and calculating, Zach was a dangerous adversary. He was a dirty, gutter fighter when he felt the need, and about now, he would definitely be feeling it.

At that thought, the door was pushed open, and Marty stepped into the room.

His gaze turned icy as he realized the other man had arranged this.

It was nothing against Khalid personally. It was the fact that Khalid had always insisted that Marty should have the freedom she needed, without her overprotective fathers restraining her.

It was a belief Zachary Jennings had never shared.

It was a belief that may now cause them more trouble than any of them truly wanted to face.

Marty stared at the three men silently as she stepped into the library. Her father looked guilty, Khalid looked frankly pissed, and her godfather seemed rather satisfied, if the tiny curve of his lips was anything to go by.

"Daddy." She walked to her father, kissed his cheek, then moved to Zach. "Dad. What are you two doing here?" She kissed her godfather before stepping back and staring at Khalid.

She watched Khalid closely, noting the icy look in his black eyes, the fury that gleamed just beneath the winter-cold depths of glittering black.

"A meeting." Zach shrugged as though it didn't matter.

She knew her fathers, though, and she knew it was much more than a simple meeting.

"A meeting?" She glanced back at her father. "Concerning what?"

"Since Zach is so forthcoming, why not let him tell you?" Joe said, though his tone was tight, almost angry.

She stared back at Khalid. "Would you like to tell me what's going on here?"

"We were discussing the attempt on your life," Khalid told her. "We were trying to figure out the source and the best way to neutralize it."

She looked at each man once again. She didn't doubt that they were discussing that, but she was betting they were arguing over much more. She had no doubt that they were arguing over her.

"I see. So did you figure anything out?"

"We figured out Khalid is paranoid and prefers not to listen to common sense," Zach growled. "And that this little meeting is over. Maybe your boyfriend here will give you the details."

"Khalid? Paranoid?" Oh boy, there was something definitely going on here.

Zach was furious, and that was something he rarely let her see. Propping her hand on her jean-clad hip, she considered each man closely for long moments.

She wasn't going to touch it, she told herself. She had enough problems trying to trail Shayne today without tipping him off. She didn't need more. She didn't have the time to fix whatever problems her fathers had.

"Definitely paranoid," her godfather snapped.

"Most likely not," her father said.

She believed her father. Of the two, it was Joe she could trust to tell her the truth, in most cases, no matter how angry it made her or how desperately he wanted to hide things from her.

Zach, unfortunately, had no problems lying to her if he felt it would protect her, or ensure her happiness. Just as he would have no qualms breaking her heart if he felt it would somehow protect her.

Joe and Zach glared at each other as she considered that, affirming her suspicions.

"It seems to me that the two of you should be more concerned about why a CIA agent is conducting an operation on home ground," she suggested smoothly. "Aren't there rules against that somewhere?"

She wondered exactly how involved her fathers and Khalid were in whatever Shayne was up to today. They hadn't informed her of what he was doing. No one had spoken much at all in the past three days about the attack against her, or how the investigation was going.

She was doing her own homework, though, so it didn't matter. At least Shayne wasn't lying to her, but he was holding back much more than she was comfortable with.

Zach turned away from her. Her father wiped his hand over his face, while Khalid merely leaned against the bar and sipped his drink, as though intrigued by the confrontation.

"There are no CIA operations being conducted on home ground." Zach turned back to her before glancing at her father. "Are you ready to go, Joe?"

Joe shook his head as he smothered a laugh. "As ready as I'll ever be," he assured the other man before stepping toward Marty. "Come see me sometime, little girl. I miss you."

He kissed her cheek before winking back at her gently and stepping away from her.

"We both miss her," Zach stated, as he moved to her and kissed her cheek as well before straightening and moving for the door. "Let's go, Joe. I have other things to do today."

As they left the room, Marty turned back to Khalid and stared at him curiously.

"I'm starting to feel as though you and my fathers are conspiring against me," she told him bluntly. "What do you think?"

"I think you should ask your fathers." He shrugged. "I wouldn't conspire against you, myself. That gun you carry intimidates me."

"Intimidates you?" Her lips pursed thoughtfully. "Somehow I doubt that."

He grinned, a smile that didn't come close to reaching his eyes. His gaze was thoughtful instead.

Setting his drink on the bar, he moved closer to her, his expression evolving from curious to frankly sexual.

"Your luncheon went well?" he asked, as he settled his hand on her hip and slowly eased her closer against him.

Her heart began to pick up speed. "Courtney is as nosy as ever, Alyssa is as quiet as ever, Terrie is certain you're up to something, and Tally wants to know if your bedroom is really filled with silk pillows and wall hangings."

"And I'm certain you informed her it was?" His head lowered, his lips brushing against her forehead as he whispered the question.

"Actually, I told her we were sleeping in a desert tent in the backyard, and that she should try it sometime. She looked rather intrigued."

He was manipulating her. She could feel it, and she hated it.

Pulling back, she watched him carefully as she moved out of his embrace.

"What was the meeting with my fathers about?"

She watched him, terrified he would lie to her now.

"Your fathers are the last thing I want to talk about," he informed her caustically. "Nor do I wish to discuss why they were here."

At least he wasn't lying to her.

"Unfortunately for you, I do," she informed him calmly as she turned away from him. "I wasn't told they would be here until I called Zach's office to ask him if he'd heard from Mom, and they were acting damn strange when I arrived."

"Then ask them." His voice was edged with impatience. "I have no desire to discuss your fathers or their issues. There are other things on my mind while in your presence."

She crossed her arms over her breasts. "What? You're going to use sex to distract me?"

And he could do a damned good job of it, she thought. She was burning for him. She had been burning for him before arriving at the estate. But she was also tired of feeling as though she were the odd person out of a very important secret. A secret that just might involve her.

"I have a feeling the hounds of hell couldn't distract you once you latched onto something." He grimaced ruefully. "You are rather stubborn, my love."

"It's called tenacity," she informed him sweetly. "It's what's gotten me this far with you, Khalid. Are you regretting it?"

"Are you?" She wished she could avoid those heated looks as easily as she could avoid his touch.

"What I'm feeling at the moment isn't up for discussion," she answered him with a bright smile as she used one of his own tactics in response to his question. "I believe you're the one we're discussing. What do my fathers think you're being paranoid about?"

"Joe doesn't think I'm paranoid about anything." He moved around her until his chest was at her back, his head lowering so he could stroke his cheek against her hair.

Subtle. Tempting. He was using her own tactics on her by seducing her, and it was working.

"My godfather does. He's usually fairly smart where some things are concerned. And it was more than obvious he was attempting to bring us to the point of an argument. So whatever you're trying to hide from me must involve me quite a bit." She sounded breathless. She was breathless.

His hands stroked down her bare arms as his lips whispered over the flesh of a shoulder left bare by the sleeveless top she wore.

"Zach is angry." His teeth raked over the rounded curve of her shoulder.

Shards of sensation raced down her spine, exploded in her clit. She was growing so wet, so slick, she had to clench her thighs to keep from moaning.

"Why is Zach angry?" Her lashes fluttered closed as his hands gripped her hips and pulled her back.

The feel of the hard length of his cock beneath his jeans as it pressed into her lower back had her breath catching in jerky response.

"Because I refuse to stay out of his daughter's bed," he stated, as she melted at the heated tone of his voice. "Because I refuse to distract you from investigating your attempted murder. Because I refuse to make you listen to my need to protect you rather than your own instincts."

His lips moved from her shoulder to her neck, his tongue sensually touching her skin. She hated the fact that his explanation was clearly an attempt to evade her, yet it still sent a rush of pleasure racing through her system to hear his apparent willingness to understand her need to live her own life.

"That sounds like Zach," she gasped, her head falling to the side in pleasure even as she acknowledged silently that he had managed to distract her without lying to her.

He didn't have to lie. He had the power of his touch. That touch was enough to fry her brain.

"Now you are guilty of leaving my bed this morning." He nipped at her neck in retaliation.

"Oh yeah. I did. I had things to do." Things like following Shayne to find out what the hell he was being so sneaky about.

Khalid's hands moved from her hips, his fingers curling in the material of her shirt to pull it slowly from her jeans. So slowly. The silk slid up her midriff, over the lacy bra, and finally cleared her head.

It pooled to a small puddle on the floor as his hands moved to cup the heaving mounds of her breasts.

Pleasure suffused her as the sheer joy she felt from his touch began to build within her. She had waited so long. She had fantasized, dreamed, ached for him, and finally, she was sharing his bed. Perhaps not his heart yet, but definitely his pleasure, and not as a third. He was her lover. It was his bed she slept in, his arms that surrounded her and held her through the night when rumor was that holding a lover through the night was something he wasn't known for.

His fingers circled her nipples, tugged at them, sent racing bolts of exquisite heated sensations racing straight to her clit. She was going to burn in his arms. She was going to melt to a puddle on the floor and beg him to fuck her within seconds.

"What sort of things did you have to do, little flower?" The front clip of her bra was tugged loose as he abandoned her nipples to relieve her of the restrictive garment.

"Things." She nearly moaned the word as his fingers caressed the sensitive sides of her breasts before brushing delicately against her nipples.

"What sort of things did you have to do, precious?" He chose that moment to exert just enough pressure on her nipples to have her back arching, a strangled cry tearing from her throat.

Reaching back for him, desperate to touch him now, to feel more of the incredible pleasure he gave her, Marty gave a low, ecstatic moan as she fought for more pleasure.

"Not yet, little flower." Catching her wrists in his hand, he locked them behind her back, keeping her arched against him as his free hand moved to the snap of her jeans.

"Push your sandals from your feet," he commanded, his tone rich with lust.

Stumbling, her knees weak, Marty did as he ordered while the zipper of her jeans gave a light hiss as he lowered it.

"Now, we were discussing the things you had to do this morning," he reminded her.

"No," she gasped, as his free hand slid into the parted fabric and eased beneath the low band of her panties. "You were discussing them."

His chuckle was low, dark. "You're being very naughty."

"So spank me . . . Oh God, Khalid." She couldn't hold back the cry as his fingertips glanced over the swollen knot of her clit.

It was exquisite. Pleasure raced through her pussy, around her clit, suffused her body.

"Spank you. I could do that," he assured her, as his hand pulled from her jeans, only to begin pushing the snug material over her hips. "I could really get into that, Marty. Watching your pretty ass blush, hearing you beg for more."

She was already ready to beg for more. He didn't have to spank her to get that.

He worked the jeans down her thighs and below her knees. "Step from the jeans, precious."

She stepped from the material, dressed in nothing but panties dampened by her desire. The silk clung to the bare curves of her sex as his hand slid up her thigh.

Her hands were still held behind her back, and she ached to touch him, to feel his flesh beneath her palms, against her skin.

"Beautiful," he whispered, and turned her until she was facing the antique, full-length mirror that sat in the corner of the library.

She looked so wanton. Arched back in his arms, her breasts swollen, her nipples flushed. Pale rose panties barely covered the mound of her pussy, and she could see the dampness at the crotch.

She watched as his hand moved to the panties. She expected him to push them over her thighs. He gripped the side, and with a quick movement the fragile material rent and fell away.

A gasp tore from her lips as the motion caused a flare of wicked pleasure to tear through her womb.

She was naked. Her pussy gleamed with her juices, the flesh flushed with need.

"Spread your legs," he whispered at her ear.

Behind her, Khalid was fully dressed, but his expression was filled with such stark hunger that it didn't seem to matter.

She spread her legs, watching in the mirror as his fingers slid between them, parted the swollen curves, and revealed the glistening bud of her clit.

"Watch," he breathed against her ear. "See what I see when I touch you. Watch the pleasure your body fills with."

The tip of his finger began to circle her clit, rubbing against it, around it, sending such electrically charged sensations tearing through her that her hips jerked against the caress.

"Pretty, pretty, little flower," he groaned, his voice becoming darker, more remote, more foreign. "Open for me, love. Let me watch my fingers take what my cock is dying for."

He released her arms, allowing them to curl around his neck as his fingers slid lower, circled the sensitive opening, then two pressed forcefully inside the heated ache of her pussy.

The sudden impalement stretched delicate tissue, revealed sensitive nerve endings, and sent her juices flowing over his fingers as tiny pinpoints of detonating heat began to flare inside her.

Feminine muscles clenched around his fingers, trembled against the penetration, and tried to draw them deeper inside her.

"Khalid, please." The plea was torn from her throat. "Don't torture me."

She felt too sensitive; the room was too hot. Perspiration gathered on her brow, her breasts. The whisper of the AC against her nipples was almost painful. The rasp of his clothing against her back had her flesh aching for his bare skin.

"Torture you?" His voice was midnight velvet, rasping over her senses with erotic intent. "Ah, sweet love, torture is the last thing I had in mind."

10

It was almost enough.

Khalid stared at the image in the mirror, watching as he fucked the sweet heat of Marty's pussy with two fingers. With his free fingers he held the silken folds apart, giving a better view of the penetration of her body.

Sweet silky juices spilled along his fingers, the darker flesh glistening against the pale peach tone of her intimate folds.

The pad of his palm brushed against her clit, perfectly timed to each thrust inside the milking depths of her sex.

It was exquisite. The little moans spilling from her throat had his cock throbbing, his balls drawing tight enough that the erotic pain was almost too much to bear.

He wanted nothing more than to sink the heavy width of his dick inside her, but this, this was a pleasure he didn't want to end.

Her body was drawn almost rigid as it trembled with the sensations tearing through her. Her gaze was locked on the mirror, on his fingers as he played with the intimate recesses of her body.

"I love the feel of your sweet pussy," he groaned, as he stroked the internal muscles and felt them clench tighter around his fingers.

"There, precious. Suck my fingers inside you. Show how much you love my cock when I get inside you."

The explicit words caused a heavy flush to stain her cheeks, and her juices flowing around his fingers.

"I love watching you," he whispered at her ear. "Seeing your pleasure, hearing you beg for more. I'd love to watch you going crazy with my cock up your ass. Stretched tight around me and screaming at the pleasure of it."

He swore she tightened to a breaking point as more of her lush cream flooded his fingers.

"You like that, don't you, Marty?" He kissed her neck gently, all the while his gaze moving between her face and her swollen pussy. "Every time I watch you walk, I imagine you bent over, that sweet, pretty ass lifted for me, my dick pushing inside as you cry out my name."

He imagined much more than that as well.

His fingers stroked inside her again, and he knew he wasn't going to last much longer. He'd end up coming in his jeans if he didn't get his dick inside her soon.

Keeping his fingers locked inside her, Khalid used his free hand to release his jeans and pull the tortured length of his cock free.

Stroking his hand along the agonized shaft he watched her, feeling the response of her body as he pulled back enough to tuck the heavy length against the cleft of her rear.

Her eyes dilated with anticipation and pleasure. Little tremors of response shook her body as her pussy sucked at his fingers and made him crazy to fuck her properly.

"What would it be like, do you think? To be taken, back and front. To know your body is the center of complete pleasure?"

She was gasping for air, and Khalid realized he was nearly panting himself. God, the thought of it. His hips rolled, pressing his cock deeper into the narrow cleft of her ass.

"I want it soon," he whispered. "To watch you, to hold you as Shayne fucks you. As his cock slides inside you while I touch you, caress you. While I see the response of your body and the pleasure tearing through you. He's dying for it as well, Marty. Merely watching is making him insane for you. When we take you together, he'll fuck you like a man driven crazy for the feel of your sweet pussy, or the tight grip of your tender ass."

A whimper left her lips, then a cry, as he slowly slid his fingers free of her and turned her to face him.

He intended to lift her, to impale her. Instead, his beautiful, adventurous Marty went to her knees as her fingers curled around his cock.

Her lips parted and, as he watched, the dark, swollen head of his dick disappeared into the heated, damp depths of her mouth.

"Ah God." His head fell back as he slid his fingers into her hair and clenched the strands desperately.

He swore the tip of his cock touched her throat as she sucked him inside. The vibrations of her moans against the sensitive flesh were destructive. He was too close to the edge, the trigger on his release was too damned touchy.

He was going to fill her mouth.

"Marty." The groan that tore from him was thick, rasping with the agonizing need tearing through him. "Sweet love. Keep it up and I'll fill your mouth. Is that what you want, sweetheart?"

She didn't stop. The fingers of her free hand curled around his balls, stroked, massaged him as her sweet, hot mouth sucked him with hungry intent.

Her tongue curled beneath the head, licked against the ultra-sensitive area that had him clenching his teeth to hold back his release.

"Suck it." He couldn't hold back the explicit words now, the need to show her, the only way he knew how, the exquisite pleasure tearing through him. "Fuck yes, baby. Suck it deep. Hell, suck it until I come, Marty. Give me that sweet, hot mouth." His voice was more strained, rougher, darker.

He could feel the impending release building in his balls. Like a tight knot of energy it began there, exploded, raced up his spine, then shot back to detonate in his dick.

His hips jerked, thrust forward, and the brilliant, white-hot sensation of tortured pleasure consumed him as he began to fill her mouth with his release.

She took it. She took him. Each hard spurt of liquid lust that shot into her mouth, she consumed, moaned, and took more.

It felt as though it would last forever. An agony, a pleasure he didn't want to end but swore he couldn't endure.

As the last tremor of pulsing pleasure raced through his cock, he pulled back from the sweet, sucking depths of her mouth.

He was still hard. Still hungry.

God help him, would he ever get enough of her?

Lifting her from her feet, there was no time for the gentle consideration he normally gave so easily. He was dying for her. A man driven insane for the pulsing pleasure that existed within this woman.

Pushing her against the couch, he gripped her hips, bent his knees and positioned himself before driving inside the liquid fire of her pussy.

He buried halfway on the first thrust, paused to feel the lightning-swift response that traveled through her body, then, with a heavy groan, buried himself in to the hilt.

It was rapture. It was the most pleasure he had ever known in his life. Fist tight, velvet soft, rippling around the torturously sensitive shaft of his dick, her heated pussy began to suck, to milk at the thick flesh stretching it.

Sweat poured down his face and dampened his chest as he fought against the heat consuming his body, the pleasure tearing through him.

Never had he known anything this erotic, this sensually perfect. Though he knew he must have, he couldn't remember a single time that another woman had created such a violent hunger inside him.

"Beautiful." He groaned as his hands lifted and stroked her from her trembling shoulders to her hips. "Sweet baby."

He began to move slowly, her desperate moans and heated cries spurring him on until he was shafting inside her with desperate lunges, rapture consuming them both as they fought for release.

Khalid swore he would die inside her grip, that when he came again, it would take his soul.

Gripping her hips, he watched as his cock thrust into the tight depths of her hot cunt. Heat swirled around him, through him. God help him, what was she doing to him? She was stealing parts of himself that he hadn't known existed. That he had been certain he lacked.

Emotions poured through him. Agonizing rapture raced through his dick and tore through his body. Electricity sizzled across his flesh, and when he felt her pussy lock around him, clenching, stroking his cock as she began to shake with the orgasm he could feel exploding through her, he gave in to the explosions detonating in his balls.

Light and sound clashed inside his head. He swore his heart was thundering from his chest, pouring from his ears as some part inside him that he hadn't known, that he had locked down, surged open.

Like Pandora's box, it rushed through him, destroyed him, remade him. Right there, buried in the sweetest grip he had ever known, Khalid felt the loss of himself as his release pumped inside her.

He gave her more than his seed. He gave her more than his pleasure.

He gave her his soul.

⊹⬦⬦⬦⊹

Marty stared up at Khalid long minutes later, after he carried her to his bed. With a warm, damp cloth he washed the perspiration and the slick excess of sex from her body.

He cleaned her gently between her thighs, the soft cloth rasping against tender flesh as he wiped her juices and his release from her sex and thighs.

He was careful, his dark face heavy with latent sensuality as his long, midnight black hair fell around his face in straight, damp strands.

He was the most handsome man she knew. Not so much handsome in the traditional sense, but utterly gorgeous in a rugged male way that he stole her breath.

As he finished drying her, she stretched languidly, her gaze remaining on his face as he laid the cloth and towel aside before turning back to allow his eyes to rove over her body.

"Where did you go today?" he asked again.

Marty almost smiled. She didn't dare tell him where she had been, but she wouldn't lie to him, either.

"I had things to do, Khalid." She shrugged before forcing herself from the bed. She tried to change the subject. "I guess I have to venture downstairs again to find my clothes?"

Also getting up, he buttoned his jeans before going to a tall wardrobe and pulling a robe from inside it.

Holding the thin silk robe in both hands, he moved to her and indicated that she should allow him to help her into it.

As she pushed her arms through the long sleeves, she turned and allowed him to tie it gently.

"I'll get your clothing later, or Abdul will bring them up." He eyed her skeptically. "You're avoiding my questions, Marty. Which means you were doing something you feel you can't tell me. As you're on vacation, I can only assume it isn't job-related."

"So therefore you have a right to know what it is?" she said, grudgingly. "It doesn't work that way, Khalid. Just because we're sleeping together doesn't mean you own me."

Following Shayne Connor wasn't dangerous, unless Khalid found out. She knew Shayne was searching for information on Ayid and Aman, and it was information she was fairly certain they weren't going to share with her.

She had no intention of telling Khalid about what she was doing, simply because she knew he would warn Shayne, tipping him off to the fact that she was indeed shadowing him whenever possible.

"It means I have a right to know when you're endangering yourself." No one had said he wasn't amazingly intelligent. "The very fact that you refuse to discuss your whereabouts with me tells me I would likely not approve."

"And your approval should affect what I'm doing? Since when?" She bristled at his sheer arrogance, not to mention the dominance he thought he had a right to.

"Since you decided seducing me was a good idea." He watched her, his expression stony now.

"One has nothing to do with the other," she stated, keeping her voice calm as she spoke against his stubbornness. "I'm sleeping with you; I'm not married to you."

"Sleeping with me comes with a certain commitment. That commitment has an underlying responsibility, Marty. Don't pretend you're unaware of the rules of a relationship."

"We're in a relationship?" She crossed her arms over her breasts and cocked her hip as irritation surged through her. "We've barely been together a week, Khalid. That doesn't exactly make it a relationship in my book. And that's besides the fact that you wait until I'm asleep then leave our bed until nearly daylight. You don't tell me what you're doing. Why should I tell you what I'm doing?"

Khalid would only get away with what she allowed him to get away with, she reminded herself. As far as she was concerned, there was no relationship until he acted more like a lover and less like a man scratching an itch and hiding secrets from her as he did so.

"I have work to do." He spoke through gritted teeth.

It amazed her how riled he was. Khalid never got worked up over anything. Even his lovers swore he was the most patient, lovable man they had ever met. He was considered the ultimate third. Intimacy during sex was his middle name, and petting and cuddling were his trademark.

She had the intimacy now. She had the petting and cuddling as she slipped into sleep. But still, she didn't have the secrets he was hiding from her.

"You had work to do." She nodded. "Well today, I had some work to do as well. Just because I'm on vacation doesn't mean there aren't still responsibilities to take care of. And until you fulfill your half of the relationship role, we don't have one."

Suspicion narrowed his eyes.

"You're pushing," he warned her, his voice deeper. "Don't pretend there isn't more between us than whatever pleasure you find in my arms."

Her head tilted to the side in curiosity. "What would that be? Perhaps you need to explain this to me, Khalid. You are, after all, my first lover, and maybe the rules aren't really clear to me."

His lips tightened.

"What responsibilities am I overlooking?" she continued. "Sleeping in your bed?" She waved her hand to the mussed bed. "You don't sleep there the full night, so why should I bother? Intimacy, perhaps? I haven't had much experience with it; maybe you should show me what it is, so I get it right."

As a hint, that was like a baseball bat against the back of his head. He didn't even flinch, though. Strike. She wondered how many of those she had so far.

She watched as his gaze flickered, his thoughts running through possibilities. He was dying to question her, but she could see the hesitancy as well. If he questioned her, and he was wrong, then the suspicions it aroused in her could work against him.

"After the attack you only barely survived, I would think you would be more careful." He peered down his nose at her regally.

Damn. He could do the arrogant royal thing really well.

"I'm being very careful," she assured him. "I was careful then, which is the reason I'm still alive today. And I've been careful enough in the past three days to identify not only the men you have following me, but also the men my fathers have sicced on me. I consider myself very well looked after at the moment."

The assassins had nearly had a jump on her. If she hadn't been paying attention, she would have taken the bullet from that gun to her face.

"So I shouldn't worry because you survive, what could have merely been the first attempt?" he asked her with cutting sarcasm. "Excuse me if I worry that your luck may run out, especially when I am very well aware that you managed to lose the men watching you for several hours today. Where the hell were you?"

"It wasn't luck, it was training." She strode to the bedroom door and pulled it open before leaving the room, thereby managing to avoid the interrogation concerning her whereabouts that morning.

She needed her clothes. It was time for her to leave. The honesty, the full truth of Khalid's past, that intimacy that came from trust, that wasn't happening so far so she may as well go home and clean her apartment. It wasn't as though he had been giving a whole lot of himself to her up till now. She didn't live here, she hadn't been invited to do so, and this was something she wasn't about to beg for. She may spend the better parts of her nights in his bed, but her days were a far different matter.

Perhaps he would get a clue tomorrow, she thought morosely, as she made her way down the stairs. It would have been nice if he had taken his clothes off, lain down beside her, and given her more than the most incredible sex she could have imagined.

She wasn't going to plead. She wasn't going to bitch over it. She'd never seen her mother have to beg for anything. Virginia Mathews had advised friends over the years that if a lover didn't give his affection willingly, then it was meaningless.

Khalid had given his affection to women who belonged to other men, but thus far, he hadn't given it to her in the same measure, and she knew it.

Once again she wished her mother wasn't on vacation. She could use some of that female wisdom about now.

"Where the hell are you going?" His tone was sharp behind her as she bent and picked up her clothing.

"Home." She kept the answer brief and the angry hurt hidden.

If she had to fight him for his affection, then it was meaningless, she reminded herself. It should be given freely. She shouldn't have to rage at him over it.

She had to repeat the refrain to herself as she dropped the robe over the back of the chair and dressed.

"You could move in here."

The suggestion stopped her cold. Dressed in her panties, bra, and top, she stood with her jeans in her hand as she turned her head to stare back at him.

"Where would I sleep?" Stepping into her jeans, she pulled them over her legs as she waited for his reply.

"In my bed." The answer was more a snarl than a suggestion.

Marty glanced at the tense set of his body, the way he kept his arms at his sides, his eyes narrowed.

"Where would you sleep?" she snapped, and zipped her jeans before pushing her feet into her sandals. "I'd hate to run you out of your bed."

"What kind of fucking game are you playing?" His voice was a hard, tight growl as he folded his arms across his chest in a gesture of building anger. "Other than the time I have spent working, I am in that damn bed with you."

"I'm not playing." She was in this for keeps, not for amusement. She didn't relish the thought of walking away from him anytime soon with a broken heart any more than she relished the thought of living without the affection she needed from him if this went further.

"Oh, you're playing," he told her, his expression tightening as the arrogance thickened. "Do you think you can fool me, precious? You're an amateur here. If you want games, just say it. I can play and show you how to do it right."

"I have no doubt." Pulling her purse from the small table she had laid it on earlier, she slung the leather strap over her shoulder and faced him with a sweet smile.

She felt anything but sweet.

"I have to leave. I need to clean my apartment and later I thought

I might see if Courtney wants to meet me for dinner. Girls night out would be nice right about now."

"Lunch and now dinner?" he snapped. "Tell me, Marty, did you want more from this than sex? Or was that all you had in mind all these years that you've chased me so diligently?"

That stopped her at the door. Turning back to him, she watched him for long, painful moments before speaking.

"Do you want more from this than sex, Khalid? Because if you do, then you have a hell of a way of showing it."

Turning away from him, she stalked through the doorway and along the hall to the main foyer. He didn't follow her.

She had hoped he would. He could have pulled her into his arms, held her, given her more than that very experienced sexuality of his. If he truly cared for her, he'd give her the explanations she needed as well. He'd tell her about himself, as well as his past, without making her feel as though she would be stepping into forbidden territory when she considered actually asking him.

He seemed to have a sixth sense for when she was about to give him the third degree, because he always found something that had to be done *that* minute.

Shaking her head at the thought, and at the tears that wanted to fall, she strode through the doors Abdul had opened and all but ran to her car.

This was hell. She needed more than the few moments it took for him to wipe the sex from her body. She needed more than the eroticism he gave so freely. She needed something to hold on to.

While driving from the estate she battled back her tears and re-minded herself that it wasn't over. She had three weeks left to cap-ture his heart. Three weeks before she made the final decision on where her life would go from here.

Glancing in her rearview mirror she glared at the vehicles fol-lowing her. He could send others to watch after her, but he couldn't take the time, or make the effort, to ensure that she stayed by his side.

Damn him. There were days she was beginning to wonder if he wouldn't really break her heart.

⋅⊹⋅⊹⋅

Khalid glared at the black BMW as it sped down the driveway to the security gates that protected the estate. His teeth were clenched, his body vibrated with frustration—and not sexual frustration, either.

She was making him crazy.

He knew what she wanted, and it was something he couldn't give her, not yet. Explanations. Details of a past he didn't want to remember, let alone talk about. But in her eyes had been the clear message that she would no longer accept anything less.

Khalid knew women, and he knew his avoidance of the questions in Marty's eyes was hurting her. And God above knew he hated hurting her.

As he ran his hand along the back of his neck, he bit off a curse before jerking his cell phone from the holster at the belt of his jeans. Hitting a speed dial number, he brought it to his ear and waited.

Shayne answered the call on the first ring with a brief "yeah."

"Have you learned anything?" The assailant who had attacked Marty was more elusive than they had anticipated.

"Not enough." Anger filled Shayne's voice. "I know what the bastard looks like now, Khalid. I know the general area where he's supposed to be hiding. But I'll be damned if I can find him."

"No information at all has come in?" Khalid asked, thinking of the contacts he had sent Shayne to for help.

"Plenty of information." Shayne sighed. "Whoever he is, he was definitely sent by your brothers to do more than just kill Marty. He's researching a target and preparing to hit it. No word on what that target is yet, other than the fact that they consider it a strategic hit."

"That could be anything." Khalid sighed. "Any word if Ayid and Aman are in the States?"

"Nothing," Shayne stated firmly. "And I've been asking. All I have for certain is that they sent someone to finish a mission. I'm assuming it's the mission you and the FBI broke up in D.C. Other than that, I really have jack shit. At the moment, we're concentrating on the target and letting you and Zach Jennings concentrate on protecting Marty."

Khalid frowned at that. "I thought you were alone."

"I was until the bastard decided to play the invisible man. Jennings loaned me some agents," Shayne grunted. "I'm on call if he's spotted, and I just finished checking the lead I managed to uncover last night. Until he makes a move, or he's seen, my hands are tied."

"Did you see Marty while you were following your leads?" Khalid asked.

Shayne chuckled. "I'm watching for her, but I haven't seen her. I figure, if she's not suspicious yet, then she will be soon. I know her too well. The very fact I've spent so much time away from the two of you will have her radar up. And trust me, it's up. She's suspicious as hell."

At least she had stayed out of Shayne's mission so far. Khalid had nightmares at the thought that she would begin poking her nose into his brothers' criminal activities.

"What are you hearing from the Bureau? Have they managed to learn anything?"

"I'm telling you what I know, man." Shayne sighed. "The Bureau managed to ID him based on the description a contact gave me. I have a picture now, and it's definitely him. But he's as slick as butter so far."

"Will you have some free time until the terrorist makes a move?"

"I have nothing but time until that son of a bitch shows his ugly face," Shayne said.

"Perhaps you would like to join Marty and myself for tomorrow night," he suggested.

There was silence on the line. So far he hadn't given Shayne an invitation that had been extended the past few nights to merely come to the estate. What he was offering right now was much more important. Khalid could feel Marty's readiness now, the tension filling her, the need, the desire to have their third finally, fully, join them. And perhaps it would distract her from the questions that he knew raged within her.

"Do you think she's ready to take it that far?" Shayne asked. "It's pretty soon, Khalid."

"I believe she is more than ready, as am I. I believe it is time we see where her adventurous nature takes her." He turned and paced to the windows, frowning as he looked into the gardens spread out before him, opposite the front of the house.

Was that what she wanted? He knew that sexually she was ready. She had been ready for years. For Marty, the knowledge of the lifestyle he lived was as familiar to her as the knowledge of sexual intimacy was to other women.

He couldn't see her stressed out over the act of a ménage itself, but perhaps she was concerned that he hadn't mentioned it, that his commitment to her required it.

"I'll be available," Shayne promised. "Whatever our black-hearted terrorist is up to, he's not moving quickly. But if he does poke his snout out of his hole, then I'll be on the run."

"Agreed." Khalid nodded. "I'll arrange everything. Meet us at Defacto's at seven for drinks before dinner."

"I'll be there," Shayne assured him. "Tell me, though, does Marty know about this little dinner date?"

Khalid grimaced. "The woman is making me insane, Shayne. She comes to my home and catches her fathers here. She should have been angry. Rather than anger, though, she was a seductress stealing my soul, only to blow cold an hour later."

"In other words, she fled your bed as fast as you fled it the first time?" Shayne's amusement grated on Khalid's nerves.

"No, I mean exactly what I said," he snarled, uncertain what to do with the frustration tearing through him.

"Marty's pretty straightforward," Shayne stated. "If she has a problem, she'll tell you eventually. Once she figures out you're too stupid to figure it out yourself. And I'd say a smart man would have already guessed that she'd appreciate the truth. I'm guessing you still haven't gotten around to tell her about Lessa."

He hadn't. He intended to. Each day he planned to, but damn if he wanted to see the adoration, even beneath the anger, change to disappointment.

The guilt that he hadn't protected Lessa, that he hadn't considered what could happen if his brothers escaped the trap laid for them. It weighed on him. The fault was with him. He had failed her, he had failed Abram, and the thought of seeing that knowledge in Marty's eyes was nearly more than he could bear.

Khalid glared down at the gardens, though the look was directed more toward Shayne's comment as well as his past. A past he couldn't change, no matter how he wished it were possible.

"She's well protected. She knows she's in danger. There is nothing where the past is concerned that could help her in protecting herself."

"You're not as smart as I thought you were," Shayne stated coolly. "Hiding this from her isn't going to gain you any brownie points when she finds out the full truth, my friend."

"She's sleeping in my bed, isn't she?" he snapped out tersely.

"No, she's not. She's having sex in your bed. She's napping in it until you get up and leave the room. She's been sleeping in her own bed." Shayne laughed as he repeated Marty's arguments. "Think about that. See you tomorrow."

The call was disconnected as Khalid brought it from his ear and stared down at it with a killing look.

To compare him to the incompetent fools who had sniffed after Marty over the years was uncalled for. She may not be sleeping in his bed, but she was definitely his. She had given him the gift that no other man had ever known from her. She had given him her innocence.

His eyes narrowed at the thought of that. She had given it to him, but she sure wasn't giving him the commitment that went with it.

And that would end now.

She belonged to him, and, he decided, it was time she figured out that gem of information.

It was time to seduce the seductress.

11

Dinner went surprisingly well as far as Khalid was concerned. Marty and Shayne had a slow, easy rapport, an awareness of each other that, in Marty's case, only revealed itself in Khalid's presence.

A new tension seemed to fill Marty, however, as they ate and then lingered over drinks to discuss a variety of subjects. It was as though she knew the significance of easing into this evening, of establishing a level of comfort within the arousal that flared throughout the evening.

She was ready for this, he assured himself. But one thing was for certain. If she weren't ready for it, she would have informed them of it long before now.

Khalid had never understood the reason his sexuality had grown so dark, why the hunger to share a lover had grown so deep. It was something he had stopped questioning years ago. It just lived inside him, like an entity all its own.

As dinner came to an end, Khalid invited Marty back to the estate, as well as Shayne. Anticipation fed the fire, and that anticipation would amplify her pleasure if the night included the sexual pleasures he had been withholding from her. He wanted her more than ready for both of them. He wanted her wet and wild for it, ready and willing to accept whatever pleasures they bestowed upon her.

As they stepped into the limo, the vibration of his cell phone in his jacket pocket caused him to clench his teeth in irritation. Pulling it from his inside jacket pocket, he glimpsed the caller ID and wanted to curse in anger.

"Yes?" he answered.

"Get to the club," Zach ordered, his voice tight, brisk. "We have a situation."

"That could be a problem," he said carefully, aware of Marty watching him with a hint of suspicion.

"I know Marty's with you," Zach growled. "I have permission from Ian to allow her into the parking area only. Tell her to keep her ass in the limo. Hopefully you and Shayne shouldn't be long."

So much for seducing the seductress tonight, he thought mockingly, as he disconnected the call and fought to hold back the aggravation growing inside him now.

"Problem?" She leaned back in the seat and watched him almost knowingly.

He glanced at Shayne. "We have to make a stop," he informed the other man.

Shayne watched him curiously. "A stop?"

"At the club."

Tension filled the limo as he turned his gaze back to Marty.

"You will stay in the limo, Marty. You know the rules there. Do us all a favor and please refrain from trying to slip in as you have in years past."

During the last two years she had been following Khalid she had made several attempts to slip into the club to see who he was meeting with, what he was doing. According to Zach, the orders to do so had come directly from her boss, Vince Deerfield.

She had no such orders tonight.

"Of course." That sweet smile didn't fool him.

Lowering the window between the driver and passenger areas, he made a decision he prayed would hold her in check.

"Abdul, we'll be stopping at the club for a while. You're to make sure that Miss Mathews remains in the limo while we're there. Should she try to leave the car, then you'll notify me immediately."

"Yes, sir." Abdul's tone reflected his hesitancy to upset Marty.

Over the years Marty and Abdul had developed a friendship that had caused Khalid more than one headache.

"Slip from the car, and Abdul will be the one who pays for it," he warned her.

Her brow lifted. "You like to play dirty, Khalid."

"Sometimes it's the only thing you understand." He sighed almost wearily.

No doubt he'd be taking her home after this meeting rather than back to his bed as he'd hoped.

She smiled again. That sugary sweet smile never failed to cause his neck to itch.

Silence filled the limo as Abdul navigated out of town toward Squire Point, the exclusive area filled with tree-shrouded estates and oceanside mansions.

Marty crossed her legs and stared at the two men sitting across from her, almost rubbing her hands together in glee.

As a babysitter, Abdul sucked. She had him wrapped around her little finger better than her fathers were.

"Stay put, Marty," Khalid warned her, as they turned into the Sinclair property and drove along the well-lit tree-lined lane that led to the estate house that held the exclusive men's club.

"Of course." She smiled back at him innocently. "I'm on vacation, remember?"

Both men eyed her dubiously. As well they should, because once she was actually on the estate grounds, getting in was going to be child's play. What she would find after actually breaching those hallowed halls, she had no idea. But she was going to have fun finding out.

She sat silently as Abdul parked in the area Khalid directed him to, a securely lit, well-guarded area of the parking lot. If Ian Sinclair knew Khalid had her in the limo, then she had no doubt extra security guards were in place.

"Be good, precious," Khalid warned her again, as Shayne pushed the door open and stepped out.

Khalid surprised her as he leaned forward, his fingers curling around her neck to hold her in place for a brief, hard kiss. His fingertips stroked the back of her neck as he lingered only moments, then slid away as he moved from the vehicle.

She sat silently and watched as Khalid and Shayne disappeared through the entrance to the club that had managed to keep itself secret from the general public for more than two centuries. The very fact that its true purpose had never come to light was a bit surprising. The club was more secretive regarding its membership than the Secret Service was in protecting the president. And that was saying a lot.

Once the doors had closed and silence filled the night once again, she turned to where the window had been lowered between the driver and passenger areas.

Propping her arms on the back of the front seat, she smiled back at Abdul as he turned and watched her warily. He knew her, and he had known the moment he had been given his orders that he would be breaking them.

"I guess you're honor-bound to contact him if I leave," she stated to the bodyguard who had befriended her when she first began following Khalid.

Abdul was older, perhaps nearing fifty. Gray sprinkled his closely cropped black hair, and wrinkles were marring his dark face. He reminded her of a loving, benevolent grandfather, though she knew he had no wife, no children. He had pledged himself to the Mustafa family, and to Khalid, as a young man and had allowed nothing to come between himself and the task he had taken on to protect his charge.

Abdul stared back at her quietly for long moments, his expression reflective as he watched her. Abdul was what she liked to call a "thinker." More than likely he had already considered this problem at some point in the past. He was a man who liked to think ahead while he was deliberating.

"He is like a son to me," he stated in his halting English, before sighing deeply.

"And he's like a thorn in my ass," she shot back in disgust, more to watch the incredulity that shot through his eyes than to simply be crude. Though there were times it was definitely the truth. But she did so love to shake Abdul's little world up.

Abdul was a friend, but one who could be rather prudish at times.

"You are a very naughty little girl," he laughed, after nearly choking on his shock. "In my country your tongue would be cut from your mouth." And he was probably not joking.

"In your country I'd have already been stoned for my smart mouth," she informed him. "Be honest about it, Abdul."

He shook his head as a lighter laugh passed his lips.

"You keep him on his toes; this is a good thing sometimes. Not many women give him the challenge he oftentimes needs."

"Women are supposed to be a challenge?" She batted her lashes back at him. "I thought we were supposed to be submissive and properly trained."

Abdul was an enigma to her sometimes. He could laugh at himself as well as at the many misunderstandings concerning his country and his religion. When it came to Khalid, though, he took his responsibility to watch over him very seriously.

"A woman is to know her place, no matter where that place is," he finally said, sighing. "Khalid never fit into the life his father would have given him. Had he done so, he would have been a leader that our people would have died for."

There was no doubt in her mind. She would have followed that conversational line if she didn't know from experience that the answers she wanted wouldn't be given.

"So, as to my question." She smiled sweetly, tilted her head, and gave him her best innocent look. "Are you going to tell on me for leaving the car?"

"Are you going to leave the car when you were warned to stay in place?" he asked in turn, giving her a mock frown of disapproval.

Was she?

"Pretty much," she answered as she pursed her lips and nodded firmly. "Come on, Abdul, it's too good an opportunity to pass up. You know that."

Abdul sighed heavily, though she could see the grin he fought to hold back in the twitch of his lips.

"If you made the promise to me that you will not leave the car, then I would take my nap." He yawned hugely, as though genuinely tired, before his white teeth flashed in his aged, sun-bronzed face. "Are you making that promise?"

She nodded quickly, all the while giving him a deceptively innocent grin. She really did love Abdul. The best thing about him was his willingness to conspire, in small ways, against his employer.

"Go to sleep, Abdul. I'm sure Khalid will be back soon."

She doubted it very seriously.

Remaining quiet, she watched as his head disappeared and listened to the sounds of him getting comfortable.

Like hell he was going to sleep, but neither was he willing to face the full force of Khalid's wrath. At least he would have an excuse if Marty got caught. That was a comfort she would have to do without.

Hell, it wasn't like he was going to kill her, she thought, as the sound of the first false snore came from Abdul. She may wish she were dead. She may scream like she was dying, and that was a very real possibility, but he wouldn't actually hurt her. Well, at least not a pain that she wouldn't enjoy.

She opened the door quietly, the metallic click causing her to grin as Abdul gave a heavy sigh.

Okay, she could be quieter but she didn't bother, simply because she knew she didn't have to.

Within seconds she was sliding out of the car, keeping low.

She knew the movements of the security guards inside the grounds, and she knew that the area this close to the house was much less secure, other than additional security guards, compared to the one leading directly here.

Still, she closed the door quietly and kept low.

Watching the security personnel moving about the front of the house, she took extra time to study their patterns and the gaps in their rotations.

Long minutes later, certain she had a handle on the security weaknesses, she moved.

There was no low music, no activity that could be heard or seen from the house. The sprawling estate was like a sanctuary of some sort, carefully guarded and intensely secretive.

The parking lot was filled with limos and the drivers who accompanied many of the members. Lexuses, Mercedeses, Jaguars, and Bentleys were parked on the opposite side. It wasn't easy to stay in the shadows and out of sight of the drivers as well as the security guards.

It took more time than she liked to work her way through the parking lot, as she kept to the few shadowed areas available.

Moving slowly, carefully, she practically crawled through the evergreen and flowering shrubs that lined the parking area.

She'd already decided on the best entrance into the house months before. She'd watched every angle that she could see from a vantage point high above the main grounds.

Every angle but the parking lot and back entrance to the club could be viewed one way or the other. Security cameras and personnel kept a careful watch and secured the house grounds against all intruders.

Until recently, there hadn't really been a weak point in the house—until the owner, Ian Sinclair, had built his main residence on the other side of the property. What had once been a wide window in the back of the house had been converted into a service door.

With just the right amount of luck and a little bit of skill, she had a chance of slipping in there when one of the employees stepped out for a cigarette. They didn't always close the door well, and beside the door was a dark, shadowed area of foliage that would be perfect to use as a cover.

She just had to get in place.

After slipping into the shrubbery at the door, it was just a matter of waiting. There were security cameras in this area just as there were in the others, but the landscaping here was more a hazard than a help to security. It surprised her that Sinclair hadn't cleared this out yet, though it did make an effective screen for those employees with the need to light up.

She had no idea what she was facing once she actually got inside. She knew the layout of the house from a few historical documents that she had managed to uncover. The Sinclair mansion was considered a historical landmark. It had been built well before the Civil War, and even before then had been known as a gathering place for certain like-minded individuals.

Men who shared their women. A place for such a man to find a third who shared his values as well as his beliefs.

It was a wonder it hadn't been burned to the ground centuries ago.

As a mocking smile tipped her lips, she suddenly tensed at the sound of the lock disengaging inside. It was simple enough to wait until the door opened and a dark figure passed. Using several leaves folded together, she quickly slid the foliage into place over the lock as the door closed.

As the employees passed by, Marty reopened the door and slipped inside. She flattened herself to the wall and ducked quickly behind a huge antique armoire that stood in the hall.

There were no security cameras in the hall, which surprised her. She wondered just how well the inside of the club was policed. She'd expected much more than she found at the moment.

Drawing in a slow, deep breath and checking the area quickly, she began advancing up the hall and found it to be an interloper's dream. There were wall insets in places, providing small, comfortable areas for work or conversation. Large antique pieces of furniture sat throughout interconnected rooms that were for the most part shadowed and private.

Getting to the stairs that led to the second story, and to many of the private meeting rooms as well as the bedrooms, wasn't nearly as hard as she had expected.

It sounded as though most of the activity was downstairs in what was rumored to be a bar and several rooms providing billiards, television, or a place for gatherings.

She hadn't seen Shayne or Khalid. At each room she'd managed to find a place to duck in to that allowed her to see inside as doors opened. It took awhile, but she managed to eliminate the chance that they were downstairs.

That meant a private meeting, and those rooms were upstairs.

As she slipped up the steps, she watched and listened carefully. Rounding the upper portion of the steps, she ducked to the side and hid by a heavy sideboard at the landing.

This was simply too easy.

Farther ahead she could see a light spilling from beneath only one closed door. There were no guards outside, no one patrolling the floors. Evidently Ian Sinclair had never had anyone slip in undetected before. It was a gross lack of security that had allowed her to get this far.

She let a small grin of satisfaction tilt her lips. She could say she was one of the few women to ever breach the hallowed halls of this elite establishment.

Sliding around the antique cherry bureau, she made her way cautiously to the spill of light reflecting from the glistening wood floors.

She could hear voices from inside, and if she wasn't mistaken, one of those voices was Khalid's. It was a rumble of sound; no actual words could be heard. Even as she stopped at the side of the door and strained to hear, she could catch no more than bits and pieces of words.

She couldn't be certain who was in the room, though it sounded as though there were several engaged, not so much in an argument but in a heated disagreement.

Biting her lip, she gripped the doorknob, meaning to turn it slowly and subtly, and hopefully to crack the panel open just enough so she could be certain of who was speaking.

As she tightened her hand on the brass knob, a familiar click and the press of cold metal against her head stilled her.

Marty felt adrenaline spike in her veins. An icy veil of pure survival instinct raced through her.

Would the person wielding the gun actually pull the trigger? She doubted very seriously that Ian Sinclair would employ anyone who wouldn't use every other means at their disposal before actually killing an intruder.

The press of the cold steel against the back of her head felt pretty damned convincing, though.

"Release the latch." The thick, heavy Middle Eastern accent kicked those survival instincts into overdrive.

This wasn't one of Ian Sinclair's security guards. This was someone else, someone who shouldn't be here either.

Marty moved. A lightning-fast flick of her wrist against the latch produced no results, but the quick duck of her head as she swung around, gripped the wrist, and swung her knee into his groin brought a definite response from him.

He was huge. A murderous mountain posing as a man. He shifted just enough to keep her knee from slamming into his cock, and at the same time his hand flew out, the back of it connecting with the side of her head and slamming her to the floor.

Simultaneously the door flew open, the mountain came over her, and the gun was pressed beneath her jaw as behind him, enraged, Shayne and Khalid each held a gun to his head.

"Mohammed!" a strong voice with a thick accent rasped from the door.

A spate of Arabic followed from the mountain called Mohammed as the gun was pressed tighter against her jaw. *Hell.* She was in trouble now.

"Abram, he has two seconds before I kill him." There was no accent, no inflection in Khalid's voice. There was cold, hard, steely death instead.

Marty met Mohammed's eyes and saw pure black fury as Abram barked another order in Arabic.

"You risk your life needlessly, woman, as well as mine," Mohammed growled, like a bear that had to fight to find the words. Even his voice was scary.

The weapon moved from beneath her jaw slowly as the giant lifted from his knees and came away from her. Marty stared up at the men who had rushed from the room and had to fight not to swallow tightly.

Abram el Hamid-Mustafa stood at the door, dressed surprisingly in jeans and a black T-shirt. He was all but an exact replica of Khalid. The same black eyes, the same thick black hair, except Abram wore a closely cropped beard and mustache that gave him a more rakish, disheveled appearance.

It was enough to have her glancing quickly from Khalid, to Abram, then back again as her imagination began to take flight and she wondered what it would be like . . . Oh no, she was not going there.

Khalid had his third, and she was fine with the decision he had made. No way in hell did she want, or need, another Khalid for a third. Her life was complicated enough as it were.

Khalid and Shayne eased slowly back as Mohammed came to his feet, and to the side of the door, where—watching in equal amounts horror, anger, and perhaps a glimmer of pride—stood her fathers.

"Someone should have told me it was a serious meeting rather than simple playtime," she remarked, as she jumped to her feet and eyed the six men warily. "I might have taken a nap instead of slipping in to see what all the interest was here and whether or not I should be jealous."

"Whether or not she should be nosy," Shayne snorted. "I'd say not, if she had asked my opinion."

"But I didn't ask you opinion, did I?"

She didn't dare meet Khalid's gaze. She turned to her fathers instead.

"Really, Dads, you should have warned Khalid about leaving me in the limo. You two know me much too well."

Joe covered his mouth with his hand as though wiping at it in frustration. He was actually fighting a grin—she hoped. Zach continued to stare at her as though he had no idea who the hell she was or from where she had come. Strange, he had helped trained her. He should have known better.

Khalid and Shayne were staring at her with the promise of a certain confrontation in their gazes as Mohammed glared at her. Abram Mustafa was the only one who appeared unfazed, in fact, a bit amused. She flashed him one of her deceptively sweet smiles as she pushed her hands into the back pockets of her jeans and wondered if her face had started bruising yet. Evidently not, because Khalid hadn't murdered Mohammed yet.

"Shall I assume we have an addition to our little meeting, gentlemen?" Abram glided to her, a grin tugging at his well-molded lips. The short black beard that covered his lower face gave him a piratical look, as the twinkle in his deep, black eyes encouraged her to join in whatever joke he was having at her expense.

As she watched Khalid and Shayne cautiously, Abram gripped her arm and urged her into the room.

"Come, my dear, let's not loiter in the hall where this slight confrontation can be witnessed, shall we?"

Marty followed, albeit reluctantly, as she watched Khalid and Shayne slowly slide their weapons back into the holsters beneath their jackets. How Khalid had managed to wear that holster without her knowing it, she couldn't explain. He had to have placed it there after entering the club.

"Inviting me in now?" She glanced at her fathers, noting Zach's grimace as all but Mohammed stepped back into the room.

"I do hope Mohammed didn't leave bruises on your delicate flesh as he pressed the gun into your neck." Abram flashed another grin at her, as his wicked black gaze raked over her face. "I'll be certain to ensure that he never makes such a mistake again."

"Abram." Khalid's voice held a warning note.

"Ah, little brothers can often be quite intense, can they not?" Abram grinned at her again as he released her arm and moved to the bar. "Would you like a drink, perhaps?"

She glanced back at Khalid as Abram laid his hand against the small of her back and led her to the bar.

"This isn't social hour," Khalid snapped. "Stop pretending it is."

Oh boy, he was pissed. It would have been amusing if the air of danger surrounding him wasn't so thick.

"I never pretend such things." Abram was clearly amused as he poured two drinks. "You have been so reluctant to allow me the chance to meet your beautiful woman over these many years, that I have decided to take this chance that has been presented so beautifully to me. I am certain Ian will forgive me for allowing this slight bend of the rules."

He handed her a drink as he toasted her with his own.

Marty lifted the short glass to her lips, gave a little sniff, then narrowed her gaze on Abram as she realized it was indeed one of her favorites. A splash of expensive whiskey over ice. She toasted him back before sipping. She continued to gaze at the other men warily.

"She's going to get herself killed," Zach muttered to Joe, as she glanced at them.

"And you're just figuring that one out?" Khalid glared at her fathers before stalking to the bar and pouring himself a stiff shot of whiskey and tossing it back; he continued to glower at her.

"I've been warning both of you," Zach snapped as he glared at her father and her lover. "But have either of you bothered to listen at any time?"

"And all of you seem to be forgetting exactly what her career is." Her father, Joe, surprised her as he snapped at all of them. "She's a trained agent, and you were all warned that she wouldn't sit back lightly once she became suspicious. For God's sake, Zach, you helped train her. You should have known she would slip in here."

That was her thought exactly.

She stared back at Zach, not really surprised at his anger. He hadn't wanted her to join the Bureau to begin with, and she was aware that it was his influence that had kept her from the assignments she had sought. "How did you convince Abdul to allow you out of the limo?" Khalid pushed his fingers through his hair before propping them on his hips.

"He's sleeping." She shrugged, covering for her friend. "I promised him I'd stay put."

"And he knows better than to believe you," Khalid barked.

"And you knew better than to think the four of you can slip in here for one of your little covert meetings. And since when does the FBI work so closely with spooks?" she shot back, keeping her voice low rather than yelling as she shot Shayne a hard look. "Give me a break here, Khalid. You and my fathers have been conspiring against me from the beginning. And you." She turned on Shayne. "You have to be sick. I've been following you for days and you didn't spot me once. Where's your head? Up your ass?"

The small grin that curled his lips assured her that he wouldn't forget that remark. Not that she gave a damn. He could have gotten his head blown off if she had been the enemy.

"Touché," Shayne murmured. "Though, I do recall that you excelled in subversive maneuvers during your training."

"I'm sure there are terrorists out there who excel in it as well," she informed him. "You haven't been watching your back. I could have kicked you more than once, and you never knew."

"Protecting her has suddenly become work here," Khalid told her fathers, the anger thick in his voice now. "And I am growing tired of this constant tug-of-war between my lover and the men who like to pretend to be my bosses."

"I don't need your protection." Her chin lifted as she faced them all, not in anger now, but in confidence. She knew her training and her limitations, she knew her job, and if there was a single one of them who thought they could change that, then it was time they learned better.

"And if we hadn't been there to get Mohammed's gun out of your face?" Khalid raked his fingers through his hair again as his black eyes glowed with anger. "What then, Marty? What the hell would you have done then?"

"We'll never know, will we? But, he was only seconds from losing his balls when he had that gun in my neck," she answered, careful to keep her voice cool. "Which raises the question, does Ian Sinclair know he has a rabid mountain roaming the halls pretending to be a man? Or is our fair Mohammed a member here, too?" She stared back at the men glaring forcefully at her. "Last I heard there was some kind of rule against members striking women. Or is that just women who are sneaking in the doors?" She rubbed her jaw. "Can we get him thrown out for backhanding me, do you think?"

She couldn't have expected what happened next. The second the words seemed to connect in Khalid's brain that Mohammed had struck her, his fist flew and landed in his brother's face. A second later his fingers were gripping the other man's neck as he threw Abram into the wall. Pure rage bled from his pores as an animalistic growl seemed to tear from his throat.

"I will kill him," he snarled in Abram's shocked face.

And Marty had had enough. It was like dealing with a bunch of high school jocks. None of them had the good sense to actually face her with the truth, all they could do was hit each other, beat around the bush, and try to pretend they weren't attempting to hide things from her.

It pissed her off. No one actually lied to her, but they sure as hell did their best to make certain she stayed in the dark whenever possible.

As the other men rushed to pull Khalid back her teeth snapped together as she turned and left the room. Slamming the door closed behind her she was met by an entire security force rushing up the stairs, headed by the formidable and much too handsome Ian Sinclair.

He came to a dead stop and stared at her in shock, as if the sight of a woman in the testosterone-laden halls of his club was too much to take in, which was far beyond the truth. His wife, Courtney, actually managed to sneak in often when she had lived in what had once been Ian's private wing of the house.

"Don't worry, I'm leaving," she informed him coldly. "If I were you, though, I'd get some cameras in these halls and the shrubbery trimmed from that back doorway. Getting in here was as easy as taking candy from a baby while it sleeps." She brushed past him before taking the stairs quickly, aware of all the eyes turning, watching her.

Below were more men. All security. The doors were closed securely to the rooms downstairs, but a few of the members watched curiously from their positions leaning against the walls.

There was Cole Andrews, Tally Conover's husband, Lucian, her rumored cohusband Devril, and several others of the social elite, who seemed unconcerned by the fact that she had seen them. Men she had danced with at balls, whose wives she had gone to school with or sometimes lunched with.

It wasn't surprising. She had known this crowd stuck together, but this should have been ridiculous.

"Sorry to intrude." She flashed them all a tight, falsely sweet smile. "See you at the next party."

With that she strode down the hall and out the double doors that a scowling doorman was holding open.

She had no intentions of returning to the limo. She would have walked home first, but, thankfully, a black Lexus that drew to a stop in the driveway was very familiar to her.

Former FBI agent Mac McCoy. That really shouldn't have surprised her, though it did. Mac was married and supposedly living on some farm several states away.

He stepped out of the vehicle, his gray eyes meeting hers as the breeze played with his thick black hair.

"Marty?" Incredulity filled his voice, affirming her sudden suspicion that he knew exactly what this club was all about. Of course he did; he was here, and that meant he had to be a member.

"I need a ride." She moved quickly to the passenger door. "Please, Mac, kinda quick, if you don't mind. Take me to my parents' place."

He slid back into the car as she opened the door, and jumped in. A second later he was speeding away from the front doors as Khalid and Shayne stood framed by the light behind them, their expressions filled with varying degrees of anger, concern, and frustration.

The Lexus sped from the club grounds as silence filled the vehicle. Marty felt the heaviness in her chest as it expanded, filling her, sinking into her muscles and tendons, making the depths of her soul ache.

She was a trained agent, just as she had stated. She had learned not just to look for lies, but to live a lie if she needed to. She had known Khalid and Shayne were hiding something, but she hadn't really expected her fathers to be involved in it.

"Strange, I can't remember ever seeing a woman walk out those doors," Mac commented, as the car turned toward Alexandria and her parents' home.

There was a note of curiosity in his tone. Mac had been a formidable agent during his time in the FBI. Strange, she had never imagined that he could be a member. There were times he had seemed so straitlaced and aboveboard.

"I'm sure you'll never see it again," she reassured him, as she crossed her arms and rubbed her hands up and down them quickly.

She felt chilled to the bone despite the summer heat. Emotion had forced her to flee, but she knew she should have stayed. She wanted to know what the hell was going on, and why Abram Mustafa, a suspected terrorist sympathizer, was meeting secretly with her fathers as well as with Khalid and Shayne.

She had known Khalid was involved with whatever Shayne was up to. She should have realized it went much deeper than she had suspected. She had assumed he was helping Shayne with his operation, but she hadn't expected her fathers to be in on it as well.

Khalid could claim her. He could fuck her. But he couldn't sleep through the night with her, and he sure as hell didn't bother to talk to her. God forbid that he should have to lower himself so far as to explain his actions to her.

"Shayne and Khalid didn't look happy," Mac commented a moment later, when she said nothing more.

"That so bothers me." She shot him an instant glare. He was a man, a member of the club, and therefore most likely in on whatever conspiracy was currently ruling her fathers' lives.

"I can tell." He nodded seriously, as though he weren't being completely facetious.

"You're a member of the club," she stated.

"Not me." There was a hint of laughter in his voice now. "I was meeting friends for drinks."

"Only members enter." She glared at him for lying to her.

At that, Mac shook his head. "Or former members. I was truly meeting friends for drinks, Agent Mathews, nothing more. And ended up playing white knight." He flashed her what she was certain he thought was a charming grin.

Marty clenched her teeth at the humor. Amusement wasn't high on her list of priorities tonight.

"Let it go, Mac," she warned him. "I'm not in the mood."

"A white knight's job is never done." He clucked his tongue as he shook his head and glanced back over at her. "Strange, I didn't imagine Khalid could get himself in so much trouble with you. I think he's been claiming you for so long that he's forgotten what it's like to realize that perhaps you don't really belong to him."

Marty turned and stared back at him in surprise and anger.

"What the hell do you mean by that?"

For a moment, silence filled the car. Mac took the turn that led to her parents' home and pulled slowly into the drive. Putting the Lexus in park, he turned to stare at her thoughtfully for long moments.

"You were eighteen," he finally said. "Khalid let everyone who could possibly be a threat to his future relationship with you know that he considered your heart his own. He was a much darker person then, Marty. A man with a lot of demons. A man who even your fathers were wary of at that time."

Marty shook her head. "I don't believe you."

He shrugged nonchalantly. "Believe what you like. But this one you can take to the bank. Khalid will catch up with you. When he does, he'll show you exactly why he waited until he couldn't wait any longer to take you. He'll show you the demons that fill him. I just hope you're woman enough to accept them."

"Woman enough to accept the third he wants in that relationship? How about woman enough to figure out when he's fucking lying to me?" She sneered. "Do you have any idea just how pompous you sound right now?"

"Woman enough to see beneath the actions, and to accept the truth of the man who just might not realize that he's given you his heart," he said softly. "And that, Marty, takes a woman who's not just strong but also understanding. I wonder if you can be both."

She couldn't be both, she thought, as she prepared to get out of the car.

Turning from him, she threw the door open and stalked to the house as the front door opened and her mother stood framed in the doorway.

Her mother was home. Her father must have called her, must have told her what was going on. Virginia looked well rested, but concerned and angry. Her gray eyes locked on Marty as a frown marred her still smooth brow.

Marty wouldn't discuss this with her. Not yet. But she could hide here until her fathers arrived and she found out exactly what they were up to with Khalid and Shayne.

12

Khalid remained calm, though doing so wasn't as easy as he had wished it was, while riding in the back of Joe Mathews's limo long minutes after Mac had taken Marty from the club. Joe, Zach, and Shayne were all silent. The silence wore on his nerves, nerves that were never tested this way until this night, until tangling with Marty.

The only man who appeared unaffected by any of this was Joe. He sat back in the leather seat and simply watched Khalid.

"This is a fucking mess," Zach muttered to Joe from where he sat at his side.

"Of course it is," Joe agreed. "We let our emotions get involved. It's always a mess when we allow that."

Amusement touched Joe's voice as Khalid watched him coldly. Beside him, he could feel the tension radiating from Shayne. Tempers were simmering, and Khalid had a feeling that holding his own in check wouldn't last much longer.

"Damn it, Joe," Zach cursed, his voice low. "She thinks we're all conspiring against her."

"You are," Joe pointed out. "All of you have been, by not giving her the answers she's all but demanded of you. I didn't make that mistake."

"You trained her too well, Zach, if you didn't want her poking her nose in places you didn't want her." Shayne sat watching them, his arms crossed over his chest, a scowl on his face. "And Khalid could have saved us all the trouble if he'd simply given her details rather than an insignificant portion of the events."

"I didn't ask for your opinion, you damned spook," Zach bit out angrily. "You only came back to the States to tell Khalid about his brothers, hoping that he would choose you as his third. And don't think we're not all aware of it."

"Enough." Khalid watched as Joe's gaze glittered with interest as he stared back at him. "It ends now. Once we reach the house I'll tell her what we must." Not that he wanted to. Hell, one question was going to lead to another, and before he knew it, the truth of his own past would come out.

Joe's brow arched. "I'd say it's a little late for that. I'd suggest Kevlar, if I were you. She's ready to shoot us all."

"If she doesn't, then I just might." Khalid forced himself to keep his hands in place at his side, rather than around Zach's neck for demanding that meeting, even though he knew Marty was with Khalid and Shayne.

"I feel like I'm throwing my daughter to the fucking wolves." Zach glowered at Khalid and Shayne.

That was exactly what he had done; it was what he had done years before, when he had allowed Marty the opportunity to join the FBI.

He had allowed his lover, Joe's wife, to convince him otherwise. He had given in to the woman and the child he had loved, and Khalid suspected he had regretted it every day since.

"She's your woman now," Shayne reminded him quietly. "Would you do anything differently? And while you're contemplating your answer, Khalid, tell me, did you ever get around to telling her about Abram and Lessa?"

"It's too late to consider what I would have done or what I have yet to do." What he should have done. He never should have stayed away from her. He should have taken her when she was eighteen, when she was young enough to be convinced to be a lover rather than a warrior.

And Marty was exactly that. She was a warrior, and she had years of training in facing the war she had chosen. Pulling her out of the fire wasn't going to happen now.

"I wouldn't blame her if she shot all of us." Joe wiped his hand tiredly over his face as the limo pulled into the driveway of his home. "God help us all. We're going to wish we were all dead now. Virginia's home."

"Then get ready to start praying," Zach warned him.

"I started doing that weeks ago." Joe stared back at his friend in irritation. "She'll kill you first, though. Think about that. She knows I would have never helped conspire in keeping anything from her. I've just never had the details."

"Because you refused to read the files," Zach said angrily.

"For whatever reason." Joe shrugged calmly. "Still, I covered my back. Let's hope you have as well. God help you if she asked you and you lied to her."

"I've never lied to her," Zach snarled.

The limo rolled to a stop as Khalid leaned forward slowly, catching the attention of both men.

"Her protection is no longer your concern," he stated, his tone icy, filled with purpose.

"Khalid . . ." A frown line snapped between Zach's brows. He was a father first, Khalid had always known that, but in his efforts to protect his daughter he had done nothing but harm her.

"She is mine now," he stated, his voice harsh. "You will not interfere in that, nor will you interfere in her life any longer. And the next meeting you arrange, you will do so in a venue that she can attend. No more secrets, period."

But he was guilty of his own secrets, and Khalid knew it.

Joe groaned. "Taking her out of it now will be impossible."

"And now she could be facing a nightmare if my brothers manage to get their hands on her." Rage ate inside Khalid like a corrosive acid at the thought of the evil his half brothers had focused toward him. "It is my past that endangers her, and I will ensure that it endangers her no longer."

With an irritated flick of his wrist he jerked the door open, rather than wait on Abdul, and stepped from the car.

Pausing, Khalid watched as the other men exited the vehicle. Shayne was the last to step out. His gaze swept the area, eyes narrowed and piercing as he searched for any threats.

Marty was like this as well. Wherever she went, whatever she was doing, she was always particularly aware of her surroundings and all that was going on.

"Time to pay the piper," he heard Joe mutter to Zach as they headed toward the house. "Virginia isn't going to be happy with us. You know, if you paid attention to me more often, we wouldn't get in nearly so much trouble."

They often bickered like close brothers. Young ones, at that.

"No one holds a gun to your head," Zach snorted. "That innocent act isn't going to get you very far with her."

"Farther than you'll get." There was a hint of amusement there that made Khalid want to shake his head.

At that moment the front door opened and Khalid nearly came to a stop as Virginia Mathews stood glaring at the four of them.

Shoulders tense and thrown back, her delicate frame nearly quivering with anger, her gray eyes shot furious daggers at all of them.

"Now Ginny, it's not as bad as she thinks it is," Joe started out. He held up his hands as though to halt the angry words before they poured from her lips.

"I can't believe the four of you." She didn't limit her anger to her husband, her lover, or the men in her daughter's life. Hell no. She was pissed at all of them.

Stepping into the house, the four men faced not just an angry mother but a furious daughter as well. Marty stood at the far end of the entryway, arms crossed over her breasts, her gray eyes narrowed on them all.

"Finished with your little visit?" She directed her ire at Khalid.

"For the moment." He shrugged as though that anger didn't faze him, when in fact he swore he could feel his balls drawing up in primal fear. She looked ready to kill. "I'm certain there will be more in the future, though."

"Come into the kitchen." Joe flexed his shoulders as though expecting a lash to descend upon them. "Hell, I'm going to need coffee for this."

"And you think explanations are going to fix this?" Virginia asked incredulously. "Joe, I've warned you about playing with her life. I've warned both of you." She shot Zach a fulminating look as well. "I have a mind to pack my bags and move in with my daughter. God only knows how the two of you have worked me over the years."

Khalid kept his expression closed, cool. He noticed Joe and Zach did the same. It wouldn't do to allow the graceful yet renowned temper of Virginia Mathews free. She was a spitfire, and one that knew how to slice the meat from a man's bones at forty paces.

"Coffee." As they entered the kitchen Zach headed to the coffeepot; Marty kept a wide distance between herself and everyone else.

She did that a lot, Khalid thought.

"Marty, Virginia, please." Joe indicated the chairs at the kitchen table. "Let's sit down."

They sat, albeit reluctantly, both women staring at the other two men as though they had grown fangs and horns in the past hours.

"Things are a bit complicated," Joe finally stated, as Zach paced back to the table and everyone took a seat. "And it's all Zach's fault."

Zach shot him a vengeful glare.

"With the two of you involved, that doesn't surprise me," Virginia snapped. "You deliberately make things difficult. And don't even bother playing innocent with me, Joe."

"We do what we have to do, Ginny." The edge of weariness in

Zach's tone had Khalid's gaze shifting from Marty's angry expression to the resolute determination in Joe's.

"Enough." Joe leaned forward, his penetrating gaze locked on Marty now. "You're angry, but without cause, Marty. No one here has lied to you. We've simply attempted to ensure you were kept safe while trying to apprehend Khalid's half brothers, and whomever they sent here in an attempt to kill you that day your car was shot at. We know they were involved in it, but knowing it and proving it are two separate things."

"Dad, I hate it when you talk around me." Marty leaned forward, laying her arms on the table as she glared at Joe. "You called that meeting tonight, knowing I couldn't be included in it because of where it was. You could have moved Khalid's brother here, or to your house, and no one would have known. Instead, you kept it there, where Khalid had no choice but to lie to me, or to have me so curious that I followed. You used him." She leaned forward, fury etched on her face. "And I don't appreciate it." Her gaze turned to Khalid, her eyes dark with anger. "And you. You allowed them to do it for most of your life."

"No one used me, precious," he assured her with a hint of steel in his tone. "If anything, I used them to achieve my own plans to destroy Azir Mustafa. We just haven't managed it yet." His gaze narrowed on her then.

"And the meeting tonight had nothing to do with you," Zach finished for him. "That simple."

"You had to get into that club," Khalid growled at her. "Just as you had to get to that meeting, despite my best attempts to keep you from it." He met her gaze directly. "You couldn't wait for explanations; you couldn't ask questions. Instead, you felt the need to slip around as though I would lie to you rather than meet your questions head-on."

Marty stared back at him, wondering if somehow the world had tilted on its axis, or if there had been a particular mental plague that affected only the males of the species.

"As though questions were going to get me anywhere," she snapped back. "You forget, Khalid, I know exactly how secretive you are, and every time I start to ask a question you conveniently have something else to do."

"Something such as protecting you. It was my fault you were in danger. It was my job to fix it."

Khalid seemed perfectly serious, and no one around the table was disputing his statement.

"What kind of game are you playing now, Khalid?" Indignation rose inside her. "Do I look as though I'm stupid? That I'm not well aware of the attempts you make to ensure my attention is diverted? That you're hiding things from me? Perhaps if you weren't so damned evasive it might be easier to believe you."

Black eyes flickered with impatience as she glared at him, refusing to blush at the certainty that her parents would know exactly the tactics he used.

"It's definitely difficult to tell you the truth. Your suspicious nature makes it damned hard to tell you what we suspect." He grunted. "Nonetheless, it is exactly that, the truth. The meetings between Abram, your fathers, and myself are for an exchange of information and security concerns. Certain factions have become suspicious, though. To allay that suspicion, we meet at the club, to make sure that Abram and I never appear as though we are working together once again, as we did in the past with your godfather."

She sat back in her chair and stared at him silently. He might be telling the truth, but none of it made sense to her.

"Why would it matter if the two of you were friends or not? You're brothers," she pointed out.

Khalid glanced at her godfather, Zach, before breathing out heavily.

"It was an impression we encouraged once I left Saudi. I cut all ties with the entire family when my brothers, Ayid and Aman, learned of my connection to the FBI and began trying to exact vengeance for it. Information I gave at the time led Saudi and U.S.

forces to the headquarters my brothers had set up in Riyadh from which they planned to stage a strike against the Saudi royal family for their ties to America. That information led to an attack where my brothers were reportedly killed. They'd escaped instead. Their wives did not. I barely made it out of Saudi alive."

Khalid managed to hold back the information surrounding Lessa's death, and his failure to protect her while, hopefully, giving her enough information to allay her suspicions. His brother's wife had been his responsibility at the time. He'd been overconfident, he'd fucked up, and she had paid with her life. How could he ever expect Marty to place her trust in him if she knew how he had failed with another woman? A woman who had trusted him to protect her?

And there was no doubt that eventually his brothers would strike again. Unless he struck first and ensured they didn't rise to retaliate once again.

Marty stared at him intently then, as did her mother. He could practically see the gears working in their heads, the information turning over, being dissected and examined.

"And you know beyond a shadow of a doubt that your brothers attacked me?" Marty asked. She could feel a lack of information, missing pieces, but she couldn't put her finger on exactly what it was she wasn't being told. One thing was for certain at this point: If she didn't ask the right question, then she would never know what he was still hiding.

"There is no doubt," he assured her.

"And that's the reason you didn't move to claim me yourself?"

She watched as Khalid's gaze became shuttered. "I did that because I could not bear endangering you because of my determination to destroy the Mustafa family."

But there was more. With Khalid, there would always be more.

"What else aren't you telling me?"

Khalid breathed out heavily. "I'm thirty-five years old, precious. I'm certain you will learn other things about me, but isn't that part of the joy of a relationship?"

She licked her lips, suddenly aware of the seriousness of his expression, the glimmer of emotion in his eyes. Could he suddenly be promising her more than just the sex? "Don't lie to me," she whispered. "It would destroy me."

"No lies." Sincerity filled his tone.

He was still hiding something from her, she could feel it, sense it, and Marty knew in her heart that that was a lie in and of itself. But she couldn't turn away from him. She couldn't bear the thought of losing him, not yet, not until she had to let go of him. "Marty, my life hasn't been charmed," he stated gently. "I've led a life filled with blood, and with nightmares that I often wish only to forget. Can you blame me for not wishing to air those nightmares just yet? Can I not take a moment of my life to simply enjoy my woman, rather than dragging her into a past that even I wish I had no part of?"

But she loved him. She had a right to be a part of that life. She glanced at Shayne, noticing that, like her father, he had found something else to direct his attention to. It appeared that the pattern of the wallpaper across the room had him mesmerized.

Turning back to Khalid, she nodded slowly. "If there's nothing more."

"For now, I swear to you, there is nothing more important than just holding you."

Marty had a feeling those nightmares now held the key to the answers she needed. The reason why a part of Khalid remained distant to her. Why she didn't have the heart of the man, as he held her heart. Zach rose to his feet and moved to the coffeepot to refill the cups he gathered from the table.

After filling cups with coffee and transferring them to the table, he retook his seat and glanced at Virginia. "We've done our best to protect her, Ginny. She might be pissed at us, but we've kept her safe."

Marty had to smile at her mother's sarcastic, less than ladylike snort.

"Why not just tell me what was going on?" She looked between Khalid and Shayne then.

"Because we weren't certain what was going on; we still aren't,"

Shayne answered her. "I came here with information for Khalid, rumors that his half brothers suspected he had helped disband the cell they sent after you, and that he was once again working to destroy them. Now, I'm trying my damndest to figure out who ran you off the road and tried to shoot you, and whether or not Ayid and Aman are closer than they should be."

"Marty, there's nothing else going on," her father promised her, his gaze filled with love, with sincerity. "I would tell you if there were."

"If you knew about it." She glanced to her godfather.

"And I swear to you, that's all Khalid is involved in," Zach promised. "I would tell you if there were more. Since the attack against you, you've had two men on constant detail to watch your back. I'm not taking chances with your life."

Her jaw clenched as she threaded her fingers together and tightened them around one another. She'd had a sense of being watched, but like Shayne, she'd been unable to pinpoint who was watching or what they wanted.

"I can't believe you two." Her mother spoke up before she had a chance to, her voice rising in maternal fury. "You suspected she was being followed, she was attacked, shot at and you never called me and warned me my daughter was in danger."

"He hadn't shared the fact that she's had a tail on her with me, either." Joe's tone lowered, became deeper as he attempted to shift the focus from his own knowledge that Marty had been in danger, and that he hadn't called his wife. "What the hell do you think you're doing keeping that information from me?"

Now, this was familiar. This was one of the reasons Marty had moved out of her parents' home the moment she had graduated high school. They fought over her, constantly. She was the only child, and the source of their greatest disagreements.

Not that her mother wasn't usually right when she argued with them, but once it began, her fathers couldn't help but bury each other deeper in trouble.

"I've had enough." Marty rose quickly to her feet, intent on getting out of the house now as quickly as possible. Staring back at her godfather, the man she had always considered her other father, Marty felt hurt rise inside her. "Perhaps when you're answering Mother, you can let me know as well why you wouldn't warn me that your men were following me. It would have been nice to know, just in case I were wondering if I had gun sights trained on me again."

"I did what I thought best." He rose to his feet, his hands flattening on the table. "Like your father, I had no desire to ruin the vacation you've looked forward to for two years, unless there was no other choice." He glanced at Khalid then. "And as much as I disapprove of Khalid dragging you into his life, I wanted you to have the time I felt you needed with him. It was bad enough you knew you were in danger. I wanted you comfortable, and I wanted you safe."

A scathing reply rose to her lips, but she held it back. She loved her parents, all three of them. She had no desire to hurt them, despite Zach's high-handedness.

"I'm going home."

Khalid and Shayne rose as well. It was easy to see that both of them were intent on following her. She hoped they had fun sleeping in the car outside her apartment, because that was where she was heading.

"You're staying with Khalid." Zach made it sound like an order.

Marty gave a light, low laugh. "I don't think so, Dad. But I'll let you believe it if it will allow you to sleep better tonight." She was angry. Her sharp tongue was impossible to control in the best of circumstances, but the hurt that rose inside her made it impossible to stem at the moment.

"Marty, you should stay here." Her mother rose to her feet and moved to her, reaching out for her with loving hands. "Give your fathers a chance to figure out what's going on before you leave." She cast Zach a glare. "And they will figure it out, I promise you."

"Then they can let me know when they do." Kissing her mother's cheek, she drew in a hard, deep breath before turning to her father, Joe. "Could I borrow the car, Dad?"

"Abdul has arrived with the limo," Khalid said. "I'll take you home."

"Nice try, Khalid." This time, her smile was tight, angry. "I think I'll pass. You and Shayne can have a nice ride alone tonight. Consider it bonding time."

"Sweetheart, stay the night." Joe was on his feet, his face creased in worry. "We'll get to the bottom of this, I promise you."

"Why are you so worried, Dad?" She gave a light, easy laugh filled with bitter amusement. "After all, Daddy Zach's agents are keeping a nice careful eye on me, remember? I'll be fine."

"You'll give me more gray hairs," Zach muttered. "You should listen to us, Marty. Stay here the night."

"I have a home and that's where I need to be." Taking the keys to her father's car, she let her gaze go over the four men once again. "You know, I think you just made a decision for me that I'd only been considering until now. You'll have my resignation on your desk by the end of the week. I'm sorry, Dad, but if you have your men shadowing me without my knowledge, then I have no business being a part of the Bureau."

"Damn it to hell, Marty, don't do that." Zach straightened in shock as she, ignoring his surprise, left the kitchen.

Behind her, Joe and Zach were beginning to argue fiercely. Khalid and Shayne were stalking behind her; she could feel them as she moved quickly to the door.

"Marty." Her mother's hand touched her arm, drawing her to a stop at the front door. "Don't make a hasty decision."

Turning, Marty breathed out roughly, staring over her mother's shoulder to where Khalid and Shayne watched her with equal amounts of thoughtful intensity.

"Go away," she ordered them both, wearily. "Just leave me the hell alone."

"We'll be waiting outside." It was a major concession on Khalid's part, she could tell. She watched as they stepped outside.

Turning back to her mother, she shook her head tiredly and fought back tears. "You know, Mom, I hate having my life played with."

Virginia's smile was loving, understanding. "You learn how to deal with it," she said softly, "when you're married to them. I love them both, Marty, but sometimes I can't wait for my vacation just to get away from them."

Wrapping her arms around her chest, Marty dipped her head for a long moment as a sense of helplessness seemed to steal over her. "I think leaving the Bureau is best," she finally said. "They can't watch over me like a mother hen if I'm not there. And I doubt Braque Sawyers will give a damn what my fathers want when it comes to the assignments I get."

Braque's private security and investigation firm was a multinational enterprise. Marty knew for a fact that Braque wouldn't consider the salary she was demanding if there was a chance of giving in to the FBI director's controlling impulses where Marty was concerned. Nor would he give in to Khalid's.

"You're growing up," Virginia stated sadly. "Just remember, Marty, they love you. They love us."

"And I love them, Mom." She sighed. "But if I'm going to keep loving them, then I need to get the hell away from them."

"And Khalid?" Virginia asked. "Do you need to get away from him as well?"

Did she? "I rather hope he's trainable." Marty groaned; she knew the chances of that were slim to none. Well, slim actually wasn't in the equation.

She doubted very seriously that Khalid was trainable in the least. If her mother's skeptical look was anything to go by, then she doubted it as well.

Marty's lips quirked with a bit of mocking amusement as she fought back a rueful laugh. Her mother didn't bother to fight back her own amusement, nor her laughter. They both knew exactly the battle Marty was facing.

She reached for her mother, gave her a tight hug, then moved toward the door. "I'll call you tomorrow, Mom."

"Do that," her mother commanded gently. "After all, I cut short sun, fun, and sand to come home and try to control your fathers for you. I, at least, deserve a call, as well as a few luncheons and a day of shopping."

Marty groaned as she left the house and closed the door behind her. She hated luncheons and shopping days with her mother. They wore her out.

Ignoring the two men awaiting her, she moved down the steps and strode purposefully to her father's black Jaguar, which was parked at the side of the circular drive.

She was aware of them getting into the limo, just as she was aware of the limo following her every step of the way as she headed home.

She was aggravated, tired, and holding on to her temper by a thread. Dealing with not one but two impossibly arrogant men wasn't her idea of a fun night tonight. But it appeared it wasn't something she was going to get out of, either.

13

Khalid watched the taillights of Joe Mathews's car as it sped through Alexandria's sparse, late-evening traffic. From his position in the back of the limousine, facing forward, he kept his gaze centered on those lights and the woman heading away from Joe's home and to her own.

Shayne sat in the opposite seat, his back supported by the corner, his gaze shuttered as he watched Khalid.

There was much about his past that this man had been privy to, Khalid knew. At a time when Khalid had felt invincible, indestructible, Shayne had been on the fringes of his life.

As a deep-cover agent for the Federal Bureau of Investigation, Khalid had worked with Shayne in the border area of Saudi Arabia and Iraq several times. Shayne had been the CIA agent in the area. They had exchanged information several times, worked together, and fought to identify terrorists and uncover the various plots to strike against America and its allies.

Until that last brutal, bloody day. Until Khalid had realized that nothing was sacred, and that no one lived forever.

"We should have never taken her onto the club grounds," Shayne said thoughtfully. "I knew she wouldn't stay put. I think you knew it as well."

Khalid shot him a withering look. "You believe I wanted to deal with this tonight? To have the woman I am trying to convince to move into my bed see that I am still conspiring with her fathers behind her back?"

He couldn't believe something so insane could have passed the other man's lips. They had endangered their own memberships by allowing her the chance to slip into the club. The only assurance they had that there would be no repercussions was the fact that both Joe and Zach were on the judicial committee that oversaw possible punishment for such offenses.

"What better way to drive her out of your life?" Shayne asked, as the limo made a turn onto the residential street where Marty's apartment was located.

Khalid's lips curled in disgust at the observation.

"It would be no hardship to choose another third, Shayne," he informed the other man sharply.

Shayne's expression never changed. The amused condescension was firmly in place.

"Try choosing one who will put up with your demands as I do," Shayne laughed, as he lifted the fingers on one hand and began counting. "Forget about her heart. Don't touch her unless you're present. You're to know every move she makes. He shook his head. "Hell, I know there's more, but it's beginning to piss me off."

The limo came to a stop on the street in front of Marty's apartment, just behind her father's car.

"Wait here, Abdul," Khalid ordered without deigning to acknowledge Shayne's mocking reference to the rules Khalid had established.

Throwing the door open, Khalid and Shayne exited the vehicle and strode purposely to the secured door of the building. The lock clicked open as Khalid reached for the handle, the security guard on duty recognizing him immediately.

"Good evening, Mr. Mustafa." The guard nodded as they moved toward the elevators.

Khalid nodded in return before hitting the elevator button and waiting impatiently.

"Any rules for this little meeting?" Shayne asked mockingly.

"Shut the hell up before I break your damned neck," Khalid said as the doors slid open.

The elevator moved swiftly, depositing them on Marty's floor in time to catch her as she slid the key in her lock.

Turning her head, she stared at them for long moments before rolling her eyes and turning the key.

"You know, this on-again, off-again stuff is going to get on my nerves," she stated as they neared her. "I'm really tired, Khalid. Would you be good enough to take your friend and go away for a while?"

Khalid paused within inches of her. "I would suggest you pack a bag," he told her. "You'll be staying at the estate for a while."

He ignored Shayne's heavy sigh.

"You know, Marty, I really thought you had better taste in men." Amusement filled the other man's voice as Marty's gaze remained locked with Khalid's. "This one isn't exactly the kind and gentle sort, you know."

"I really thought he had better sense," she said mockingly.

"It would appear he doesn't." Shayne shrugged as Khalid crossed his arms over his chest and stared back at Marty demandingly.

Shaking her head, Marty pushed the door open.

Khalid had only a second's warning. He saw the shadow from the corner of his eye gaining speed as it moved toward the door and toward Marty.

There was that split second that adrenaline tore through him, that strength rushed through his body. Gripping her arm, he jerked her back, threw her into Shayne, and tried to block the intruder rushing toward them.

"Fuck!" Shayne yelled behind him as Khalid felt a bulldozer plow into his chest, throwing him into Shayne and he heard Marty yelling about guns and getting down.

A rapid, muffled retort of gunfire had him trying to throw himself over her. Unfortunately, she was one step ahead of him and Shayne.

As the black-garbed intruder threw himself around the corner of the hall, Marty was chasing after the fleeing form, a weapon held closely against her thigh as she rushed past them both.

Jerking the Glock from beneath his jacket, Khalid was on her ass, with Shayne running fast behind him as they all stopped at the corner.

Raising his hand, Khalid glared at Marty as she began to duck and peek around the corner.

Bending low, Khalid also gave a quick look, jerking back as gunfire sounded from the open window and the fire escape outside.

With a quick gesture indicating he was heading to the next floor via the stairs, Shayne rushed from his position and pushed through the stairwell doors.

"Now what?" Marty turned her head and arched a brow tauntingly.

"You go low, I'll go high." Adrenaline coursed through his body as she flashed a bright, honest-as-hell smile before giving a quick nod of her head.

Behind them, apartment doors were opening, voices were demanding explanations, and all Khalid could do was feel a strange, unfamiliar sense of completeness.

He'd never had a lover who could match this side of him. That side that hungered for danger.

"High, low," she mouthed back. "One. Two . . ."

On three, they moved.

Marty threw herself to the floor, rolled, and came up across the hall with her weapon aimed at the now empty window and unoccupied fire escape.

Almost simultaneously they were up and running at the same time to the window. Marty went low, he went high. They both stared at the empty fire escape for a long moment.

"Bastard's gone," Shayne called out from the level below them. "No car, no nothing, just gone."

Gone. That meant that whoever the hell was after Marty was still out there.

"Get up here," Khalid ordered, his voice harsh as he gripped Marty's arm and began pulling her back along the hall.

Residents at the open apartment doors stared at them in curiosity and shock.

Ignoring them, Khalid continued to draw Marty back to her apartment.

"Everything's fine." Marty waved them back toward their apartments. "You can go back to your homes. Have a drink for me. Don't worry, this is your building's owner. Nothing to fret about."

"Shayne will be here in a minute." His voice was harder, demanding. "Get some clothes together or do without them, it's your choice, but hurry."

The door slammed closed behind them.

"Of course you would." Marty jerked her arm out of his grip as she bit back the need to roll her eyes at him. "Let me guess: A club member can help you out of this under the right circumstances."

She moved to her bedroom and jerked the overnight bag she kept handy from beneath the bed. It was filled with several changes of clothes and needed supplies, as well as an extra weapon and ammunition.

"Your fathers can take care of anything I need where the police are concerned," he informed her. "I'd just prefer to be on home ground."

"Fine. I'm ready." She slung the strap of the heavy backpack over her shoulder as she turned to face him. "Let's go."

His gaze flicked to the backpack, but he surprised her when he didn't make a comment. Instead, he held out his hand to her.

Marty stared at that hand for a long moment before placing hers in it. Feeling his fingers curl around hers as he drew her quickly through the apartment back to the door sent a strange feeling of warmth surging through her.

He hadn't gripped her arm and pulled her along. He'd extended his hand and invited her to go. There was a difference, and that difference sent a wave of unfamiliar emotion washing through her.

"Abdul has the car waiting." Shayne met them at the elevator as the doors slid open. "I called Joe Mathews. He's chomping at the bit to race out to your estate, but I convinced him to hold off until morning. Someone will be coming out for his car tonight."

The ride to the lobby was made quickly. As the elevator doors slid open, the manager rushed from the security station toward Khalid.

"Mr. Mustafa, security has been sent to Miss Mathews's floor and the police called."

"Cancel the call to the police and get security back in place, everything's fine," Khalid ordered, as he led the way through the lobby at a quick pace. "I'll be in contact with you soon."

"But Mr. Mustafa . . ."

Khalid pushed the door open and led Marty outside.

Marty felt the strangest sense of unreality as they passed through those doors, as though she had entered another world rather than simply left a building.

Abdul waited by the limo, concern marking his face as they rushed inside. The door closed behind them, enfolding them in privacy as he quickly slid behind the wheel and put the vehicle into drive.

The sound of oncoming sirens could be heard as the limo sped away quickly from the apartment building.

"Mathews wants a report asap," Shayne told them, his expression tight and closed as he stared at Khalid before turning his gaze to the traffic around them.

"That makes two of us." Marty breathed in roughly. "I didn't even have a chance to get a look at his face."

"His face was covered," Khalid stated.

"And my apartment was very professionally searched," she reported. "There was just enough out of place to show he was in a hurry."

What could he have been searching for? Marty never brought files home;

her computer was used for personal e-mail and business records only. She wrote about or logged her reports from her office computer.

"The search was a smoke screen," Khalid informed them. "They weren't after information."

"They were after Marty," Shayne finished.

Marty stared back at the two men as she tried to make sense of what they were saying.

"He was there to kill me." She had known that the second she had realized what was going on.

The gunfire hadn't been loud; the assailant's weapon had been silenced. She had known the sound of that *pop-pop* as the bullets had been fired from the fire escape.

Something flashed in Khalid's face then. It wasn't just fury; it was pain, an agony that went far beyond the thought of what could have happened.

It was there and gone so fast that she couldn't be certain of the emotion she had seen there.

"He was there to kill you," Khalid finally agreed. "We need to figure out what the hell is going on." Khalid glared at Shayne. "When we get back to the estate I want you to pull in as much information as possible from your sources. Don't scrimp, Shayne; we don't have much time. That assassin was too close. If they follow previous patterns, then they're here in Alexandria. They would want to be close. They would need to see me suffer. They wouldn't wait in Saudi and merely guess at my reaction."

"If your brothers hate you so much, then why come after me rather than you?" she asked.

"Oh, they will," he promised her. "But they would want me to suffer first, Marty. Killing you would ensure that suffering, even more than they could guess. Before they kill me, they want me to know they've taken my woman, destroyed her. They'll be satisfied with nothing less."

"Have they threatened the girls you look after?"

There were six young women who his father had sent to him years ago as sex slaves; at least, that was the rumor. Khalid had adopted them instead.

"The girls have never been threatened, because they were a gift from my father," he sneered, his voice deepening, darkening with a ragged agony that tore at her soul. "Until he dies, Ayid and Aman won't tempt his patience with them by harming them."

"But your lovers are fair game?"

"My lovers are fair game," he agreed quietly, but the echo of rage in his voice was clear. "Over the years I've cost my brothers a lot, love. Even more important, I've steadily worked at destroying them. The last cell we captured was more important to them than most. The mission they were on was one that would have brought glory to Ayid and Aman among the terrorist community. Taking that from them ensured that they would strike against me."

Marty stared back at him, not in horror but in confusion.

"Why?" She surveyed his expression carefully, watching the subtle emotions that flickered through his eyes. "When you first went to Saudi fifteen years ago, according to the file I had on you, there was a sense of alliance between you and your three brothers. What happened, Khalid?"

"They found out I was working against them," he stated baldly. "And in doing so, I was responsible for the attack on the headquarters of a small cell based in Riyadh that was planning to infiltrate the royal palace and blow it to hell. The strike the government made against those headquarters resulted in the deaths of their wives. They swore then they'd destroy any woman I claimed as my own. It hasn't helped matters that I've continued to attempt to destroy them over the years."

Silence filled the limousine as Marty stared at him in surprise and pain. The grief that seemed to envelop Khalid drove a wedge of pain inside her chest. To see him, his black eyes flickering with sorrow, tore at her. A sorrow that his brothers had destroyed any hope of a future with any woman he could love, any child he might have.

Marty saw the agony he felt, that at no time had he ever been safe. That his friends, his family, that everyone he loved could be struck at any time. The weight of the knowledge must have been horrible.

Breathing in tremulously, she considered the options they had.

"What do we do next, then?"

"Tomorrow, I'm taking you to the club," Khalid said, causing her lips to part, first in shock, then in mounting anger. "Ian has agreed to allow you to stay in a specially prepared area beneath the club for those members' lovers, wives, children who are in danger. You will be safe until this is finished."

Marty couldn't believe what had just come out of his mouth.

"Ian is not going to allow me back in that club," she informed him. "Not after tonight."

"The agreement has been made," he informed her. "The rooms beneath the club are safe, Marty. Neither Ayid or Aman, nor their assassin, can get to you there. You will be completely sheltered."

She looked at Shayne. Once again, he had found something else to direct his attention to.

"The fucking scenery isn't that interesting," she burst out as he stared out the window. "Did you know about this? Did my fathers?"

Shayne turned to look at her and cleared his throat. "It's a rule. All members have to be informed in the eventuality of this. No names are given, nor the location of where you're staying. Simply that you are staying on the property and that your protection is assured by the club. That means we're all responsible for your safety and well-being." He stared directly at her then. "And we take it very seriously.

"Well, bully the hell for you and your club members!" she sneered. "But you can count me out. I do believe I have other plans."

"And those plans are?" Khalid wasn't happy, but at the moment, she really didn't give a damn. She couldn't believe he would dare attempt to stash her someplace safe while he and Shayne got to run around having fun catching terrorists. It wasn't going to work out like that.

"Anger Thornton is hosting a party in two nights," she informed them both as she sat back and crossed her arms over her breasts. "I'm scheduled to be there, as are the rest of the very powerful and elite here in D.C. There's enough gossip at those parties that if a person catches the right whispers, they may very well get a clue as to what is going on."

"We attend the party and do what?" Shayne asked. "We have no idea who to watch, question, or kill. You're reaching Marty."

"As long as I hide, Ayid and Aman will never show their faces or their intentions," she snapped back at him. "Put me out there. Show them we're not frightened, that we intend to fight back, and you'll piss them off. You'll make them move."

"And risk your life?" Khalid said as he leaned forward and all but shoved his nose against hers. "I don't think so."

Marty watched Khalid. It wouldn't work without his cooperation, without his help. He would have to be there with her as well as Shayne to present the correct image and to incite the brothers who hated him so desperately.

"I don't need your permission," she stated coolly. "Don't make this mistake, Khalid. You can work with me. I can even follow your lead. But I'm not a helpless little homebody that's going to be content to sit in some basement and twiddle my damned thumbs while you're out having fun catching the bad guys."

"I can't believe she's pissed off because she thinks we're going to have fun!" Shayne said.

"Call it what you will." She shrugged negligently as Khalid leaned back slowly. "Either way, you can work with me or I can work alone. Anger's party is perfect for this. There's always a fair number of Saudi businessmen in attendance, and trust me, those guys gossip worse than any other men I've ever met."

Khalid glared at her. She glared back. She wasn't backing down. She wasn't going to hide and play dead and hope the monsters went away. She was going to fucking slay them.

Long moments later elation seared through her at his slow nod.

"Under the right circumstances, the right controlled conditions," he agreed. "And with your fathers' supervision."

She wanted to roll her eyes at the thought, but a part of her also agreed with him. Her fathers could ensure her safety as well as lay a trap that could catch anyone who may be watching or tailing them. If they caught the assassin, if his brothers were in the States, then the mole would be revealed, it was that simple. Khalid's sexual lifestyle was a sore point with the royal family, considering he was distantly related to them, she knew. Their faith didn't allow for the extremities which Khalid had made a part of his life.

"Dad and Zach can arrange the security we need as well as any extra surveillance to watch for your brothers and their assassin," she said. "It could be the chance we need to put an end to this."

"If they take the bait," Khalid pointed out, his voice, his expression dark and brooding now.

"We're the bait," she told him. "The very fact someone has already struck at me assures it."

"My original suggestion stands," Shayne drawled, his tone dangerously low now. "Someone would be doing the world a favor if Ayid and Aman simply disappeared."

Marty couldn't help but agree, from a personal standpoint. As a law enforcement agent, though, it was a harder call.

Khalid simply said nothing. His gaze remained locked on her, his eyes black, a flicker of light, like white-hot flames, gleaming in tiny pinpoints with the raw emotions she could feel tearing through him.

"Come to me." He held his hand out to her once again. "If you have to risk your life in such a way, then I'll at least have what you're willing to give me for now."

Marty restrained an instinctive flinch at the harsh tone of his voice. But she couldn't deny him. She knew how he felt. Knowing the danger he faced, that he had faced most of his life, left her insides shaking with fear.

Moving slowly she closed the distance between them, allowing him to draw her into his arms.

The second he did so, she melted. The warmth that surrounded her abated her previous anger and struck a spark to the flames of arousal that simmered, ever present, within her.

The intimacy she had missed in his bed was there now, as though he needed to hold her, to cushion her against his chest to assure himself that she was safe, that she was his to touch.

And he intended to touch her.

Tipping her head back, he didn't ask for permission to kiss her. As though the very thought of the danger she could be facing spurred the need he felt for her, his lips and tongue took hers with a hunger that burned through her.

Holding her to him with desperate hands, and lifting her closer to him, Khalid ate at her lips, licked at them. He drew her into a sensual, heated world where nothing mattered but his touch and the desires raging through her now that she was in his arms.

It felt as though it had been ages. Centuries. It had been too damned long. It had been since this afternoon, and as far as she was concerned, that was a lifetime ago.

As he kissed her, as his hands roved over her back, her hips, she felt the touch of another's hands at her thighs.

Shayne.

It wasn't a shock; it was an addition to the pleasure, a sensual, erotic enticement that stoked the fire burning inside her higher, hotter.

"I've wondered who held your heart." Shayne's voice was a caress against her senses as Khalid's lips stroked from hers to her jaw, her neck. "Then I wondered if I had a chance at being his third."

Fingers pulled her blouse from her jeans; she didn't know whose, she didn't care. All that mattered was the touch, the pleasure, and Khalid.

All that mattered was the feel of the fingers slowly unbuttoning her blouse, pulling the edges apart, and revealing her lace-covered breasts as Khalid's lips brushed from her neck to her bare shoulder.

Sensual weakness filled her muscles, making her feel dazed, mesmerized. Their touch mesmerized her. She had expected pleasure, but she hadn't expected what she was feeling now.

The front clip of her bra was released, the lace was peeled away from the swollen mounds. Marty's head tipped back on her shoulders as Khalid supported her, held her against his chest and stared down at the fingers brushing over, against, around her breasts.

The window between the front and back had been raised. She didn't know when he had done it; she didn't care.

They didn't undress her, though she felt as though the material of her clothes were too rough against her sensitive flesh. Heat burned her bared flesh as the tips of calloused male fingers rasped against it gently.

"I want to watch," Khalid whispered against her ear. "I want to see your pleasure, Marty. I want to see the hunger in your eyes. I want to watch your face flush with pleasure."

The overwhelming desire, the need, roughened his voice and sped through her own system like a wildfire racing out of control.

Her eyes opened as she felt his arm brace the back of her neck, lifting her head to meet his gaze. She felt too drowsy, too inundated with the exquisite pleasure tearing through her to protest anything he wanted at the moment. Perhaps not at a later moment, either.

She didn't pretend to understand the need the men of the club had to share their women. At the moment, she didn't care. At the moment the pleasure racing through her was all that mattered.

"So pretty," he whispered, his gaze moving from her face to where Shayne was caressing her breasts. His palms cupped the swollen mounds, his thumbs rubbing over them as Khalid leaned back and shifted her body until she was facing Shayne.

He leaned forward, his dark blue gaze heavy-lidded, his cheekbones flushed with lust as he watched Khalid's palm curve around the side of her breast, lifting the tight, hard nipple to him as though in invitation.

A whimper left her lips as Shayne's head lowered. Her hands

clutched at the outside of Khalid's thighs, and her head fell back against his shoulder as Shayne's lips covered the ultrasensitive peak of her breast.

Heated moisture surrounded her nipple as Shayne sucked it into his mouth, drawing on it, his tongue flickering over it with wicked intent as Khalid drew her arms up and back until she curled them around his neck.

The taut arc of her body seemed to make her nipples more sensitive, as though it stretched the nerve endings, revealing more of them for Shayne to torture with the sensual licks of his devilish tongue.

"Feel good?" Khalid's lips brushed against her neck as a hoarse cry tore from her throat.

"Khalid, please . . ." Each heated draw of Shayne's mouth sent sizzling sensations down the neural pathway from her nipple to her clit. She swore she could feel each lick of his tongue on the tight, hard knot of nerve endings between her thighs.

"Oh, I intend to please you, baby." His teeth raked against her neck. "Shayne and I both intend to please you all over."

All over. She was shaking, trembling with pleasure as she tried to arch closer, to bury her nipple deeper into Shayne's mouth as he sucked at it hungrily.

"Damn, that's pretty," he breathed, his voice rough with hunger as a hand curled around her other breast and fingers began to pluck at the hard peak.

She tried to writhe against his lap, the feel of the heated length of his cock pressing against his slacks had her pussy throbbing and spilling her juices into her panties.

When Shayne drew back, she watched in an agony of need as he slowly drew the cups of her bra back over her breasts and fixed the latch.

His gaze locked on hers, he drew the edges of her shirt together and buttoned them.

Marty fought to breathe, the act of having Shayne redress her as

Khalid held her in place was almost as erotic as being undressed by them.

"We're home," Khalid told her softly, as the last button was pushed through its hole.

The limousine came to a stop in front of the house as Khalid let his lips caress the sensitive flesh just beneath her ear.

She wanted to scream out at the intrusion of reality. She wanted to order Abdul to keep driving, to stay in the car, to give her just a few more moments of a pleasure that she hadn't imagined could be so exquisite.

She wanted just a few more minutes in their arms.

14

Khalid had promised himself years ago that he would never allow himself to love a woman—not that true, undying love that could destroy a man when his woman was gone, as it had destroyed Abram. As they neared the house, though, he was beginning to wonder if he hadn't broken that rule without even knowing when or how it had happened.

The thought of losing Marty left him in a cold sweat. The thought of what his brothers would have done to her if their hired killer had managed to take her left his guts cramped with fear.

Sitting on his lap in the limo, she had been the most beautiful woman in the world. Locked in pleasure, her lithe, slender body arching, reaching for more. She had nearly had him coming in his jeans.

As they stepped from the limo he watched as she blinked, trying to force her mind to clear, her senses to steady. He knew almost the moment she managed to reenter reality. And if the thoughtful, suddenly contemplative look on her face was any indication as they started up the steps to the front door, then she was coming up with more questions already.

"Tell me, is Anger Thornton a part of the club?"

Of all the questions he had expected her to ask, that wasn't the one he would have expected.

"You know I can't answer that one." He almost grinned at the narrow-eyed ire that filled her gaze.

"You know, the members of that damned club make it rather hard on their women" she muttered.

"I never promised it would be easy."

It wasn't easy. Few things in his life had ever been, though, he could assure her, any problems with the club would be minor in comparison to others.

She turned her gaze to Shayne. "You'll need to coordinate with my fathers. We'll need several teams conducting surveillance and watching the Saudi guests that attend to see if any of them meet with Ayid or appear to be acting for them."

"You think I want your fathers screaming at me over this?" Shayne lifted a brow mockingly. "Not hardly."

"Call him, Shayne," she ordered firmly. "Trust me, they'll scream at me louder, and then I'll just get mad, and then I'll be stressed out when we arrive at the party."

Shayne grinned as Khalid shot him a warning glance. Neither of them wanted her fathers screaming at her.

"I'll call." Shayne finally chuckled as they paused at the landing. "But I'm not promising they'll listen to me, any more than they would listen to you."

They would listen to Marty much quicker, Khalid knew, but she was still uncertain of her ground with her fathers at this point. The previous anger, and deceptions on their part, had left her wary where they were concerned for the moment.

As the heavy doors opened and the butler stepped aside, Khalid entered the house, his hand settling against Marty's lower back.

"Come to my suite," he told Shayne, as he turned up the stairs, urging Marty ahead of him. "I'd like to discuss the Thornton party."

He really had nothing to discuss where the party was concerned until later tomorrow. But sometimes a woman had more gentle sensibilities than they let on.

"I rather doubt you would get along well with AT." Marty sighed with amusement as she used Anger's nickname. "He doesn't normally like men as arrogant as he is."

"There's someone as arrogant as Anger?" Shayne snorted as they reach the landing. "Somehow, I rather doubt it."

There was an air of casual rivalry between them, but Khalid was aware they both had their hands close to their weapons as they moved to the suite.

Shayne opened the door and went in first. As Marty started to slide in behind him, Khalid pulled her to him, then very neatly slid her behind his broader form.

Those few seconds gave him an edge in case there was trouble inside the room.

Pushing past him, Marty shot him a hard glare before following Shayne and quickly checking the room. After locking the door, Khalid watched as the two secured the room, and then checked for any listening devices before Shayne turned on the stereo and allowed the sultry, sexually heavy strains of music to filter through.

This was his life, thought Khalid. It had been his life for far too many years, and he was growing tired of it. The secrecy, ensuring no one knew if he had his own lover, taking care to simply never care.

Turning to the bar, he poured drinks for them all before picking up his and Marty's and moving toward her.

"Let's sit." Indicating the seating arrangement in the center of the room, Khalid moved past her.

There was no doubt she would follow. She was much too curious for her own good sometimes.

As she took a seat in the chair facing him, rather than on the couch next to him, Khalid had to restrain a smile. There were times when her innocence reminded him a great deal of Lessa, in a faraway time, a faraway country, the young woman who had entranced him and Abram.

Lessa had had that same sense of excitement, bravery, and courage. Marty's was better honed, her sense of caution more developed,
and her passion deeper, hotter. But that familiarity was still there.

She terrified him at times with the courage. She was a trained
agent, he understood that, but she was also his woman, a woman he
had to trust to know her own boundaries and her safety. And he had
to ignore that little voice in his head that warned him that there
were law enforcement officers with the same training and the same
boundaries who died every day.

Sighing, he stared at her. "I'm sorry, little flower," he said, as
Shayne took his seat on the matching sofa to the side of Khalid's.

"Why?" She was watching him with that caution now, as though
deciding if she'd let him live another day.

"For the protective impulses that will always irritate you," he
finally stated. "They are a part of my nature, though I do attempt to
rein them in whenever possible."

Her gray eyes darkened before her lashes lowered for a second, as
though to give herself a chance to hide her emotions.

"It would help if he hadn't been trying to find ways to protect
you for the past eight years or so," Shayne drawled, drawing Marty's
surprised glance. "Khalid doesn't trust fate overly much."

"I don't need his protection, or yours," she told them both flatly,
as she stared back at them.

Frustration ate at her. Khalid could see it in her eyes. She needed
to follow her dreams no matter the inherent danger she faced.

"This is insane." Rising to her feet, she paced several feet from
them before turning and glaring at them. "You've been focused on
me since I was eighteen years old, and yet you couldn't let me know.
You had to wait until I was assigned to investigate you? For God's
sake, this is like the night from hell. What other little secrets are you
keeping from me?"

He could hear the hurt in her voice. The attraction had been
there between them, even when she was younger, but not the matu-
rity she needed to handle his desires.

"You needed to mature," he answered softly. "You were simply too young for what I needed from you, Marty. Too young and too innocent."

Instantly, as though his words struck fire to a fuse, sexuality flamed through the room. Lust began to beat in his veins as he watched her eyes darken, her face flush. She knew, and she wanted.

"You're dying to share me," she stated, her voice husky, sweetly aroused.

"I want it more than my next breath," he revealed, though a part of him regretted the pain that it might cause her.

"Have I been protesting?" she whispered, her voice filled with arousal now.

"There have been no protests," Khalid assured her then, his voice soft as she stared at him.

Khalid knew that Shayne was convinced that Marty was in love with him. He'd warned Khalid on many occasions of the hazards of breaking her heart.

"None whatsoever," she promised before moving slowly, easily, toward Shayne.

Khalid watched as she moved, the determination that flared in her eyes, the excitement and energy that seemed to flow from her body. She was going to test herself as well as the two of them, he could see it in her face.

"Beware, love," Khalid warned her, watching as Shayne rose from the sofa. "You could tease too far."

She moved against the other man anyway, brushing her sweet, lithe body against his side.

"Really?" The temptress began to emerge.

Khalid felt his dick harden painfully, his balls tightening in pure white-hot lust.

"Shall we see what your limit is, then?" she asked as she moved back from Shayne, watching them as they watched her, her body moving sinuously to the music echoing through the room.

As he watched, her hands lifted, her fingers moved to the buttons of her blouse, and his mouth went dry. Sweet God have mercy on him. The acceptance suddenly filling her face nearly had him coming in his slacks.

Rising to his feet, Khalid paused, waiting, as Shayne moved, striding to her, his fingers sliding into her soft hair as the blouse dropped from her shoulders. Fisting his hand in the silken strands he pulled her head back and lowered his own.

Khalid watched as Shayne's lips moved over Marty's. As though electricity connected them all, Khalid felt the tingle of pleasure, the tearing hunger, and the demand for more.

Moving to the couple, Khalid came behind Marty, his hands touching her shoulders as the muscles there tensed, seeming to tighten to near the breaking point.

Hearing the broken moan that escaped the demanding kiss Shayne held her with, Khalid unhooked the clasp of the lacy bra she wore before edging the straps over her shoulders.

Shayne's hands gripped her wrists, lowering her arms from his shoulders as Khalid stripped her of the fragile garment.

"Khalid." She jerked back from the kiss, panting as Shayne turned her to Khalid.

Shayne lowered his head to her neck, the curve of her shoulder. His hands slipped around her body to cup her breasts, his fingers toying with her tight nipples as Khalid sank slowly to his knees.

He held her gaze, watching her eyes darken, her breathing roughen, as he removed her sneakers and socks. His hands lifted to the clasp of her jeans, the zipper, and as a muted cry echoed around him, he drew the material slowly from her hips.

She was wet. He could see the sweet dew clinging to the soft curls shielding her pussy and had to force himself to hold back from her. No woman had ever made him so hot so fast. He was desperate for her. The hairs on his arms tingled with the pleasure rushing through him, the pleasure he could see on her face as his fingers caressed her inner thighs.

Forcing himself from the temptation of her heated juices, Khalid rose to his feet, cupped her neck, and held her still as his lips lowered to hers.

Kissing her burned through his senses. Her lips were like silk, her sweet tongue like satin touched with sugar. Small nails pierced his shoulders as she gripped them. His cock pressed against the soft heat of her belly, her flesh cushioning the steel-hard erection tormenting him.

Running his hands down her back, Khalid gloried in the hitch of her breath, the lick of her tongue against his as he cupped her rear and lifted her to him.

It was a short distance to the bed, but it seemed to take forever. He needed to lay her down, to see her pleasure, to see the wild excitement he could feel overtaking her.

Behind him he was distantly aware of Shayne undressing quickly. Khalid could feel his temperature rising as the air in the room became heated, sultry.

"Damn, she's pretty, Khalid." Shayne groaned behind Marty.

Lifting his head, Khalid glanced at where Shayne was kneeling in the bed, waiting, aroused.

Turning his gaze back to Marty he lifted his hand to touch her flushed cheek.

"She's beautiful," he whispered, as her tongue licked over her lips before she swallowed nervously. "No fear. There's no pain, no reason for apprehension, sweet."

"Of course there isn't." Her voice was breathless, filled with wariness and hunger as Khalid eased her to the bed and the man awaiting her.

It was incredibly sensual. There were things as erotic as standing back and watching as a woman begins drowning in her own sensuality. And Marty was drowning.

Her gaze locked with Khalid's as Shayne cupped her breasts, his head lowering to take a hardened tip into his mouth.

Khalid began undressing, desperate now to join them, to aid in stroking his lover into the pure white-hot flames of arousal. Shedding the clothing, he moved to where she lay against the pillows, kneeling beside her as he caught her wrists in his hand and pulled them above her head.

Her head thrashed against the pillow as Shayne's lips moved from her breasts, lower. He kissed, nipped, licked his way down her stomach as Khalid watched with a rising need.

Frissons of fiery sensation raced over his flesh as he felt Marty's fingers curl against his wrist. She arched in Shayne's caress, her eyes opened to mere slits as she stared up at Khalid.

He needed this. This pleasure, this incredible arousal flowing from his lover. Like a man with a sweet tooth and denied his sweets, he was starved for it.

His gaze moved from her delicate face, lower. Shayne moved between her thighs, his hands spreading them wide, his chin brushing against the wet curls between them.

Her clit was like a little pink jewel between the folds, glistening and heated. Khalid wanted to see it caressed, wanted to watch her body, feel her response.

As Shayne spread apart the plump flesh, Khalid jerked, his gaze racing back to Marty as her tongue swiped over the crest of his cock.

"Brave are you, darling?" He groaned, freeing her hands to allow her to touch as she dared. "Be careful, you may tempt too far."

He received a broken moan and the feel of her mouth enveloping the head of his dick in response.

It was like dying, he thought. This must be what dying would feel like. A sense of flying, of freedom, and the lash of the sun against his flesh as her tongue licked over the sensitive crown.

As she sucked him in, a cry tore from her throat as her body arched almost violently. Khalid tore his gaze from the sight of his cock fucking her mouth to watch as Shayne's tongue flayed the damp pearl of her clit.

"Yes, precious," he said, his voice thick. "Feel how good. Feel the pleasure we can give you, baby."

Her moan sent electric flames searing into his balls, drawing them tighter. So much pleasure. A hunger he couldn't deny. His woman finally giving in to her fantasies, her hungers.

Marty was lost. She knew she was lost and wondered distantly if she would find herself again as the sexual pleasure blistered her nerve endings.

She wanted, needed to touch, to pleasure Khalid. Needed to destroy his senses as he was allowing another man to destroy hers.

A scream tore from her throat as she felt Shayne's hands slide beneath her ass and, a second later, his tongue fucking into her pussy.

Pulsing, destructive sensations shot from her core to her soul. She couldn't process the alternate pleasures quick enough; her brain was fried in the lash of heat searing her body.

Khalid's fingers played with her nipples, caressing, rubbing, tugging at the sensitive tips. Shayne's fingers were sliding inside her pussy as his tongue returned to torture her clit, and pure, undiluted sexual hunger was burning inside her.

Adrenaline coursed through her, racing through her bloodstream like wildfire through a forest. She hadn't known it could be like this. She wasn't certain if she could survive it.

"So fucking good," Khalid moaned above her, as she sucked his cock deeper and fought to hold on to just enough control to torture him in return, in some small way. "Suck my dick, sweetheart. So hot and tight."

He was fucking her mouth slow and easy as she felt Shayne's fingers slide along her rear. They were cool, slickened heavily.

A sharp flare of knowledge rushed through her system a second before those fingers rubbed over the entrance to her rear, lubricating it, easing against it, then retreating.

She stared up at Khalid as she fought to breathe. He was watching Shayne's fingers, and Shayne was making damned certain Khalid could see as they disappeared between her thighs.

Again and again they returned, slicker, sliding more firmly against her anus as she jerked and shuddered against the sensations. She was terrified, exhilarated, and burning with lust.

"Look at me," Khalid demanded as her lashes fluttered closed. "Feel the pleasure, Marty. See it in my face. Watching your arousal is the sexiest damned thing I've ever seen."

Shayne's finger slid deep inside her ass as a cry ripped past her lips, and she arched with a sharp, jerking motion that only drove him in deeper.

"Feel him there. Your ass is so hot, Marty. So sweet and tight. The thought of sinking my cock inside it makes me crazy. The thought of fucking you while Shayne works his cock up that tight little ass has me insane with the need."

Before she could stop him he pulled back from her lips, touching them gently with his thumb before easing along her body.

"Khalid, please." She clenched her hands in the pillow at her head. "I can't stand this."

"Just a bit longer, baby." His voice was so heavy with lust that Marty felt the sound of it clear to her soul.

Just a little longer? Would she survive a little longer?

She couldn't.

She screamed as Shayne pressed two fingers inside her sensitive rear, sending scalding arcs of sensation racing, tearing through her.

She was dying. She could feel the pleasure destroying her and had no idea how to stop it. She had to have more. Needed more. Nothing mattered but the incredible ecstasy and the pure hunger in Khalid's voice.

Flames were racing through her, building, pulsing. Her orgasm was only a breath away when, suddenly, it was gone.

Her eyes flew open to stare down her body as Shayne moved. They pulled her to her side as a whimper left her throat.

This was it.

She stared back at Shayne as his lips moved to her nipples once again, sucking at them, nipping at them as she felt Khalid settle in behind her.

Shayne's head lifted, his gaze locking with hers as he moved against her, aligning his body with hers. Khalid lifted her leg, laying it over Shayne's thigh as she felt his cock nudge against the slick folds of her pussy.

"So pretty," Khalid crooned, as Shayne's hips began to move. "That sweet, tight pussy is so hot, isn't it, baby? It's so sweet, so very snug."

She was being stretched, burned. She was shaking as she felt Shayne thrusting inside her, easing into the swollen tissue between her thighs.

"So tight." Khalid's fingers moved into the cleft of her rear. "His dick has to stretch you. Does it burn, love?"

Her lashes fluttered open to stare up at Shayne as Khalid's voice washed through her.

"Fuck her easy. Slow and easy," Khalid told the other man.

Shayne pressed inside her slowly, taking her with slow, stretching strokes, and she felt her rear entrance stretching slowly as Khalid began to slide his fingers inside her. The stretching, burning impalements were too much. Marty felt her nails digging into Shayne's shoulders as a broken cry rasped in her throat.

"More." She couldn't hold it back, she couldn't fight it. She needed it all, now. "Please, Khalid. More."

A second later Shayne thrust hard and deep inside her as she felt Khalid's fingers sink inside her ass, past the tight ring of ultrasensitive muscles, to caress the nerve-laden flesh beyond.

She was ready to come. She could feel it. She clenched on Khalid's fingers, on Shayne's cock.

"Not yet," Khalid said roughly.

Shayne stilled. A second from orgasm, Shayne stopped, his thick cock buried inside her, throbbing as Khalid's fingers eased from her ass.

"Khalid, please." She tried to scream, but the sound was more a breathless moan.

"Yes, love." His lips pressed against her shoulder as she felt him spoon against her, his cock pressing into the cleft of her ass. "I'm right here."

He was right there.

The head of his cock rubbed against her anal opening as her leg was shifted, her body angled closer to Shayne's chest as she felt the head begin to stretch the tender opening.

Pleasure and pain began to race through her. It was like a narcotic, a drug that hypersensitized every nerve ending and held her in a grip of sensation that she didn't know if she could bear.

Should pain be pleasure? Should the fiery, burning sensation of his cock stretching her, opening her, sinking inside her ass have her screaming for more?

Each stretching advance of his dick inside her body sent waves of agonizing pleasure washing through her. She could feel Shayne buried inside her pussy, his cock throbbing, his body dampened and tense as Khalid worked the thick flesh of his erection inside her rear.

"More," she gasped. "Oh God, Khalid, please. Please."

Slow impalements, retreats, advances. His cock worked inside her slow and easy until finally, blessedly, she felt the length of it thrust fully inside her before he stilled.

She was filled. Taken. Possessed.

"I knew you would be so hot you'd burn me alive," Khalid whispered at her ear. "So tight and fucking hot I'd die for you."

The sudden fierce desperation in his voice had her vagina and her ass clenching around their intruders, sucking at them, and triggering a response in the men's lust that suddenly blazed out of control.

She was suddenly locked in a world that pulsed with a rainbow of color and showers of fire. Pleasure was agony, it caressed through her pussy, along her clit, inside her rear. She clenched on the throbbing erections as they thrust deep and hard inside her now.

There was no mercy, and she wanted none. They were fucking her as though they were dying for her, as though she would die without it. And she just might.

With each burning impalement she could feel the ecstasy building. It rose inside her like a tidal wave, surging, encompassing her senses until she felt herself exploding like a star burning out of control.

She screamed at the rapture. She shook, shuddered. Sensation whipped through her like a sharp-edged dagger raking over her nerve endings and burning through her flesh.

She was only barely aware of Shayne's groans; it was Khalid's voice at her ear that she heard as she felt him pumping inside her ass, his cock hot and throbbing a second before he moaned her name and stiffened against her.

She hadn't realized they'd sheathed themselves with condoms. She felt their release, heard their pleasure, but the wash of wet heat was absent.

In that second she realized how far she had slipped into this pleasure, and just how addictive and destructive it was. Destructive enough that she had forgotten to protect herself. Addictive enough that she was terrified now that it was a pleasure she would always ache for.

15

The sleepy, irritated grumble Marty gave as Khalid finished cleaning her with a damp cloth brought a smile to his face.

She hadn't jumped from the bed the second they'd finished in order to shower. She'd mumbled something about sleeping an hour, then immediately drifted off to sleep.

Sitting next to her on the bed, dressed in the slacks he had worn earlier that evening, he brushed a strand of silken hair back from her face and fought the impulse to hold her to him in a grip no man would ever be able to break.

He was aware of Shayne as he stood by the opposite side of the bed and watched thoughtfully. Sometimes Shayne thought too much, Khalid mused. He was always looking for angles, always searching for answers and solutions. Sometimes there simply was no solution.

"Who knew she could burn us alive like that?" Shayne finally spoke, his voice reflective. "I think she exhausted me."

Khalid ran his fingers along the slope of her jaw.

"I knew." Khalid had always known exactly what she would do to his senses. She filled them. She burned through his mind to his soul and left her imprint in a way he knew he would never be free of.

"You love her," Shayne remarked.

Khalid remained silent. He couldn't allow himself to love her, but neither could he find the voice to deny the statement. She was important to him, he assured himself. She was a part of him. That didn't mean it was love; it simply meant he was very very good at lying to himself, perhaps.

"She's not Lessa, Khalid. Marty can protect herself. She knows what she's doing."

Khalid's jaw clenched at the statement. "I know this." But a part of him couldn't forget the past or the lessons learned from it.

A heavy sigh sounded from the other man, as though he had run out of arguments or explanations. Shayne had argued for years that Marty was more than mature enough to handle the hungers that tormented Khalid. He'd urged Khalid on more than one occasion to secure her to him before another man did.

Staying away from her had been nearly impossible at times.

"I'm heading to bed," Shayne finally announced, when Khalid said nothing more. "We'll have this taken care of, Khalid, one way or the other."

Something would have to be done about his brothers soon. Khalid had just enough suspicions that Marty's boss was working with the brothers determined to destroy him, that Deerfield was risking his life at Khalid's hands. They had dared to try and harm Marty now; if Joe Mathews and Zach Jennings didn't finish this soon, then Khalid would be forced to do so.

Tightening his jaw at the thought of that, he rose from the bed, pulled the blankets over his sleeping lover, and paced to the shower.

After stripping again, he adjusted the water in the large shower, and then stepped inside.

Liquid warmth caressed his flesh, reminding him of Marty's touch, of the sweet velvet rain of her release. She truly had burned them alive. He could feel the blisters on his soul already.

Even Lessa hadn't burned so sweet, so bright.

That thought had him grimacing as it sent a surge of guilt tearing through his gut. Lessa had been filled with laughter, with life. She had touched him with her laughing dark eyes and heady passion, but she hadn't been able to touch that inner man, the part of him that Marty seemed to fill.

Lessa had loved him. She had loved him and Abram with everything inside her, and that love had gotten her killed.

Those years in the desert with his father had turned into a nightmare, Khalid acknowledged. Sweet Lessa. She had been Abram's first wife. She had been his first love, and he had shared that love with Khalid.

Khalid had known for years of the dark desires that raged inside his brother. It was impossible not to know of them when their father berated him often for them. Still, in the darkness of the night, away from prying eyes, Abram often gave in to those hungers himself, and he invited Khalid to share in the warmth.

Those desires had nearly destroyed Abram and Khalid in the end, though. With their father's help, the evil of their brothers had struck with terrifying, unexpected force and left them reeling with shock.

Khalid had been drugged, kidnapped, beaten, and left for dead in the desert his father so loved, as Abram had been sent to oversee the return of his brothers' dead bodies. Brothers who hadn't died. For three days Khalid had struggled to make his way back to his father's palace. A broken rib, bone-deep bruises, and dehydration had sapped his strength. He wouldn't have lived if it hadn't been for Shayne searching for him.

Khalid returned to his father's palace certain that justice would be dealt to the men who had dared to strike against the sheikh's youngest son, only to learn that it had been the brothers who had struck him. They had learned of his deception, his betrayal, and they had struck back at Khalid and what they believed was his ungodly affair with his brother Abram's wife.

Khalid leaned his head against the shower stall, reliving the memory. Stumbling into the palace, he'd heard Abram screaming, enraged. Ignoring the servants, Khalid had pushed his way into his father's suite to hear the damning words that had torn from Abram's lips.

"You bastard, you let them kill her!"

Abram's face was damp. The stoic, often cold heir to the minor throne had shed tears.

"A whore. A blight to your life!" his father screamed back at Abram. "She is better off dead, just as you are better off without the blight she brought to your soul. She let your brother touch her. She allowed another to desecrate the garden you tended."

Khalid stared at them in horror. Abram swung around as Azir Mustafa had realized what he had said at the second Khalid stumbled into the room.

"Lessa," Khalid whispered, staring at Abram, praying he'd heard wrong. Praying she was safe.

"They killed her," Abram snarled, his dark eyes burning with such livid rage that Khalid backed away from him. "That bastard let them kill her."

Abram stalked out of the room, swearing he'd kill them with his bare hands. As the large doors slammed behind him, Azir sighed wearily, as though dealing with a child's temper.

"He won't find them," he finally said, shrugging. "They will not return until he has regained his senses. It is regrettable, but the girl brought it on herself with her unholy desires." He had glared at Khalid. "Such women do not deserve the lives they are given."

To this day, that memory was so vivid, so clear in his head. The scent of sandalwood, the breeze that blew through the opened windows. His father's bronzed features twisted into a scowl, his black eyes burning in fanatical judgment.

Something had died inside Khalid that day. He remembered staring at the man who had helped create him and thinking that monsters truly did exist in the world.

Azir's gaze had flickered over him then, as though only then realizing that Khalid had been harmed. A frown had formed between his brows as he reached out for his son. Khalid had flinched, turned, and left. His broken rib had been no more than an ache. The pain in his soul had shattered him.

He'd showered, changed clothes, then stolen a vehicle from the palace garage and driven himself the distance to Riyadh, where he'd called his mother in America. She'd arranged his return. She'd been waiting for him after he'd healed enough to fly, and had tried to heal the wounds his soul had been inflicted with.

Khalid had tried to put the past behind him; he'd put his father behind him and disowned the bastard as well as the half brothers who had never known a moment's punishment for what they had done to Lessa.

Abram had taken care of her body. He'd had her cleaned, dressed, and buried as his faithful wife. He had gone to her funeral, and as he had written Khalid not long after, he had buried his soul with her.

It should have been over. His ties to the desert and the family he hated above all things should have been severed. They had been, until the suspicious death of Abram's second wife and unborn child.

Ayid and Aman were determined to ensure that Abram and Khalid paid for the deaths of the women they called wives, the desert vipers who had been as merciless, as vicious as their husbands could ever hope to be. But even more they wanted vengeance for the loss of respect and the money Khalid had cost them each time he managed to track down and destroy one of the terrorist cells his brothers controlled.

After finishing his shower, Khalid dried himself, and then padded naked back to the bed. Marty was still sleeping peacefully in the same position he had left her in. Curled in the middle of his large bed, she looked much too small, too fragile to be the lover she had been such a short time ago.

Lifting the sheet, he eased into bed beside her. His heart clenched as she shifted, moaning a little before turning and rolling into his arms.

She fit against his body perfectly. Her head rested at his heart, her slender legs entwined with his. She was a warm, precious weight, one he feared for more than he wanted to admit.

He would protect her, he promised himself. Her fathers were watching out for her, as was Shayne. He wasn't alone in protecting her and, unlike with Lessa, he knew the danger was there. He wouldn't lose her to them. They wouldn't take this woman and the life he had built for himself in the past ten years. He would kill them before he allowed it.

His brothers had marked themselves when they had struck at her. He wouldn't rest now; he would never lower his guard or his determination to destroy them. If he had to destroy the throne to destroy them, then he would do so. Abram had better prepare himself, and he had better bring his part to the table quickly. Because Khalid wasn't playing anymore.

16

After Shayne's early morning meeting with her fathers the next day, Marty typed up her resignation, dotted all the i's and crossed her t's, ensured that the proper wording was there, then handed it to her godfather after his meeting with Shayne.

Zach's expression had been quiet before he stared back at her, his gaze flashing with sorrow and regret before he gave her a sharp nod and turned away.

There was nothing left to do then but turn in the letter to her boss. The protocol irked her. Deerfield was an irritation she would have preferred not to deal with right now. The moment Marty walked into Deerfield's office, she knew she should have just stayed in Khalid's bed that morning.

Deerfield had shed his jacket and tie. His sleeves were rolled up and his hair was standing on end, as though he had plowed his fingers through it countless times. Hazel-green eyes stared at her with a hint of censure and brooding disgust as she stepped to his desk and laid the resignation on it.

"I'll consider the rest of my vacation as advance notice of my intent to resign," she stated, as she stared back at him with chilling regard. "I won't be returning."

"Sit down," he ordered, his tone calm but steely with a muted fury.

Taking a seat, Marty watched him warily, wondering at the flush on his pale face and the glitter in his eyes. She could almost swear he had been drinking.

"Went running to Daddy, didn't you, Agent Mathews. And here, according to our last meeting, you hadn't done that since you were a child."

Her chin lifted at the insult.

"The harassment in this office has gone beyond acceptable boundaries," she said, as she crossed her legs and placed her hands confidently in her lap. "Your agents are on edge and your office is filled with backbiting political backstabbers, with the majority of them fighting to gain your acceptance and the support they need to do their jobs. I refuse to continue to work in such an atmosphere of complete disrespect and disregard for the laws we're to uphold."

He sneered back at her as he lifted the paper and glared at it again for a long moment.

Finally, Deerfield leaned back in his chair and simply watched her contemptuously.

"I'm certain you're aware this office is now under investigation," he stated. "Your godfather, our esteemed director, has decided he doesn't like how it's being run. I have no doubt you weren't behind the information he's received."

Marty shook her head and let a small, mocking smile tilt her lips. "I was unaware of his plans until I began my vacation and learned of it," she assured him, though she really hoped he didn't believe her. "Any decisions he made, he made without my input. But I don't disagree with it."

"You and your father are a plague." His lips pulled back from his teeth in a display of primal fury. "Neither of you want to accept that we're not safe. That the country our agents die to protect is under attack, and that Khalid is a part of the disease moving into it."

Marty sat silently; she wasn't arguing Khalid's innocence any further. Her last report stated all she had left to say about it.

"Your resignation." He sat back in his chair once more as flicked his fingers toward the paper still lying on his desk. "I'll file it. Collect your belongings and get the hell out of here. But when you're staring into that monster's eyes facing your own death, don't say I didn't tell you so."

Marty moved to rise from her seat.

"Agent Mathews." Leaning forward, Deerfield had her sitting back slowly in her seat. "The attack against you last week ties directly back to the Mustaffa family. Are you aware of that? He's ready to rid himself of you and you can't even see it."

Marty didn't speak. She stared back at him silently, following her godfather's advice to allow him to dig his own hole to see how deep he was involved in this.

"If his family doesn't kill you, others will. Mustafa has enemies." He grimaced as, she suspected, he realized she cared very little for whatever he had to say. "Those enemies will kill you, simply because you're associated with him."

"I've known Khalid most of my life." A small, knowing smile tipped her lips. "I've followed him for the past two years, and I know things about his life that I'm certain even he is unaware of. I believe by now I know exactly the man this Bureau has been harassing."

"Harassing?" His voice sharpened angrily as he leaned forward. "This fucking office doesn't harass anyone. We are investigators, Agent Mathews. We are all that is standing between the evil of this world and the country we are sworn to protect, this United States of America," he yelled back at her. "That son of a bitch has never known what it is to suffer. To fight to rise above poverty or to fight for justice. He doesn't know any fucking thing but the silver spoon shoved up his ass when he was born."

Perspiration popped out on his forehead as his face flushed a dark, ruddy red. Anger sparked in his gaze and his lips pulled tight as he glared at her while she refused to speak.

She sat calmly, though she allowed the contempt to reflect in her face. It was better not to argue with him. At this point, it would be much more productive to allow his paranoia to build instead.

"Get the fuck out of here," he snarled, when she said nothing. "I hope you sleep well at night." His hand brushed the paper violently to the side of his desk.

She was dismissed that easily. Contempt glittered in Deerfield's gaze, as did an edge of fear.

Rising to her feet, Marty moved to the door.

"He's nothing but a fucking disease and you don't want to see it," he told her as she gripped the doorknob."

"If he's such a monster, then his enemies would already be taken care of, wouldn't they?" she asked him. "Khalid is innocent, Deerfield. You simply refuse to accept it."

She didn't give him time to reply. Pulling the doorknob, she left the office quickly and strode past the secretary watching her suspiciously as she left.

The office was filled with suspicion and plots. Everyone watched everyone else with the knowledge that a meeting with Deerfield could signify yet another spate of harassment or suspicion of their character or their investigations.

No one was safe here when it came to having their character sliced and diced.

While entering the elevator, Marty clenched her teeth to hold back the curse trembling on her tongue. Damn Deerfield. The bastard made her want to rake his eyes out. He was condescending, superior, and completely neurotic. She had never been so certain of her decision to resign as she was at this moment.

After leaving the elevator, Marty walked quickly through the exit to the outside parking lot. Sunlight speared through the shelter of trees that filled the barriers between each section and lent a measure of shade to the overly warm day.

Stepping to the curb, she waited as the limo came to a stop in front of her. Stepping quickly from the driver's side, Abdul rushed around the vehicle and opened the door for her with a flourish.

Marty slipped inside where Khalid and Shayne waited silently, their gazes on her.

"I can see a pleasant time has been had within the offices of the Federal Bureau of Investigation," Khalid drawled knowingly. "Is Deerfield still living or should I start purchasing alibis and having federal surveillance videos acquired?"

He sounded much too certain that he could do exactly that, and in her experience, given enough money, most anything could be accomplished.

"He's still alive," she breathed out roughly as she pushed her fingers through her hair. Anger still washed from her in waves, instilling a heated tension in the air that had Marty's nerve endings suddenly more sensitive than they should have been.

Or perhaps it was simply the fact that the two men were in the back of the limo together. After the past night, she found herself too aware of them, too aware of herself. It hadn't been a problem after she had left the limo earlier to enter the federal building. That sensitivity had evaporated as though it had never been present. The moment she stepped back into the limo, though, it had increased in strength and depth.

"He's riding a fine line." Marty swallowed tightly as she tried to ignore the sexual intensity wrapping around her. "He's been riding it for a while. And that's a shame, because he was once a well-respected agent. He should have never been promoted to bureau chief."

"Having me branded as a traitor and locked away would make it much easier for my brothers to get to me." Khalid shrugged. "It would also implicate Abram and almost assure his execution. I feel no sympathy for him, love, and neither should you."

"I don't feel sympathy for him," she sighed heavily. "Just for the agents working under him."

"Agreed." He nodded at her. "And it's something Zach will be taking care of with the investigation he started. Deerfield ruined his own career when he targeted you as he did."

Khalid moved to sit beside her, his hand lifting and curling around the back of her neck to stroke the sensitive flesh there gently.

The stroke of his calloused fingertips over her skin sent a shiver racing down her back. She was still sensitive, not sore exactly, but the flesh between her thighs knew it had been thoroughly ridden the night before.

The thought of it had her thighs clenching, as a sudden wave of heat flushed through her body. She could feel her pussy becoming sensitive, swollen, needy.

Breathing in deeply, her gaze lifted, suddenly becoming locked with Shayne's.

"Shayne becomes very wired when he allows his anger free," Khalid stated, as Marty felt her heart begin to race. "He's furious that you had to go into Deerfield's office and be subjected to his abuse alone."

"I can handle Deerfield." She had to force the words past her lips. "And I'm not a toy to relieve the stress with." She shot Khalid a challenging look, knowing what it would do to his lust. She wanted to be their toy, just for a little while. A favorite toy. A much loved toy.

"I'll be your toy," Shayne said, as she felt Khalid's hand move to her side, his fingers bunching in the material of her T-shirt to begin lifting it.

"Allow me to see how gently he would play with your perfect body, precious," Khalid crooned, his dark voice filled with lust now.

She couldn't breathe. Her chest felt constricted as Khalid shifted her, lifting her to his lap as he pulled the shirt from her body.

She shouldn't allow this. Oh God, she was melting right there for them, allowing them to do whatever the hell they wanted to do, as though she were the toy she had said she wouldn't be.

She had to admit, though, the thought of how wicked he could be in the back of the limo was burning through her now.

"We have several hours before we arrive at my mother's estate to ensure my family's protected," Khalid whispered against her ear, as Shayne released the catch of her bra and spread the lace from her breasts. "How many different ways could we make you come?"

A lot, she was betting.

"I want your ass this time." Shayne cupped her breasts as she stared back at him, dazed. "I want to watch my cock stretch you, watch you take me as you scream for more."

She whimpered. Her pussy was so wet she swore she was soaking her jeans.

It didn't take long to undress her, then themselves. Within minutes the back of the limo was steamy with sexual tension as Shayne lifted her to his knees, spread her thighs, and ran his fingers through the generous wealth of juices gathered between the folds of her pussy.

She only had eyes for Khalid now. One broad hand curved around the base of his cock before he stroked upward, caressing himself as he watched Shayne's fingers find her clit.

Marty flinched at the wave of excessive pleasure washing through her as she watched the thick width of his jutting erection and remembered the feel of it in her mouth.

"Such a sweet wet pussy," Khalid murmured, as he nodded to Shayne.

A second later Shayne slid back into the corner of the seat, leaning back and pulling Marty against his chest as his knees held her thighs spread wide.

Khalid reached out, his fingers sliding through her thick juices as Shayne's fingers began to torment her nipples.

Khalid parted the folds, rubbed against her clit, then slid lower to find the clenched entrance to her vagina.

"Oh God!" she screamed a second later as he plunged two fingers deep inside her and began stroking, fucking inside her with dominant, powerful thrusts.

"Come for me," he said roughly, his black eyes blazing with lust now.

Marty shuddered, her hips trying to move with the plunging force of his fingers as she felt her body flying closer to orgasm.

"Fuck my fingers back, baby." He was powerful now, demanding. "Take it like you'll take my cock. All of it, Marty. Give it to me, baby." His fingers reached deep inside her, stroking beneath her clit, sending her exploding with such sudden force that she could do nothing but let it have her.

She felt her juices soaking his fingers, her orgasm ripping through her and spinning her into a velvet sea of sensation.

"Sweet baby." His fingers eased from her as he knelt to the floor between the seats. "Let's see if you can come another way. With my tongue fucking that sweet little pussy and my fingers buried up your tight ass. I want you ready, precious. When Shayne leans over you and sinks inside that special little place, I want you ready."

The image he planted in her mind was too much: bent over, Shayne taking her from behind. She nearly came from the force of the response as she felt Khalid's lubricated fingers easing into the cleft.

This time, he was slow and easy.

His tongue licked through her folds, circled her clit, and then sucked it gently into his mouth as his fingertip pierced her anus.

"You're shaking, Marty," Shayne whispered at her neck, his lips pressing against her flesh. "Does it feel good, baby? I know what he's tasting. The sweetest pussy I've ever laid my lips on."

Marty jerked in their grip, crying out as Khalid whispered a moan against her clit. Another finger joined the first, pierced her anus, then sank inside the nerve-laden entrance.

"Is your pretty ass tender?" Shayne's fingers tugged at her nipples. "I felt him riding you, his dick plunging in as I fucked your pretty pussy."

She shook her head. She couldn't talk. She arched to Khalid's mouth, his tongue, the fingers moving inside her, stretching her.

She couldn't hold on like this. With each retreat Khalid slicked his fingers again, then penetrated again. She could feel her muscles sucking his fingers in, eager for more.

Eager for Shayne's cock. She wanted more—the burning, agonizing pleasure that sent a razor-sharp edge of ecstasy tearing through her.

Khalid's tongue plunged inside her pussy as his fingers thrust inside her again. She was going to come. He was licking inside her, fucking her with his tongue, spearing into the tight muscles, and flickering over them with loving, demanding licks.

When it hit, she couldn't breathe. Her orgasm shook through her, powerful, blinding, as she felt Khalid's fingers sink deeper inside her ass.

She couldn't handle it. It was too much. She was whimpering with the ecstasy pouring through her now.

As the waves of painful pleasure eased, her lashes drifted open. Khalid was watching her, stroking his cock, his black eyes demon bright.

"Ride his cock," he whispered. "Take it up that sweet, tight little ass while I watch. Let me see your face, Marty. I want to watch as you allow him to stretch you, to take you in this way."

She was, for that moment, more than willing to do anything he asked. Shaky, whimpering with the intensity of the wicked pleasure tearing through her, she let Shayne lift her so he could sheath his erection in a condom. Kneeling above him, she felt his hand wrap around the base of his cock before he brought it in line and tucked it against the too tight entrance Khalid had prepared before drawing her back against his chest.

She watched Khalid's face. Bracing her back against Shayne's chest as he held his erection steady, she pressed down on the thick width invading her.

Khalid's gaze flared. His fingers tightened on his cock as he watched her take the impalement, watched as her tender flesh stretched, burned.

"Khalid!" Her head ground against the chest behind her as she felt the agonizing pleasure blooming through her rear, spreading to her pussy.

"Beautiful," Khalid groaned. "Take it, precious. Take him inside you. All of it, baby."

Shayne's hips arched as his hands gripped her hips, holding her in place. Each shallow thrust took him deeper, spread her farther as she fought to clench on the impalement.

"Khalid, I can't . . ."

She couldn't take any more. She couldn't bear the sensations.

"You can," he crooned, as his hands gripped her ankles, drawing them up until her feet rested on Shayne's knees. Shayne's cock slipped in farther, spearing inside her with a burning thrust that had her screaming and fighting the hands holding her hips.

She was gasping, shuddering, as waves of intense sensation raked over her nerve endings and filled her senses.

"Fuck, hurry Shayne," Khalid said, panting. "Let me see you fuck her. I won't last much longer."

She was dying with the sensuality, the white-hot lust and burning need wrapping around her.

Shayne did as he was bid. His hands tightened on her hips as he began to fuck her, drawing back then sinking inside her rear with careful, deep strokes that had waves of piercing sensation tearing through her.

"Marty, baby." Khalid moved closer, a grimace of agony on his face as he tucked his cock against the folds of her pussy, as Shayne stilled. "Sweet baby. Tell me if it's too much." He began to stretch her, pushing apart the tender folds and easing into the clenched entrance as Shayne stilled behind her, still filling her ass, stretching her as Khalid began to penetrate an entrance that seemed already filled to overflowing.

Marty reached for him, her hands gripping his shoulders as the broad crest pierced the entrance to her pussy and sent pure, painful ecstasy racing through her.

It didn't hurt, yet it was agony. She was burning, freezing. With each shift of his hips, each additional inch pushing inside her overly tight vagina, she was clenching harder on him, crying out in an agony that was pure rapture.

She had never imagined this. A pleasure that bordered pain. An agony that was a wash of pure ecstasy. Sandwiched between their hard bodies, pierced by their thick, heavy erections, Marty felt purely female. At their mercy. An integral part of them, and their pleasure.

She had called herself a toy, and she had demeaned what she felt at the moment both men filled her. She felt powerful, and yet submissive. She was their pleasure, just as they were hers. They were entwined, connected through more than just the flesh.

Holding Khalid's gaze she saw something in his eyes she had never seen before, as he thrust his erection to the hilt inside her. Here he was at peace. Here, wrapped in the pleasure she gave him, he was more than just a man. He was her man. And for these moments, she knew she held him body and soul.

"So tight." His lips lowering to hers as she fought to adjust to the heavy presence of the two cocks penetrating her. "Sweet Marty. So tight, it's agony."

Yet he was moving. Slowly. They were both moving inside her. Each thrust in, out, pushing in deep, then pulling back, drove her higher, sent her flying further into the dark, sensual depths of this adventure she realized she had nearly missed.

Her body was hypersensitive, each thrust shafting inside her had her gasping, crying. Her nails dug into Khalid's shoulders, her head ground against Shayne's chest.

"Marty." Khalid's voice was ragged, desperate. "God, baby. I can't hold on."

Leaning back, his head also fell back as his hips began to move harder, faster. They moved in time, retreat and thrust, fucking into her and pulling back, their thrusts increasing, speeding up until she was screaming, trying to scream, gasping for air, and then exploding in such sensory overload that she wondered if she would survive it.

Shayne was coming. She felt him tightening, heard his groan

behind her and the powerful throb of his cock up her ass. A second later her eyes flared open, her gaze locking with Khalid's as he spurted his release inside her.

This wasn't the first time. With the first fiery blast of his seed inside, her pussy tightened around him further and her body shook in another orgasm that left her spinning out of control. Each heavy throb of his cock sent another pulsing wave of heated warmth inside her and another explosion of intensity.

She couldn't survive this much pleasure, she thought. She couldn't survive if she lost this pleasure, and that thought sent a wave of fear rushing through her.

Khalid's pleasure affected her own. His need, his hunger, his very touch and the knowledge of his desires fueled her own fantasies.

That made her weak. It made her want to give; it made her hungry for more. And she was terrified that Khalid had nothing more to give than this. His body, his desires, his hunger, and more pleasure than she had ever imagined could exist.

What would she do if she ever lost that?

Holding on to him now as he lifted her from Shayne and eased her into his lap as he sat on the opposite seat, Marty tried to tell herself she would be okay when it was over. All things come to an end, she reminded herself. At least for her.

"Come here, precious." His voice was a velvet croon as he lifted her chin and touched her lips with his. The kiss was gentle, easing. It sent an easy feeling of warmth through her soul and almost settled the painful thoughts filling her head.

"You make me breathless," he whispered against her lips. "You steal my control when no other has ever managed to do so."

Her lashes lifted to stare into his sexually sated expression. Nothing had ever been so damned sexy as Khalid sexually sated.

"What the hell am I going to do about you?" she whispered then, her hand lifting to stroke his rough jaw as a small smile tugged at his sexy lips.

"Take me often?" he suggested. "Keep me lazy and sated, and I will follow behind you like a puppy begging for a touch from your silken hand."

She almost snorted at the words. *Yeah*, she could see Khalid trailing behind her like a little lapdog. *Not*.

"Now, are you hiding a shower in here?" She sighed, desperate to keep from sinking into the emotional trap awaiting her.

"No shower." He kissed her lips quickly. "Trust me, though, sweetie, I know how to clean that sweet, pretty body of yours."

She hoped he did, because she was slick, wet, and definitely in need of a shower. Even more, she was in need of a sense of balance. Some way to place a guard between her heart and this man who she could feel stealing it, touch by touch.

If she wasn't very, very careful, she was going to end up with a broken heart and a very lonely life.

17

Anger Thornton's guest list made up the who's who of politics and power in D.C. and Alexandria. He didn't stint on the wine, champagne, and buffet. It was the best of everything, and everything was perfect.

The band was subtle and excellent, the music wafting through the air with a gentle presence. The place was filled with the clink of glasses, the murmur of conversation, as well as an air of privilege and refined arrogance—rather like Anger himself.

At six-four, broadly muscular, with piercing blue eyes, and thick black hair, Anger was a man who most others knew to watch out for. He was rough-hewn; no one could call him handsome. He was more striking, and completely domineering, than "handsome" could ever describe.

The Thornton family had been one of the social elite in the area since the inception of the colonies. They had thrived, risen, cemented their hold and held on to it with steel-reinforced claws. Anger continued the tradition, as well as the tradition of making money in an import-export business that had been in operation nearly since the family had stepped foot in the colonies.

The three-story mansion Anger resided in boasted two large

connecting ballrooms. That night, guests milled in both rooms, as well as in the large outer rooms and well-lit gardens. It was a ball that most of the female guests planned for a year in advance. The right dress, the right shoes, and, of course, the perfect escort if they weren't married or that option were available.

For Thornton, it was the business event of the year. He'd managed to acquire many a government contract over the years because of the excellence of this one party.

Entering the main ballroom, Marty had to hold back a smile of mocking amusement as heads turned, the arrival was noted, and varied looks touched many of the faces. Marty wasn't a regular to the parties that kept the social matrons buzzing through the years. Tonight, dressed in a gown that Khalid had managed to procure at the last moment, Marty knew that she was easily competing with even the most expensively dressed women there. Somehow he'd managed to acquire an original by one of the most exclusive dressmakers in the world.

Never underestimate a determined man, she thought. The royal blue silk-and-taffeta concoction bared the upper curves of her breasts, lifted and cupped the rounded globes before tightening beneath them and shaping her hips. From there it fell to the floor in a glorious array of material and stiffened petticoats. Sapphires glittered at her ears and throat, while her long dark blond hair had been upswept into a loose, graceful style that complimented her neck and shoulders.

Beside her, Khalid was dressed in a black silk evening suit with a tie that coordinated perfectly with her dress. Shayne was dressed similarly, though his tie was a slate gray rather than a royal blue.

They flanked her, one on each side, and Marty knew the tongues would wag that night and come morning.

"Marty Mathews, you've finally decided to grace one of my parties." Anger stepped from a nearby group of aging men, his fit, dominant features at odds with the wrinkles and gray hair that surrounded him. "Khalid, Shayne, good to see the two of you again."

Marty almost arched her brows at the familiarity Anger extended toward Shayne. *Another member of the club,* she assumed. She glanced at Shayne and almost snorted at the amused look he threw her way.

"Anger, an impressive crowd," Khalid stated as they shook hands.

"As always." Anger chuckled.

He sounded amused, but with Anger, one could never be certain. His blue-eyed gaze was cool, his expression placid, barely registering emotion.

"I hear congratulations are in order as well," Khalid said. "A very lucrative contract with the State Department?"

A hint of a smile touched the corners of Anger's lips. "Someone has to transport their dirty laundry, may as well be me."

Khalid inclined his head in acknowledgment as Marty caught sight of her parents across the room. Joe and Virginia Mathews stood with a small group of friends and acquaintances. One of whom could be a contact to the Mustafa brothers.

She had no doubt that someone there was in contact with Ayid and Aman. They wouldn't move with such confidence, such ease, unless they had help within their own government as well as in the States.

Her parents were there as well as her godfather, though. They would be covered. She just prayed she was right. The suspicion that Ayid and Aman would have friends in this crowd had arisen only after she had read the file on the Saudi operation. Someone had sent the brothers that message, and that person could have only been among a very small group of government individuals.

"If you'll excuse me." Marty smiled to the group. "I see my parents."

"Of course." Anger's gaze flickered with curiosity for the briefest moment. "I spoke to your father and godfather earlier. They seem rather pleased with your association with Khalid. I wish you both the best."

Marty nearly choked at the good wishes. Her fathers were obviously sick tonight. They were both furious at Khalid as well as at Shayne, for her resignation as well as her refusal to stay at her parent's home while Khalid's brothers were still on the loose.

"Thank you, AT," she murmured. "If you'll excuse me."

"And I as well," Khalid stated behind her. "I believe I'll accompany my lovely companion."

Anger chuckled and Khalid's hand settled once again at the small of her back as they moved across the room.

"Your fathers are good," he murmured, as he bent his head to her. "No one will have any illusions that you are now sharing my bed."

She flicked a glance up at him. He was so smooth, so confident. She felt like stomping his toes just to see his reaction when that amused arrogance showed itself.

She might have if she hadn't caught a glimpse of Vince Deerfield moving slowly from the group her parents were a part of, as he cast her a look that indicated he wanted to meet with her. His eyes were narrowed on her and Khalid, tracking their movement across the ballroom as he drew farther away from them, heading from the ballroom to a hallway at the other side that she knew led to guest bathrooms as well as a small library and a sitting room.

What the hell did he want?

She made the decision to follow him, hoping that if she let him get whatever he had on his chest off it once again, she wouldn't have to worry about a public display of idiocy.

He wasn't above it.

"Excuse me, I think I need to make a trip to the ladies' room." She excused herself to Khalid as she looked around and saw Shayne moving toward the hall from another angle, his gaze flicking toward her.

"Be careful," Khalid warned her softly, as his touch retreated from her back.

"Always." Throwing him a pointed smile, she moved in the direction of the hall as Khalid stepped over to the group her parents were with.

Once in the hallway, she strode as quickly as four-inch heels allowed along the corridor, wondering where Deerfield had gone off to and if Shayne had been following him as well.

As she rounded a corner she glimpsed a door farther up the hall that had been left open. As she moved closer to it, she hid her surprise as her former boss stepped into the doorway and motioned her in.

The small study was designed simply. There was a large desk and bookshelves and, at the side of the room, a luxurious couch and matching chairs.

Closing the door behind her as she turned to face him, Vince Deerfield glared at her.

"Everyone is wondering how long he's going to keep you in his bed," he snapped. "Have you lost your mind, Agent Mathews? I can't believe you'd flaunt this affair so publicly. Hell, I couldn't believe you were actually involved in it until I heard the gossip tonight."

"Others can wonder whatever the hell they want to," she told him briskly. "Now, what did you want? I need to find a ladies' room and I had assumed we no longer had anything to talk about."

He shot her a malevolent look and strode across the room to the small bar in the far corner.

"I always assumed you had more class than to allow yourself to get mixed up with that bastard, no matter the rumors that circulated concerning his interest in you. He has his own harem, for God's sake."

He has six girls his father had sent to him as children who he adopted and now raised as sisters, Marty thought. *Unfortunately Deerfield had never believed it, no matter the proof he had been given to the contrary.*

"I'm hoping to enjoy the party," she finally said, shrugging. "And he'll miss me soon if I don't hurry. What do you want?"

Deerfield shot back his drink with a hard grimace before slapping the glass back on the dark gleaming wood.

"Your godfather seems particularly proud of this relationship that everyone assumes has developed between you and Mustafa," he said. "I had more respect for Zach Jennings than this. I never imagined he would allow you to make such a decision."

Marty arched her brows slowly. "Why wouldn't they be proud? Neither my father nor my godfather runs my life for me, Vince." The use of his first name was a deliberate insult and a reminder that he no longer had any power over her.

"Does your father know the bastard shares his women?" he asked snidely. "Did you know?"

She stared at him as though he had lost his mind.

"What are you accusing me of, Vince?" she asked him carefully.

Pushing his fingers through his short brown hair in agitation, he narrowed his eyes and stared at her angrily.

"Don't try to deny he's shared his women," he ordered her.

There was no denying that one.

"That simply means he has a past." She shrugged. As well as a future, but there was no sense in lingering any longer here than she had to.

He grunted at that. "I would hope you would be smarter." He didn't sound as though he believed she was, though. "I'd be careful, though, if he brings that brother of his for a visit. The last woman they shared they murdered."

She didn't try to hide her surprise, or her disbelief. "And that's not in our files, why?"

Deerfield grimaced. "Because it was taken out by your god-father." He sneered. "'No proof, supposition only,' was his damned argument. We couldn't find proof."

Now wasn't that a familiar scenario.

"Perhaps because no proof existed," she suggested, as she gripped tightly in anger the small purse she held in her hands.

"But the proof was there, proof I wasn't allowed to use because of international implications." Deerfield sneered. "And I suspect be-cause your godfather thought more of his friendship with Mustafa than he did of his country."

"I'd be careful, Vince. My godfather wouldn't cover up murder. Nor would he pull information he believed was relevant," she stated.

His lips twisted furiously as he turned and poured himself an-other drink before turning back to her. "He wouldn't accept the proof," he told her, his voice rough. "Eyewitness accounts. Witnesses who saw the girl's body, saw the sexual abuse inflicted on it. She'd been raped, Agent Mathews, horribly. An autopsy confirmed she had been raped to death by two men at the same time. And Khalid's and Abram's depravities together were well-known. She was Abram's wife, and evidently he simply grew tired of her."

Shock filled her. "This isn't information that I uncovered, and I've researched every facet of Khalid's life."

"Then you didn't research enough," he snapped. "Abram is as depraved as Khalid. He disgusts even his own people. He'll never succeed his father as ruler, because the religious hardliners will never accept an unmarried king who allows others to fuck his whores as he watches. His second wife died before she could even give birth to his child, and he has no intention of acquiring another wife. He gets tired of them and he kills them. Men like him and Khalid are a disease, Marty. One that requires a cure."

Hatred gleamed in his eyes as the fury seemed to build within him.

"That's not your call, Deerfield," she argued. "And a man's sexual tastes don't define him, nor do they make him a murderer."

"They do when he kills the stupid bitches willing to fuck him and his brother at the same time. Silly little whores who fool themselves into believing those men love them, only to learn they're no more than a toy. Then you're damned right, it defines him."

"You're losing your objectivity," she said, backing slowly to the door. "Nothing you've said here warrants the Bureau's harassment of him. If you're not very careful, he's going to have a lawsuit against the entire Bureau."

Deerfield smirked at her warning.

"Worry about yourself, I'll worry about the Bureau. That's my job, and I'm damned good at it."

He's not stable, she thought. *He is slipping over an edge that could end up causing irreparable damage between the United States and a potential ally.*

"My job is nearly over," she warned him. "Khalid is no traitor, and he's no murderer—"

Deerfield broke her argument off with a sharp, derisive laugh.

"You've fallen for him, haven't you? Wouldn't your father be proud to know how far you'll end up sinking for that bastard? Would you betray your country for him, Agent Mathews? Would you let him watch as another man fucks you?"

"You've lost your mind," she breathed out roughly.

"Ask him about her," he snarled, his expression twisting into lines of fury. "Her name was Lessa. She was Abram's wife. A tiny little thing who they broke." His gaze flicked over her in scorn. "I hope you never experience the horror she must have faced as they fucked her to death."

"I don't have to ask him about anything. Khalid isn't a monster, and he'd never hurt one of his lovers, or anyone else's. And I will remind you, you're the one who put me on that assignment to watch him. It was your responsibility to tell me everything, no matter the fact that someone else believed the information irrelevant."

"I didn't tell you to fuck him!"

"Speak to me like that again and you'll regret it." Marty's fingers clenched her purse even tighter as anger coursed through her. "I've taken your abusive tirades long enough, Deerfield."

"For God's sake, do you think I'd bother to berate you if I didn't think you'd make a damned fine agent one of these days?" Surprise seemed to reflect in his expression now as he held his hands out in supplication. "You're risking your life and your career with this man."

"And I will remind you that it's no longer your concern." She could feel her heart racing, adrenaline surging through her as she recognized the fact that her boss's sanity just might be slipping.

"I thought you were smarter than this." He shook his head slowly. "Damn. I thought you were a better agent than this."

Marty gripped the doorknob behind her and stared at him in fury. "I think you should sit down and think about what you're doing, Deerfield," she told him coldly. "You're the one risking your life. You're the one whose career is already shot to hell. Don't make it worse."

He smiled slowly, confidently. "I'll win in the end."

"Don't bet on it." As she jerked the door open she threw him a hard, enraged look before turning and stepping back into the hall.

She was trembling with anger as she slammed the door closed and came face-to-face with Shayne.

His blue eyes were as cold as ice, his body tense with anger as he stared at her, then at the door.

"You heard?" she asked.

His jaw clenched. "It was hard not to. And you're damned lucky Khalid didn't. He would have killed the bastard for talking to you like that."

As she moved away from the room, Marty glanced back at the door, wondering what Deerfield was doing inside.

Marty shook her head at the instability she had glimpsed in her former boss before drawing in a hard breath and asking, "Who is Lessa Hadad, Shayne?"

Silence met her question for long moments. "She was Abram's wife," he finally said. "If you have any other questions concerning her, then you should ask Khalid."

"Khalid hasn't mentioned her yet," she pointed out stiffly. "What did she mean to him?"

He stopped her before they stepped back into the ballroom.

"Ask Khalid about this, Marty. Let him explain Lessa to you. But be very careful. Remember, Khalid is the way he is for a reason. Sometimes, once the darkness takes hold of you, you don't want to ever return to the memories that caused it."

As Marty walked away from him, that statement stayed with her. There was definitely a darkness raging inside Khalid, one he battled often when it came to standing back rather than interfering in the career she had chosen for herself.

That would be hard for him, she admitted. *A man like Khalid didn't just stand aside while his woman endangered herself. Yet, he had done exactly that more than once.*

He was allowing her to be who she needed to be. No matter his disagreement with it, he was standing back. She could see the torment in his face when he did so, just as she had glimpsed his fear for her more than once.

As she moved across the ballroom, she caught sight of several familiar faces. Men she knew were members of the club had gathered around AT at the other side of the room. They were talking quietly among themselves, several of them nodding seriously.

AT was always plotting and planning.

Ian Sinclair was part of that group. He watched AT with narrow-eyed intent before he nodded carefully and glanced out over the room and saw her.

Amusement marked his expression. Evidently there were no hard feelings about the fact that she had managed to slip into his club.

She returned to where Khalid stood with her fathers and mother.

There was a sense of readiness that filled the three men. As Shayne joined them seconds later, that readiness intensified.

"Everything's in place." Her godfather leaned close to her. "We've picked up two transmissions from here since you and Khalid arrived. They spoke with Ayid, who promised to be on a plane to D.C. ASAP, since the man he sent here couldn't seem to do the job right. We have assets moving in there to let us know when he moved."

Staring out over the ballroom, Marty hoped the operation worked out quickly. She had a feeling that if it didn't, she and Khalid could be facing more danger than she had imagined. "Then he isn't here in the States yet?" she asked as she turned to Khalid.

He pulled her to his side, his fingers clasping her hips possessively. "Not yet."

Marty nodded slowly. It wouldn't be long, she told herself. Ayid Mustafa would take whatever chance he had to destroy Khalid.

As she stood next to Khalid, she noticed something. The way he held her, close to his side. The way his body turned into hers. She had never seen him hold another woman in quite that fashion. Had never heard of him keeping one at his side.

He loved her.

She stared at him, admitting silently that she had loved him most of her life. She had loved him with a certainty, a confidence that the day would come when she would have at least a chance to steal his heart.

Had she managed that?

There were times she thought it possible. There were times she feared she still might have a ways to go.

Feeling his hand settle possessively at the small of her back once again, she turned to stare up at him with all the fears, all the needs that were becoming harder and harder to hold inside her.

"Dance with me." Taking her hand he stepped back, watching her, waiting on her to accept. "Shayne's meeting with a contact tonight, but we'll be leaving soon, ourselves."

He was dominant, but he wasn't overbearing. He was arrogant, but his arrogance was always tinged with logic, with reason.

"Always." Her hand tightened on his as she let him draw her out onto the dance floor.

As he took her in his arms, Marty felt the familiar heat he ignited inside her rising once again. He was the spark inside her soul.

Laying her head against his shoulder, Marty closed her eyes and let herself simply enjoy his touch, the slow glide of his body, the warmth of his arms.

She didn't understand the need rising inside her to simply exist here, to hold on to this moment as long as possible, to hold the memories inside her.

"It will be over soon." His whisper against her ear was soft, though the tone of his voice reflected a steely strength that made her lift her head, her eyes meeting his.

It wasn't fear she glimpsed in his eyes; it was a certainty that if his brothers weren't dealt with, then he would lose more than he could bear to lose.

He would lose her.

"One way or the other, it will be over soon," she agreed.

"I won't let them win, Marty."

"I know you won't." Confidence gleamed in her eyes, and that terrified him.

He'd let Lessa down. How could he bear failing Marty in the same way?

Khalid couldn't stand the thought of losing her. As he stared down at her he knew that nothing in his life, no other woman, had ever been to him what Marty was becoming.

Strength glittered in her gray eyes, mixed with compassion and a sense of fun. She never took herself too seriously, and she never let him do the same. Yet, at the same time, she understood the danger revolving around her. There was no denial of it. She didn't fight it. Hell no, she was jumping right in to attempt to solve it.

Staring up at him, Marty saw the emotions shifting through his eyes. Dark, desperate emotions that she wanted nothing more than to ease.

As the song came to an end, Khalid led her back to where her fathers stood.

"We identified our caller." Joe edged close to them, keeping his voice low. "He's part of the Saudi ambassador's entourage." He nodded to the tall, heavily robed middle-aged Arab speaking to the ambassador. "He received a call two minutes ago. We think he's preparing to meet with the assassin."

"Why?" Marty asked, her voice low. "What information could he have?"

Zach shook his head. "That's what I intend to find out."

"We'll leave, as well," Khalid stated. "Let us know the moment you have anything."

"The very minute," Zach agreed, before bending his head to kiss Marty's forehead gently. "Be careful baby," he whispered. "Your mother would kill me, and rightfully so, if anything happened to you."

Saying their good-byes to their host several minutes later, Marty wondered what could have warranted a meeting so quickly.

She didn't have the answers she needed, and the questions tormented her. There was a new one to add to the list, as well.

What had happened to Lessa, and what had she meant to Khalid? Had he loved her? Had he already lost the woman he felt his heart belonged to, even though she was his brother's wife? Even though he had been the third rather than the first?

Glancing at Khalid beside her, she took in the quiet expression, the flat, almost unemotional glitter in his eyes. That look had been there since the moment they stepped from the dance floor. "My parents have invited us to lunch next week," she told him quietly, as the limo drew closer to the estate. "I told them I'd have to be certain your schedule is free."

She watched his nostrils flare as he breathed in deeply.

"I'm free," he finally said.

She watched him curiously, wondering at the reserved air she was seeing.

"They'll be glad to hear that." She began to shift away from him, the distance she felt around him making her vaguely uncomfortable.

"Where the hell are you going?" Before she had moved more than an inch he was pulling her back to him, then going a step further and lifting her into his lap.

"What are you doing?" Surprise shot through her as she felt his arms suddenly surrounding her, his warm chest against her.

"Do you think I will let go so easily?" There was something definitely dark and dangerous in his expression now.

"I wasn't aware you owned me." She wasn't pretending to be unaware of the fact that he was trying to become totally dominant.

So why the hell was her heart racing as though she were excited, as though a potential confrontation with him were turning her on? And why was she growing so wet?

Khalid stared down at her, feeling things he had never imagined feeling as they rolled through him. Most surprising was the edge of possessiveness. Never had he known an obsession such as the one he knew for this woman.

He had shared her easily. The pleasure, the pure eroticism of each adventure had been more than he had ever known with another woman, at any other time. Yet, seeing her walk from that hall with Shayne, his hand on her back as he stood protectively behind her, Khalid had felt a shaft of possessive lust unlike anything he could have expected.

Shayne didn't love her. He wanted nothing to do with love or possessiveness. Shayne wanted to stay on the outside looking in, a part of the relationship but never truly committed to it.

"I never stated that I owned you," he growled, feeling his cock harden to painful tightness as her little ass wiggled against it. "I merely stated that I would not let you go easily."

"And I'm telling you that if I decide to go, then you'll have no say in it." Her voice was sweet, but beneath it he could hear a threat of determination and lust boiling inside her.

"Don't believe I'll have no say in it," he told her, hearing the harshness entering his voice. "I did not begin this relationship with you, Marty, to lose you so easily."

Her eyes widened. *There was definitely lust there. Arousal*, he amended. The heat in her gaze held emotion, shades of anger, hunger, and a glimmer of feeling that he had never seen in another woman's eyes.

Or did he only wish he was seeing that emotion there? When it came to Marty he was never certain of what he felt, or what she was feeling.

"No, you began this relationship because you were under suspicion for treason by my boss," she shot back.

She was a quick little thing, he thought. *But that wasn't exactly accurate.*

"No, I began this relationship with you because staying away from you was no longer an option," he stated, gripping her hip to hold her in place as she made a move as though to leave his lap.

He liked her exactly where she was, in his arms.

"You act as though I had nothing to do with the decision." The anger flared in her gray eyes then, and sent a surge of pure lust ripping through his balls. "Excuse me, Mr. Mustafa, but I made the first move, not you. I seduced you, remember?"

"That you did." Threading his fingers through her hair, he pulled her head back and stared down at her, dying to consume her. "And I'll be damned if I hadn't grown tired of pushing you to do so."

Before she could argue with the statement he took her lips and stole the kiss he needed. His tongue pushed passed her parted lips, stroked against hers, and tasted pure, sweet female a second before he felt her sharp little teeth snap against his tongue.

Jerking back, he stared down at her, eyes narrowed, before he threaded his fingers into the back of her hair, letting the thick, silken strands tumble over his hand. Clenching, he held her still, lowered his head, and nipped her lush, lower lip before flicking his tongue over it gently.

He kissed the pout on her lips and held her head still, and as he stared into her dark, hungry eyes, kissed her again. His tongue flicked over her lips, teased, and stroked until her lips parted again, and her tongue reached out for him.

Hunger was a driving ache in his balls. His cock was engorged, throbbing in such need that he wondered how he bore it. Never had he ached like this, hungered like this.

Turning her, he lay her back on the seat, coming over her with a muted groan that tore from his throat. Kissing her was like bathing in fire, in sweet, white-hot pleasure. His lips took hers again and again, feeling the deepening need as it bloomed inside her, the rush of blood thundering through his body, the heat pouring from her sweet flesh.

Lowering one hand, he raked the heavy taffeta and silk of her dress up her leg, over her thigh. Satiny flesh met the stroke of his hand as her knee bent, her thighs parting beneath his touch as he held her firmly, his lips devouring her.

He could feel the sweet wet heat of her pussy just inches from his fingers. Her juices dampened her panties. The thought of delving into it nearly had him shaking like a young boy.

The feel of her fingers in his hair, tugging at the heavy strands were a pleasure he was certain he had never experienced before. At least, he had never felt such pleasure from it.

Touching her was the most erotic thing he had ever done in his life. Fucking her was nirvana. It was the greatest pleasure in the world.

What made this one woman so different? That thought was barely a presence in his mind as her hips arched to his fingers, which were stroking over the damp panel of her silk panties. A fragile moan passed between them as he felt her melting further beneath him.

"Do you know what you do to me?" He groaned as he tore his lips from hers and stroked them over her jaw. "You make me lose control, Marty. Something I swore I would never do."

"It's only fair," she gasped, as he nipped at her neck. "I swore I'd never let you do the things you do to me, either."

Such as sharing her. Such as letting him watch her take another man's cock and seeing the erotic pleasure that suffused her face. His cock hardened more, and he hadn't thought that possible.

"I give you such pleasure, though," he said, his hunger amplifying at the thought of it. "Tell me I don't, precious."

She couldn't, he knew she couldn't.

"Is pleasure enough, Khalid?" Her voice was husky, torn from her as he rubbed at her clit through the silk of her panties.

"With us?" His thumb smoothed over her sweet clit. "Ah, love, the pleasure will never be enough. Because I don't believe I can ever touch you enough, take you enough. You are my eternal hunger."

And he was her guilty pleasure, he thought, with an edge of dissatisfaction. She was never certain if what she was doing would harm her tender heart or strengthen it.

"I will always ensure your greatest pleasure," he promised her, as he lowered his head to rub his lips against hers, knowing they had little time for much else.

He felt her gasp as he rubbed her clit between his fingers, the silk barrier of her panties adding to the friction. She was so responsive, always so ready for his touch.

Looking up, he restrained a curse as the limo pulled into the estate. He didn't know how much longer he could wait to have her, to sink his cock inside the velvet fist-tight grip of her pussy. The way she took him, milked his flesh, and stroked him to completion was a hunger he couldn't seem to sate.

Straightening from her, he helped her to slowly sit up, taking his gaze from her only long enough to watch as the front doors opened and the security personnel gave him the go-ahead to exit the vehicle. Abdul opened the limo door.

He trusted the men he had hired—men he knew could not be bought by his brothers, and whose loyalty was tied to him through the club.

"Khalid." Their commander stepped outside, well armed, his piercing gaze scanning the darkness for threats before turning back to his boss.

"Any problems tonight, Braque?" Khalid asked, as he stepped from the limo. He turned and helped Marty from the car.

"We had some visitors by the north fence." Braque strode down the steps with one of his men. They flanked him and Marty as they moved to the house. "No one got in, but I wanted to be here myself in case they tried again."

Hard-eyed killers, that was how many men described Braque's elite security force. Khalid considered them more of an insurance policy. Better his enemies die than Marty be harmed further.

Braque and his men escorted them into the house. Khalid noticed with a sense of amusement that Marty showed not so much as a shred of recognition where Braque was concerned. He knew the other man had made her several offers to join his security teams. Offers she was actually considering.

"We've kept a constant check on your suite as well as the rest of the upstairs rooms," Braque assured him, as he and Marty moved to the stairs behind one of the other guards. "Will you be going up now?"

"Yes, we're retiring now," Khalid assured him. "Should we need to leave my suite, you will be informed."

Braque nodded. "I took the liberty of having a tray of food sent to your room when you arrived. I know what Anger's buffets are like."

"Filled with calories with no staying power," Marty remarked with a light laugh.

"Exactly." Braque's answering grin was filled with amusement.

And he liked keeping his clients alive. The easier it was to keep them to one general area, the better he liked it. Hence the food waiting for them in the suite. It would keep Khalid and Marty from wandering the halls in need of a midnight snack.

While moving up the stairs, Khalid kept his eyes on the men ahead of them. They were spread out, less obtrusive than many bodyguards he'd had over the years, and much better at their job while staying well back.

At first he had been hesitant about accepting Ian's suggestion that he hire them until this situation had been resolved. Now he was thankful he had. Someone had tried to slip onto the estate the very night that Shayne hadn't been with them to help secure the house.

Even Abdul had been unaware that Shayne wouldn't be there until they had left. Whoever his brothers had hired to attack Marty hadn't worried about facing Khalid as well as two FBI agents. Fortunately for Khalid, no one had known until this evening that Braque and his men were watching the estate.

"When did you hire them?" Marty asked, as they stepped into the suite.

She turned to stare at him as though trying to read past whatever answer he would give her.

"Several days ago," he informed her. "They've been staying out of sight until tonight."

"You didn't trust Shayne and me to protect you?" She laid her little purse on the antique table just inside the door.

"I hired them as backup, not protection. Besides, you're my lover, not my bodyguard," he answered her. "I had them secure the house when I learned Shayne wasn't returning with us tonight."

"I see," she murmured, moving farther into the room. "So, will they be here permanently?"

"I would imagine they will be. At least for a while," he told her. "I sleep easier with you in the bed sleeping with me. Neither of us will have to worry about the security of the estate this way."

Khalid followed her slowly, crowding her closer to the large bed on the other side of the room.

"Do you have a problem with this?" he asked her silkily.

"Would it do me any good to have a problem with it?" A delicate brow arched mockingly.

"We would, of course, discuss it," he promised, as he shed his evening jacket.

"Oh, I just bet we would." Eyes narrowed, she watched as he toed his dress shoes from his feet.

"I'm always willing to discuss any problems you might have, dear," he assured her, as he began to loosen the buttons of his shirt.

"Somehow I doubt it would be an acceptable discussion." The edge of mockery in her voice had his lips tilting in acknowledgment.

"I would always do my best to accommodate you," he promised her, as his gaze flicked over the ballgown she still wore. "However you need."

"And if my needs didn't include sex at the moment?" Her head tilted as her arms crossed over her breasts. "What if the discussion topic was something that required words rather than actions?"

His brows arched as though in surprise. "I assumed all discussions require words rather than actions. Have the rules changed?"

"Whenever you decide to try to change them," she shot back.

Khalid almost chuckled. She was a fiery little thing; he loved that about her. He would never manage to get anything over on his Marty; she would always see him for the man he was. Whether or not that was a good thing, he wasn't certain at the moment.

What he was certain of was the complete hunger raging through him. He needed her. His dick was a fiery throb, his lips ached to kiss her. Like a drug he had been too long without, his entire body was edgy for her.

"You should inform me when you make these decisions," she told him, as he moved closer to her. "Don't pretend I know everything that's going on here. And this decision to hire a mercenary force without my knowledge is bullshit. You should have consulted with me first."

His nostrils flared. "I do not have to consult with anyone where my protection and the protection of my woman are concerned."

He watched her expression tighten. Her chin lifted to a stubborn angle, her gaze darkened. He hadn't thought he could feel hornier, but that look proved him wrong.

"I am fully trained." She bit out the words, ire punctuating every one. "Have you forgotten that?"

Khalid was treading a very fine line, and he had the sense to know it. Just as he knew that if the ground rules were not established now, then the problems down the road would only amplify.

"While you are in my bed, sleeping in my arms, I am your protection," he said, as he gripped her waist and pulled her to him. "Hear that, Marty. Know it. You may call the shots at any other time. But during those hours that you are my lover, I will ensure your protection with my life."

He didn't give her time to argue. As far as he was concerned, there was no argument. His lips covered the words ready to spill from her, his tongue stroking along the satiny curves before pushing in to tease her tempting little tongue.

"This is no way to win this fight," she gasped, as he pulled at the skirt of her gown, jerking it up her leg to allow his hand to stroke beneath it.

"This fight has already been won," he informed her, trying to breathe through the hunger pounding through him. "The unit is here, they are on guard, and, by God, you are in my arms. I win."

He was certain she would have said more. The woman could argue for hours, he knew. Rather than give her the chance, his hand slid to the wet triangle of silk between her thighs and cupped her firmly.

Instantly, her expression softened, a flinch of pure pleasure shook her body, and Khalid couldn't hold back the growl that tore from his throat at her response.

"I want to be inside you." Lowering his head to her ear, he nipped at the lobe as his fingers found the delicate little nub of her clit and rubbed it sensually. "I want to watch my cock sink inside the snug heat of your pussy, Marty. I want that with every breath inside me."

She was melting in his arms. As he pulled aside the elastic curving around her thigh and slid his hand inside the minuscule material of her panties, he felt her melt against him.

Parting the curl-shrouded folds of flesh, his fingers slid instinctively to the clenched, tight opening he sought.

Marty knew she should fight this. She should demand her independence here and now, because later might well be too late. But, oh God, the pleasure. Her head fell back on her shoulders, her hands gripping his neck as his lips traveled to her shoulder to kiss the sensitive flesh there.

His fingers, broad and heated, the tips calloused and sensually rough, parted her flesh and began to work inside with such sensual pleasure that Marty felt her senses skyrocketing.

Heated dampness spilled from her pussy, spreading along his fingers as he moved them inside her, caressing and rubbing the most sensitive spots with erotic destruction.

It was like setting a match to fuel. Her heart rate thundered as perspiration coated her flesh and her sex became hotter, slicker.

"Ah yeah, sweet baby," he crooned, the rough, sexual vibrancy in his tone making her womb clench. "I could make you come now. Feel you tighten on my fingers and spill all those sweet juices for me to lick away later."

She nearly came in that second. What he did to her should be outlawed. It shouldn't be possible. Her knee bent, her leg lifted along his as she fought for a deeper touch, a harder thrust from those diabolical fingers.

"There, precious, open for me." Approval thrummed in his voice as he sank deeper inside her, his fingers shafting her slow and easy as she began to shudder from the pleasure.

A distant part of her was aware of him moving her. He lifted her with his spare arm, angling her back as his fingers continued to possess her.

She expected to feel the bed as he stopped. A little surprised gasp left her lips as he lifted her instead, pushed her back along the table behind the sofa, and stepped between her spread thighs.

"God yes," he said, as he pushed the skirt of her gown to her waist, the taffeta bunching above her thighs as his gaze centered on where his fingers sank inside her.

"Khalid." She cried his name out, one hand gripping his wrist at the side of the table as her hips arched to one hard, fierce thrust as his thumb raked over her clit.

"So damned beautiful," he breathed out roughly. "You have no idea, Marty, how beautiful you are to me."

His fingers stroked, eased, stretched her. Flames surrounded her, white-hot and intense as they burned through her nerve endings, leaving her gasping, shuddering in near painful pleasure.

"Here." His hand lifted, breaking her hold on him before he gripped her wrist and brought her fingers between her thighs. "Play with your pretty clit for me. Let me watch, baby. Let me see your pretty fingers as you pleasure yourself."

She had never done that. Never had another watched her masturbate, or aided her in the pleasure as she touched herself. A flush stole over her body, burning her higher as she let her fingers circle the sensitive knot of nerves and she felt his fingers moving inside her.

Her back arched at the first caress against her clit, as he timed the thrust of his fingers inside her. Sensation shot up her spine from her sensitized sex, washing through her body in a blaze of heat.

Her head thrashed against the table, and a long, low moan escaped her lips. It was so good. She stroked her fingers over her clit again, her teeth biting into her lip as his fingers shafted inside her, deep and strong, nearly sending her soaring as they stretched and filled her.

It was exquisite. Pleasure was a steady stroke of intense sensation and breath-stealing vibrancy as it shot through her, then rained over her nerve endings like a shower of heat.

Her senses became dazed, lost in the pleasure as her fingers moved faster over her clit, while his fucked her harder, thrusting inside her pussy with sure, deep strokes. The explosion when it came had her upper body jerking up, her free hand clenching his shoulder as their gazes locked and a wildfire of sensation began to spread through her.

Gasping, crying, Marty shuddered in reaction, shaking with the intensity of the storm inside her as Khalid pulled his fingers back, gripped the thick stalk of his cock, and jerked her to him.

The crest pushed past trembling folds of flesh to burrow into the clenching, tightening entrance of her pussy. His hands locked beneath her rear, lifting her, holding her steady, as he began pushing inside her, his erection stretching her, filling her as it burned along sensitive tissue and stretched her nerve endings.

Her clit, throbbing in orgasm, began to peak and explode in pure unimagined ecstasy. The explosion rocked through her body as she felt his lips at her breasts, his chin pushing aside the snug bodice of her dress to find the hard tip and suck it inside.

"Yes. Please. Oh God. Khalid." Desperate cries welled from her lips as his hips began to churn, his cock shafting inside her, parting her, burning her. She tightened further around him, her body melting, consumed by the ever-growing wave of pleasure. It was destructive, unending. The pure rapture of his possession of her stole her senses and consumed her mind until she felt herself exploding again, clenching on him, her juices flowing between them as he gave one last, hard thrust. Burying to the hilt, she felt him spurting inside her, his cock throbbing, jerking against the sensitive inner flesh of her pussy and peaking her orgasm higher.

Crying out his name, Marty held on to him, certain that without him she would be lost somewhere between the darkness and the fire consuming her without end.

There had never been anything as intense, as brilliantly hot and consuming as exploding in Khalid's arms.

As she fought to catch her breath she felt him pull back from her. A muted moan vibrated in his throat as his cock slid free of her, while a shudder raced through her body.

"Come, precious." His voice was sensually rough, rasping along her senses with a quiet stroke. "We can shower together."

In the past week she had found that she loved showering with him. He took forever beneath the hot spray, using incredibly soft cloths to clean every inch of her body.

She slid from the table with his help, staring up at him as he released the zipper of her dress and helped it pool at her feet. Leaving her in nothing but heels and stockings, his black gaze flared again with decided male interest.

"I can't get enough of you." He sighed as he stripped off the remainder of his clothes. She had no idea how he'd managed to shed his shoes and slacks without her knowing.

Slipping her shoes from her feet, Marty moved slowly away from him, heading to the shower.

"We need to talk," she said, all too aware of him behind her as he watched her walk.

"Some discussions need to wait until daylight." Amusement lingered in his voice.

"Not this one." Turning back to him, Marty watched him as she felt the ache in her heart begin to intensify.

He was the ultimate in male arrogance, dominance, and supreme sexuality. Tall and broad, dark and brooding. He was the epitome of the male sexual animal. Enough so that her womb clenched with a renewal of spiraling, fiery need.

How could she ever let him go? Khalid wasn't known for his long-enduring affairs. What if she became nothing more than another notch on his bedpost? It was something she needed to be prepared for.

And it could come sooner rather than later if she didn't have her questions answered. She needed to trust him. She needed to know that no matter how strong was his need to protect her, he would always be honest with her.

Pausing at the bed, she shed her stockings before continuing to the shower. She hated the knowledge that she had to confront him for information; some things he should have volunteered.

If he had been accused of murdering a young woman, then that was information she should know. It was information that could have aided her in the investigation into who was trying to murder him, and why.

And on the heels of that thought: *Why hadn't her fathers told her?*

18

Khalid found himself clenching his teeth as he followed Marty into the shower. He should be well beyond the fiery lust that he felt as he watched her rounded ass tighten and shift as she walked ahead of him. Hell, he'd just fucked her until they were both nearly exhausted, and still he could feel the white-hot bite of hunger clenching his balls and tightening his dick.

What the hell did she do to him? What was it about her that had his back teeth locking against the urge to bend her over and sink inside her again? Balls deep, his cock surrounded by the fist-tight, slick velvet depths of her pussy.

Hell. He was damned near sweating with the need now.

"Deerfield had some very interesting information when I met with him," she commented, her back still to him as she moved to the shower door and reached in to adjust the water.

"Did he?" He'd waited impatiently, torn between the need to jerk her out of the room with the bastard and protect her and the need to allow her the independence he knew she demanded.

As he moved into the shower with her, Khalid watched as she stepped back, grabbed her shampoo, and began lathering her hair.

Silence but for the pounding of the water filled the shower stall as

Khalid watched her expression closely. She hid her emotions when she deemed the situation warranted it. Her face was calm, composed; there was nothing but the eerie sense of impending doom that circled his head to warn him of danger ahead.

"You haven't asked me about the meeting." She stepped beneath the spray to rinse her hair as she spoke. "Were you waiting on Shayne to discuss it with him?"

"We've been rather busy," he said. "Is there something that should concern me other than the manner in which he spoke to you?"

There was a trap in her question; Khalid could feel it, and he didn't like it.

"Is that all that concerns you?" She opened her eyes as the last of the shampoo ran from her hair and stared back at him, her lashes spiked with moisture.

"Why not get to the point, Marty?" he growled. "You obviously have something on your mind here."

Even the sense of impending doom did nothing to affect the jutting erection aimed her way. Damned stubborn cock. The woman had an effect on him that he simply couldn't fight.

"Why haven't you told me what happened in Saudi Arabia before you left? What happened with your brother's wife, Khalid?" she asked him as she pulled a soft cloth from the towel rack and dampened it.

Khalid's nostrils flared as he dipped his head beneath the spray, closed his eyes, and concentrated on the answer for a second.

"You don't have to make up a lie for me."

His eyes snapped open as he reached for shampoo and tried to occupy himself with the shower rather than with fucking her against the shower wall and stilling the anger he could feel building inside her.

"I have never lied to you," he snapped.

"Then you don't have to find a way to delay or avoid the question." Her slim shoulders shrugged nonchalantly, though her demeanor was anything but.

Rubbing the cloth over the scented soap, his luscious little lover began washing delicate, silken flesh with rough strokes. Khalid almost winced at the force she used. He would have stroked her, caressed her, washed her with delicate sensuality and much pleasure.

"Deerfield believes you and your brother Abram shared, then murdered, his first wife."

Khalid's gaze jerked up in shock. "This has nothing to do with the investigation."

Marty watched as Khalid turned his back on her and soaped a cloth with a bar of creamy soap that she knew was made especially for him.

When he was finished, the soap was slammed back onto its small tile shelf. With rough, furious strokes he began to wash himself silently, his shoulders tense, the air in the shower suddenly thick with tension.

"It's not your place to decide if this pertains to the investigation," she informed him. "Vince Deerfield knows about it, and he was particularly volatile over the subject. I want to know what happened, Khalid."

"This has nothing to do with us." His tone was icy. Despite the warmth of the water flowing over her, Marty could feel the chill of it licking over her flesh.

"Do you really want me to get my answers in other ways, Khalid? Do I have to search for them?"

She watched as the cloth stilled for a moment. When it resumed, it was with efficient deliberation. He washed, tossed the cloth to the corner of the shower, then stepped beneath the spray once again to rinse.

Amazingly, he was hard. His cock stood out stiff and heavy from his body, the thick, engorged crest throbbing enticingly as rivers of water and suds flowed around it.

Marty resisted the urge to lick her lips as she jerked her gaze to his face.

A flush stained her face as she caught him watching her, his black eyes narrowed, the sign of emotion in his expression being the glimmer of hunger in his black eyes.

"There is no need for you to search for answers," he said, his voice still cold. "I told you. Lessa has no more to do with this than Abram and I had to do with her death. It requires no more explanation than that."

"I'm sorry, but it's not that easy." After wringing the excess water from her hair, she reached for the shower door as she stared back at him intently. "I need to know what happened, Khalid, and I need more than you gave me as an explanation for your brothers' behavior. Otherwise, I'm going searching for answers whether you want me to or not."

"Is that a threat?" he asked, his tone snapping with ire.

"It's an alternative," she informed him. "It's information I deserve to know, whether it's part of this investigation or not. If a woman died because she was a lover to you and to your brother, then as your lover now, it's something I need to be aware of. Something I deserve to be aware of."

"Damn it, it has nothing to do with you," he growled, the anger she knew was brewing in him shading his voice.

"It has everything to do with me." Emotion erupted as her voice rose slightly, the pain she was beginning to feel tearing through her now. "You have all of me, Khalid. You have parts of me I swore I'd never give a man, and you share them. Don't you bloody well tell me that I have no right to the answers I need. Don't you dare even think you have a right to deny me those answers."

Marty was shaking. She felt the tears rising to her eyes and stepped quickly from the shower, slamming the door behind her as she placed a stranglehold on the screaming pain beginning to radiate through her.

Why this hurt so desperately she couldn't fully explain. She was fighting to protect him. She had lain her own career on the line even before becoming his lover to protect the innocence she believed in. To protect the man who already held a part of her heart.

He'd refused point-blank to ever discuss the time he had spent with his family in the Middle East. She'd assumed it was because of the ill feelings he harbored toward them. She had never imagined it was because someone had died, that there had been a woman, one he had shared with his brother, whom he hadn't been able to forget.

That was what hurt. She'd seen the look in his eyes, the sudden chill that had filled his expression. Khalid felt something for the mysterious Lessa. There was a part of him that still belonged to her.

How the hell was she supposed to fight a dead woman for his heart?

Jerking the towel from around her body, she dried quickly before heading to the bedroom. She dressed quickly as well. Panties; loose, dark blue pajama bottoms; and a matching T-shirt that fell well below her hips. Sitting down on the side of the bed, she gripped the thick socks she held in her hand and fought to breathe past that hurt.

She felt chilled, uncertain. Naked.

God, what was she doing to herself? She felt as though a part of her was splintering from the inside out in pain.

"Why is this so important to you?" His voice was low, brooding, as she jerked her socks on.

Marty lifted her head and stared back at him in pain.

"I have the right to know." Perhaps she didn't; she could be wrong. Her heart assured her she wasn't. He was becoming so much a part of her that she wasn't certain anymore where she ended and he began inside her soul.

Plowing his fingers through his damp hair, a heavy sigh left his chest as he moved into the bedroom and jerked a pair of loose white pants on over his dark, muscular legs.

Silence filled the bedroom. It was thick, heavy with tension, as Marty waited to see what he said, or what he would do.

"She was our lover," he finally said softly.

Marty stood slowly, turning to him only to find herself staring at his back as he stood in front of the heavily tinted windows.

"Yours and Abram's," she said.

He nodded. "More Abram's. She was his wife." He shrugged as though in afterthought.

She watched his profile as he rubbed at his face and grimaced heavily.

"What happened?"

He gripped his neck tight for long seconds before blowing a hard breath and turning back to her.

"As I told you before, we thought Ayid and Aman as well as their wives had been killed in that explosion. We didn't know Ayid and Aman had survived. I was attacked hours later, taken out into the desert and nearly killed. Abram went to Riyadh at our father's request to learn what had happened to Ayid and Aman. Once we were both out of the way, Ayid and Aman returned to the palace." He closed his eyes as he turned away from her and fought back the tightening of his gut at the knowledge of how Lessa had been found.

"Ayid and Aman did it?" she asked.

He nodded. "They weren't where they were supposed to be. Their wives were there, but they weren't. The moment the building was bombed, they knew I had betrayed them. They knew, because I had been at their home and seen the paper that the location was written on. They knew that. Ayid caught me reading it. I told him it was near my favorite coffeehouse. We laughed about it."

Marty felt the raw agony that glittered in his eyes.

"There was no reason for them to believe I would think anything of it." He breathed out roughly. "No reason to think it would affect their plans. After all, I was no more than the bastard brother who wanted nothing more than to make the world my playground."

Marty sat silently, watching the emotions that flitted across his face.

Hatred and fury flashed in his eyes for a second before he shook his head and moved from the window to the small sofa that faced the bed. Sitting down, he laid his arms on his knees and stared at the floor for long seconds.

"Shayne found me in the desert," he continued wearily. "When I made it back to the castle it was to find Abram screaming in rage at our father. As strong as he was, as unbendable as he could be, still, he cried when Azir called his wife a whore. Then he admitted he knew that Abram had shared his wife with me, and that because of that he would do nothing to Ayid and Aman for her murder." He turned away from her for a long moment before continuing in a voice thick with grief. "I had sworn to protect her as I would my own wife. I swore to love her as I would love my own. And I failed her." When he turned back to her his gaze was bleak with sorrow. "You have always watched me with such pride, with such confidence in my strength. To have you know the truth, to know I failed Lessa when I swore to protect her, to love her with all I was . . ." He gave his head a hard shake. "It was a truth I did not want you to know."

"And you think this affects how I see you?" she whispered painfully. "That I would blame you?"

"I blame me," he stated simply. "I failed, when I should have been more diligent."

"Your father failed." A tear slipped down her cheek as she read the pain in his eyes, in his face. He had made a promise, a vow, and the knowledge that fate had conspired against him had obviously nearly destroyed him.

"I watched that crazy old bastard that day. I saw a monster who had helped create me, and I wanted to be sick." He jumped to his feet and paced the room again as Marty watched, aching for him.

"She was so young." He turned back to her, his gaze tortured. "We were so young." A sharp laugh left his throat. "So stupid to believe that we could ever change what hasn't changed in the history of the world."

"Did you love her?" she asked.

He shook his head slowly. "I cared for her, deeply, but she was Abram's wife. Abram loved her. And I saw his face that day. He was lost inside. A man now free without the anchor sustaining him." He shrugged his shoulders heavily. "I left that night. I went to my rooms, showered, and patched myself up as best I could before calling

Mother. She arranged my transport home. I left the palace that night, I contacted Shayne, and left Azir's lands. I've never returned. Azir refused to do anything about the brothers until he was ordered to by the ruling family. Then he appealed to Abram, begged him to save his lands and his people at a time when Abram was making plans to leave Saudi and immigrate here to America."

That was new information to her. "Did Azir know Abram was planning to leave?" she asked.

Khalid shook his head. "He couldn't have known. If he had, he would have killed Abram himself."

"How would Aman and Ayid react to that information?" she questioned.

"They would kill him faster," Khalid stated. "That would disgrace the family. It would be a stain on their honor that would forever mar their lineage. When Abram's second wife and unborn child died under mysterious circumstances, Azir sent Abdul here, supposedly to protect me," he sneered.

"Why were the facts of her death covered up?"

Khalid sighed wearily. "To protect Abram. If it became public knowledge that we had shared her, he would have suffered. He would have been persecuted for it. Ayid and Aman remained silent because as long as it was unknown, they could hold it over his head, or punish him however they chose. Deerfield shouldn't have known of this, though."

"Well, trust me, he knows," she stated roughly.

"It doesn't matter what he knows, or how much he hates me." He moved to her as he extended his hand. "Come to bed, little flower. Let me hold you for a while."

She gave him her hand and let him draw her to the bed. As they settled in, her head on his shoulder, Marty couldn't shake the feeling that there was something going on that she hadn't yet put her finger on. And a feeling, an intuition, that things were building around her that she couldn't control.

A dark cloud was rolling in on them, and if she didn't figure this out, if they didn't neutralize Khalid's brothers, then that dark cloud could destroy them.

And she had a feeling that she didn't have much longer to take care of it.

19

Finishing her shower the next morning, Marty dried her hair before wrapping her towel around her body and moving into the bedroom. Shayne and Khalid had gone to separate showers earlier. They'd been quiet, looking at her intently.

There was something especially watchful about them that morning that had put her entire system on overload. Her senses had gone on full alert, her body humming with anticipation until they left the room.

She was still off balance. The brooding sensuality in Khalid's expression was impossible to put out of her mind. The way his gaze had flicked over her before meeting her eyes. There had been a message in them, one she couldn't decipher before he left the room.

While shaking her head, she moved to the dresser. As she reached for the first drawer, her head turned as the door opened and Khalid and Shayne stepped inside once again; staring at the two men, she felt her womb clench with a little, slow, electric sizzle that shot straight to her clit.

Shirtless, Shayne wore loose sweatpants; Khalid had donned a pair of black silk pajama bottoms. The differences in the two men had never been more apparent. Khalid had a smooth, dangerous sophistication that hid the animal lurking beneath, while Shayne didn't bother to hide anything.

There was something more intently formidable about the fact that cool sophistication cloaked the man Khalid was. It made him less predictable, more inherently sexual than she had ever seen Shayne.

Breathing in deeply, she turned back to the drawer and pulled free a pair of lacy bronze panties and matching bra.

"You won't need those quite yet." They were plucked out of her hand as Khalid stepped up to her. "Not for a quite a while."

"I have things to do," she informed him, her voice breathless.

Damn. She was panting for him, and they both knew it.

"Not for a while yet."

The towel slid from her body as he pulled at the tuck between her breasts.

Her breasts became immediately sensitive, swollen, her nipples hardening to the point that they ached.

She would have protested. She should have protested.

Khalid's hand slid into her hair, his fingers tangling in the damp strands as he gripped her hip and turned her slowly to face Shayne.

"I want to watch first," he growled against her ear as he nipped at it. "I want to watch him fuck you. Watching your face as his cock sinks inside your sweet body and drives you to climax."

Marty wanted to whimper as Shayne shed his sweatpants, his expression tight with lust, his eyes darkening with it. Between his thighs his cock stood out, heavy with lust, the crest dark and tight.

"I want to hold you, control you," Khalid whispered at her ear. "I want to ensure that you know who controls your greatest pleasure." His hand slid to her thigh as he used his foot to push her legs apart. "I control it." Hard, thick with lust, his voice stroked over her senses as Shayne's hand slid between her thighs, his fingers opening her.

"Is she wet?" Khalid growled, as Shayne's fingers slid through the slick, sensitive flesh.

"Wet. And hot." A tight grimace contorted Shayne's face as

Marty arched and cried out at the sudden thrust of two fingers deep inside her aching pussy.

She felt the instant thread of response that tightened between her pussy, her clit, and her impending orgasm. His fingers slid back, thrust home again. For long seconds they fucked inside her, driving her to her tiptoes as a wailing cry left her lips.

"Enough," Khalid ordered, as Marty flew to the very edge of release.

Just that fast Shayne stopped. His fingers were still embedded inside the clenching depths of her vagina, the muscles of his arm and chest straining as she shuddered between them.

"I'm going to watch him fuck you like that." Khalid's hand slid over her stomach, caressing the clenched muscles of her abdomen. "So hard and deep, you'll be screaming for more, begging for it to stop."

She was ready to scream now and wanted nothing more than to beg to come.

"I ache for you." A gentle, soft kiss smoothed across her neck as she fought to breathe.

Shayne's fingers flexed inside her, drawing a strangled cry from her throat as the tips of his fingers rubbed inside her, stroking high and deep and stealing her breath with the sensations.

"I ache to watch your face, hear your cries, to see your sweet pussy or that tight little ass stretch until you're screaming from the biting pleasure."

Shayne's fingers slid from the aching depths of her sex as Khalid picked her up and carried her to the bed. She was laid down gently, but the kiss that came immediately afterward was anything but gentle.

It was filled with hunger, with need. Khalid took her lips and stole her senses with his lips and tongue as he lay beside her, his hand caressing from her neck to her breasts.

Her world became limited to the two men and four hands.

Khalid's kiss was like wildfire as it sank into her. He ate at her lips, sipped at them, as Shayne's lips traveled along the breast Khalid left free.

She couldn't focus on just one touch; it was impossible. Hungry lips took hers as suckling lips drew a tight, sensitive nipple into a hot mouth and began to work it with a hungry tongue.

Hands touched, stroked.

They parted her thighs.

Marty arched as desperation began to claw inside her. Two strong male fingers sank inside her pussy, working into the clenching flesh as Shayne began to kiss his way down her body.

Fire tore through her. It wrapped around her clit, blazed across her nerve endings, and left her shaking, shuddering in need.

As Khalid's lips lifted from hers, her eyes opened to stare into the hungry eyes of the rough-hewn man who held her heart.

"Do you know what you do to me?" he whispered.

How could she ever do more to him than he did to her? He stole her mind with his touch and stole reason with his kisses.

"You make me dream, Marty." His lips settled at her ear, his voice a breath of sound.

She made him dream?

Her breath caught in her chest. He was her dream, her greatest fantasy.

"You make me come apart at the seams."

"Oh God." The cry tore from her at the same moment, at the feel of Shayne's tongue delving into the folds of her pussy.

A second later it was gone, and fierce male lips were kissing her thighs, teeth raking her flesh.

Shayne's lips traveled lower, kissing behind her knees as his hands stroked and soothed her flesh, even as he built the fire inside her higher, hotter.

"Khalid." She was dazed, on fire as she lifted her lashes and stared up at him. "You're killing me."

"Pleasuring you." Male satisfaction gleamed in his eyes as hers widened at the feel of Shayne's fingers easing inside her pussy once again, while his tongue moved back to the swollen knot of her clit.

She was stretched so tight she trembled, her body shuddering at the pleasure.

"There, little flower," Khalid soothed her, as his head lowered once again and his lips eased over her neck, then to the swollen nipple nearest him.

Licking it sensually, he stared up at her, the exotic planes and angles of his face giving him a wicked, hungry expression.

Gasping for breath, Marty tried to hold on to her senses just enough to understand which lover was touching which part of her body.

She was losing that ability, though. Her lashes drifted closed and the erotic sensuality of the moment took over.

Pleasure built and burned inside her.

Shayne licked at her pussy, circling her clit with flickering quick little strokes that had her reaching, fighting to throw herself over the edge of ecstasy as his fingers stretched and eased inside the delicate tissue of her pussy.

Hips arched, her hands buried in Khalid's hair, she moaned their names as the escalating pleasure whipped through her senses.

She couldn't have imagined it could be this good, this erotic.

"Sweet love." Khalid groaned as his head lifted, his lips moving to hers once more. "Little flower. How beautiful you are. You're lost, aren't you, Marty? Lost inside the pleasure. I see it in your eyes, feel it in your body."

He stared down at her, his expression reflecting such hunger, such pleasure that she had to wonder what drove him to these lengths.

"Nothing matters but this," he whispered. "Seeing you. Watching the pleasure transform you. Knowing the ecstasy you find in this will never be forgotten."

It was for her. It wasn't just for him. As she stared up at him that realization tore through her. He loved watching her pleasure. He loved seeing her reaching, tightening for release rather than becoming lost in it with her at these times.

"There, precious." His voice was thick, rough, as she fought the climax now, wanting to hold it back, to make this night last forever, to see this expression on his face for all time.

He smiled down at her. "I won't let you fight it, baby."

Shayne's lips closed over her clit as his fingers began to move faster, harder inside the clenched recesses of her pussy.

"Let me see it, baby. Let me see you come for us."

Shayne flicked his tongue over her clit as he sucked it deep, his hungry mouth surrounding it in heat as his fingers shafted inside her with pistoning strokes.

She couldn't hold back. She wanted to. She ached to.

The world exploded around her. Bright prisms of light detonated in front of her eyes as powerful waves of electric sensation began to electrify her flesh.

It sizzled, a phantom stroke that became too much to bear, throwing her through that barrier of light and tossing her into a world of such extreme sensation that she wanted to scream in agony but could only gasp in pleasure.

"Yes, baby." Khalid's voice was guttural now. "Come for us, Marty. Suck his dick with your sweet pussy. Take it, baby. Take it all."

She was dying inside from the excess of sensation. She was unraveling, coming apart with the pleasure.

No sooner had the wave of orgasm peaked and begun to ease, then they began building her higher.

Who eased between her thighs she wasn't certain. Her eyes were closed tight, her fingers fisted in the sheets beneath her.

Her thighs were lifted, placed over powerful thighs.

Khalid. She knew his body, she knew the touch of his cock against the sensitive folds of her pussy.

Her eyes opened to mere slits as she felt Shayne moving in beside her. His lips covered her nipple as she watched Khalid, watched as he lifted her hips closer, his gaze focused on the aching flesh of her pussy as he began to push inside her.

Her back arched. This was pure rapture. The sensation of Shayne's touch was erotic, exciting, but the feel of Khalid taking her was like feeling electricity pound through her entire body.

His cock eased inside her, working through the tight muscles, stroking them, caressing them with the wide head of his erection, and then the heavily veined shaft.

Her hips arched closer, cries began spilling from her lips as the overwhelming sensations began to arc through her body. It was like tidal waves, never ending, laying destruction to any hope she may have had of retaining any part of her soul where he was concerned.

But there was already no hope. He'd stolen it along with her heart.

"Fuck. Sweet Marty," he moaned, as he worked deeper, deeper inside her. "So fucking tight. Like a fist clenched around my dick."

She clenched tighter, the involuntary reaction to his words slamming through her womb with spasms of sensation bordering on pain. The pleasure was too intense, too incredible.

Shayne's lips drew tighter on her breast as Khalid began to move inside her, deeper, harder. He was taking her on a roller-coaster ride of such incredible power that she couldn't do anything but hang on for the ride.

And the ride was incredible. As Khalid's cock thrust and stroked inside her, Shayne's lips played with her nipples as his fingers slid down her stomach to the distended bundle of nerves between her thighs.

She was being stroked, taken, caressed, in ways she couldn't have anticipated. They drove her higher, sent her spinning through a sensual universe so filled with pleasure that it was almost agony.

She was crying, trying to scream. She writhed and arched into the driving strokes of Khalid's cock as she fought to take him deeper, harder.

"There, sweetheart," Shayne's voice began to croon at her ear. "Fuck, you're pretty, taking that dick. All flowered open and slick and sweet." His fingers strummed against her clit now, driving sensation through the core of her as her pussy tightened around Khalid's thrusting cock.

She couldn't bear it. She was dying. There was too much pleasure, too many sensations. God, she had never imagined there could be too much pleasure. It began to swamp her. Sensuality drowned her. She couldn't breathe. She couldn't move.

Her body tightened to a breaking point, began to shake harder, to tighten until her orgasm tore through her with a violence that threw her over the edge of reason.

She didn't slip over. She didn't slide.

She was catapulted into a shimmering sea of brilliant, pulsing sensation and explosive rapture.

Crying out Khalid's name, Marty felt him slam deep just before the deep heavy throb of his cock signaled the fierce, heated jets of come spurting inside her and driving her higher.

Beside her she felt Shayne's fist moving over his cock as the fingers of his other hand stroked her clit to a blistering release. He was moaning her name at her side as Khalid groaned above her, his body arched back, perspiration gleaming on his shoulders and chest as the flames of pleasure continued to flicker over them.

As the final violent tremors of orgasm eased through her, Marty collapsed back on the bed, fighting to breathe as exhaustion moved through her.

How the hell was she supposed to get through the rest of the day now? All she wanted to do was curl back into Khalid's arms and go to sleep.

She was only distantly aware of Shayne groaning as he finally moved.

Khalid was collapsed at her side, his arm thrown over her waist as he gasped for air as well.

"Fuck me," Shayne breathed out roughly. "I'll have a heart attack at this rate."

He moved from the bed, stumbled, then padded off to the bathroom.

"Kids, I need a nap," he announced long minutes later, as he came into the bedroom and moved back to the bed. "Rest, sweet thing." He kissed her gently on the lips before she felt him move away. Seconds later she heard the bedroom door close softly.

"I think I did have a heart attack," Khalid mumbled at her side. "I felt my heart rip out of my chest."

She turned her head and couldn't help the smile that curved at her lips as she asked, "How do you figure that?"

As he lifted his head he stared back at her, his expression somber, serious. "I lost my heart," he said then. "You stole it, Marty. When I wasn't looking, you took it right from my chest."

What was he saying? She stared back at him in shock.

"I love you, Marty," he said then, and she saw the truth of it in his eyes, in his expression. "I love you until there's no tomorrow without you. Until I think I would die a cold, lonely death without you."

He loved her.

She stared back at him, still not entirely certain that she was awake. Had she fallen asleep? Had she somehow managed to slip into her greatest fantasy to hear the words she had needed to hear for so very long?

"You're not saying anything, Marty." He reached out, his finger-tips caressing her cheek, then her jaw. "What's wrong?"

She had to swallow tightly to speak.

"Say it again." Was that her voice? So desperate, so filled with hope. "Please, Khalid, say it again."

"I love you, Marty Mathews," he said simply, softly. "With everything inside me, I love you."

He loved her.

She wasn't dreaming. This wasn't a fantasy. It was real, and she wasn't losing her mind.

"You love me?"

"I love you." He gave her a small, gentle smile. "More than you can ever know."

She couldn't stem the tears. They filled her eyes and slid slowly down her cheeks as he stared back at her, a small, confused frown darkening his brow.

"I've loved you since I was fifteen years old," she whispered. "So much, Khalid. I've loved you so much."

Her arms went around his neck as she buried her face in his chest, fighting to stop the tears. She didn't want to cry. She didn't want his face blurred because of her tears. She wanted to memorize it. She wanted to preserve this moment in time.

"He loves you so much."

They both froze for one second before jerking around to stare in shock at the figure who stood in the doorway, an automatic rifle cradled in his arms.

Aman Mustafa.

Marty knew his scarred face instantly. The thick black hair was pulled back into a ponytail; a ragged, ill-kept bushy beard covered the lower part of his face.

She couldn't move. She stared at the barrel of the rifle as it pointed toward her chest, the evil smile on his face as he moved into the room, terrifying her.

There was no mercy in that gaze. There was no compassion. There was only evil. Pure, black-hearted evil.

"This was so easy." He laughed at them as he moved inside, an arrogant swagger in his step that screamed conceited confidence.

Her weapon was tucked under the edge of the mattress, so far away. She lay against Khalid on his side of the ultra-king-size bed, the edge of the bed a good body-length from her.

"Aman." Khalid's tone was ice, his body tense against her.

He stared around the room curiously as he moved to stand at the foot of the bed. "I'm surprised you have no third with you tonight. I expected it."

He didn't know Shayne was there.

"I didn't need one tonight." Khalid held her close as he sat up fully and stared back at his brother.

"Ah, surely you are not giving up on such pleasures?" Aman propped his foot at the bottom of the bed. "I thought for certain that if you did not give them up for the memory of Lessa then you would give them up for no woman."

Marty kept her eyes on Aman, but her senses concentrated fully on Khalid. Aman was trying to piss him off, to hurt him. The memory of Lessa was one Khalid had never let himself forget, nor had he ever forgiven himself for her death.

There was also a sense of hope. Shayne was in the house. There was a chance, a slim one at best, but a chance that he could return to the bedroom and distract Aman.

"Does it matter why I gave it up?" Khalid asked, further drawing Aman into the belief that no one else was there. "Tell me, Aman, how did you get past my security guards?"

"They were easy." Aman smiled as he shrugged. "Very complacent in their abilities and their technologies. Unfortunately, I was here long before the full force actually arrived. Your poor cook slipped me in this afternoon, just after you and your lovely Agent Mathews left the house."

"And the call that the Saudi ambassador's assistant made from the party last night?" Khalid asked.

Aman smiled. "To Ayid, as I'm certain you know. I've been here for a while, brother." His gaze slid to Marty. "Long enough to nearly kill your whore the night you almost caught me in her apartment."

It wasn't an unknown assassin. Aman had been here all along.

Khalid breathed in deeply behind her. A controlling, patient breath as Marty clutched the sheet tighter to her breasts.

"Americans amaze me." Aman sighed, as though they were children he didn't understand. "They believe they are so full of wisdom and answers. But living is the understanding that such things cannot be controlled. Allah controls all things instead, and he reaches back, forsaking us when vengeance is owed us." He glared at Khalid then. "Vengeance is owed, Khalid. Allah provided a way for me to strike."

"I thought you said the cook provided that?" Khalid drawled.

Aman's glare intensified. "You mock me, Khalid?" He snarled.

"You mock Allah further? The unholy alliances you partake of with other men's wives is a sin against all men. You should have been stoned as an infant. Destroyed before you could infect others with your perversions."

And Aman believed that, Marty saw. In his deep brown eyes she saw the conviction he felt.

"I've heard this all before, Aman." Khalid sighed. "It's becoming boring."

"Then hear this, traitor . . ."

The rifle went off.

Marty flinched then screamed as the bullet tore a hole in the pillow no more than a breath from her head.

"Fuck you, Aman!" Khalid yelled furiously, as he pulled Marty closer to him, despite her attempts to throw herself to the other side of the bed and the gun within easy reach if she could just make the distance.

"Perhaps I am only trying to liven things up," Aman sneered. "As you tried to liven them up the day you killed mine and Ayid's wives. The day you and Abram thought you could destroy our lives and our plans, forever."

Marty dug her nails into Khalid's wrists in an attempt to force him to release her.

"Abram did nothing," Khalid snapped.

The rifle fired again. A volley of bullets tore into the mattress beside Marty as Aman screamed out furiously. "You bastard liar! We know better! We have always known better! Tonight I came to kill your whore. Ayid will be with Abram now, ensuring he never breathes another night. But you, my brother, you will live to suffer as no man on earth has ever suffered."

He was insane.

Marty fought to hold herself in place, to still the need to fight Khalid's hold until it eased just enough to tear herself from his arms at the next opportunity.

She was halfway behind him now as he jerked her back and came forward. His muscles were tense and bulging as he held his rage in check, obviously waiting as well.

"You won't live to make me suffer," Khalid assured him. "Trust me, Aman. I'll hunt you both down like rabid dogs."

Aman chuckled at that. "I may die, but you will suffer. You will suffer the truth. The knowledge that your actions have caused you to lose the only woman you have ever truly loved. Ah, yes." He smiled. "I heard your vow of undying devotion to your little cunt. Words you have never given another woman. They have signed her death warrant rather than the mere raping I had intended for her."

She would rather die than have him so much as graze her with his demonic touch.

"Don't force me to destroy you, Aman," Khalid warned him, his voice powerful despite its softness. "I will. Harm her, and I'll make certain you die in agony."

"No more agony than you will know, my brother." The rifle lifted again and aimed toward her hip.

"Aman!" Khalid screamed out his name as the weapon fired.

Agony streaked along Marty's hip as she threw herself from Khalid to the edge of the bed. Her hand flew to the separation of the mattress and box spring, her fingers curling around the butt of the gun as it slipped free.

Simultaneously Khalid threw his weight over her body as more gunfire sounded.

She fought him. Trying to ignore the horrifying agony at her hip, Marty fought to turn, to aim the weapon she had managed to snatch at the bastard daring to endanger the man she loved.

"Move!" She was picked from the floor like a rag doll as Khalid threw himself toward the bathroom door.

Aman's curses were like the screams of a demon as Khalid threw the door closed, locked it, then forced Marty to the back of the room and into the sunken tub.

She stared at him in shock as she glimpsed the small, lethally powerful P90 personal protection weapon he carried in one hand.

"Put this on." He threw a white robe to her as he grabbed the white, comfortable pants he had worn in their suite and jerked them on.

"You won't escape so easily, Khalid." The sound of Aman's weapon tapping against the door was like listening to Satan peck his nails against it. It sent chills racing down her spine and horror filled her soul.

"Are you okay?" Khalid sliced a look at her as she tied the robe.

She nodded with the lie. She wasn't okay. She was bleeding like a damned stuck pig and her fucking hip was burning like the flames of hell were flickering over it.

"Do not play this game, Khalid."

Khalid threw himself into the tub, covering her as bullets tore through the bathroom door, the lock shattering. A foot against the panel, and Aman was staring in at them with a smile on his face before he threw himself to the side, barely escaping the gunfire Khalid spewed toward him.

"Ah, you are getting smarter," Aman called out. "Come out and play, Khalid. Come, my brother, and perhaps I will share your woman with you before I cut her depraved cunt from her body."

20

Where the fuck was Shayne?

Khalid crouched over Marty's body, fighting to protect her, to give Shayne time to hear the weapons firing and to come running.

He knew she was lying to him. She had been hit. Her blood had sprayed his thigh as the bullet tore through her hip. Jumping for the opposite side of the bed had most likely saved her life, as Aman had been aiming for another shot even as she moved.

"You're fucking up, Aman," he called out to the other man. "You won't leave here alive."

"Do you think I came alone?" Aman was laughing. "I came with friends. One has bound Abdul to keep him safe, the others search your home now to ensure we missed no one. You are isolated, Khalid. No one will help you now."

Khalid breathed in roughly. Shayne was a damned good agent. He wasn't that easy to catch unaware. "Your father won't like having Abdul harmed, Aman," Khalid reminded him.

"Father is a sentimental old fool," Aman called back. "But Abdul will live, as per his orders, just as you will, brother. Though I doubt Father will shed many tears for Abram. You know he sent us for him."

Khalid stilled. That was impossible. Azir would have never sent his sons to kill his heir.

"Abram thought he could leave his home, his country," Aman called out. "He thought he could abdicate the future of his throne and his father would tolerate such a betrayal. Azir ordered Abram's death. Just as he will one day order yours."

He felt Marty moving behind him, her breath catching in obvious pain as she slid around him.

"Come, Khalid, let's not draw this out any further than we must," Aman chided him. "Let me kill your little whore, then I will be gone from your life again. At least, until you find another diseased bitch to take your depraved cock."

"Bastard," Marty snarled. "I want to cut his fucking dick off."

He stared back at her almost in shock. His ladylike little Marty had a mouth on her that could possibly almost match his own. He'd have to discuss this with her.

If they lived.

God, if they lived.

He narrowed his eyes on the door frame, watching the shadow that moved just outside it. The light spilled over Aman in a way that allowed Khalid to track him by tracking his shadow. His brother still hadn't learned to watch his ass. He had always depended on his father to watch his back. His father wasn't here now.

"We need to distract him," Marty whispered softly behind him. "We need to get him to edge closer to the frame. The P90 will pass through the wall, Khalid."

Khalid shook his head. "It's reinforced. I suspect Aman knows this, as my employees did. It will do no good to shoot anything other than the door. The bullets will be stopped by the layer of steel within the walls."

She sighed heavily behind him.

"My cell phone is in the bedroom," she said. "We're fucked if we have to stay here."

Their ammunition was limited, whereas he had glimpsed the backpack Aman carried. No doubt his brother was fully stocked.

"We'll just have to make every bullet count," Khalid told her quietly.

"I believe before I kill your whore, I want to fuck her." Aman was trying to push every button he thought Khalid possessed. "It was I who cut Lessa's betraying cunt from her body, Khalid. She was alive as I did so. She cried and begged, and in the end she screamed for her depraved husband and her bastard lover. But you weren't there, were you?" He laughed viciously. "Do you think my wife screamed for me when she died?"

"I think she died instantly," Khalid called back. "I doubt she even thought of you, Aman. I would guess she was happy to leave this life and her insane husband behind."

No doubt, Khalid thought, *the woman had been as crazy as Aman was*. She built many of the bombs that went into the vests of suicide bombers and helped Aman to plot many of the merciless attacks that had been made by the terrorist cell he led.

"Ah, you think you can speak such lies and hurt me," Aman called back, his tone furious. "Allah has sent me to punish you, Khalid. I am vengeance."

"I doubt Allah had anything to do with your insanity, Aman. Your father should have drowned you like a diseased dog when you were born."

Silence met the words. Khalid stayed carefully behind the rim of the tub, praying the sunken design of it would protect them once Aman stepped clear to fire inside the room once again.

"You are a part of Satan," Aman accused him sadly. "Father refuses to believe it. You have bespelled him. But it will not last much longer."

No, it wouldn't. Khalid was going to kill Aman before he ever left this house, then he would go searching for Ayid. He just had to be patient, he warned himself.

Behind him, Marty shifted, a soft curse falling from her lips from the pain the action no doubt caused. *The flesh wound on her hip would be a deep one*, he thought. The blood that had splattered over him hadn't been minute.

"Check the window," he ordered her softly. "See if anyone is outside."

She moved behind him. The wide windows looked out over the back of the estate and the gardens below. There was a small balcony outside, one for looks rather than actual use, but it would hold their weight if they could slip outside.

"Nothing," she whispered back.

"Khalid, I grow weary of this game," Aman called out to him.

"Then come on, Aman. Let me kill your ass and get it over with," Khalid called back, as he glanced over his shoulder.

Marty was struggling with the lock, trying to disengage the heavy metal latch.

"What are you doing, Khalid?" Suspicion filled Aman's voice. "Do you think you can escape me?"

Reaching behind him, Khalid gripped Marty's robe and jerked her back as all hell seemed to break loose.

Aman threw himself into the room, his body flattening against the floor as his weapon began to spit a rage of gunfire that seemed never ending.

Ducking over Marty, Khalid laid the barrel of the P90 over the tub's rim and began firing himself. He knew the general area. He had only one chance.

Glass showered around them as bullets sliced through the window. He was aware of Marty ducking, covering her head as he lay over her, his heart racing, fear clogging his throat as his weapon began to click.

His ammunition was exhausted.

Holding her to the floor of the tub, Khalid waited.

Silence filled the bathroom as he slowly eased Marty's Glock from her grip, his eyes meeting hers as she turned her head to stare back at him.

"I love you," she spoke silently, her lips moving as her pale face reflected her fear that Aman was only laying in wait to see if his bullets had struck before moving again.

Bracing one hand beside her head Khalid began to lift himself to check.

What he saw caused a breath of relief to ease from his lungs.

Aman lay on his back, his eyes staring up silently as blood pooled around him.

Shayne stood in the doorway staring at the body with icy eyes as Khalid calculated the number of hits his brother had taken.

His aim, despite his inability to do more than lay the weapon over the tub's edge, had been on target.

Shayne lifted his gaze from Aman's body to Khalid.

Rising from the tub, the Glock now held loosely in his hand, he helped Marty up.

"Fuck me," Shayne breathed out roughly. "Do you know how many of these bastards I had to go through to get here?" He indicated Aman's still form. "I bet he had a dozen men in this fucking house."

Stepping over the body, Shayne gripped Khalid's arm and helped him from the tub as Khalid lifted Marty against him.

"We'll need the doctor here," Khalid ordered. "She's been shot. Call her fathers and check on Abram. Ayid was sent to kill him."

"Got it." Shayne moved quickly as Khalid swung Marty into his embrace and carried her to the bed.

Staring up at him, Marty reached out, touched his cheek, then his lips.

"It's over," she whispered.

As he laid her on the bed, Khalid sat slowly beside her, his gaze lingering on her face as Shayne spoke on the phone behind him.

"It's over," he agreed.

A tremulous smile shaped her lips. "Still love me?"

"Like the sun loves the flowers that brighten its day," he whispered. "Like a body loves the heart that beats for its life. God help me, Marty, I love you until I know I would die without you."

He couldn't exist without her. There was no life, no heart, no soul if he lost the spirit that kept him alive. Marty was the life, the heart, the spirit that had kept him reaching for a new day since he'd met her when she had been no more than fifteen.

A part of him had known then. His soul knew now. The pleasure she gave him, the warmth she filled him with, the touch that kept him centered to the earth was more than he could bear losing.

She was his heart. She was his soul. She was a pleasure that held no guilt, no shame. A pleasure that met his, matched it, and heated the coldest night.

His Marty.

"I love you, Khalid," she whispered.

And he smiled. For the first time in more years than he could remember, he truly smiled.

"And I, precious, love you."

extracts reading groups
competitions books new
books discounts extracts
competitions
books new
reading groups extracts events
events books extracts discounts reading groups
new reading groups
interviews
discounts events extracts
new books events
events new events reading groups
discounts extracts discounts books
www.panmacmillan.com
extracts events reading groups
competitions books extracts new